THOMAS CHURCHILL

CENTRALIA DEAD MARCH

CURBSTONE PRESS

This publication is supported by a grant from the
National Endowment for the Arts
in Washington D.C., a federal agency

The author wishes to thank the Oregon Historical Society for use of its resources; Charles Sydney Everest for permission to use the back cover photograph; the University of Wisconsin-Green Bay for time off to finish this work, and Alexander Taylor and Judith Doyle for many helpful suggestions.

published by
Curbstone Press
321 Jackson Street
Willimantic, Connecticut

For Cathy and Julia

Part 1: **Wesley Everest**

They go wild, simply wild over me,
I'm referring to the bedbug and the flea;
They disturb my slumber deep, and I murmur in my sleep,
They go wild, simply wild over me.

Oh, the "bull" he went wild over me,
And he held his gun where everyone could see;
He was breathing rather hard when he saw my union card,
He went wild, simply wild over me.

from "The Popular Wobbly"
by T-Bone Slim /Valentine Huhta/

The nickname, "wobbly," for International Workers of the World wasn't a derogatory tag laid on by hostile people; we gave it to ourselves from a machine called the "wobble-saw," because it cut in both directions.

from interview with Herb Edwards
I.W.W. member, Seattle, Wash.

Where is private property's most sensitive spot? One learns the answer whenever a business man announces that his son will be taking over the business. . . . The ultimate *locus* of private property is in the private parts.

from "An Un-American Chalk Circle"
by Eric Bentley

I

He sat on his duffle bag nodding with the steady clack-clack of iron on iron and saw his father dimly by a fire at the ocean beach when things were good, the family tight, and no war hunkering like a beast out in the blackness of the sea. He thought of the drafty old immigrant trains his father had described to him, new settlers--his grandad among them--making their way to the northwest from Michigan and Wisconsin. Wrapped in blankets, they huddled around wood stoves that blasted heat in a three foot circle and left the rest of the car shrouded with cold. Wes was only riding from Tacoma to Centralia, but the car was crowded with people who looked as lost and uprooted as the shawly peasants he had gotten used to, spread out along the country lanes in France. An old woman, seated and trying to steady herself with a cane against the rocking motion of the car, leaned towards him and spoke loudly: "Why do you want to go back into those awful wet woods? City's a place for a young man. . . I lost a grandson in that war--you're lucky to have your hide, big strong man like you. Logging's as bad as the front from what I hear."

He smiled at her, wanting to settle it. The talk had whirled around like leaves piled in a windy place--(So where are you from? What've you done with your life besides wastin' it in the army?")--he wanted to say something final but all he could think was, "Logging's about all I know how to do, 'bout all I want to do."

"Don't you have folks, can't they get you decent work? Goodness, I had one cousin went to work logging down in Pacifica, and he came out *bits*. Just bits was all that was left of him."

"There's just my uncle back in Tacoma, he's got nothin' but a night watchman's job at St. Regis. . . lost his candy business down in Newberg, Oregon with the war boom," he said, hoping to sound ironic. "Been in the woods since I was thirteen, ma'am, with time out in the service."

"Hey, that's my stop coming up. . . you take care now--" He struggled to his feet, feeling pin-pricks striking his cramped legs.

"*You* take care!" she said, raising her cane.

About a block from the train station he found a bar and restaurant called the Olympic Club, with an open air glass counter that came right out of the place and greeted you on the sidewalk. He went in and ordered a beer, which the bartender bought because he was in uniform. It was a fancy place with big plate mirrors behind the bar. The bar was a reddish wood with brass taps and fittings, and two red and green glass chandeliers hung down from a ceiling that was twenty feet high. The urinals when he went to take a piss were damned near up to his shoulders, with copper pipes running all over the place and a floor that was inlaid tiles. If he'd slipped and fallen he might still be in there, those urinals were so big.

A rat-faced guy the bartender called "Heinie" was playing solitaire, placing cards carefully on the bar to avoid little rings of beer.

"Say," Wesley asked, "I'm trying to locate a camp that's hiring loggers. Know any around here?"

The bartender kept on polishing glasses, but the rat-faced guy looked up quickly--"That your calling, soldier?"

"That will be."

"They got loggers in the army?" The man's eyes aimed away from one another in his narrow face, so when he looked at you he tilted slightly.

"Who d'you think built all those trenches?"

"You do that?" the man asked, licking foam from his glass.

"Oh, yeah." He watched the odd-looking man lift a match stick from the bar, quickly bring the end to a point with his pen knife, pick an object from his teeth and dispose of it with a swipe on his pants.

"Well, I'll be go-ta-hell," he said, "y'get gassed down there?"

"Not so's you can still smell it," Wes answered. Heinie laughed and hit the bar.

"You're all right, soldier. . . say, I'll tell you one thing I know about the army--" He winked at the bar man and pointed at Wesley's overseas cap, limp beside his hand. "--I know what you call that there hat." He cast one bent eye expectantly up the bar as if he figured no one had heard it and said excitedly, "A cunt cap!"

He and the bartender had a laugh over that one.

"A cunt cap? Right, soldier, ain't that what they call that cap? Thought so. What's yer name, anyway? There's a big operation out at Michigan Hill--"

"It's Wesley, Wes--"

"Well, Wes, you'll find it, you take the train out of here towards Aberdeen. You get off at Independence, cost you ten cents. . . Hey, where the hell y'goin'?"

He gripped his duffle bag. "Thought I'd head out there."

"Not so fast. John, give this boyo a beer." It was already poured and waiting for him.

"You wanta watch it, son, you go out there to Michigan Hill. Them goddam wobs got a foothold in the mill. . . had one in this town, too, right across the street, but we kind of stepped on it."

He winked again with his sideways eye.

"Oh, yeah?"

"Had us a blind man across the street, sold red newspapers. Don't see nothin' of him over there any more, do you, fella? Maybe some scraps of paper and shingles and shit like that. That's all she wrote for mister wob across the street."

"What happened to him?" Wes drank and watched the ugly man's fingers jerk and twitch as he rolled a cigaret and lit it. The ends of his fingers were yellowed and broken open. He plucked all his cards, slammed them edgewise against the bar and slipped the pack into his vest pocket before answering--

"Some of our boys here in town got fed up with him yellin' dirty lies from them papers of his. He ain't about to come back here, don't worry."

"Blind, you said?"

"Oh, that he was and dirty, too. Slept with goats, what I hear. Him and his wobbly buddies, they had their hall right over there in that building across the street--"

The brick building next to the lot where he'd pointed was gutted and empty as the socket of a rotted tooth.

"Burned 'em out, huh?"

"You said it, soldier. Some of us been busy here on the home front while you boys was overseas. . . course, the bastards relocated up the street. How long that lease is gonna last is another question, tho."

He hoisted his bag. "Thanks for the beer."

"You ain't finished it--"

"It's all yours."

"Hey, if you're goin' out to Michigan Hill tell them Heinie Huss sent you. . . . That's my kind of man," he heard him mutter to the bartender as he let himself out.

Wes stiff-legged his bag along the sidewalk and warmed to the thought of blood jumping from the man's bad eyes if he'd crashed a glass on the bar, as he'd been tempted to do, and jabbed the stump in his face. Blind men? They went for blind men in this town? He saw a soldier, his blouse all undone, one leg off at the thigh, sleeping in a little cart drawn up tight to the railroad building.

He rolled a cigaret shakily, trying to swallow his anger and rid his mouth of the taste of beer that the shabby little bastard had bought him. He popped the match on the bricks and brought it to his face aware that the guy in the wagon had come awake as though struck by the match.

"--hold that light, fella," the wounded man commanded. He'd found a butt in his shirt and was pointing towards the end of it. Wesley bent his two good legs, eyeing the tucked-up trouser and offered his own cigaret, which the guy eagerly took. His jaw tightened, lips pursed, his blue cheeks sucking smoke.

"What kind of a town in this, anyway?" Wes asked him as though they were buddies agreed to hightail it out.

"Kind of a town I'm leavin'," the wounded man said, squinting at him. "Takin' the next train out of here to Everett."

"Good luck," Wes said, wondering at the man's choice. Two years ago he'd unwrapped the package of broken cookies his aunt had sent, sat down on his bunk to enjoy them, and just as he'd got his boots off, toes stretching in the web of stinking socks, he saw the headline--the wrapper was news of home, two weeks old but leaving him cold with fury. The Verona had pulled its way into Everett harbor, packed to overflowing with wobblies from Seattle come to start a free speech fight, invading Snohomish County, but a sheriff's posse was waiting for them and no sooner had they docked than they were blasted with sniper fire. He'd seen in his mind's eye fellow workers grabbing at their throats, fumbling for guns of their own, toppling overboard, and fifty guys like Heinie flattened their noses against rifle stocks and fired at men whose struggle turned the water red. The Heinies of the world had an answer to free speech: they'd put a bullet in your mouth.

How could you fight them? That day he'd left the pile of cookies, wandered off with the paper in his hands wishing he'd never joined the army, or joined only to steal an automatic weapon, wishing for the power to know ahead of time--yes, to have known they'd be waiting for you and you at the wheel of the Verona with an arsenal of Browning automatics. He'd ended up getting drunk. He was in Georgia. Four men in Everett were dead, two weeks ago. He was in the wrong place and no way of getting back.

He bought a ticket, watched the big engine slow, pushing steam against his legs. What use was guilt? Before Georgia there was Herbie Berkoben down in Coos Bay, a lanky, gentle man with sloping shoulders and a rounded pot belly. With his mass of curly hair and soft eyes, he was the last guy you'd expect to find in the woods. He wasn't a very good logger, but could that guy *talk* and he got it all from his little red book, the wob's bible. Two months of Herb's prodding and Wes was carrying a union card proudly. He felt part of something solid for the first time.

One day he and Herb were half way through a log that would have yielded 25,000 board feet when this guy comes running up, yelling, "We're on strike!" like he'd just struck gold. So they whooped, too, and headed back to the bunkhouse. That night they were still pinching lice from their clothes--no strategy yet--when a company dick showed up, all policy and quiet talk, wondering if any of the boys wanted to step over to the office with him, this trouble could be settled without any violence. No one moved. The guy stepped out politely but the next day they woke up to dogs howling on the edge of camp, clubs rattling against trees, guns blasting. Caught with their drawers down, he and Herbie had to run through the damn'd woods in their socks, chased by three big company dudes armed with pick handles. They finally hit into the sunlight of a highway. Wesley knew there was a recruiting station two miles down the road. "Where you headin'?" Herbie yelled at him. "I need boots, man," Wes hollered back, "I'm joinin' up, screw this life!" "Oh, Christ--" Herb started then waved him off. "You're hopeless, Wes. . . good luck." Wes watched him heading north at a trot.

So he'd run from the first human contact outside his father and mother who'd helped him towards a conscience, but he hated to be chased--he ought to be the one chasing and for sure the army would give him that chance. He felt lucky not to have gotten clubbed, lucky after that to land at Fort Ord, not shipped right away to the east coast and France. When he found out that there were men being trained at the Presidio to snoop out radicals in lumber camps that were making parts for aircraft, he and a couple of other workers thought maybe they could ease their guilt for having joined by working from within. They started performing what they called "vigilantes" on members of the Spruce Division and the Four L Crew, drifting late into the Monterey bars and picking fights for no reasons they ever stated. No politics, they kept it dumb, but when Wes broke a guy's jaw and the M.P.'s tagged some innocent sailor, he asked for a shift of scene.

They shipped him to Fort Benning in Georgia. He worked in the pine woods and in the swamps, pulling out the giant cypresses. Chiggers gnawed a ring around his belt line and ate into both calves where his boots stopped; they bored into his crotch. When he complained to his sergeant that the work was damned tough and not quite kosher, the man told him, "There's a war on, don't forget. Lumberjack like you don't like cuttin' wood?" "We're pullin' wages right out of the labor force, doing this," he told him. "You don't like your job?" the sergeant repeated. It was useless to argue, then the following Monday found Wes with two squads of men, all armed, trucked across the border into Florida to report to an outfit called C.H. Barnes and Sons. Florida had no state prison; the Barnes company leased out hundreds of convicts at fifty cents per man per day. They kept them in hand using guards and bloodhounds. He saw men whipped. The effects of malaria were obvious in their swollen eyes and shaking limbs. Men worked barefoot, many were crippled, their feet torn and poisoned from the saw palmettos.

There was scarcely a white man among them. They waded in the swamps, girdling cypress, digging canals for pullboats and laying railroads. "They ought to use elephants for this kind of work," he told the man beside him. "Shut up," the soldier said, "and don't ever talk about this shit outside of here." It was lunch time, they'd stacked rifles, he'd wandered off to take a leak and a company doctor was showing him the way to the cafeteria. Coming around one of the bunkhouses, they stopped short at the stench of rotting flesh. Ahead of them in the baking sun was a wild hog, rooting into a dead man. The doctor roared and fired his pistol at the hog, who went grunting into the woods on quick short legs.

Wes came back to camp sick and desperate. He couldn't strike here, that was the freedom he'd lost joining up. Couldn't show his colors. Now he wrote a letter to the I.W.W. headquarters in Chicago. What could he do, he wanted to know. They replied to a civilian P.O. box in Columbus. They told him to contact the circuit judge in Phenix City, Alabama; the man had a good labor record. Big Bill Haywood himself congratulated

Wesley through the mails for testifying in private chambers that the company of Barnes and Sons were engaged in acts of peonage. It was a big day for him. He knew from that moment on he had the cunning it took to lead, now all he had to do was to stay alive and get some men behind him.

He also knew that it wouldn't take long before they linked him to that testimony. He told his C.O. and his sergeant--"I got to kill a hun or I'm no kind of man." They clapped his back shipped him off, but he kept his logger's M.O.S.--he was more valuable to the army rebuilding trenches than shooting a gun. So for the last two months of the war he worked in mud, diving before the scream of shells. He wondered at the colossal maze of trenches, logs shipped in from every ally who supported the war, and from some who did not. An Irish soldier with the British Foresters told him that the whole western edge of his country had been leveled to build these bloody trenches. Lumber was their living, here it was all wasted--all the labor involved in its getting and the lumber itself. Wes returned a wreck. He'd found his aunt's spotless house in Tacoma a good place to dry out, except on those nights when he and his Uncle Jim just had to go out and get themselves loaded.

Watching the fields maundering past the windows of the train, he thought, my god, that was just last night Jim and I went out. Seemed years ago. The old man had tucked him into bed, giggling and stomping around till his wife called him to come downstairs.

Wes stepped off the train at Independence and one appraising look sent him a view of farms in a flat valley between rounded hills, and grass the kind that pushes against your knees when you wade through it, thinking of surf, and the old free days when he was young and all his friends were Indians. He never wanted to be a cowboy when he took to the ocean in July. Down the gravel embankment of the railway a deep river ran by, and a hundred yards or so up from the station was a bridge over the river. It was painted silver, its girders delicate and webbed.

Independence was a station, a store and some farm buildings near the store. He mosey'd into the store looking for directions. He couldn't see at first if anyone was attending. Sausages hung from the ceiling, fresh dill in big clumps dangled in his face--and the air in the store was dim, light brown, it seemed, like the plump eggs in mesh baskets that lined the counter-top. He lifted a dipper of fresh milk to his lips. From deep in the store he heard a woman's voice say, "Are you paying for that milk, mister?" He licked his lips and moved his head from side to side, peering through the gloom. The difficulty with seeing was that the only light entering the store was concentrated around his head.

"Hello. . . ? Yeah, I guess I am--" He brought a large penny from his pocket, snapped it between thumb and middle-finger so that it spun, a hoop of glowing copper, dancing like a top over the counter as she came into the light on the other side, a young woman with long brown hair and pleasant, easy lips. She spread both hands out flat on the glass and leaned forward, watching the spinning coin, her elbows locked. She wore a white blouse, open at the neck--in a flash she'd scooped the coin as a lithe river animal might snatch a fish. Pinching it by the edge, eyeing him, she said, "The milk's on me," and flipped the coin, his hand coming up to part the air between them and squeeze it.

He caught the odor of scented soap so fresh when her arm came up that he let his eyes go free to run along her breasts and down the smooth flow of her hips. He imagined a milk white pitcher on a maple table, sunlight in the room, and she unbuttoning her blouse.

He asked about working in the woods; she told him to skirt the big turtleback ridge behind the tracks and look up Mr. Bob Thompson, the mill operator.

"This the company store?" he asked.

Her reaction surprised and pleased him--"What? No, this is the Neimi Store."

"Well, good. . . and you must be a Neimi, too."

"I'm Lucy." Her skin was clear, his gaze steady. "And who might you be, soldier?" she asked, just slightly sarcastic. He hadn't been aware of being in uniform since coming in the store.

"It's Everest, and when I change clothes I'm a logger." He saw her brow come up at this. "--you can call me Wes if we see each other again."

"That's a mighty big name," she said and brought her hand to her mouth. He laughed with her though the joke wasn't new to him, and watched with interest two cherry-like spots color her cheeks.

From pond to drying yards the Michigan Hill operation was a pretty efficiently run mill. They'd installed automatic drop sorters to control length, electric air dogs to grab and turn the logs on the saw carriage. They had automatic roller dryers and stackers and moist air dry kilns: he guessed the place must have cleaned up on government contracts during the war and wondered if the workers up here had shared in the profits. No, of course they hadn't, it couldn't be different here. They weren't slaves in the northwest and they had struck, for whatever good it did them. Bad tactics, he wondered, to go out during war? For all the wartime demands, they'd gotten less for their work--wages had dropped from '15 to '17 and the I.W.W. had led the whole northwest woods out on strike, bringing out Uncle Sam's meanest side. Wesley kept up--a lot of local lawmen, interpreting congress as loosely as they could, had argued that it was "treason" to belong to the union during the worst times of '17 and '18. They did what they had to, what would he have done? Instead of answering himself he found that he was conscious of a lightness at his right hip. He'd left his gun at his aunt's. . . but he'd wanted to leave it.

As he walked from station to station in the tearing noise of the mill, men stared at him with a look of shrunken fatigue he thought he'd left behind in the trenches. One old man stood gray-faced in the incessant buzz of a machine that was new to him. When he brought his hand to his face to brush away sawdust, Wes saw that his thumb was trimmed from the fatty underpart to the nail like a sharp wedge. Another guy coughed and spat pink phlegm as he leaned a board into a planing machine.

The machinery of the mill was well oiled, things just hummed along but he saw no protective guardrails around the saws, no ventilation. He was beginning to cough from the dust when he saw a worker with some authority limping towards him. "Boss'll be here shortly," he called, and gave Wes a quick looking over. Later he learned that this man was Britt Smith.

Bob Thompson was going to turn out to be one of those *friendly* bosses. Wes could see that right away in the manner of his greeting--all smiles, big handshake. He felt he'd calculated rightly to come as a soldier instead of a roughneck, still he laid it on eager with his eyes wide. Oh, he was a tough, raw-boned stud of a choke-setter, sawyer, pond dunker, mule skinner--if Bob was looking for such a man. And mind the rain? "Why, I'm a webfoot from way back," Wes bragged, "rain'll run right off my tail."

"I got a mule and a wagon of supplies goin' out of here in an hour," Thompson said. "You just ride along with it and look for Commodore Bland, or Ole Olafsen or Johnson, the foreman out there, if he's sober. Make sure you talk to the timekeeper and speak nicely to the cook. You got yourself a pair of corks?" Wes patted his duffle bag. "--good." His round face opened up to show a lot of teeth.

Light streamed down on him through tall hemlock, spruce and fir. It was a pretty good feeling to be in the woods with the sun going down and nothing to do but ride behind a mule, and he couldn't help thinking, why if only conditions were better it wouldn't be such a bad job. He'd known plenty of men who worked in the woods because they liked it. What Herbie Berkoben always argued: "It's not the weevils in our food and the bedbugs in our bunks that makes it a good job. It's the air, god dammit, and the sunshine--when it shines--and just the pure pleasure of choppin' one of those big cusses down to size--right, Wes?" "Right, Herb," he'd answered, feeling the blast of heat from their campfire in his face and waiting for the *chunk* of Herb's axe as he lashed into a Douglas fir for emphasis. He could be dangerous when he got the urge to speak.They were on their own and liking it, three days to cut a new section line through to the bunch from Tillamook. "Yeah, it's hearing your blade cut through the air--" His forearms went winging through the sparks of their fire, and his torso spun drunkenly.

Wes slapped a mosquito, sucked blood from his hand and chased it with a swallow of acrid tasting whiskey. He handed the jug back to his friend. "Ain't that it, Wes?" "That's it, Herbie." "But the thing that gets my goat," Herb went on, holding the jug and jabbing at the black sky, is the question without an answer--Why do some men live off the backs of others?"

"I don't know," Wes said.

"You bet you don't. Why do they have to?" he asked the trees. "You read that book I got by Engels. It's about working people in England. You think we got things bad here. . . "

"We do have things bad here."

"No, you read it. Engels says it's not just in a man's nature, when you got the means, to strangle the man who doesn't. Men choose to do that. You read that, then you read Bill Haywood: 'The I.W.W. aims to use any and all that tactics that will get results. The question of right and wrong does not concern us.' Big Bill pissed a lot of people off with that but you got to say *amen*, Wes." His face was strange in the light beyond the flames. "'Right and wrong' are always the bosses words, and the only words for the bosses ought to be. . . *fuck you*," he said quietly.

So Herbie had him not only joining the union but learning its slogans and its structure. No other union in America had been able to organize migrant workers, Negroes and Mexicans. The union had its own college in Duluth, and during one trial in Weed, California they claimed to have read the whole town dry (really, it wasn't that big). But their problem was that they were so gangly-limbed, hands and feet so far from the heart of their organization. Herbie said that as a midwesterner he thought it was his duty to bring a bit of Chicago daily to the west coast. "Some wobs out here are still praising Jesus, Wes, do you realize that? You got to keep reminding them that He would have made a good carpenter if He'd stuck with his real old man."

The loggers on Michigan Hill laughed at Wes when he pulled in at dusk slumped on the back of that mule, dead asleep. They kidded him at supper so he played the rube to please them, eating rows of beans off his knife. But even as he warmed to this old life and these people, his people, he knew that the food he was shoving into his mouth would turn his firm civilian stool into water again before the sun came up. And two hours later--unable yet to face the four-holer--he hunkered down over a log, head down to his knees and Oregon grape pricking his ass, thinking with all his might, "Herbie, give us a sign. If you're alive, cure this shit."

He sat on the edge of his bunk in clean long johns, perched above the others who crowded around a table playing draw poker. He looked down on the head of Bert Bland. They called him Curly--he had a part up the middle and two big clumps of tangled hair jumping out on either side of the part. His brother, O.C., who everybody called Commodore, sat across from Bert. O.C. frowned into his cards. He was maybe ten years older than his brother and nearly bald except for about fourteen strands of hair that he dragged across the top of his head. He was better looking, though--he didn't look as wild as Bert.

Bert slapped down a card. On the end of his foot locker were pasted a couple of stickers: A Worker, *Yes* - A Hired Gun, *Never!* The other said, Man of Crust or Doughboy? Join in that Grand Industrial Band.

The stove at the end of the bunkhouse had wires running out in all directions; pants and shirts and about a hundred rotten socks steamed, hanging limp from the wires. This stove had a pipe rising out of it, an improvement over the one in the last camp he'd worked which had no pipe, just a hole in the roof. The air was heavy up where he was sitting, and sour like someone had opened a bottle of vinegar and poured it in his lap. A man lay on the lower bunk across from him, wheezing. His right hand came over the blanket and the first joints of every finger were trimmed neatly off. He had a nail only on his thumb.

A third at the poker table was a young lad called Loren. Wes asked them, "What d'you do up here for excitement?"

"Ask Ole, here, he learned a good cure for the piles," Commodore said, indicating a blond man whose back was to him. Between massive shoulders, yellow hair curled over the top of his long johns. There were brown sweat marks at his arm pits and a bottle of whiskey plunked down near his right hand. He didn't turn around but kept pondering his cards.

"Ya, I vass vorkin' on dat river with the blood yoost a-runnin' down my legs, den I got me an idea and I soaked up a wad vit turpentine and shoved him up m'hole and I haven't had no trouble since."

"Then we have our mouse-trapping contests," Bert threw in. They waited for him to bite.

"Oh, yeah? How's that?"

"Well, you see that big split shake over there by the stove? When the mice get real bold and come beggin', you put a piece of bread on the floor right under the big end of the shake, then you press your foot on the bevelled end and lift up the thick end till it bows real tight, then--bam!--you let loose and flatten the little bugger like a bunkhouse pancake."

"Right, Ole?" Commodore said.

"Oh-ya, I ban eatin' them little beggars ever' morning with my aiggs." He washed his mouth with whiskey and swallowed it. He didn't seem to mind their nagging. He slapped down an ace of spades and an ace of hearts and won a dime pot. "There, by gol--"

The door at the other end of the bunkhouse opened and the foreman stuck his head in: "Ole, you drinkin' all that hooch? Thought we went halvers on that bottle."

"Oh, yah, don't vorry about it, sveetheart."

Commodore Bland broke in, yelling over his shoulder--"Johnson, did we get that new flywheel on the number four donkey, or do they expect us to break our asses again tomorrow, doin' everything by hand?"

"Ole, how 'bout it with that whiskey?"

Ole answered by throwing down another swallow.

"You hear me, man, where's that flywheel? They expect us to risk our hands and necks--"

"All right, all right, Bland, as if I didn't hear enough of y'r bitchin' all day. . . you don't have to work it if you're afraid--"

"Not me, Johnson, every man-jack in this camp."

"Okay, okay. Company's breakin' its ass to make enough money to stay afloat and you buggers have the gall to ask f'r special favors."

Bert yelled--"Get y'r butt out of here, you fuckin' drunk!"

"You know I got my eye on you, buddy--"

"Out! This is man's quarters. Go on back to your cooky!"

"Lay off now, Bert. Let's have some peace." Commodore pointed firmly at the bottle and Ole poured half of it into a tin canteen and carried it to the foreman, who was red with anger.

"That's some drinkin' buddy you got, Ole," Bert said as the Swede came back and picked up his cards.

"No buddy a'mine and he pulls his veight, drunk or sober."

Commodore said, "The trouble with Ole, Wes, is that he's still holding out for the sixteen hour day. He keeps wishing he was back in Michigan with Paul Bunyan. Men were men, right, Ole?"

"Dam'right, all day and all night, too. . . go into Escanaba, get drunk wit d'whores, walk home ten miles in below zero veather. I used to sleep in d'snow, vake up in the morning two feet down, th'breath all turned to ice on my face. All you boys know is Strike and don' let the bedbugs bite, and clean sheets lak you vas some kind of fairies--"

Bert asked him who'd got him his steel spring bunk.

"Lak lead that bunk, and I sleep light."

The youngster Loren threw in, "Like the night you dreamt a dog had you by the nuts and when you woke up it was only a bug in your crotch."

Everyone yelled out laughing; it was all for Wesley's benefit, so he figured it might be his turn: "You got lice here?" he asked.

"Does d'bear shit in d'voods?" Ole asked.

"--shit on your shoes, smells like," Loren said.

"The thing you want to do for lice," Wes continued, "is to get you ten pounds of salt and spread that all through your underwear. You sleep in that and you work in it--"

"--heard this one," Loren said.

"--shut up," Ole told him.

"--you keep that salt between you and them lice for a week. Then you get yourself next to a river and take off all your clothes till you're down to raw skin and you lay the clothes out nice and neat on the bank-- long johns last. Then you step back because them lice are gonna be movin'." The others started to laugh. "They're gonna be hoofin' it down to that water, be so thirsty they'll run you over if you aren't careful."

"--good advice," Commodore said.

"--heard it," Loren muttered.

"How do you know when there ain't no more?" Bert Bland wanted to know.

"That'll be when the king louse goes down--can't miss him--big balls on him, bandy legs, a big gut and a gold wristwatch--" They were all laughing now except the man in the lower bunk across from him, who looked up with red-rimmed eyes.

"How about you, mister," he said, "where you been gettin' bit lately?"

His cheeks were ruddy and a part of the back of his scalp was shorn off in such a way that Wesley thought of mange.

"First I was down at Ord, then down south for a while, then I was overseas."

"Oh, we got us a reb." The man coughed hard and spit into a Prince Albert can.

"No, I'm from Oregon. . . spent a year down there--Georgia and Florida."

"Things worse down there than here?"

"Well, if you're a black man or a wob, it's tough. The combination could get you killed." They were uneasy with him for a moment, but the Blands looked up with interest.

"You better stay out of the I.W.W., Ole," Loren Roberts said, turning his longish face towards Wes. "He's our white nigger up here--look at that kinky hair."

"Deal the damn' cards," Ole told him.

"Everyone's on poor Ole's back," Commodore said. "One time the Four L's came through here and got all excited about Ole's accent. Said it was Kraut if they ever heard it--" Ole was burning as the laughter picked up. "They dragged him out of his bunk and one fart out of him and they'd have deported his stubborn ass. All he said was, 'I know y're just doin' yer job!'"

Olafsen banged his whiskey bottle down to quell the laughter:
"Deal!" he shouted.

When the bunkhouse quieted down Wes asked how they'd made out during the war contract years. Worse, he was told.

"--paper ran editorials so hard against us we hid our cards and pins when we went to town," Commodore said. "We go in groups of three or four--you come with us in that uniform next time--"

"What's this I heard about some blind fellow--a wob, sold papers?"

He heard Ole mutter, "Blind Tom Lassiter, used t'drink wit him. . . bugger's likely dead now."

"Yeah," Bert said, "like my little niece. . . it was a piss poor strike, except maybe we rocked a few folks."

"Your girl, Commodore?" Wes asked him.

The man folded his cards briefly. "That was the worst of it, friend-- we had a little girl with hair like Bert's got real sick when we were on strike, died after it. . . maybe she's better off. My wife's never got over it. Some folks took Jenny's dying to be evidence of god's will, that we were

20

wrong, see?"

"Your wife think that?"

Bert Bland shook his head. "No, lord. O.C.'s wife's too smart for that. She's practically a damn'd red. No, we're just talkin' about the way the neighbors want to see you. Crazy, you know?" Bert had started this new mood, now he pointed at Randall. "All of us suffered during the war, Wes, but nothin' like what Stu did. By god, he went through hell and back on the Verona, that's why he's so sour. We can't cheer him up, no matter what we say. . . don't blame him none."

"That's right," the man said excitedly, missing Bert's irony. "That's right, pure hell. And that's about the time I quit your organization." He wheeled his torn head back to stare at Wes. "What about you, son? You a big he-man red?"

"Nope. Seems like every time I think I've found my own red angel, someone comes along and beats the living shit out of him, then claps him in jail."

"But you're a free man, yet," Randall insisted, "just like we were after the Verona. 'Cause here you are, still workin' and still lookin' fit."

"But you got a change of venue, that was your freedom. In Everett they would've rigged the jury or deported you. the sheriff still rules in Everett, anyhow, doesn't he?"

"Oh, they've got their methods, I don't deny you that. No, I admire these boys here--" He indicated the brothers. "But that one boat ride was enough to last me my lifetime. Sheriff's boys had us in a wicked crossfire, you know. We couldn't do a damn'thing but back that leaky tub out into the Sound again."

"Yeah, I read all about that business."

"Well, you know a lot, don't you, son? You must have a hankerin' to get yourself all joined up and hit on top of the head."

"Well, you got to have strong feelings for a man like Bill Haywood. Why, shit, if you lived in Georgia. . . he goes into the deep south and he tells them, 'If it's against the law for blacks and whites to work together, then you better change that law.'" Wes shook his head as if it were just too good to be true, for a man to be that forward-thinking. "Stu, I lived in the south. The man's got to have guts, saying something like that. And that's the leader of a new union, going places. . . it's just--" He gestured as though he lacked words to say it.

Young Loren had lost his concentration on the card game. Stu Randall had his face right down inside the Prince Albert can, spitting. He wiped phlegm off his chin.

"Well, I'll tell you something, newcomer, that there Big Bill Haywood is one of the principal reasons I left the wobblies. When you start talkin' about this kind of freedom and that kind of 'equality', and givin' half of my pay to a nigger, then you are talkin' *bolshi*. And that man is just too much of a bolshi for my way of thinkin'."

"Now there's somethin' to what he says, dere," Ole put in.

Bert Bland was finally exasperated--"Oh, Jesus Christ, Olafsen, you are one hopeless, block-headed Swede, I swear. You wouldn't know a bolshevik from a Bull Moose."

"Now, yoost a minute--"

"Ah, *bool*shit," Bert mocked, and looked up at Wesley, wanting to clinch something with the new man and embarrassed for the others. "Wes, there's a worker in town I want you to meet. He was on that boat and he's a stronger wob than ever because of it. Forget these hopeless dicks."

"Good for him," Randall mewed. "--fuckin' Mick McInerney, had an automatic pistol, what did I have, huh? No one told me they'd cut loose. Just let me ask our smart new greenhorn, here, how come--if things is so bad in these parts--how come he come back to the northwest, anyhow?"

"Like I told you, I was raised here. It's like I had to come back."

"Like the salmon, huh? Come back here to spawn and die."

"That's the she-salmon, isn't it? The she spawns. I'm not a she, at least at last check."

"I say too bad for us you're not." Stu rolled away to face the wall, exhausted but triumphant in his narrow way. Best take Bert's advice, Wes thought and lose that one, let the poor fish die out of water. But Ole. . . Ole was tempting.

The night wore on like a small but stubborn tug boat pushing through the fog. He stretched out, started to nod, breathed in the same old stink of sweat, and listened to the bullshit mount as the cards slapped the wooden table. Ole growled and moaned and they tore at him mildly, as dogs might worry a large but meatless bone. How used to each other they all must be. Wes figured they must have been together now for five years at least, then came alive again at the mention of women. "She's a cute little Finn," someone said. It sounded like Ole had complained that she hadn't any "brains", then Loren came back with, "She's got more brains in her ass than you got in that pighead of yours, Ole." "--must have an extra brain in her ass, the way it moves," Bert said.

"God dammit, Bland, you know she ain't any more my girl than she is yours. . . she's the reason they call this place Independence. Her and that dang mother of hers with her big tits."

"--didn't say she was your girl; that was your claim."

"That lady at the store," Wes said suddenly, then lay there reddening as he listened to the silence he'd created.

"We're talking about her daughter," O.C. finally told him.

"Yeah. . . " They didn't have to know he'd met her. Allies in work weren't necessarily allies in love. "She pretty?"

There was a slap of cards. "I'd say so." O.C.'s voice was flat and studious.

"What's her name. . . the daughter, I mean?" He was still examining the ceiling above him for possible leaks.

He could tell that Loren didn't want to but he said it: "Lucy. Lucy Neimi. Known her all my life."

He drifted off again, thinking of Lucy. Lucy Neimi. To have known her all his life. Would that have changed his life? Had a kid by now, a farm? "That's a mighty big name," she'd said. Remembering her made him warm all over.

Bert had jumped on Ole's back again, "You're busted, aren't you, Swedish pancake? God damn, if you couldn't use more cash for us to take. 'Are you poor, forlorn and hungry? Are there little things you lack? Stiffen up, you orn'ry duffer--Dump the Bosses off your Back!'"

"Yingle-yangle, lit-tle lass, if you din't have a brother, I'd yump upon y'r ass!" There was a general roar from the table, and Wes sat up to cheer with them. My god, Ole was a real lumberjack. A blond block-head of a giant. The buttons of his long johns strained apart and hair curled out of the holes. He came by Wesley on the way to his bunk and squeezed his leg above the knee. The bite of that middle finger was like a peavey hook, and it was all Wes could do to keep from crying out.

"I hope you von't be yankin' yer yingle-yangle tonight and keepin' me avake," he warned.

"Okay," Wes agreed and checked into his pale blue eyes. It was always a wonder to him why guys like Ole were so hard for the union to win. And, god knew, they could use a few like him. The sonofabitch just liked to wrestle with the woods, he guessed. Randall was snoring, both the Blands rapped him on the knees and smiled as they filed down the crowded alley of the bunks. Before he fell to sleep, he remembered stories they fed you in school, about how great it was out in the woods or in the army. They wanted you to believe that to be rugged and good you only had to join something grand, or go to sea--but never talked about a union. His father had not prejudiced him; he just said, Men have got to join together if they're getting bled. But it was the Men thing that moved in on him every time he landed in a camp. He liked it and he didn't. He'd been in a man's world ever since he walked out of Newberg with a pack on his back and peach fuzz for a beard, and there was something about this *man* thing that had always struck him as unnatural. There was the one-armed cook's assistant out in his shed. Someone had remarked earlier that if you buttered him up he made a pretty good girl. Suffering Jesus.

He strained to see his friend Herbie's face in the darkness of his brain. . . . You're the only man I ever loved, he felt himself saying, almost the way he used to pray as a kid. . . Where're you sleeping tonight, Herb? What's your secret? You're dead, aren't you, pal? They got you, didn't they? Six missing on the Verona, and he'd felt that private, inside grief of someone who just *knows*--they always get the best ones. It was the Verona, too, that had nailed him to the union. For better or for worse.

He rolled to his other side and soon was undressing, button by button, the lovely woman at the store. Bert had commented, "She's the only person in Finn Valley who speaks pure English." He thought of her throaty voice saying his name, and despite Ole's warning reached for the man between his legs. Life was not exactly beautiful, he supposed, but at least if there was saltpetre in the food it hadn't gotten him yet.

II

The dream was no surprise to him, he'd had it before: he was crew on a large ship, wide as a bunkhouse, its top deck high above the plunging, black-tipped waves. Though the ship was big enough to house a crew, it was never stable enough to stand upon, so he lashed arms to the deck and gripped his fingers into the rotting gaps between the planks. He might have expected the dream after that chilling talk of the Verona, but he knew its source was the fishing boat that had taken his parents down into the sea. Fishing was "balancing the budget," his father used to say. "Teachers have summers off so they can learn what real people do." What surprised Wes that morning was the screech of a siren, sometime very early that felt like four o' clock. It sent him diving out of the bunk to hit the floor and clutch his hands up over his ringing ears. Some nearby him already pulling on boots, laughed at him, then stopped as they must have sensed the terror he'd lived with overseas. He climbed back into his bunk, lay for a minute resting his head, cursing his life, then like the rest of them, got up, pulled on canvas pants and laced his boots. He'd forgotten, also, the way a bunkhouse day began with a blue greeting to the gods of work: men bending, grunting, freely letting gas. A regular chorus of wind, and again it came to him--he had to get out. I am thirty, he said to himself, and I've still got all my hair. I need a woman and a farm. If I don't get out I'll die of the stink of men.

The dream was a familiar one: it was often like that, with his face down on the deck, his fingers digging into planks, the ocean weather gray and thick as the past. The dream ship was as big as the Verona, and when it shifted course to avoid a black sunken hull floating belly-up, the whole thing leaned to starboard, water coursing to the second deck, and he thought that one day he must go down with them. The dream was more real to him than wandering to the cookhouse half asleep. He'd forgotten the din that forty men could make eating off metal. The clack of forks on tin was unnerving, it almost made him sick. He'd forgotten the old bunkhouse names for food: "Pass the murphies," someone yelled. They called beans "firecrackers." "Red horse?" the potent man beside him offered. He looked down at what might have been corned beef. "No thanks." He saw a smear of orange hardened rutabaga from the meal the night before and urged it off the tin plate with his thumb. Oleo had been discovered by the civilian populace, for it floated like mucus in the

24

middle of his grits. The egg was hard boiled and cold, the coffee so dense and hot in the surplus canteen cup that each time he brought it to his mouth, he had to take it away fast from his burning lower lip. There was another corporate roar, this time of wooden benches shoved back, and he was off somewhere, led by the mob to stumble into the damp darkness outside the hall. He breathed in mist. It was fresh with a fragrance like blossoms, though soon enough his head would fill with the potent odor of resin and pitch. He wasn't sure what he was to do because he'd never found the foreman, and having seen that bitter man in action from a distance couldn't stand the thought of talking to him.

Olafsen had him by the arm and was propelling him along a narrow, wet path, treacherous with sprouting nettles. "--all vorked out, pal, all vorked out. Don't vorry, you're wit me. C'mon, c'mon, you vork wit me today."

Ole was a river pig. He worked with peavey to free logs heading for the mill in town that had gotten themselves tangled and criss-crossed in the Chehalis. He remembered having heard the term but loggers in Coos Bay, who worked the Willamette River, had called themselves jam-crackers back before the war. It was one job Wes avoided; he could swim but he was no acrobat, and everyone agreed that working river jams, hanging out over one taut, springy log, trying to free it--your only security another log part of the same traffic--was just about the dumbest thing a man could do if he preferred to live awhile.

Ole pushed along the green path, ripping holes in spider webs that sparkled in the first light, swollen with dew, whistling, happy as an oyster at high tide. He walked in a pair of street shoes; over his shoulder he clutched by the laces what looked like a new pair of boots.

"Dere she is." Ole's voice was hushed and reverent as he pushed aside the branches of a tall, sweeping cedar to show the river that moved silent and green a hundred feet ahead of them.

"So, what's so great about this job?" Wesley wanted to know.

"Vell," Olafsen sat down on a stump. "I vill tell you." He cradled his new boots in his lap. Straight out towards Independence the sun cracked over the horizon and brought grainy tears to Wesley's eyes. Though it carried no real warmth to him, staring at it could convince you to relax your skin and cease shivering. Ole had his knife out. "--dere is gud vork here. But da'river is the best. Vhy? Because cooky follows us. Four meals a day ve get, 'cause it's hard vork and ve are special."

"Jesus, what the hell're you doing with those boots?" The crazy yo-yo had cut through the toe of one boot and was lopping it neatly off.

"Dis? Dis is d'only vay to let the water out." He offered the knife to Wesley. "You vant to try?"

"No. Christ, no. These are new. I stole them just before I mustered out." He'd started to shiver again as the sun slipped up under an eyelid of gray clouds.

"Soot y'rself." He worked the knife into the toe of the other boot and the round of leather came off as smoothly as a cut of laundry soap. "You'll be valking all sq'vishy." He bent double to lace the boots, steam rising around his head. "Ya, dis is gud vork. My grandad vas a river-pig in Maine. Dad vas a logger, too. He brought us all to Escanaba ven the woods closed down out east."

"And now you're stuck here. What the hell are you going to do when we clear these woods and the river's nothing but fish again?"

"Dat'll never happen. Too many trees here." He stood triumphant in his newly manicured boots, stamped the ground, perhaps expecting it to quake or for his great blue ox to come pushing through the trees. "Let's get to gettin'. Grab y'r peavey. Company's payin' us for workin' not for sittin' on your tokus."

It was as Wes figured it would be, only worse. They found the first jam a mile down the river, the gap was narrow, though probably you couldn't drown in it unless you got trapped. But before he knew it Ole was out there on the end of the bowing log, balancing with peavey like a veteran circus man, and of all things, calling for help! What was he to say? I'm afraid of water? Of rocks? Of suddenly going crazy? But out along the log he came, trying not to hear the water booming through, or to think of the enormous pain if he should slip both sides and go right down on this lively log, bouncing on his balls. Ole was shouting something over the roar of water. No, not there, cinch it *there*--he was weaving a small circle up and down, pointing at a spot on the trapped log beneath them where Wes was expected to grip with his peavey and pull. But, god, wouldn't that bring both logs together, bruising in on him and Ole? Where was the logic? Nowhere, of course, just like the army. He did as he was told, sunk the peavey hook and hauled downward and away. But it was as he'd feared; quickly the log they shared started easing with the other into a slow, terrifying roll. So Wes released the hook and was running at a slant, sideways back to shore, sliding and poking along with peavey, the log still circling and shifting laterally. Five feet from the river's edge he leaped, a head-first dive into sand and stinging nettles, then pushed off his heaving chest, looked wide-eyed for his pal as the two logs that had been freed mated and crushed, bucking down into the flow. Across the gap of river there were four or five big ones still knotted like arthritic fingers. He scanned the bank for Olafsen and was surprised at himself for feeling, Ah, good, he's drowned--that means a day off. I'll quit this foolishness. Then he heard the boom of his partner's laugh behind him. "Fun, huh?" Ole was yelling. "God-dam dat's fun. You're gud, Vesley. Natural."

"How'd you get up there?"

"Lak dis." He sprinted along the sandy bank, stuck the peavey in and vaulted ten feet up stream, splashing down into a shallow of the river's eddy.

Somehow Wesley lived through it. The working day was done. They had indeed been followed four miles down the river and been given not one lunch but two. Thus, "pig," he was made to understand. It was a good job because you got to eat more. And you got to vault over logs that might bring certain death. Might dash your brains out the other side of your skull, for instance. A lovely job but, no thanks, Wesley told his buddy at the end of their exhausting encounter with that intractable, freezing river. He thought for a time that your boots need not get wet, that Ole's action in cutting his was an exaggeration, like his appetite. Till midday his feet were still warm, toes huddled nicely together. Then in an instant it seemed Ole had him plunging towards a log jam off shore where there was no access but to wade in over his thighs, his breath jolting in and out. The cold was like fear, and he kept waiting for it to feel warm, as when you stand naked in a shower and first the water's needle-cold, then when finally the temperature evolves your skin flames up and you stand there bent in lovely steam. The water he was struggling in stayed cold.

He kept the news of his change of heart from Ole till the last, after the Swede had shown him all around the camp, as proudly as an owner. They stood on top of Michigan Hill, Ole pointing like a man on a galleon discovering land, surveying a stumpy saddle of blackened earth that plunged away abruptly. The hillside was a maze of donkey engines, cables strewn like arteries along the ground, pumps still steaming hot in the mist though work was done, huge saws tilted against shacks and trees, and further down they could just make out a railroad ribboning through. On the tracks were a string of flat cars and beside these, two company trucks. "Dat's somet'ing," Ole said, "An'so, Wes?"

But the next day Wes squared it with the foreman and hooked up with Stu Randall setting choke. This at least was ground work. The tree was felled, you scrambled through the underbrush dragging your cable-choke, set the mammoth hook, then stumbled back as the giant log was first dragged then jerked high in the air by means of pulleys anchored to cement blocks that weighed a ton. It was nothing like the holy terror the river had been and the dream he'd had that first night working the river had been extremely clear. He was lost in a tentacled woods. He was leading a small troop, they might have been young men, innocent. There was a river they must cross and to accomplish this he'd found a long but rickety catwalk that led out from the brush across the deep and swiftly moving stream. It was just old boards nailed to two long streamers of logs that stretched away through hanging branches so close to the river that the catwalk might just have touched water. There was a handrail on both sides but he couldn't trust it--it was too shaky. He moved out cautiously, he must get them to the other side. He heard the pock pock of boots on hollow boards, he was leading, pushing branches from his eyes. There were boards missing; he stepped over them, the river coursing through the gaps. Half way across, the catwalk ended.

Now he must turn and hustle back but as he did the end of the narrow bridge began to sink and come apart. He was into painful water, yelling to the others, "It's breaking up--go back, go back!" Then somehow he knew--as he began to sink--those others weren't troops. They were children.

He explained all this to Commodore, the only one patient enough to listen. Frankly, dreams to him were messages. It was more than clear that he had to get off that river.

Ole asked him, "Vhat's the message ven I dream of tits?"

"Tits?" Wes was gathering up his cards.

"Ya."

"Just tits?" There was a red Jack, two fours, a Queen and a nine.

"Ya. Big vuns, little vuns, skinny n'fat vuns."

The others were roaring. "Is this another damn' joke?" Wes wanted to know.

"No yoke t'me. Yoost acres of titties, and me wit'out my boots on, runnin' vild!"

You've got to be in good shape to set choke because you're constantly ploughing through elderberry and brambles, salal and blackberry vines like to tear your wrists off, and Oregon grape as high as your arm pits. Dust and grit, sawdust down your sweating back--itch?--most of the time his whole hide felt like it was swarming with chiggers. His ass and balls were raw from itching and of course Ole put it around that he'd brought back a monster case of clap from overseas.

"French crabs," Ole said. The worst kind.

In the first three weeks working there, he saw two donkey-engine cables snap. One of them whipped right over his head with a sound like a bullet whine. Randall, setting choke beside him, had gashed his arm badly, plugged it up with pitch and lay in the bunkhouse now with a fever. Wes was doing his work besides his own. The day after Stu was hurt a coupling broke on a flatcar and it went rocketing downhill, overturning with a load of logs.

Bert and O.C. Bland said the work could've been good, like Ole said, and that Thompson wasn't all that bad a boss at times, but he was inconsistent. He didn't mind the improvements in bunkhouse life, was even installing a shower with heated water, but in matters of life and limb he was still a he-man at heart and expected his men to agree. "Ole's just about his favorite son, I guess," Bert said.

One day in April they were out there after five straight days of pretty heavy rain, and everyone was slipping and slopping around. Bert argued with the foreman to get some extra puncheon laid in all the cutting areas.

"No, no--get on with it, y'r always bitchin'," Johnson said. "Just takes time and money and we can't afford luxuries. Get on back t'work."

It was blowing cold and the rain slid off the branches of the evergreens right down their necks. Wes and Ole were trying to get out from under it but the branches kept opening up and showering them. Ole was giving Wes a hand because the river was so swollen from rain that all the major jams were broken, and it was deadly to work it for sticks with the water rising. In heavy weather his blond hair beaded with water and kinked up tighter on his head. Wes had been talking to him every day and hoped that he was pushing him closer to his side. Ole pleaded that things had to get better one day. Sure, Wes would say, then he'd start to sing, "Work and pray. . . live on hay--" Ole would bash him on the back. "Ya, I know--'pie in the sky.' Dat's me." Wesley knew that he wanted the man badly yet he questioned that wanting. O.C. had warned him: "You're not going to penetrate that man's skull, so forget it." But Bert, who mocked the Swede pretty much to pass the time of day, thought that maybe Wes could bring it off. "If anyone can push a boulder up a hill, it's Wes," Bert said. It was nice to hear that already he was making his mark, but sometimes Ole looked bigger to him than your average mountain stone, whose mossy sides might shelter him from wind and rain.

They were standing on the downwind side of a hill, away from the fall line, waiting for Bert and O.C. to cut and capsize this monster of a fir that had been struck by lightning. One whole side was scarred black, from which limbs stuck out like smoky ribs. Otherwise it was a giant Christmas tree.

Bert yelled, "Tim-ber!" They felt the hill shudder, looked up to watch the slow majestic teetering of the thing, then heard Bert's whistle blast. Wes had his eye high up on a broken dead limb as big as a mule's thigh, cracking away from the main stem. He scrambled over a fallen tree and threw himself between it and the one beside it, but Ole had taken a step in the other direction and was cursing the mud. Wes heard a rush like a great-winged bird descending--he was coated by an ice of fear that quickly blossomed into joy as he heard the thing hit and knew that he'd been spared. He thrust his head up.

Ole's feet were stuck in mud up over his ankles and the rest of him was bent forward, driven to the ground. The huge blackened limb had dropped butt first on the hump of his back and drilled the air right out of him. There was a ring of charcoal like a target on his mac--his hands were the only part of him still moving. Wes watched the mud rise slowly between his fingers as he gripped into earth.

They were too far from the bunkhouse to get a mattress, so they slashed cedar boughs to place beneath him. Wes lay on one side of him; at the steeper places in the road, Bert pulled a rope tied to the rear of the cart and O.C. led the mule down the ridgeline to the mill. It was a rough and ugly trip. For a long time Ole seemed not to be breathing and when he came to he didn't know them. He only moaned and bit his lip to a bloody mush.

Bob Thompson came running up all sympathetic and dumfounded when they pulled up beside the pond. "Oh, Christ, why Ole?" he cried.

"My best worker!"

Wes stayed with the Swede; the Bland brothers were sent to town in one of the company trucks. When they came back an hour later O.C. told him, "Who'd we get but Bickford--he's the man who lost our Jenny. He says, 'Bring the man in here.' I says, 'We think he's got a broken back.' 'Who the hell's the doctor here?' he says."

"I'm for takin' my gun back with us," Bert said.

His brother told him to shut up and get behind the wheel. They lifted gently but Ole cried out so painfully in his own tongue that Wes fought to keep his mind right here at home. This hill was home, but from deep in the woods came the boom and hollow echo of explosives. They had two mattresses under him now; they gave no comfort. His eyes rolled in his head like a madman's or a devil's.

"No butchers, please, Vesley," he asked. "Oh, god, just roll me off the side."

They got to town at six o'clock. The R.N. on duty in the emergency room stood back from the counter, eyeing them.

"Where's Livingstone?" Bert asked.

"Doctor Livingstone is coroner now," the woman said.

"Well, then, where's Bickford, can you get him in here? We got a man hurt--"

"Frank Bickford is the only doctor working now and he's taking a well deserved rest--"

"--can you get him in here, we got a man out back hurt bad."

She pointed to the wall. "There's the phone, here's his number." She handed Wes a card. "You know how to use a phone?"

The brothers had pointed out to him Bickford's green shuttered house with the broad front lawn when they came down Pearl Street. Wes imagined him waving his wife off, moving slowly to the ringing phone, wearing a bib. He was all pissed off, his mouth full of steak but he said he'd be right over as soon as he finished supper.

Wes found that he was only vaguely aware of the man when he did arrive and they had moved Ole into the examining room, because he'd phased into that dull and fatal mood he'd learned so well in France: whenever a friend was hit, expect the worst. If it was only a scratch, expect gangrene. If a pal were to lose a tooth and want a stitch, know that sawbones would find a cancer of the jaw. Reputations could be firmed up quickly on the battlefield. Snip snip, a civilian career was being made. His only wound, a tiny shrapnel burst through the palm of his right hand, he'd cured himself with Cognac baths and lots of licking. He squeezed his hand shut now--it nearly closed into a fist.

Bickford was in there with Ole about fifteen minutes, then he came out. He jammed his spectacles with his finger. "You fellows better face it," he said. "That man will be lucky if he doesn't last the night. He's got two vertebrae in his lower back breaking up. He's going to be completely paralyzed from the waist down."

Wes broke in, "But Commodore told you that when he came in here earlier--and us bouncing him all the way to town in that truck."

His inky black hair was parted in the middle; he fixed Wes with a poison look. "Look, mister whoever-you-are, when I want your medical opinion and your criticism in my hospital, I'll ask for it."

Wes watched his lips--they were limp and nervous. The fist was good now, it had finally come tight.

"And my coming into the woods I'm sure wouldn't have made the least difference in his condition."

"Look, doctor, it's only Olaf I'm worried about. I know men get maimed and die. I've seen them. It's just that he's our buddy."

"I'm sure you're very concerned--you people have been badgering that poor man for three years to join you. . . and I'm wondering if he isn't better off as he is than to be whole and end up in your camp--"

"Don't say it!" Bert had yelled from across the hall where he'd been staring out the window. Commodore brought up his finger to jab and make a point, then he jumped to help restrain Bert as he crashed across the floor.

"Bickford, I wouldn't send my horse to you."

"Bland, you haven't got one."

They had their hands full. Bert's flannel shirt was sweaty and rank. He heaved about, his eyes red--"You're just like the lousy bosses in this town, you won't take any blame, you're too good to go out there!"

Bickford didn't flinch but stood with his arms folded, staring them down. "What you'd really like is to change places with me, isn't that true, Bland? You and your whole clan."

"Our clan's one less because you wouldn't come around--"

"--that was her father's fault," he yelled, "and he knows it--"

Commodore's huge hand was bunching the white coat into a ball-- now it was Bert and Wesley pulling him back, saying, "Easy, man, easy!"

Bickford marched the few paces to the desk and yanked the phone from the wall. "One more word from you scum," he said, "and I'm calling the police."

"Come on," Wes told them, bumping them back. "Bert, move out-- he's not worth the powder to blow him up."

They came out on Tower, hooked a left and headed for the wobbly hall. It was a good night to get a new card.

It was some encouragement, feeling as bad as he did about Ole, to find so many men gathered in that rough, wood-floored lobby of the Roderick Hotel, members of the I.W.W. from all over the area. There were miners and railroad workers as well as loggers from Onalaska, Raymond, Tenino and Chehalis.

Wes wiped water from his hair and face and rubbed it on his mackinaw, then he shook a couple of hands. Britt Smith, the secretary,

31

came up and introduced himself.

"What's the verdict on Olafsen?" he asked. Wes told him what the doctor had said. "The poor bugger, that's like gettin' clobbered on your day off." His jowls were puddeny, his eyes bright blue. Wes had heard nothing but good things about him from O.C. and Bert. "Oh, they'll put it around that it was nobody's fault, except maybe Johnson. He's an easy scape', but the real enemy's ol' Hubbard--owns damn' near every mill in Lewis County."

"I feel rotten, still," Wes protested.

"Well, I know. But remember this, old man--you're still alive and fit. You were spared. . . oh, sorry," he said as two men pushed up and Wes thought, And who's going to feel 'spared' when I go down? "This here is Ray Becker, Wesley. And Jim McInerney--Wesley Everest."

"Hello, good to meet you both." Becker was the smaller of the two but his handshake was stronger. His eyes were brown, his hair dark and dropping over his forehead. McInerney was about Wesley's size, with a glowing, forthright Irish face. "Britt's gonna move in here and get paid for bein' a wobbly now," he said. "But I can't say much for his choice of livin'quarters. They raided us, you know, about a year ago."

"I heard that." He had a sudden memory of that little man with the wide-set eyes, staring at him slant wise.

"We were up the road a ways. They dropped us very cordially out of town--"

"--by the ears," Becker finished.

Someone outside their group yelled, "Is that the Mick?" It sounded like Bert. "Hey, Wes, want to go for a beer?"

"Yeah," he called and turned back to McInerney and Ray Becker. "You were on the Verona, I heard."

Becker pointed at the Irishman. "--that's this one."

"You were wounded?"

"I was and tried for it, too."

"Did you know Olafsen?"

"I've had the pleasure--he put me right on my head in the drink last logger's picnic."

"I feel sick about him," Wes maintained. McInerney dropped his head and Becker glanced from him back to Wesley.

"Maybe you ought to save some of that feeling," he said evenly. "When the going gets tough, there'll be union men who suffer twice as much."

"--what do you mean, if they're killed?"

"No, because they're on our side." The voice was icy, articulate. It brought McInerney's head up again and he was looking at the other man as if to say, Oh, no, too soon with your opinions, Ray. Wes put down the urge to punch him. He'd been looking for fibre and here it was, if the guy could back up his words with action. Still he was burning.

"For god's sake, Ray," McInerney put in. "The man's just seen a friend bad hurt--have you no heart?"

"I've got plenty," he said, "and even more for people who are on my side."

"I understand what you're saying," Wes told him, sweating with the effort to be diplomatic and remembering Ole's bleeding lip.

"I'm sure you do--and I didn't mean to be hard." He eyed Wes closely--"I heard you were in the army."

"That's right. What about you?"

"I resisted the draft," he said.

Bert yelled at him to come on. They were going to some place called the Timber Inn.

"How 'bout you, Ray?" Wes asked. He could still try to be friendly.

"No thanks, I don't drink." He headed for the table of pamphlets near the steps that led upstairs.

There was a commotion at the glassed doors of the entrance. He heard a voice raised and saw a newcomer peeling off a yellow sou'wester under the dim overhead light.

"Bloody Constable," McInerney said.

"--no, no warrant," the man was telling Britt Smith.

"Well, then, I guess you won't be stayin'. . . sorry we can't invite you along for a beer."

"On duty," the man said stiffly. "Sorry, Britt, but Doc Bickford says it was some outside agitator with the Bland boys over at Scace not an hour ago, threatenin' to blow it up--"

Wes started to laugh, then he was staring at the constable through a corridor of men.

"You find that funny, do you, son?"

"Yeah, I find that funny."

"Careful, Wes," McInerney warned, "this one's all right."

Smith stepped in. "Luther, we got forty-five men who'll swear there's not a single one of us in this hall who comes from more than fifty miles away."

The men crowded around him started to laugh, but the constable was aiming his hat at the brothers. "Blands--Commodore, Bert--I see you. What about this business?"

"We ain't been near that hospital in over a year--"

"How'd Ole get in here, then? Did he walk?"

"No--Bickford came all the way out to Rochester on foot, worked on him in the school infirmary, and carried him back--"

"To hell with all you mugs," the man said, jamming his slick yellow hat back on his head. "Try to be decent. . . "

"The doctor doesn't pay your salary, Luther," Bert called after him. "We do." The doors slammed so fiercely the glass nearly broke. He'd reminded Wes of someone--his uncle. He felt a little guilty now for

33

sounding off, new as he was to the place.

On the way out Wes saw Bert collar Loren Roberts. He hadn't seen Roberts around Michigan Hill for about a week because, as someone said, he'd gone home to help his mother get her shaky house in order. Inside the Timber Inn they got seated around a big oak table and Wes slid in next to Loren. Commodore sat across from him with John Lamb, a man in his forties with a long, slanting ski jump of a nose, hair that was a brown and gray mix, and a quick smile that bunched the skin at the edges of his mouth. Right away he brought out a flat tin that Wesley assumed was snuff. "Here, son," Lamb offered, "I know the size of the lice where you're workin'." "What's this?" "Salve, my friend, and very effective." "Well, sure. How much?" "Cost you two beers." He laughed but he'd meant the sale. Lamb's pockets were bulging with tins like the one he'd slipped him.

Bert was talking with a miner named Gene Barnett, who had been a union man since he'd started out as a kid, digging coal in North Carolina. He had the handsome face of a movie cowboy and wore a ten gallon hat cocked back on his head. When he rode into town on his roan-colored mare, kids could hardly contain themselves.

"You must have joined tonight," Wes said to Loren Roberts, trying to draw him out. He'd struck him as not particularly friendly in the bunk-house and, he had to add, not particularly bright, but he had the cunning of the best soldiers Wes had known. He was a tough country nugget.

"Oh, yeah," he said. His bib overalls had a kind of pathetic sag to them, and Wes doubted that he really understood the union's language of international brotherhood, but he guessed that he could put up a good fight if he was asked to.

"You hear about Ole?"

"I heard. . . damn' near the same kinda accident that got my dad. Damn' near the same spot, too, 'what Bert told me."

"Your dad's--?"

"Ended up he couldn't move anything but his head. Died of pneumonia 'bout a year after."

"I'm sorry."

"Nothin' to be sorry about. Better be ready than sorry, I figure." He was only about nineteen, and it wasn't any Boy Scout determination in his eyes. His eyes were pasted on underneath slit ovals of skin. Wes decided he could like him well enough but talking to him wasn't easy. There were quick sure answers then long gaps in the conversation.

"This must be a bad town," he said abruptly, "with doctors like that." Then he looked around the room. They were off the stern of the bar, the bartender up front, busily polishing glasses, the white sleeves of his shirt held up by stretchy bands. A big tired plant with leaves like a rhododendron pressed its face against the window, while outside-- through the streetlamps--he could still see the petering rain. Two old mounds of men, formerly woodsmen, he guessed, spoke in whispers in a forward booth, weaving the smoky air from their cigarets with spidery fingers. He found he was checking the place for Heinie--he owed him one. Behind the polished cherry wood of the bar was a long, washed out mural of a fantasy logging operation. The greens were pale and the sky a putrid blue. Who knew what the sky really looked like in western Washington? The trees in the mural were hacked off clean at the roots and the loggers all had arms like Paul Bunyan.

"I don't get in here much," Wes said, "except on weekends. Probably be coming in more now I joined up."

"Wouldn't be surprised. . . where'd you say you come from?"

"Oregon, originally."

"What did you want to leave Oregon to come up here for?" His hair was short and the features of his face mobile and expressive, almost elf-like when he smiled, but his hands were big and bold, nicked like a veteran's. His nose was long and thin, his teeth small as though he'd ground them down.

"Had to find work."

"I guess so. . . well, there's work enough. You like workin' out there?" He didn't wait for an answer. "I got to get out of there--things close in on me. Goddam trees, they close in on you. I think that's why I like cuttin' the sonsofbitches down."

Someone had put a nickel in the electric piano and it was banging out a tune that made him think of a black haired villain at the railroad tracks tying down a long-legged woman.

"You sure of your dedication to the union?"

"My what?"

"You like all the men?"

"Yep. That's why I joined--one of the reasons."

"What do you think of that man, Ray Becker?"

"He's crazy."

"What d'you mean?"

"Oh, I don't know--he's okay. He's just one of them--you know--fanatics. His dad's a preacher back east somewhere. Milwaukee."

"You raised here, Loren?"

"Yep."

"Right here?"

"Nope, out to Grand Mound. That's on the way out to Independence and Rochester, half way. That's what they call me, 'Grand Mound.'" He couldn't tell if Loren thought the naming was a good deal or a bad one. He'd made it sound like fate.

"'Grand Mound,' huh?"

"Yep. Went to school out there, too."

"Family?"

"I got me twin brothers, and my mom."

"What're they like?"

"Oh. . . who?"

"Your family--what do they think of your joining the I.W.W.?"

"The little ones don't know anything and my mom's just mixed up. She ain't been the same since the old man died. I guess it's just a union to her."

"Well, it is a union."

"Yep."

He turned to the other men for the sake of conversation but suddenly Roberts was pouring it out:

"You know about all the shit that come up a year ago, when F.B. Hubbard and his association boys raided the old hall on First and Tower and burned out Tom Lassiter and auctioned our stuff off in the streets? That sonofabitch Van Gilder still has our Victrola and our desk is sitting right now in the Chamber of Commerce--"

Wes looked at him and remembered the distorted features of a man at Coos Bay who came running to tell him that his buddy had his head torn off by a flying cable. "Yeah, the boys on the hill have been filling me in pretty good."

His face broke into a smile, became a boy again.

"Well, I got me a gun. Fact is, I got me more than one gun--got three. And I know how to shoot 'em."

Wes sipped his beer and caught some of the talk beside him, Bert Bland saying, "I wanted to strangle him, Gene. . . "

Barnett said, "If Olaf had been a wobbly, the doc would have killed him while he had him stretched out, then called it an act of God."

Loren was going on--"Then they shipped Tom Lassiter out of town, after burnin' him out. They found some kind of tore up body about five miles down the Chehalis, below the staircase rapids, but it'd been in the water too long. Coroner says, 'It could've been anybody.' And I said to myself, 'Then why wasn't it him in that river, or Grimm or Scales,' them Legion peckers."

Barnett mentioned the name of Elmer Smith, a lawyer in town very much on the union's side. He'd tried to bring up the matter of Lassiter's property getting burned before the city council and Hubbard told him that there was no place for Tom's kind in their town.

"Elmer's taken it to Olympia right to the Attorney General, and he's damn well gotten nowhere." Barnett swept cigaret ash from the table with a rush of his cupped hand.

As though he was still in private conversation, Loren said, "--and the worst of it is Lucy all the time telling me, 'They're not all bad men, Loren.' And I said, 'What about Dale Hubbard?' She says, 'Lookit how he's raised.'"

Bert caught him up: "Well, he has been raised, Loren, he's the upper crust."

36

"The hell with you and your dumb jokes, Curly Bland--it's okay, she don't really like him. Trouble is, she don't like me, neither."

When they stopped laughing Wesley asked, "Is this the girl whose family runs that store?" He remembered the rich, cheesy smell of the place, the likeable young woman behind the counter. 'This is the Neimi store,' she'd said.

"Hell, she might as well be your girl as mine, and you probably never even seen her."

"Probably not."

"Well, you will, you stay out there long enough."

"Who's this Dale Hubbard, anyway--F.B.'s boy?"

"No, he ain't got no boy, I doubt he's got any balls. That's his nephew. Big V.F.W., American Legion type. Half the time he wears his uniform. Played football, belonged to a ferternity house. I give a shit. She don't care for him, anyway. One time he come out there, meaning to impress her. His uncle owns the mill and the goddam railroad, so he has this idea of takin' the tires off the White truck down at the mill and tryin' to ride down the tracks. Come to the first big curve and dumped it right over in a ditch, damn'near drowned and when she heard about it she laughed her head off. Another time he got his uncle's private car, filled it full of flowers and wine and perfume, and tried to get her to go for a honeymoon ride with him up to Aberdeen--"

"Honeymoon?" Bert asked.

"Well, you know what I mean. Now let's just shut up about her, okay? And about that other one, too. I don't want to talk about him no more."

"I don't blame you, Loren," Gene Barnett said. "He works their side of the street just like all family does. He's the youngest dead man I ever saw--especially from the waist down; bet on it. They ought to stuff him and put him in one of their windows. If she liked a dude like that she ain't worth worrying about."

"Don't worry," Bert said, "she's lookin' for another kind of man."

II

It was a foggy morning likely to clear. They had finally convinced Thompson to install hot showers in the bunkhouse and Wesley felt grateful now that his pores were open. He and Bert Bland spent the time between waking and breakfast squeezing lice that lived in the lining of their clothes. He checked himself to see if this new warmth at meeting her again would make him itch. Not so, he felt only lucky. The day at least was lucky--the fog would burn off. The store was, as before, dimly lit and smelling richly of dill.

"I know that's you. . . Lucy--?" His face quickly heated, as he realized the woman counting apples into a bag might be the mother.

"Oh, hello," she said, turning and coming into focus. "I thought you might be back."

"It's Wesley," he said.

"I know. Would you like something to eat?" She lifted a round wooden cover to reveal a block of cheddar and a knife.

"Sure, why not?" It might not be a bad idea to mix something strong with the grease he'd eaten that morning. Bacon, they called it. It was fat with one lean line running through.

"--and some fresh baked bread?" she tempted.

"You know the way to a man's heart," he tried.

"Uh huh," she said. "Let's just say I know what they feed you up there." She moved into the darker regions of the store to find the bread.

He chewed slowly, working on composure. Though he thought of himself as a bold man, it did not do right now to look at her directly. Yet, there he was, straining to see her in the glass, her slender arms crossed under her breasts, her belly pressed against the wooden edge of the counter, moving in and out as she breathed. "--what?" he had said and she'd repeated, "I said, it doesn't seem to have done you any permanent damage, yet--the food up there."

"No, no," he came back, wiping his mouth. "And if it's too bad we can eat the plates. . . or pitch. Pitch is good."

"At least you don't rub bacon in your hair like some of them do to make themselves more. . . " She was looking at him with such direct interest that he had to stare back, noting that her eyes were gray, and her brows, despite the lightness of her hair, were dark and thick, like wings. "--more appealing or something. Makes them stink like a bear. But you-- it looks as though outdoor life's improving your complexion."

"It's a lousy life," he said, "let's face it. And you're the only one in this place worth looking at."

They were surprised at how easy it was, each time they met, to push the friendship on ahead, and how simple to find the time to meet again. They were unhurried, liking the casual rules friends establish when there is no one but themselves, and there is nothing to do after work but find your way down the hill or up the hill, calling to each other as they closed the gap to meet along a path. The first thing that hit them, after they'd found how pleasant it was to embrace, was that they liked talking to one another. Her family table was quiet, she said, her father difficult with others but easy with her. Men in the camp never knew where they stood with the store, because he refused credit, Lucy encouraged it, and her mother stood somewhere in between, going more or less on mood. "Whenever my father's in here," she told him, "Loren Roberts waits--he does--stands over there smoking in the shadow of that barn, and waits till I take over." "Hell, he's in love with you," Wesley offered.

"I know that, and so should you be."

"Oh, I am." he said and kissed her.

She was more advanced in her thinking than many in the camp who wore the pin and kept the little red book. She disliked the men who ran the town as much as Loren did, but she could talk about them reasonably and make sense, where Loren could only get silent at the mention of their names, then angry and violent. She knew all of the union men, talked with them on the front stoop of the store while her father glowered behind the screen. She knew O.C. Bland's wife, Martha; had ridden her bike into town to help her out when she'd lost her little girl.

Wes asked her once, in a teasing way, how she had managed to improve her mind stuck way out here in Finn Valley. It was daytime, they'd walked the whole stretch of road from just below the store to her schoolhouse, which sat white-pillared and solid in the sun.

"It's not everywhere you can go to school and be taught in two languages," she said. "Then I have my Aunt Eva, you might meet her today, and my Uncle Oscar. Aunt Eva's a progressive! Really--don't laugh," she added and pushed up her sleeves, then marched ahead like she was going to walk right up and punch a copper in the nose. "You'll love her, Wes. She's clever--she's learning to take pictures now, and my Uncle Oscar's the nicest man in Finn Valley. Eva's not from here. She wouldn't be caught dead living in this place permanently."

As they came down the road the clouds made them first cold; then when they parted it was like mid-summer. All the grass in the fields spilled drops of water. A crow ca-cawed from an apple tree green with tiny fruit. They knew the river was tumbling beyond the edge of the fields all the way along the road.

They came by a grayed barn, bursting with swallows and hay, turned a road to a whitewashed house among cedar outbuildings. "This is Uncle Oscar's place," she said. She pointed to a round sign, bright orange and pale green on white that was stuck like a lozenge to one end of the barn. "He made that, that's his own personal hex sign."

"What's it say?" he asked, straining to read the foreign words.

"It's Finnish. Something like, 'No stranger stops here long.'"

"Sounds dangerous. This is your uncle?"

"No, dummy, it means you don't stay a stranger long. He's my mother's uncle, Eva's ex-father-in-law. She's fascinated by him. He was the only good reason to marry, she says."

"Where's the husband?"

"Off somewhere in California, dead as far as she's concerned. George--he was nice but a little slow in the head for Eva. Then she got to be more interested in causes and in girls than George could tolerate."

He looked at her as though she'd changed colors. "Oh?"

"Not in me."

"No?"

"Not especially," she said and winked the sun from her eyes.

Before they reached the top of the rickety back stairs, a woman pushed open the screen and came out. She wore a long black skirt and a white blouse with ripples of lace going up the front, the sleeves shoved up on strong, browned arms. Her hair was short, curly, drawn back with ivory combs. Her eyes swept over him as she took hold of Lucy and held her tight.

"Hello, beautiful girl. Hello--" She took his hand firmly. He guessed that they liked each other instinctively and gave up the idea that he was to be judged. "You're Wesley, obviously," Eva said. "I'd invite you both in but Oscar's gone off to the outhouse with his paper and his pipe--he could be decades. C'mon. Anyway, it's too perfect to be inside. Lucy, you look great, you're tanned already. Here, Wesley, give me your arm, too. Do you like stories? Oscar's been regaling me with tales, as usual. It's too bad George didn't inherit his narrative skill, we might have had a better marriage." They headed quickly up the dusty road, past the barn full of blue and gold swallows.

"--Oscar's always going on about Finnish loyalty. Don't I know enough about that subject! I met George at a strike in Portland and we actually shook hands.

"You may not be aware of this, Wesley, but Finns have very little use either for the law or for logic. They often punish their own murderers and adulterers and so on without any interference from the sheriff. . . .Oscar told me that back home in Marikiva there was an old man who played around with his own daughter and had a child by her. The fool confessed to someone and a group of elders took him out and strapped him to a tree stump very cleverly by his genitals. Then they piled pine boughs all around him, leaving a little alleyway, then they set the boughs on fire and sent the girl's lover down the alley with a straight razor to give the old man.

"He could do one of three things. He could stay there and burn, he could slit his throat. Or he could cut himself loose from the stump by cleaning himself out entirely."

She paused to let them marvel at the story.

"Those are Oscar's words, of course, the 'cleaning out' part."

Wesley laughed uneasily then looked at her, puzzled. "--whatever happened to the child, I wonder?"

"--beg pardon?"

"The child. . . by the man and his daughter. Is that part of the story or is it just left--"

"Well, that part's just left hanging there, I suppose," Eva concluded with a smile of assurance. "Typical of his stories, to leave you pondering things like that. Though, I must say, you have a rare instinct for the wrong end of the story. I'd watch him, Lucy."

They had come to Neimi's store.

"How's your father, Lucy?" Wesley heard the woman ask.

"Oh, you know, Aunt Eva, private and kind of sad."

"I suppose I do--still reactionary right down to his butter patties. How's your beautiful mother? Is she at home these days?"

"She's in the store today."

"Is she? My goodness, then I can talk to her, never can tell when I'll be out here again. Listen, sweetheart--and you, too, Wesley--drop back by Oscar's when you get through with your little walk and we'll have some of Oscar's lovely cakes and dreadful black coffee he's so proud of. Then I'll chaperone while everyone else takes a sauna bath--"

Lucy protested with a quick look.

"No, now never mind. It's quite proper, Lucy, in this little cultural fjord. In fact, I may join you. I'll bring the birch whips."

With that she disappeared under the ringing of Neimi's door bell.

He ventured, "She's even more lively than you said she was."

"Isn't she? I forget from time to time, now I see her less. She always used to come visit us and take me into town on the train-- she took me to Portland once. I love her. She's a breath of fresh air. She's told me more than once that one day I can live with her and travel wherever we want."

"Has Loren met her?" he asked, trying to keep the jealousy down.

"Oh, yes, he can't stand her. Calls her 'high and mighty!' She doesn't go over very well out here. She can't stop laughing when she meets the average country boy." She looked at him, her brows meeting. "She *liked* you."

"Well, sure. I liked her, too. She reminded me of someone."

The river through the trees was powerfully bright, like dancing crystal down past the railroad bed. They noted the sign at the station: INDEPENDENCE ELEV. 114 POP. 65.

Fog blew high above them, running out from the ocean. He told her that yellow and green were the colors of May--dandelions in a field of grass. He kissed her tanned forearm. Her eyes in the strong sunlight were pale green with flecks of brown.

They passed the station and got half way over the silver-girdered bridge. The planking was torn from horse hooves and truck traffic. On the other bank, below the edge of the bridge, stood black and white cows eating grass, up to their necks in purple thistle. The deep green of the slow moving river drew him down so that momentarily he lost the sense of being there, rooted on a bridge. A sweaty spot on his lower back went chill as wind swept up the hollow that tall firs made sticking up along the banks.

"Let's find a spot," he said.

"All right. . . "

She knelt in the sand above the wet, beadlike rocks of the river's edge. When the sun broke through the sky was electric, a blue so bright they could hardly face it, and the river where they stopped seemed to dance, spanking around an island of young alder.

"Did you ever answer my question about what to do out here to improve your mind?" The warm weather made him want to tease.

"I told you, I talked with Eva when I could. What does anyone do? What did you ever do?"

"My father taught school," he said, leaning his face on his hand. "Then he was postmaster, then he died. He talked all the time about ideas, he read alot. He used to tell me about old David, his dad, come out to Oregon in the '40's as a homesteader. Had him an ox team. I barely remember him--stains in his beard. He was a good old guy."

"What about your uncle?"

"He's all right, but I worry about him. It's the wife I have trouble with."

"She's a nag?"

"She nags at his work. He was all right when he still had the candy store in Newberg. She grew up out here; she's convinced she comes from 'pioneer stock' up in Port Townsend."

"I've heard that's a pretty place. Have you ever been up there?"

My brother and I spent a couple of summers on the peninsula. We hiked up the Hamma Hamma till it got so wet we couldn't light a fire, then we came out."

"Who did Eva remind you of?" she asked, sliding down beside him. "What?"

"Eva, you said she reminded you of someone."

"Oh--an older woman I knew before I went into the army."

"I see."

"A small flirtation."

"What did you name it?"

He laughed, then put his head on her breast and slid his arm beneath her. She had him dead to rights--"No, no," he said, "it's just, a woman reminds you of another woman and, you know, certain feelings rise."

"I know. I can feel them." She pushed up on her elbows. "Look, you don't have to try to make me jealous."

"I know."

"What about the other summer?"

"Oh, out here? That was the other end of the peninsula, Neah Bay."

"When was that?"

"Year before I left home, I was sixteen, Charley was fourteen. . . we worked the cannery up there, got in fights every night with the Makahs. Then we had an old buddy at work used to take us fishing, way out, mostly because he drank so much he needed a couple of steady men at the oars."

"How far out did you go?"

"To where it starts to roll. In the ocean, rollers are like breakers that haven't yet found the beach."

42

"I'd be frightened," she said.

"You'd row back before they amount to anything--they just roll and sway, it's kind of strange, especially when it's foggy, which it is out there most of the time. You know, I always thought when I was out there, it wouldn't be so bad, if you were going to die, to go down in the sea."

"If you're really intrigued by that sort of thing, I guess. . . you've really seen and done things. I've only just seen the Sound, when we drove up to Hood's Canal. That was so beautiful, the mountains come right out of the water, and there you were those two summers, just on the other side of them."

"Why not hit the road? Take yourself a trip?"

"Women can't do that," she said, half-joking. "My father's always talking about moving us to Los Angeles for the weather."

"I could think of other places he might go."

"Ah, don't--he's not that bad, just a little mixed up."

"Hope he doesn't get sick and die of it."

"Wesley--"

"Sorry, love."

"I told you before, it's when you talk that way--you're on such close terms with death, honestly, it bothers me."

"Don't forget who built the trenches. . . and I work in the woods. Like Loren says, 'Things close in on you.'"

"Tell me something--I've wondered. . . did you ever kill a man? No, I mean--that you knew about?"

It wasn't a story he often told. He set it up for her so as not to brag: they had a lieutenant, an obnoxious little O.T.C.'er from the Plains, a college kid filled with authority. He used to head out every night to find the battalion C.O., who trafficked in Cognac, used to deal it and play cards for it. The lieutenant had money and liked to get drunk with the brass, then he'd abuse his men all day because of his throbbing head. One morning there was someone crawling through the firing zone; the sun had not come up. There was a password and he and two other men called for it. What they got back was something like, "Go fuck yourselves," in garbled English. Naturally they shot him.

"My god. Just like that? Didn't you guess it might be him--?"

"Could have been a Hun."

"Wesley, that's awful. . . stop it now." He had rolled her over in the sand, tickling her. "Stop it," she cried.

He kissed her and ran his hand up her dress, touching her through the fabric of her drawers, until he felt his fingers wet. "Tell me something," he said, "what did you ever do for excitement before I came to this crazy place?"

She squinted her eyes at the sun and spread her legs so that he could slide his fingers in--"Well, me and my girlfriend used to sit up to our necks in Indian Creek and read *20,000 Leagues Under the Sea* to

43

each other. Stark naked."

"Want to try that again?"

"What, you've got Jules Verne?"

"No. We've got the river. There's that pool out there off the end of the island."

"What'll we read?"

"I've got my red book."

"Let's stick to the bathing."

"All right," he said, plucking the globe-like buttons of her blouse.

"All right." She moved on top of him, pulling down his suspenders so his arms were briefly pinned, then went for the buttons of his fly.

They returned to Uncle Osacr's farm that afternoon and got their picture taken. Eva warned them, "Don't move now. Hold it just like that." Inside they met the old man standing at his stove, lifting a porcelain coffee pot. His white hair blossomed around his head, rimless glasses shone above high cheek bones--the cuffs of his heavy black pants hung over his boots. These were his Sunday clothes. He wore a vest of the same material as his trousers over a gray flannel shirt buttoned to the neck. He was pleased to meet Everest. Eva sat at the table admiring him.

"This is Oscar, Wesley," she said. I suggest you watch him, he's a *noita*." The remark amused the old man--he laughed and shot up one eyebrow, up and down, as he poured black coffee into blue china cups. Lucy said that a noita was a sort of Finnish wizard, someone who does tricks and is tricked in return.

Oscar hadn't the heavy accent of Ole, in fact scarcely any accent at all. He seemed a wise, clever person--not really fatherly, more like an old sailor who'd finally retired. He said metter-of-factly that he'd known one or two "noitas" in his lifetime: "There was one man right here in Finn Valley could tell you every time when the ocean fog was coming in. . . 'every damn morning'."

He stirred his coffee and held a cake that was made from an iron mold. "I was born in the province of Pori, Mr. Everest, and I lived in Marikiva before we moved to the upper-peninsula in Michigan. One of my sons, George, the one who married Eva, came over with me and lived here. The older one stayed and fought in the Russo-Finnish War and refused to leave his homeland." Wes got the feeling that maybe it was too bad--if Eva was destined to meet him and his family-- she hadn't met Jussi instead of George.

A pretty girl of about ten came into the room. "This is Ilsa, my youngest," Oscar announced. He spoke to her in Finnish and she smiled. She said hello with great effort, but when Oscar asked, "Do you know Lucy might be your teacher next year?" she blushed and ran off.

"Ah, there she goes," he said, "wild as a cat. She'll be gone for hours now, hiding in the barn or someplace." They sat at a great oak table, the women moving back and forth from the kitchen through the glass doors.

Wesley was aware now that the cakes and coffee were just preliminary to a larger meal. He watched steam rise from a mound of mashed potatoes. "Ilsa came to me when she was three," Oscar was saying. "Her mother's dead, hemorrhaged, father's a drunk--he doesn't dare come around here. She wouldn't talk for the longest time, then out in the shed one day I pointed to a shovel and asked fast, 'What's that?' She said *shovel* in Finnish before she could think, and I grabbed her up and ran in here--my wife was alive then. 'She *can* talk!' I said. Oh, my, she was so scared.

"When I was a boy I guess I was a lot like her. I was small but I was strong. I remember I nearly was sick when my father made me hold the sheep to be slaughtered, but from the time I was ten I could hold an axe straight out." He gestured, grimacing, with his fork. "--easy for a lumber-jack like you, huh, Wesley?"

"No, as a mater of fact, it's not," he said. "My right hand's not what it ought to be. . . I can still fire a pistol--" He felt Lucy grip into his shoulder as she set down his plate and he smiled back at her to make her think he was joking.

"I, too, had to serve in the army," Oscar said, "very much against my will. Then I came back as a 'trenki'--that's a hired man. The lowest. I had done well in school, but there wasn't money for me to become a scholar. Instead I worked myself nearly to death with jobs I hated. I worked in lumber camps in this country and was nearly blinded helping a blacksmith. Sparks flew in my eyes." His eyes were big and milky behind the lenses of his spectacles.

"I don't regret coming to this country. In Finland the lakes were full of fishes but we couldn't fish them; the woods were full of game but we couldn't hunt unless we poached because the land was owned by our 'betters'. Is it any wonder I left Finland to come here, Eva?"

She seated herself beside him and touched his hand. "If you hadn't I would never have met you and I'd be the loser for that."

He looked to Wesley once more. "I know what an American working man's up against--I'm not stupid--you're right to organize. The wobblies have my sympathy. More than that. . . for what it's worth."

"It's worth a lot, I'm sure," he said.

"Everything is how Eva says it--'relative.' The lumber bosses in this country are rich, just like our noblemen back home. It's the same all over the world and it has to be changed. Men will die but it has to be changed." He went on more brightly: "You've got to have the toughness of a Finn to survive a labor fight. You can't believe what a Finn can stand. I saw a fight between two Finlanders right out there in Rochester during the '17 strike. A little fellow who was a wobbly sympathizer come into the store and slapped a big company man so hard he knocked his hat off. The big one, John Lonzo, pulled out a gun and shot a bullet right through the little one's hip. We set little Aljo up on a grocery shelf and wanted to fix him up. He just laughed and said the bullet had come out, so he'd walk home and be down again in the morning. He was dead in the morning!

"They got the big guy later though--Finns don't forget. The company protected him but after the strike he took a job down in Portland for more pay. Two local men followed him and put the finger on him and some of the workers down there pushed him off the side of the road and dumped wheelbarrows full of gravel over him."

Eva said, "I thought the climax of that story was that Lonzo emerged two days later from the pile, spitting gravel--"

He winked, "No, no, we're not that tough."

She went on, "You see they get brutal from those steam baths. I've seen them in their saunas pouring water on the hot rocks until the steam is so thick you can't see. Then they beat each other with birch branches to whip up the blood. Tribal, really." She added, "Men and women together--"

Uncle Oscar was back in the game--"After they get hot enough, they run out naked and jump in the snow to cool off, or chop holes in the ice and go swimming in Lake Superior."

"Is that why so many Finns have t.b.?" Lucy asked.

They moved outside to a cool, brilliant sunset of deep orange and blue running up to a middle sky of indefinite green. "Won't take me long to fire that sauna," Oscar said.

Wesley knew that they were going to do something he had never done before. The feeling of wonder located itself in his flesh, but it was not what he had known that afternoon with Lucy stretched naked over him. They sat on a bench drawn up against the outside of the sauna shed. Eva reached towards him and asked if he smoked--"Thanks," he said and leaned across Lucy's breast to take a light. He knew that what Eva had said that afternoon about joining them was now to be fact. He wondered why he'd felt threatened by her earlier, figured it must have been that remark of Lucy's about her "liking girls," and knew that things of that kind oughtn't to bother him because. . . well, he'd been around, he was human. Wasn't everyone set down naked in this life? His own meanderings began to amuse him, wishing Herbie were there, sweating out the wait, dying for a look. The women turned to see him grinning to himself. "--looking forward to this," he explained, lifting his hand with the cigaret and gesturing back towards the sauna. Way out east, along the horizon, things were going black. The ends of his and Eva's cigarets gave them their only light but at his back he felt the walls of the sauna warming up. He was aware of a richness: beside him, maybe deep in Lucy's womb, was seed--his and hers. He was aware, too, that he wanted to see Eva naked.

They were in a place like a miniature locker room, all cedar, outside the door to the steam room. Wesley started out pretty boldly undressing, following Oscar's lead, but here in this suddenly public place he found that it was his own nakedness that consumed him, not Eva's. He cast a look just at the level of Oscar's groin and was shocked to see the old man's genitals hanging down like those of a horse. He'd always thought himself moderately endowed and for a moment wished himself without eyes or with the secret instincts of an ostrich, seeking sand.

Thank god, he thought when Lucy, perhaps in tune with him, grabbed a towel to wrap herself. He did the same and fig-leafed his way into the other room. Eva walked ahead of him, towel-less and apparently unperturbed. She had breasts, he noted without passion and a rounded behind--like Lucy's, like his own without hair. Oscar's buttocks were like the blades of a plow.

They walked up two steps to a narrow platform and sat on a bench with their backs not touching the wall because it was charcoaled black. He was taken by the simple steam system, which consisted of a nearly invisible iron oven, weighted down under a heap of river rocks. They glowed red. The lamp cast strange shadows on the blackened walls, then Oscar from the other end of the bench, dipped into a bucket of fresh water at his gnarled feet, leaned over the railing of their perch and flung water from the dipper onto the rocks with a terrific hissing sound. The steam rode up on the far wall and crossed the ceiling fast to the level of their heads and shoulders. Soon they were running wet as he repeated and repeated the operation.

When they came back down the two steps a half an hour later, Wesley carried his towel limp in his hand. Each of them took a turn in front of Oscar as he washed the sweat from their bodies with dippers full of lukewarm water. They quickly rubbed themselves dry in the outer room and dressed without care of their nakedness, then walked outside to night air that was heavy with scent as a blooming tree. His body felt like a waterfall, clean and full of strange motion. He and Lucy left to grope their way home. Eva leaned on Oscar's arm as he lifted the kerosene light above his head. He was a friendly jack o'lantern in the darkness at the end of the porch.

"Goodnight," Eva said. "You're both sweet."

"Goodnight, Aunt Eva--"

"What do you think of Lucy's man," they heard her ask.

"He'll never be a stranger in this house," the old man said quietly.

As they turned by the mailboxes to find the road, Wesley started at a sound that seemed to come from the branches of a nearby apple tree.

"What the hell's that?" he asked her.

"Just Ilsa, probably," she guessed. "Oscar lets her roam around and sleep where she wants when it's nice."

"Pretty kid. . . "

"Um hmm, and smart."

"She must know everything that happens here," he said and squeezed her to him.

IV

"Why the silence?" she asked him. They were sitting with their backs to the barn wall. Across the loft he could see rain falling softly through a window that was just a hole framing a square of night.

"My silence--?" he said, stalling. It was true, for the past few minutes he'd fixed his eyes on a rope that dangled from the beams fifty feet above them. Ilsa's swing. He wondered what made it twist and slowly turn. There seemed no breeze in here at all. "--I was thinking about the men."

"Which men?"

Why all of them, he wanted to say. They groused and bitched each day at camp, they worked long hours for nothing more than pitch and sweat, and last week a non-union donkey engine man had got his face burned off, the result of a faulty valve. No safety checks, it was the same complaint. His stomach boiled at the unfairness of it, and still the union men held tight. He was furious with their bitching, the molasses way they held back from taking things into their hands. Sometimes he feared he'd backed the slowest guns in the west. And Lucy? She, too, was part of his mood. He couldn't quite say it to himself--she'd come to him so quickly, somehow.

"Wesley--?"

"Well, Loren, for one," he said. "He's so damn'd. . . I don't know."

"What do you mean? I know he's a little peculiar."

"Yeah, 'peculiar'--do you know he's got a hunting knife he keeps in his boot?"

"That's not unusual, is it?"

"--and every day at noon break he stands with his back to a tree, he whips out the knife and spins around and throws the god damn'd thing. . . wham! Bounces it off a tree. I told the crazy bastard, if he hits me with it--"

"He threatens you?"

"No, why should he? No, he thinks I'm a god or something. It's just . . . he bothers me when he talks about the businessmen in town, like they were giants in a fairy book and he was Jack. I mean, he's got things so distorted--he has no sense of organization or tactics--"

"But he's unique, isn't he?"

"I'll say he's unique."

"Is he the only one who's bothering you? I know he goes around provoking. My dad won't have him in the store and my mom doesn't know what to make of him. His own mom's scared one day he'll hurt himself. But he's just a kid to me, it'll take him time to understand the union. He just needs a hero. . . and here you are. He's probably just showing off with the knife."

"But how could he think that someone like me would be impressed by a show like that? He's dizzy--"

"He's a boy. And I'll tell you something maybe you oughtn't to hear, you're such a grump tonight. You're a real man." He shifted uneasily away from her. "--no, listen, that's important out here. You're not a he-man, you're something new to them. You've got strength and brains and courage. They're not used to many men like that."

The compliment was nice but it settled on him heavily. He wondered if it were entirely her view, if maybe Eva'd said it first. He breathed deeply, pushed his chest against her once again and listened to her.

"But that scares me, too, knowing you're like that."

"What scares you?" She spread herself over his chest, locked one leg in his and breathed warmly into the hollow of his neck. Outside the space of the barn a riverbird cried upstream, a frozen sound, as the rain swept calmly on the rooftop. For the first time since they'd scouted out this alternate to their crushed bed by the riverbank, he felt that they were being watched. He looked over her shoulder into the semi-darkness below the loft and saw only the rope and dust ambling in the shadows of the tall supporting posts.

"Nothing," she said. The bird cry came again, closer. He imagined he heard the flap of wings moving through the heavy mist. He saw her now, a huntress with eagle eyes. "I'm scared sometimes you'll go too far, and not just you but other men, like Ray Becker--he's so dedicated--and maybe take Loren with you. . . or Bert. They're still so young."

"You think Becker's dedicated?" he picked up.

"Don't you?"

Wes had talked him into leaving the union hall the night before, got a beer inside him and soon Becker was challenging him--"You think we don't know about fire?"

"You don't know what it's like to be fired *at* is what I said."

"That's not the issue. You said, 'Someone just about has to die in a real fire fight.' Okay, because the town's ready for havoc--the paper's running hot editorials, the Bland and Lamb kids getting spit on. . . "

"Yes, what I said was someone just about has to die, and you aren't ready for that yet. Not as ready as they are."

Bert spoke for the first time--"We been through this before."

"And what happened? In April of '18, when Lassiter went out of town and never came back, workers got clubbed and tarred and feathered, and took it--"

"God damn," Bert shouted, "*you* weren't here."

"No," Becker said, "he was off fighting for Uncle Sam."

"I was building trenches, I was in a fight. There were bullets."

"The fight was here. Bullets, and yesterday another editorial calling us enemies of property. Men fought back. I was in jail, you know that," Becker challenged. "That's a fight."

"--for the love of Jesus."

"Do you know Elmer Smith's had his life threatened again. . . and he sticks it out, five miles away from any hall or friends like us."

"Is he a wobbly or a lawyer?"

They said in chorus, "He's got a card--"

"--and he's a lawyer, too," Becker finished.

"Maybe you're more ready than I thought," he conceded.

He had been looking away from her, towards the far corner of the barn, aware of the odors of old cow flop. of her sweet soap and his own sweat. "You know something?" he asked.

"What?" She was suspicious and brought her head up so that he had to stare back into her eyes. When he used this tone of voice it was best to get him eye to eye. He could be miserable otherwise, they'd both agreed.

"It's just--maybe all that talk about my being manly. Maybe in a way it's what you want me to be."

"Oh, Wes. . . that's so unfair."

"Maybe you want me to be a hero."

"How can you say that?" She'd moved away. Do you need to be propped up? That's just cruel."

He didn't like himself for saying it but the change of emotion was good for them, he thought. It was getting so stagnant up there. Next they fumbled for their clothes, shaking out the straw. It took him ten minutes, it seemed like, to lace his boots. She'd climbed down from the loft and stood across the barn in the shadows of the posts, her back to him.

Late in June the *Hub* ran an announcement:

> Business men and property owners of Centralia are urged to attend a meeting tomorrow in the Chamber of Commerce rooms to meet the officers of the Employer's Association of the state to discuss means of bettering the conditions which now confront the business and property interests of the state. F.B. Hubbard, Secretary-Manager, says in his note to business men: "We need your advice and cooperation in support of the movement for the defense of property and property rights. It is the most important question before the public today."

If they had spies among the workers at the hall, the union had its own informants. Elmer attended the meeting and told Britt Smith that one of the points Hubbard made was that "the radicals are better organized that the property interests." He also claimed that what the businessmen needed was a special organization to protect rights of property from the encroachment of the enemy. It was a murderous speech against all labor, including the A.F. of L., but he came down especially hard on the I.W.W. He named them the "most dangerous organization in America." It was the duty of every honest citizen to crush them out of existence.

Hubbard went further: he asked that they lay the groundwork for a group they would call the Citizen's Protective League. He didn't suggest that it have any laws to speak of, or any records, just eager members with one flaming cause--to silence wobs and any other related "foes of government." Of those members Elmer was sure of, Hubbard was to be chairman; Coroner Livingstone, secretary; Bill Scales, Post Commander of the Legion, was to be sergeant-at-arms; and Warren Grimm, a lawyer who'd taken an O.T.C. commission and served overseas, was named treasurer. Warren was a burly man who had played football at the University of Washington. An all-coast guard and president of his fraternity in his last year, he was one of the most admired young men in town.

The *Hub* reported on this meeting the next day, saying that the "labor situation had been thoroughly discussed" and that in order for the property interests to handle the problem a "temporary organization" had been formed with the President of the Eastern Railway and Lumber Company as chairman--it went on to say that Hubbard was empowered to "perfect his organization."

"What the hell does that mean, Elmer?" Britt Smith asked him. They were sitting in the hall by the windows. The door was open to the street and Wesley noted that their lawyer's hair matched the color of the bricks outside.

"It means what it usually means," Elmer said in his quiet way. He was leaning against an oak table their proprietor, Mrs. McAllister, had given them to spread out their magazines. Britt kept trying to arrange them in stacks, his hair was combed straight back and thinning, his blue cotton shirt was unbuttoned to his adam's apple. "--it means they're fingering their weapons with an aim towards using them."

"On us, you mean?" Britt asked. Wesley flicked a cigaret butt past both men into the sunlight of Tower Avenue.

"I have the feeling they'll be around in person one day pretty soon-- as long as you men are here, you're a cancer to them."

"Then I guess it might not be a bad idea to be ready for them," Wesley said. The two men looked at him with interest; and Gene Barnett, a few feet away and slanting down in a chair holding his cowboy hat, raised a finger and pointed it at him like a pistol.

"I hope you don't have any fancy ideas about shooting down your fellow citizens, mister, 'cause that could get you in a lot of trouble." Wes could never tell what he thought of this man--it was as though he was always joking or pushing him. Gene was a miner, the head of his local. They saw each other only on weekends and he hadn't yet got a fix on him. He certainly carried their red card and was big enough to bring down three men if he got angry enough.

"I didn't say anything about shooting, Gene. Those were your words."

"You put 'em there," he said and left them to join a group outside.

Gene Barnett made quite a stir on their annual Logger's Day Picnic, wearing his ten gallon hat and chaps, riding up with his wife and kid before him on his big gray horse. She was a pleasant, soft-spoken woman with a bonnet on her head. Gene had long sideburns, wide sunburned cheeks and talked with a Carolina drawl.

"Still in a fightin' mood, Wes?" he asked.

"This is a day of peace," he told him as Gene tied up the horse and his youngster went tearing off towards the other kids gathered near the water. "--unless you're talking about our log rolling contest."

They were gathered at Fords Prairie in a park by the Skoocumchuk River among firs and larch and blooming rhododendron. The biggest part was a ball park and the river behind the diamond backstop was wide and deep, a natural pool. They had trucked in some logs that morning for the contest.

Lucy's mother had come with her--she was sunny and nervous to be around her daughter's lover. Loren had brought his mother and two younger brothers. Wesley introduced the Barnetts and the three families made their way across the grass. Up ahead he saw Bert Bland pushing a wheelchair towards a long table of food near second base. Bert was having trouble with the big-wheeled rig of a wooden, cane-backed chair that bumped along over the rutted turf. A brass plate at the back of it read, Scace Hospital. He ran to them and called, "Bert, where'd you pick up this lug?" "Ah, relief," Bert said. "Ole, here's your new male nurse."

"Howdy, Olaf," Wesley said.

His head bobbed, a grin ran away from one side of his mouth and he whispered, "Howdy, yourself, Vesley." His neck was wrinkled and sprouting, his legs had turned to sticks under the woolen pants. Wes sat on a bench and put his hand on the Swede's paws that sat inertly in his lap.

"How you been keeping, old buddy? I guess you know Lucy, here, and her mother."

"I do," he said and they nodded to him. His curly hair had grown longer and more tangled. "You know, Vesley, I t'ink I become more of a yoon-yun man since I been down at that veasel vorks of a hospital."

"What d'you mean, Ole, you were always a union man at heart."

"Oh, but I'm all for d'eight hour day now."

"Any special reason."

"Ya--so Vesley Everest got more time to visit an old buddy."

"Okay," he said and saw that Ole's legs had started to hop at the knees. "Okay, pal, you got me dead to rights. . . " He got up to help Mrs. Neimi with the food because he could not confront the hurt look that had come over Ole's face.

"Bert!" Ole cried, "where's dat skinhead brother of yours?"

"My goodness, look at the food," Mrs. Neimi was saying as Wesley brushed her plump body going for a basket full of plates. She was a lot like Lucy only silkier and more severe. They were still getting used to each other.

"Those are my blackberry pies down at that end, Wesley, so be sure, you know--" She blushed at failing to finish her sentence. "Do you know about picking blackberries?"

"What's there to know?" He looked up to see Bert propelling Ole across the field.

"Why, there are about four varieties around here, only one fit to cook with." Her fingers were stained dark blue.

No one was eating yet, there was a crowd around the table and talk of moving the whole thing over to the side so they could get a ball game going. The men wore stagged pants and red flannel shirts, though some had peeled them off already as the sun eased up the sky. He saw Jim McInerney with a guy called Hanson, an okay sort, a logger from out Tenino way. He waved at them and at John Lamb, who sat in the bleachers with his son, Dewey, smoking his pipe.

Mrs. Neimi was fussing wildly with a bumblebee that threatened her pies. "Just clear off, Mr. Bee, or someone's going to take care of you."

The bee flew away. She looked at him admiringly as if he'd done it.

"--there, now, Those are lovely berries. You have to get the little ones. Where I grew up alongside Hoods Canal it's all just huckleberry scrub and wild blackberry. The year my dad died was a banner year--we had to call in extra help. All my sisters come over from Port Orchard and first we had buckets, then we had big copper wash tubs and the berries were black and ripe as you please. We hung all the buckets down the well, it was the only cool place. Why, we was canning berries three whole days."

"Mama!" Lucy had rounded up Ray Becker and a nervous-looking roughneck with a big wave of brown hair dropping over one eye. He looked Lucy over slyly when she turned her back. "Mama, you remember Ray I told you about. Here he is, and this is Tom Morgan, one of his friends from where he was in the seminary." She laughed at her own joke--the roughneck drew back.

Not wanting to appear annoyed, Becker forced a laugh--"Everyone doesn't know that, Lucy, least of all Tom, here. He's never even seen the inside of a church--you'll scare him off."

"You was a preacher?" Morgan said with distaste. "That why they call you that?"

"Seminarian," Ray said. "--oh, forget it," he added. "See what you started, Lucy? This is Tom Morgan, Wes--you know him. He may be joining us."

"We can always use fresh blood," Wesley said, taking the man's limp hand.

Morgan regarded him vacantly. "I hope you won't be needin' any of mine. . . "

"What a pair they make," Lucy said as they trudged away.

"C'mon, ball game!" someone yelled.

"Let's go, Lucy," Wes said, pulling her. "You be in the outfield with me."

She shook off his arm to stump on one foot, removing a shoe. Now she took off running through the dandelions and passed him as he pumped along thickly in his logging boots.

They threw the ball back and forth waiting for teams to set up. Loren Roberts, Bert Bland and O.C. had gathered at the relocated table with Olaf, who hoisted a bottle of beer to his mouth. Some of it glistened down his chin. "Take me out to d'ball game," he sang. "Go on out dere," he scolded Loren. "Make us proud of you--hands out of yer pockets." Loren trotted out to join them. Lucy yelled at him when he came in at her side and bowled her over, interfering with a ball hit to her. The ball went for three bases. With a bottle of beer in his back pocket, he picked a garland of dandelions for her. It withered by lunch time and by then everyone had drunk a lot of beer.

They had to scout the whole park to get enough benches and tables to accomodate the crowd. People were happy with the day and the numbers who'd turned out. The dresses of the women were faded tissue thin, the children's overalls were patched and their teeth turning brown. But a group of them sang, "No more school, no more books--no more teachers' dirty looks," and tied together the laces of those men who had dozed off in the sun.

"Try some pickles," Lucy said, shoving a sparkling dish at him. Wes bit a dill with a juicy snap. She had grass stains on the hip of her pale green dress, the first one he'd seen her pull over her head. He put his hand on her thigh where no one could see and rode the dress up a ways. Her leg and her dress were hot from the sun.

There were wicker baskets full of fried chicken and plates of Boston baked beans. Besides the pickles were home canned beets and tiny corn cobs that you ate whole. Bottles of beer stood in wash tubs filled with water from the river, Gene's wife and Mrs. Lamb poured hot coffee. There were two apple pies at their end of the table, lying beside the blackberry that oozed blue stain from its crust. A mound of yellow cheddar cheese sat unmolested in the middle of the cedar table. Mrs. Neimi said in a clear voice, "Well, who'd like to cut the cheese?" From the other end of the table, Bert Bland said, "I believe you ought to turn that job over to Wesley--he's good at that. . . "

The sun had come down a ways since they ate. The men unfastened their top buttons and sprawled on the grassy river bank, the sun dazzling off the shifting Skoocumchuk. In the spread out pool were two big logs, wired to spikes in the centers of the ends and these were securely anchored. A log could still spin but it couldn't get away. Women lay in the arms of men, sucking grass, very warm in the lazy sun. Cattle moved near them, chewing dumbly. There were only about two clouds in the sky that anyone could see. Someone had pulled Olaf to the edge of the bank. There was a crowd now, pretty much everyone. The trash had been put away, the baskets were packed with empty jars, dirty plates and spoons.

Mrs. Roberts wouldn't let Loren's younger brothers roll the logs. They were soaked to the skin anyhow and their noses pickled by the sun. O.C. told Wes that his wife had wanted to come but she was ill again. She'd said that sometime she wanted to meet him.

The competition over the logs was getting pretty thin. Few were left whose clothes weren't soaked, though most of them had removed shirts and wore only suspenders over their skin. Wes could see some pretty sore shoulders coming to work on Monday if they didn't get to them quick with oil and iodine.

Tom Morgan had been down at the pool's edge all day practicing. McInerney got on the other end of the log in borrowed corks two sizes too small, about a dozen beers in his gut, stags but with a white dress shirt. Thirty seconds later Morgan was teetering fantastically on one leg, then--*whoop*--the other. He spun his ass around, went all shaky with the arms; again he storked on one leg and fell backwards in the drink.

Jim took a beer, chug-a-lugged it while everyone cheered him, then jumped on with sober Ray Becker. There weren't any more non-union men left in competition.

Wes was trying to follow Ray's technique, just to see if there was any, but he was just plain merciless, as far as he could see. Ray faced the other in a boxer's crouch and didn't do anything but hop up and down with the other man's effort. Pure defense, and when Jim got tired--the sweat popping out and shining in the sun, running down the sides of his shirt, his friend Hanson no longer cheering because he *knew*--he just pitched head first with the spin of the log and took a welcome plunge.

So people were yelling, "Okay, Wesley, it's up to you to stop the Preacher. Uphold the honor of us heavy drinkers--come on, pal!"

And he considered it as Big Jim came fanning water at him with sweeps of his long arms. He thought he'd just get on and do the same thing Ray was doing, let the other man move it, but he quickly saw that it would be a pretty stupid contest with no one spinning the log. About like two men drawing guns in the street and staring at each other till the sun went down and the town went cold and quiet. Instead he stood up, hoisted Lucy beside him and told them, "Sorry, folks, no. We got to say so long. Thanks for everything--" He spoke like a family man while people on the bank jeered back, but friendly.

He came home with Lucy and her mother, then stayed on at the house. At ten her mother took a magazine to bed. They went outside to the porch. Around midnight her father appeared as a dark form on the other side of the screen door. "Lucy," he said nervously. "Lucy--"

"I won't be long, father," she said. "Don't worry about me."

He hesitated then disappeared. The wind got cooler, raising goose bumps. They held each other tightly.

Wes stayed the night with Uncle Oscar out in the haymow, which he and Bert called the Wobbly Hotel. The next morning he spied Oscar's ward, Ilsa, down on the barn floor, sitting cross-legged, reading in the sunlight that was milky with the early morning mist. He stood at the top of the ladder, then tapped his pockets and realized he'd misplaced his little red book. As gently as he could he said, "Hello."The book flew up in the air like a dime novel and she ran out of the barn before it struck the floor.

Outside he hit water into his face from the well's edge. His shirt off, he examined his red shoulders. He caught sight of her again at the side of the barn, coming with a basket of eggs.

"Hello, there--"

She flinched away and clutched the basket tighter to her belly.

"Do you spend a lot of time in the barn?"

Even from a distance he could tell she was blushing. She squinted and held up her arm to shield her eyes.

"How's Oscar?"

She shrugged her shoulders way up to her ears and pointed towards the door of the house.

He went inside and was offered breakfast. Wes worried at times that the old man's muddy coffee might make a person sterile. He ate an egg, densely peppered, fried in bacon fat. He bit hard bacon with his bad tooth and out of gratitude for the food kept from wincing.

"How is Lucy?" Oscar asked him.

"She's fine," he said and was surprised at his own tentativeness.

"That's good. You must take good care of her." Wesley couldn't think of doing anything else, yet the more he knew the old man, the better he understood his special love for Lucy. Finished with her breakfast, Ilsa clattered dishes on the counter and ran off shouting, "Going fishing!"

Oscar said, "Oh, that little one--such a tomboy."

"It must be nice to have someone like her around."

"It is, it's wonderful. You should try it someday."

"I'd like to. . . I'm sure, like anyone else. It's just that--you know, I've often wondered if I'm ever meant to have a child."

The old man mulled his toast. "What d'you mean? Whyever not?"

"My circumstances, I suppose."

"Say what you mean--be like the sun."

"Can't a person have certain ideas about himself? Sometimes I lie in my bunk just wondering what's going to happen to me."

"Are you happy, Wesley?" he asked while his porcelain clock ticked off the morning.

"As much as anyone, I guess. I've still got my arms and legs--"

"You wish for offspring?"

"Sometimes."

"Take little Ilsa."

"How--?"

"How? When I die. I'm an old man, she's a little girl. I will *will* her to you," he said, and from the porch Wesley heard a sudden pounding down the stairs.

V

Labor Day had begun cold and drizzling. Wesley sat in O.C. Bland's back yard and flipped with him to see who'd get to cut the head off the chicken they had picked out for supper. The flip went to Wes and he found it wasn't as easy as it looked to hold the flopping chicken by its big yellow feet and keep the head from squirming all over the block. He sang as he maneuvered--

Scissor Bill, he is a little dippy.
Scissor Bill, he has a funny face.

The chicken bought time with a sudden flutter of wings. "Scissor Bill, gets his reward in heaven," he sang and had the head off so neatly that some part of the chicken thought it was still functioning and weaved bright circles of blood around the yard.

There was a pine table and some chairs besides the stove in the kitchen. An old striped dog heaved a sigh as though in his dreams he'd ended his last chase with his muzzle in a rabbit hole. Martha Bland smiled at him as she cut the chicken open and said, "That dog makes a better rug than a dog."

Lucy asked if she could help with dinner. "Sure--you scrunch up this loaf of bread, while our men here sit on their duffs and guzzle beer."

Martha was an ample woman with a clear skin who liked to rag her husband or poke some part of him when she was near enough. She had white lashes and blonde hair, and her eyes were red because often when she'd start to laugh at something funny, tears would spring. She'd wipe them with a swipe of her arm and go on talking as though there was nothing odd in her behavior.

"I wish you'd been a farmer, O.C.," she told him, looking at Lucy to see the effect of her remarks. Lucy stood at the other end of the table, shaking pepper on a rising heap of dressing.

"Need land to farm, sweet. . . land we haven't got, unless I steal it."

Wes liked the way the couple spoke to each other, practiced and mocking, but even when the Commodore joked back you could feel the care for her feelings, which stuck out in everything he said. There was a boy and a girl in and out of the hot room, the girl wrapped up so close around the throat with a candystriped choker that only her blue eyes peered out.

"Now, stay in or stay out!" Martha warned. "You'll catch your death--"

"Have another beer, Wes," O.C. offered.

"I'll stay with this awhile, thanks." Martha had her arm to her eyes again. The kids were out the door, shouting up the back yards.

In the front room there was a couch O.C. had built, just bed pillows on a platform. On either side of the front room were tiny bedrooms. The boy and the girl slept in one bed. You reached the outhouse by walking through the woodshed.

"You would have made a better farmer than a woodsman," she kept on. "Lucy, my father had a lovely farm out towards Raymond, but he sold it rather than have it fall into dangerous hands--" She pointed at O.C., who sat so mildly with his beer that Wes could as soon see him behind a counter as hacking trees. She came over and planted the chicken gizzard on his bald head. He shouted and ducked his head fast to catch the organ then sat there looking at it as if wondering how far he could go in front of guests. As quick as a cat he had her around the waist, pulled open the front of her dress and slipped it against her belly. "Oh, ish-- Commodore--stop!" Her face flamed. "My best and only dress," she said. She put the gizzard in a pie dish and asked Lucy, "Does that one ever get violent with you?"

"All the time."

"Oh, what am I talking about? You likely get a damn' sight more loving care than I do, been married ten years. One and a half days a week I see this stranger," she cried. "And then we spend half a day working out the money and how we're going to get through the week. Fighting and what not--"

"Ah, hon. . . "

"But Sunday. Why we hardly stir from bed all day. So I guess it works out." She turned to open the oven and look in. The dog sighed, a ball crashed against the side of the house and she moved to rap the window and scold.

"Oven's almost ready," she said. "How's that stuffing?" She put a greasy finger in O.C.'s mouth.

"Spicy."

"Good."

Lucy gave a final squeeze to the mass, leaving finger holes, then helped her fill the chicken's meager cavern. Martha patted the end of it. "In you go," she said, opening the oven again. It breathed hot air at them. The women sat at either end of the pine table with cups of tea.

"Lucy, when are you and Mr. Goodlooks here getting married?"

"That's the first I've heard of it," Lucy said.

"You young people, I'll bet you're a scandal out in that queer little community."

"Who sees us?"

"Who knows us?" Wes asked. "Who speaks the language?"

"Well, the Lord knows you!" Martha said thunderously.

"Come off it, Marty," O.C. laughed. "She's the biggest atheist, commie-lover I ever met."

"Commie-lover," she mocked. "Oh, Commodore, you and that little union of yours. . . what do they know? Look here, here's your union--" She held up her teacup with tapered fingers. "Now, you believe in certain ways the world should be run. . . you look around and you can't miss the fact there are some others who feel the same way you do. But you won't join with them, you say they're all just talking pie in the sky." Commodore was frowning in protest but she waved him down.

"Well, you say they let the workers down with their big words, but the truth is that you're not really international. Why, you're hardly national, split the way you are. The average worker out here wouldn't know an east coast wobbly if he saw one--"

"Dammit, Martha, us and the I.W.W. in King County sent more money to Lowell in 'thirteen than any other union in the country!"

"No, let me finish. Lucy, I've been with your Aunt Eva. She and I were in Everett, we worked the kitchens there and led the singing. In Aberdeen we stood in line and got hosed clear across Fourth Avenue, up against the courthouse steps. And what'd we get out of that--new beds in the *bunk*house."

"Which is one hell of a concession."

"For *you*, maybe," she said, her color rising. "But for me the best improvement they could have made in *my* bed would be to have you back in it on a nightly basis!"

They ate mounds of potatoes, more starch than chicken. O.C.'s and his mother's yards were back to back. Bert stayed weekends on the other side of them with a third brother named Walter. The three families kept a community garden which put out spuds and carrots and peas. Wes tried not to be greedy but he was as hungry as the little ones, who literally shovelled food, their cheeks bright. The day had cleared by now, sun surged through the windows where big droplets formed outside and fell--plunk, plunk like liquid time. The children were grateful for the food but didn't overdo the thanks. Martha often looked at them and tried hard to keep from scolding them for their manners. Touching the girl's flying hair, she nervously said, "We lost a pearl last year."

The kids glanced from mother to father to see how the subject was going to go this time.

Martha calmed, realizing that Lucy and Wes must know about the child.

"She was a beauty," O.C. said, trying for a neutral voice. "Marty did herself proud with that one."

"She looked like you, Commodore. With hair."

Bert came in.

"--don't you ever knock, Curly," Martha scolded. "My god, he walked into our outhouse last weekend, bold as you please, said he wanted paper."

"--need a lamp in there," he said and plunked down a bottle of wine as dark as blood. "Or get you one of them brass candle holders. . . here this is on Walter. Wop miners out in Tenino made this."

"Wops?" Martha called.

"Eye-talians, then," he said, hitting Wesley on the shoulder as he left. "Made it with their feet."

"Thanks, brother," O.C. said and went to the cupboard for glasses.

"Brotherhood of bigots," Martha was mumbling.

The kids went out to play in the remnant of the sun. The oven slowly cooled as sunset came on and they sipped the wine and the men rocked back in their chairs. A knock came from the front door and their lawyer, Elmer Smith, joined them. He wore a dark suit that wouldn't have won any style shows. Even the leather on his frayed cuffs was worn shiny and smooth. He held a fruit glass of wine admiringly to the light and toasted Lucy and Wes: "Best looking couple I've seen in this town since Marty dragged O.C. to the altar."

"Only reason I got stuck with him was that you wouldn't fall. Redhead," she added.

"Where you been all day, Elmer?" O.C. asked him.

"Been down to City Park, sitting under my umbrella listening to a very inspirational labor message by Warren Grimm."

"What's he up to?"

"He's going to be the new commandant of the Legion, did you know that?"

"Scales got the clap, or what?"

"No. He's not tough enough. Warren's tough. He had a word for you boys today. Called you 'the American Bolsheviki.'"

Through their laughter Martha asked, "Where does he get this Russian malarky?"

"When I was at the Presidio," Wesley said, "there was a bunch of O.T.C.'ers wanted to kiss army brass, volunteered to stay on for a chance to go to Siberia. That was about the time that we trained across to Georgia. They were mostly anti-red, in love with the regulars, and the army figured they'd be useful citizens if the war ever broke down."

"That's our man," Elmer said. "He went there, came back an expert. He asked me afterwards what I thought of his speech. I told him it was dangerous and stupid and he turned mute. He really thought that I would approve. I told him his kind of Americanism was exactly this town's excuse for running Tom Lassiter out, and he said, 'How can you say that? That's the proper way to treat such a man.'"

"The man's insane," Martha said. "He's as dangerous as Hubbard."

"He's worse," O.C. said. "He's Hubbard's gun."

"Grimm told them the criminal-syndicalist act isn't working. 'Not a single I.W.W. in the northwest in jail on this charge as I stand here. . . ' I almost lost my head and cheered."

"You would have lost your head."

"Did you hear what they did after I showed up at your gathering for Tony Brinks? Look at this--" He pulled a crumpled note from his pocket: "Are you an American?" it read. "You'd better say so. No more I.W.W. meetings for you." The scrawl was backhanded and the dots for the *i*'s were little circles.

"The hell of it is, I can't get in the Elks Club anymore. They've got meetings coming up we just have to have access to. Every scrap of news is vital now. We're practically at war."

At the end of October, Wesley found this Halloween message from the Tacoma *Tribune* tacked to the union bulletin board:

> At Centralia a committee of citizens has been formed that takes the mind back to the old days of vigilance committees of the West, which did so much to force law-abiding citizenship upon certain lawless elements. It is called the Citizens Protective Association, and its object is to combat I.W.W. activities in that city and the surrounding country. It invites to membership all citizens who favor the enforcement of law and order. It is high time for the people who do believe in the lawful and orderly conduct of affairs to take the upper hand. Every city and town might, with profit, follow Centralia's example.

Tacoma was the town he'd come to after the war and briefly thought of adopting. His uncle had chosen the place after working forty years in Newberg, bringing a candy store from a one to a two clerk operation and at last had decided to give up to take a night watchman's job with St. Regis Paper for the years before his retirement. St. Regis was principal among the outfits that gave Tacoma its distinctive aroma, which was like opening the tent of a witch doctor living on a diet of green kelp, breaking wind for a solid week to build his reputation as a wise and potent man.

He guessed that his Aunt Violet backed the move north: her own Victorian family home sat high above the sandy bluffs and the Weyerhauser stacks of Port Townsend. She had lineage and class and just enough money to keep the old man humble and to create a tension between her and Wesley that still held him short of taking her in his arms and kissing her whenever he returned to the place.

He lay in bed at the Queen rooming house in town, Lucy for a change neither beside him nor in the center of his mind. He'd read hostile newspaper articles before but, god damn, "vigilance committees" and "law-abiding citizenship," "*certain* lawless elements." And "force." There it was spelled out, so bad smelling and evil that you could reach right out and touch it. Didn't everyone know what vigilantes did? His dad had read to him about Quantrel when he was just a kid. This kind of editorial would bring all the Huns out of the closets.

He'd not pulled down his shades--rain as usual sprayed against the glass. He saw his Aunt Violet reading the paper through her eyeglasses, sitting next to the lamp hung with crystal pendants. Were they working class with him at the mill? Well, except for the flowered wallpaper and the cherry wood piano brought over from Holland and the inlaid floors. He used to wonder what she did with the little money his uncle made-- turn it over entirely to him, earmark all his cash for his hobbies, fishing and chickens and those long hikes down the Oregon coast with his nephews and their father that last summer he was alive? Uncle Jim liked Wesley's dad and listened to him. Maybe that's why he moved away--no one to talk to. With Wes and Charley his uncle opened up. He walked taller along the beach than he did in his own dry parlor.

He saw his uncle sinking deeper into his own private deafness, while she mechanically played that smooth piano that for years she'd been trying to coax into sounding alive. She had no politics whatsoever, not needing any. Surely she couldn't see any more point in the union Wes had joined than she could in his uncle's job, or his life.

But straight upstairs from the room where she sat reading was another formal room and a bed with a multi-colored quilt, a white pitcher on an ornate walnut stand, a brilliant view of Commencement Bay when the smoke and weather cleared. Where he had stalled three weeks after he'd come home from the army, the old man really old: "Wesley, do you think you can make it up the hill to Jerry's for a beer with your Uncle Jim? Wanta show you off to the local hicks--" "It's you who ought to worry about making it up the hill," she told him.

In that room with the quilt-covered, boxy bed and the white basin and the antique stand was a matching walnut dresser. And in the top right drawer of that matching walnut dresser was a forty-five service revolver. He left it there thinking he'd never have use for it again.

His Aunt Vi's house, seen from the street above and looking out to the peeled blue of the bay where seagulls tossed aside logic and dove down from the higher air, was as Victorian and stark and sticking-up on a corner of the street as any fine house in Port Townsend, though smaller. How *white* it was on that blue day, the first of November-- light, light cool air and the gingerbread scallops above the pure white siding were like bits you could pull off and eat. The tiny, crisp back porch was something embedded and whole in his mind. Over the top of the house--the chimney curling out wisps of clean smoke--you plunged through time and space down to the cold blue waters of the Sound. The house faced the sea; Wes looked at its back and one side and a portion of the roof--there, behind the green shutters on that second floor dormer room was the object he sought. He wondered if she'd found the gun and hid it. No, more likely, she'd have sent it back to the family seat to leave under glass with a card:

.45 automatic revolver
carried by Wesley Everest
the Great War
1914-1918

Would he tell her about Lucy? He doubted it.

"Wesley, dear, what a surprise!"

Behind him the air was bright and cool on a north wind, and beyond her was a well ordered cave where he could feel that his uncle sat brooding. She was as parchment as ever; almost perversely he wanted to crush her till he felt her breasts move against him. He thought of Lucy, so far from him, fifty miles away. And probably pregnant.

He ran his fingers along the covered keyboard and watched the slow transition of his uncle's face as he took in the fact of his coming back, unannounced and looking fit. His chunky thighs were crowded in a paisley chair and from inside her house the bay through her spotless windows was as sweet as English tea, but when Wes showed up his eyes began to glow.

Uncle Jim got them out of there as quickly as diplomacy allowed.

"Jerry's Bar, then?" he offered, getting into stride. Wes put his arm across the broad, bent back. In the cool sun he was turning puckish. There was no hair on his freckled pate, but beefy gray sideburns stuck out aggressively.

"Why not? It's on me."

"Like hell it is."

"You hear from Charley?"

"Not much, he's down to California last we heard."

There was no one in the place but Jerry, the owner, and a tough looking pensioner with a cane. His arthritic hands were like some higgledy form of knotted wood, and he looked around expectantly as though he dealt in opinion. For the first time since joining the I.W.W. Wes felt self-conscious. He hardly knew men critical of the union, though they were the big majority, because he and the Blands and Becker and Smith stuck so close together. In this cool, piss-stinking bar he grew self-protective, or, more accurately, protective of his uncle. He didn't even know what Wesley had been up to since leaving for the woods. Neither wrote.

Before he knew it the arthritic one was into a tirade. Like talking to himself, except that they were only two stools away.

"--but I tell you one thing, my friend, they ain't a-goin' to get away with it."

The owner sat comfortably with his back braced and one dazzling shoe sticking up over the inside of the bar. He was bored to dizziness. The sun kinked his oily hair.

"--oh, I know--"

"I've told you this before, Jerry, if I've told you a hun'erd times. . . the wobblies is as dead in Centralia as they was in Everett, as they'll be in Tacoma if they ever try anythin' in these mills again. Now, ain't that so?"

"--oh, I don't know."

"--damn right." He took a drink from his schooner of beer. He also looked over a glass of muscatel and something disgusting he was eating off a folded paper sack. Wesley was tense--but, funny, not from the urge to argue or to kill him. Here in Tacoma he didn't count. The tension came because of his uncle. They'd never talked about his being in the I.W.W. Wes was frightened that he might wade right in there with the cripple and let go a blast that would--coming from such a fine old gun--half sink him.

"Oh, hell, Riley," his uncle told the man. "If you'd joined the wobs in oh-six when they first came to St. Regis, you might be getting drunk on something fancier than that cheap wine you drink."

The other flashed a look their way. He might have been speaking directly to them the way he bristled and chewed, and his uncle wasn't smiling any longer. Wes saw it--they disliked each other.

"As for you, Jim Burnham, you been wrong in the matter of our country's honor before--you know that." His face was dark gray, wine-soaked where his anger showed. His nose was a stepped-on strawberry. "And maybe wrong about comin' to this town in the first place."

The nastiness was stupid but it shook his uncle, who fixed his elbow on the bar and pointed at the man--

"When you start to heave that stuff, Riley, turn your head the other way."

"Well, to each his own poison is all I got t'say," the man answered. ". . . that one down there don't know the meaning of the word patriotism," he added, thumbing them and speaking to the bar in general.

"I've got an idea," Wes offered mildly. "What if me and my uncle just grabbed your ass off that stool and threw you in the shitter?"

"What's that--?" The man's head switched rapidly from them to the bartender and back again on its buzzard's neck. The bartender's heel slapped the floor like a broom falling and now he was standing with his hands up as though surrendering. His face began immediately to sweat greasy drops and he kept repeating, "Now take it easy, boys, take it easy--"

Wes could hear his own voice intoning, "Or Uncle Jim could pull that pig-sticker he's got hidden in his shoe top, poke you in the throat and watch you bleed to death."

"Now that's enough, fella, that's enough," the bartender was urging them. "You gotta go, we can't have any of that kind of rough stuff here. . . everyone's tense, I know, but I'm surprised at you, Burnie," he pleaded but Uncle Jim was laughing and hitting the bar with his fist so that he scarcely heard. Wesley led him out of the place.

"Oh, nephew!" Jim called to the empty street, "that was fun. . . now that was really fun. God *damn,* I wish you'd move back in with us. Never see you any more, for cryin' out loud."

"So where'd you meet that terror of the world, Uncle James?"

"Who--that pimp, Riley, back there? Well, like a fool I once argued with the man. I said that maybe Wilson wasn't the Prince of Peace we made him out to be. Like a bigger fool I told him that the war was all for capitalists." He laughed sheepishly. "To hell with him, he should get a cancer of the liver. . . oops, no, I've got to watch that kind of wishin'. The old boy upstairs could get mixed up and send that wish in my direction, the way I've been cursin' and grousin'. But, god dammit, Wesley, you know, I ain't been so well. Up and down, up and down, that's me for the last three years."

Wesley shifted things back. "Is the anti-wobbly feeling strong in this town?"

"'Strong?' You should read the paper."

"Oh, I have. . . "

"You mean today? What's in there today?"

"No. . . we get it in our union hall in Centralia."

"Oh."

Clouds had joined up along the horizon to the north and west of them but it was still light. The sun was giving up the ghost.

"What else could I do," he asked, "but join them?"

"What else could anyone do, who's got any balls? No, don't say it, Wes. I envy you. And I'm scared for you, I can't help that."

"Do you know why I came home?"

His face darkened. He didn't answer.

"--to get my gun."

They stiff-walked a few paces, steeply downhill. Her house came smartly into view.

"God knows it's no use to any of us here," his uncle said. "Unless to blow our brains out."

VI

Centralia depot, Sunday night, cold, dripping rain. He picked up a day old copy of the paper on the benches in the deserted station: "If the city is left open to this menace, we will soon find ourselves at the mercy of an organized band of outlaws bent on destruction. . . " He crumpled it up and threw it in the street. They actually cut down trees to use for that kind of ass-wipe. What a waste--well, that was essential capitalism as far as he was concerned. That and butchering pigs, the slave trade, and bloody-fingered twelve year old girls in the mills of Lowell, Mass.

He'd arranged for Bert Bland to pick him up early Monday morning at the Queen rooming house. Before dawn he heard his friend's piercing whistle and rolled off the bed fully dressed. The rain still fell. He shivered with the wet and coughed violently as they plodded through the dark streets. They were clearing an easy slope not three miles out of town in Ford's Prairie, and they'd be burning slash, which at least was warm work.

"What's the news, Bert?" he asked. "Any changes?"

"For the worst, you mean? We know for certain they're plannin' another parade--for the Armistice."

"They wouldn't want to miss that day of all days."

"I don't know, pal--some say it means something, others say it don't. Now, me, I tend to think it does."

"Jesus Christ, Curly, who says it doesn't mean anything?"

"Well, Faulkner, for one, doesn't think they've got the guts to raid us in broad daylight."

"That's because he's scared himself--doesn't want them to. He's just a kid. . . like Loren."

"Well, don't get all jumpy and keelhaul my friends, pal. Lots of us is getting nervous."

"He's my friend, too. 'Fellow worker,' for Christ's sake. . . . How's Martha?"

"Huh?"

"Martha. Your brother's wife."

"Oh, she ain't feelin' too good. O.C.'s maybe thinkin' of stayin' home from work today."

"That bad, huh?"

"She ain't too well. Her nerves, you know."

"I know. I swear, I wouldn't want to be married to one of us blokes. Not just now, anyway."

"No, sir," Curly said and shot his head so drops flew from his bush of hair.

"God *damn* this weather!" Wes cursed and a horse whinnied agreement from a barn across the road. "What's Britt been up to?" he asked.

"Gettin' ready a flyer. He's going directly to the people with the strongest words he's ever used."

Britt Smith's circular was still wet when he handed it to Wes to read that afternoon. He took a stack of about fifty with him to pass out to the farmers in Rochester and Finn Valley.

TO THE CITIZENS OF CENTRALIA WE MUST APPEAL, the flyer said:

To the law-abiding citizens of Centralia and to the working class in general: we must beg you to read and carefully consider the following:

The profiteering class of Centralia has lately been waving the flag in order to incite the lawless elements of our city to raid our hall and club us out of town. For this purpose they have inspired editorials falsely and viciously attacking the I.W.W., hoping to gain public approval. These profiteers are holding secret meetings to that end, and inviting returned servicemen to do their bidding. In this work they are assisted by the bankrupt lumber barons of southwest Washington who led the mob that looted and burned the I.W.W. hall a year ago.

These criminals call us a band of outlaws. They do so in an attempt to hide their own work in destroying our property. They say we are a menace and we are to all mobocrats and pilferers. Never did an I.W.W. burn public or private halls, kidnap their fellow citizens, club their fellows out of town, bootleg or act in any way as lawbreakers. These patriotic profiteers throughout the country have falsely charged the I.W.W. with every known crime. For these alleged crimes thousands of us have been jailed in filthy cells, often without charge, for months and in some cases years, and when released, re-arrested and again thrust into jail to await a trial that never takes place. The only convictions of the I.W.W. were those under the espionage law, where we were forced to trial before jurors, all of whom were at odds with us, and in courts hostile to the working class. This same class of handpicked courts and juries also convicted many labor leaders, socialists, non-partisans and pacifists, guilty of no crime except their loyalty to the working class.

Only last month 25 I.W.W. were indicted in Seattle as strike leaders, belonging to an unlawful organization, attempting to overthrow the government, under the syndicalist act passed by the last legislature. But the court held the I.W.W. to be a lawful organization and said their literature was not disloyal nor inciting to violence, though the government had combed the country from Chicago to Seattle for witnesses, and used every pamphlet taken from the halls in raids as evidence against them.

In Spokane 13 members were indicted in the Superior Court for wearing the I.W.W. buttons. The jury unanimously acquitted them.

In test cases last month in the Seattle and Everett Superior Courts the presiding judges declared the police had no authority to close their halls, the padlocks were ordered off and the halls opened.

Many I.W.W. in and around Centralia went to France and fought and bled for the democracy they never secured. They came home to be threatened with mob violence by the law-and-order outfit that pilfered every nickel possible from their mothers and fathers while they were fighting overseas.

Our only crime is solidarity, loyalty to the working class, and seeking justice for the oppressed.

He jumped a freight and swung off when it slowed at Grand Mound. Lucy was to be at the Roberts' place, too. She often helped Loren's mother, who was feeling ill again. The bond between them was solid as stone, but he hadn't seen her except just to speak in four or five days. She knew nothing about the gun, of his real reasons for going home.

The wood range was grimy and roaring, heating the two rooms of the Roberts' place, which was two surplus tent tops over two shells of houses. He and Lucy were seated in the main room and from the other they could hear the Roberts' children calling out for water and "stories." Loren was rifling through the pantry, searching for something to eat.

Lucy had just washed Mrs. Roberts' hair, using a metal pan that sat on the countertop next to the hand pump which worked directly into the sink. The sink drained into a bucket hidden under the counter by a piece of cloth stretched on a string. Lucy had wrapped a white towel around Mrs. Roberts' dark hair; her skin was flushed from the stove and she kept leaping up to charge into the other room and yell at the twins who she claimed always got "rambunctious" whenever Wesley showed up.

Lucy read Britt's circular with one foot propped on Wes's chair and her hand on his knee.

"This is good," she kept insisting. It's all true what Britt says. . . Loren, read this."

"--read it." Loren came away from the pantry with a jar of peaches, one hand on the lid, strangling it. "Down at the office. Down there when he ran it off last night."

His mother came back in and started passing around dishes.

"What is this?" She took a sheet suspiciously.

"Oh, my. . . oh, my," she said reading. "It's come to this. Oh, dear, if there was only some way of slowing those people down. That Hubbard fellow--and Sammy Agnew--and *Scales,* I knew him in school. He always looked sick and his eyes were funny. We used to call him 'Snake', and that awful fat nephew of Hubbard's--Dale--remember, Lucy, how he followed you out here that day in his uncle's private car?"

"Oh, yes, I remember Dale, all right. He'd get in these dumb debates in Civics class, then he'd sit next to me and he sweated so bad he stunk just like a bull."

"All of 'em stink. Bunch of thieves, pigs and Robber Barons," Loren offered, slurping a sliver of peach and syrup from a thick white dish.

"Loren, now you just settle down," his mother warned, motioning with the paper.

"Oh, hell, what good's a leaflet going to do? You know, Wes--I'm only passing it around for Britt's sake."

"It's well written--"

"Don't I know that. There's fancy words in it, but hell it ain't no gun, is it?"

"No, Loren--!"

"You might as well know, Ma, I've been cleanin' Daddy's old twenty-two."

"No, I said it. You ain't going to do it!"

Lucy stared at them, then glanced at Wes. Neither of them liked the way things could just ignite in that house. Wesley didn't mind the fight so much this time--it took the pressure off of him.

"I already done it, Ma. I'm only doing what makes most sense."

"Sense? Sense, says the boy with the brain of a pea! Where d'you get off saying that carryin' a gun makes sense? You have no sense, if you ask me."

"No one asked you--and I ain't got no pea brain, so just get off that."

"No guns. . . no *trouble*. That gun belongs to me, rightfully, anyhow."

"Well, that's just too bad, because it's already stashed away. And you don't need to bother yourself looking for it."

"Stashed? *Stashed?* What kind of lame-brained, Chicago gangster talk is that? Is that the kind of words they're throwin' around in that union hall of yours? Oh, they're fancy talkers down there, all right."

"Wes, tell the old lady what's goin' on, for Christ's sake."

"Well, these are the facts, Mrs. Roberts. Before Saturday as far as anyone knew, we weren't going to have a parade in this town--Chehalis is the rightful spot for it because it's the county seat. Now there is going to be one. The paper prints a story about the parade, and right beside it they run an aggravating story about the I.W.W. We sense a 'plan,' as the boys in the union say," he finished, trying to make his voice sound light.

She was befuddled. "I just can't believe it, Wesley, after last year and that poor blind Tom disappearing." She stared him down. "Are you in on this, too? Tell me honestly. You're the only union man I've ever met with any sense."

Lucy was fingering the edges of the flyers nervously. "Well," he started, watching the older woman's face turn to stone. "I'm not exactly a member of the Legion--but I'm bound to wear my uniform if there's a parade. Armistice Day and all--"

"Get on out of here, the three of you," she told them. "Lucy, thanks.

Here, take your mama's towel." She stood with her hair hanging wet around her shoulders, her back to them, her hands trembling over the heat of the stove. "I've got kids to care for--you go on out in the rain and agitate."

The three of them hitched up a buckboard and a couple of the Roberts' horses and rode out into the neighborhood with the circular.

The Linnankoskis and the Klipis couldn't read English and would scarcely suffer the paper to be put in their hands. Some were just plain hostile:

"If y'ask me, I think they ought t'do what they done before with the wobs."

"Run them out of town on a rail, you mean?"

"You people wobblies--how 'bout her?"

"No, we're Russians," Wes told him. The man stood on his porch, overalls loose about his naked shoulders. Behind him his wife leaned out, gawking, with a lantern.

"And y'better not turn your dogs loose on us," Loren told him from the rig.

""No, I never planned on it."

"--'cause if you do, we'll shoot 'em," he concluded. They drove up the road, somehow it did not seem that they'd gained support.

They came to Oscar's place. "It's too bad Eva's not here," the old man said. She'd get them to listen--come in out of the wet, for goodness sake, and have some coffee." Wesley was tempted but told him they had to get on with the job. Oscar wanted to come along, but they said no. He could intimidate his preachy neighbors by deliberately working his fields on Sunday, but it was too much for him to be sticking I.W.W. leaflets in their hands. "Be good," he called. "Be careful, there are terrible rumors." His voice stayed with them as they rattled down the road in the mist. They decided to drop Lucy off at her house and the two of them work the north end of town instead of the farms.

"Hurry up, now, dammit," Loren yelled to them from the rig. "Don't leave me here freezin' while you two snuggle on the porch."

"Oh, can it, for cryin' out loud," Wes threw at him. "You want to wake up the old man?"

"Don't stay out all night, Wesley," she warned. "You want to get more rest. Is Bert picking you up again?"

"All this week, as long as we're on slash."

"Do you still love me?" she asked, twisting herself around the pillar and moving higher up the steps.

"Why do you ask that now?"

"Because you've changed. Something about you's changed."

"Nothing's changed," he insisted.

"No? Do you have a gun stashed like Loren?"

It bothered him to know that he was going to lie to her. She shouldn't have asked, she should just have known--

"Not with me, love. I sold it."

"You did? I thought you left it in Tacoma."

"Yeah, an army forty-five. It wouldn't have been much use anyhow."

"Why not?"

"Not accurate enough."

"I see. . . kiss?"

He moved quickly to her level on the porch and kissed her, squeezing her close. Was she bigger in the belly? She brought her hands away slowly along his beltline like she was frisking him.

"Pleasant dreams--"

"Goodnight, sweetheart."

"--'bout time," Loren scolded as he leaped into the rig.

"Shut up, and haul ass into town."

They stood before a cafe on a sidewalk not two blocks from the union hall. The only light came through the windows, past the words AX BILLY'S painted in black across the glass. Inside they could see through a haze of smoke about a dozen heads bent over coffee cups.

"We ain't thinkin' of waltzin' in here, I hope to Jesus Christ on a painted stick," Loren offered.

"Why the hell not?"

"Well, why-the-hell-not is what I mean by the fact that right over there's the editor of the *Hub* newspaper; and that big bohunk talkin' to him is Warren Grimm, post commander of the Legion, and that there ugly little dude with Scales is Heinie Huss. There's the fuckin' undertaker--"

"So that's his name. . . ?" He remembered the feeling of slime upon his face from talking to the little man in the Olympic Club when he first came into town.

"--and that there's the god damn sheriff and the President of the Trades Council."

"Well, then, in we go. We're safe as houses."

"Wait!"

"Didn't you say this place was run by an ex-logger?"

"'Ex' is right."

At first the light from the cafe was warm and blinding and when the odor of coffee and cigar smoke broke over him in waves, he wanted badly to burrow into some quiet corner and stay there the rest of the night. Before he gave in to that need, however, he saw three sets of eyes pick him out, and one phrase reached him from the table he bore down upon:

"--decent labor ought to keep hands off."

From the other side of the room he heard, "--what's that stinks like a polecat?" But no one picked it up. Moving straight for the main table through their ferocious stares, he knew his strategy would work. "Mr.

Grimm," he said and the huge back shuddered, the handsome frightened face turned towards him. "Little circular material we want you to consider; Mr. Editor, wouldn't want you to have only one side of the story--" He was whipping them out and, stunned, they took them and involuntarily started to read. ". . . Mr. Sheriff, nice to see you again, and Mr. Dunning--is it?--good to see that Labor has a voice in this little gathering."

He was aware that Loren had scarcely moved from the entrance and that Huss had ferreted up to him, demanding a paper.

"Christ!" he exploded now, flapping the sheet with the back of his hand and digging at his nose. "--did you read this, men?"

Wesley pushed past him, sensing his mission was done, hooking a finger into Loren's ribs as the other man bleated, "Not so fast, boyo!"

"'Boyo' my ass," he told the man and shouldered through the door. They walked fast to the waiting buckboard. Four men came out of the cafe after them, spilling light from the open door. Loren grabbed one hand onto the reins and with the other held his rifle. Ducking down, Wes reached under the seat then brought his hand up so that it was hidden between his thighs.

"Are you the author of this. . . " the portly Grimm was trying in his rage to get out.

"--this hogwash," the editor put in.

He watched Huss strut before a silent and cadaverous figure standing back from all of them.

"That's right," he said.

"You're Smith?"

"We're all Smith," Wes told them.

"Hear that," Huss was informing the streets, "that's pure Bolshevik if I ever heard it." Other heads appeared as silhouettes in the window of the cafe and the horses began to prance and draw the rig out from the curb.

Grimm was pointing, "Mister, I'd think twice before I showed my face around this neck of the woods again."

"Maybe next time we meet it'll be in cleaner quarters--"

"Never with the likes of you!"

"Hit it, Loren! We'll see you in hell, then--"

"Brazen bastards," they heard behind them as Loren was whipping the horses hard and rattling curses at his friend for being such a damned fool.

There must have been 150 people in the union hall on the Sunday night before Armistice Day. Britt had lined up John Foss, a wobbly shipbuilder from Seattle, to speak to them. Wesley moved up and down the aisles with Ray Becker and McInerney, handing out Smith's leaflet, waving at friends. Many in the crowd were new to him; some were just kids. It was an encouraging show of confidence in the union but people's nerves were bad. The day before the paper had printed a map showing the proposed line of march for the paraders: from City Park to Third Street and Tower Avenue, then back again. The I.W.W. hall was located in the Roderick Hotel between Second and Third Streets on Tower Avenue. Since usually parades marched only to First Street, the union men had little doubt that the hall was the marchers' specific objective.

Foss's speech was blunt and well shaped but mainly a too general appeal for solidarity, considering the particular situation they were facing. When he was finished he stood like a stump to one side of the podium while Britt made the usual plea for questions. A big bearded man wearing a brown mac, who'd joined up just the week before, rose painfully and demanded, "If they raid us again, what're we going to do about it?"

For a moment there was quiet; it was the question on everyone's mind that no one thought to ask, then Wes heard Loren say, "That's what I wanta know. . . "

"Then, by god, we'll fight--" someone stage whispered. Wes swept eyes across the gathering to see if he could pick him out. There were the Barnetts near the front struck dumb. Bert Faulkner, John Lamb, O.C. Bland and his brother sat shoulder to shoulder in the second row. None of them really wanted a fight. Ray Becker stood two men down the aisle from him. They checked into each other's eyes, Ray obviously wondering if it was Wes who'd spoken out.

"If the law won't protect us, we've got a right to protect ourselves--" a man in the back had yelled.

Several were on their feet. "How about it, Britt, what're we going to do?"

Britt was still in charge and he wasn't about to advise them to arm up in a public meeting. "You've got every reason to be mad!" he yelled back. "Just keep your eyes on them. . . don't let them be the ones to force you to attack. That's what they want--and, then, just hope to Jesus nothing happens!" He brought his hands up, Foss was watching with approval. "C'mon, now. Let's have one more song that'll shake the bosses of this town right down to their foundations. C'mon, you've got your song-books. Let's hear from you, 'Workers of the World Awaken.' You know the tune. . . "

Wes watched the folks settle back and reach into purses and pockets, then pull the books out like little hymnals. He remembered saying to his mother one Sunday morning bright with sunshine and the promise of trout: "No, Mom, I need a break--"

"*Why* don't you like it?" she'd demanded of him and for the first time in his young life he'd heard in her voice, not the need for him to tell, but to inform her.

"Because the organ makes me think I'm dying," he'd said and she'd drawn back, then smiled at him, then packed him a lunch.

--If the workers take a notion,
    They can stop all speeding trains:
    Every ship upon the ocean
    They can tie with mighty chains--
He looked to see if Lucy was singing and saw her jaw descend, hold a note, then rise again.
    --Join the union, fellow workers,
    Men and women, side by side
"'Like a sweeping, surging tide. . .'" he heard himself sing, the only lines he'd try, because he saw his mother drowning, sucked down--
    --Workers of the world, awaken!
    Rise in all your splendid might--
Sucked down, caught in her tangling dress, her hair surging up in the gray waters of the ocean. . .
    --No one will for bread be crying,
    When the grand red flag is flying
    In the Worker's Commonwealth
    We'll have freedom, love and--
"--health,'" he finished in tune with the congregation. He bent his head, trying to erase the picture of her slow descent and when he brought it up he was staring straight into Lucy's eyes.

She lay in the crook of his arm on his two-bit bunk in town. They hadn't touched one another and weren't even breathing very well. He'd turned out the lamp in the room and outside nothing moved, not a thief or an owl.

"I thought I felt it move," she said.

"What--?"

"What 'what?' Whatever it is inside me."

"You think it's a girl?"

"Maybe. . . are you ever going to marry me?"

"Soon, love."

"Can you be careful? I mean, with your life. It's part mine, in a way, you know."

"It's as much yours, and hers, as anyone else's," he said, stroking her belly. "--but I wish people around here would remember, I'm one of the few people on our side who's actually shot at someone."

"Does that give you an advantage or make you more dangerous to yourself?"

"I've shot at people, I did it to keep myself alive."

"What about the lieutenant?"

"What lieutenant?" He wished he'd never told her. "It might have been a Hun, how did we know?"

"There are 'Huns' here?"

"What the hell's Grimm, if it's not a kraut name?"

"Wes." She sat up, propping her arms on his ribs. "--don't play the fool with me now."

"Sorry, Luce--"

"And tell me something--truth. What's all the talk about shooting? Don't turn away. . . tell me."

"I didn't sell the gun."

"Oh." He felt her arms go slack and saw her eyes like a night animal, staring at him.

"It's under the foot of the mattress--and I've got three clips of ammo. Lucy, honey, please, don't worry and don't try to stop--" She was up and moving to the window:

"Don't say anything. I'm on your side. I understand you and I accept what you're doing." She pulled aside the windowshade and stared into the dimly lit street, speaking distractedly--"I know the people who run the town. We know what they've done before--" She started to falter, and he felt her difficulty across the dark room. "--but, why? I want to know why--"

"Why what, hon."

"Why are they so cowardly and sick? God, Wes, I do understand. I guess that I could kill one of them, too. If it was a matter of my child, I could."

"It's always a matter of your 'child,'" he said, sitting up. He hadn't quite meant that. "I mean, otherwise conviction is just a toy or it's grubby."

"I love you," she said. Her hands gripped her upper arms tightly. "Come over here, keep talking--"

"No, it's nothing," he said, staying on the bed. "I love you, too. But tell me why, you know, why you could kill someone for your child."

"No," she said. "No, maybe I couldn't. I'm me, you're you. We're all just accidents. It's just their makeup. It's an accident, why they're like that."

"A man burns someone, or carries a rope--he doesn't have a choice?"

"I don't know. Why are you staying there?"

"To me they're unnatural. It's funny, when you think about it--they used to justify slavery by saying it was part of nature."

"So when do we start saying what's natural?"

"When we win, I guess--when we've got the power."

"When's that?"

"Maybe never."

He saw her staring at him, arms crossed, an angry nurse trying to get her patient off his ass--"Don't you believe in what you're doing?"

"I do, but I never much believed in the place where we're stuck down."

"Here? America? This town? Say where."

"Anywhere you name. . . all right, America. It can't work here."

"So you don't--and those men, they work so hard and they're beautiful."

"Too beautiful, Luce--"

"No, that's not fair. Who are you, then?"

"They're not tough enough--wait--" He held up his hand. "You've got to be a bit of a Hun to kill a Hun."

"Then you. . . that means you're like Grimm and Scales--"

"No, love, I said a *little* like one. And it's not the issue you started. I think this--I don't think we're going to win a real class victory, not in my lifetime."

"Why do you have to be honest now, and why do you stay sitting there?"

"Listen. I was raised that way, just my folks. I loved them both for that--that way of saying the truth. When they drowned that summer at Tillamook, I think that's when I felt things could never be right again. It was like the whole world lied. Everything I've done since then's been by rote."

"You frighten me."

"I'm sorry. . . I hardly ever think about it quite like that." He told himself the lie was necessary to keep some part of her spirits up.

"I'm afraid," she said. "I'm afraid I may be the one to lose the most."

They both were silent, listening to the sound of her words; then she was anxious--"I'm sorry, Wes--I'm really sorry."

He came to her at the window. She'd turned from him and he took her shoulders in his hands. "Listen, love, if I'm not around after this parade--"

"No--"

"Yes. We've got to be ahead of things."

"A-head? How backward can you be?"

"Listen, we're not sentimental. If I die--yes, just like in the prayer. 'If I die before I wake. . . ' Then what's left of me carries on." He turned her around and felt the bulge of her belly pressing into him. "You, for one, get out of here."

"No."

"Yes."

"What kind of place must this be where we have to plan like this?"

"It's America. I fought for it."

"You're killing me. Don't talk like this. What are you saying? I run to Mexico?"

"I'm not killing you. Other people might. No, not Mexico or Canada, just anywhere where you can meet someone and live a decent life."

"No, damn you--"

76

"--and have the child, and raise it."

"Then I'll raise it here. I live in America, Wes. I can't run to some limbo. This is stupid. You're going to live."

"I know I will. . . through you and this baby. Kiss me."

She did, then they made love. Then she crept down the street to seek out Loren and a ride home. Wes slept only an hour or two, it seemed, before Bert whistled. He dreamed there was a knock on the door and he smiled waiting for his mother, but it was Aunt Violet come in to fuss with the covers. She replaced them too high, covering his face and even his damp hair.

VII

Bert was standing in his room, his hands looking small and white. He'd left his gloves at home. For a moment Wesley lay there, his mouth dry and cottony, wanting badly to drink beer. There was something he could not get straight--what day was it?

"What the hell? Where's my pants? Sorry, Curly."

"No hurry, pal."

"What time is it? Christ, it's light already." He'd ripped aside the shade and was scratching fiercely at his backside.

"Damn'near ten." Though Curly had seen him naked a hundred times in their makeshift showers on Michigan Hill, now he turned away. "No hurry, Britt says. Just show up."

"--ten! Jesus. No--oh, yeah. I forgot."

"Yeah. Day off, pal. Parade's today." Bert sat quietly on the edge of his bunk while Wes kicked off the canvas pants he'd just pulled on and went to the closet for his uniform. He was conscious of Bert's eyes, watching him dress, wondered about his interest. "There," he said, finally, the twenty-one brass buttons smartly buttoned. "--there." He brought one boot up on the bed, then the other, fixing his puttes at the backs of his calves. "Snappy, huh?"

"I guess so."

"You don't sound too convinced, Curly. Don't I make a beautiful soldier?"

"Well, I suppose prettier than the ones we're gonna see today."

Wesley struck his back and squeezed his shoulder through the raspy wool of his shirt. It was pretty clear what was on his mind now.

"Maybe you won't even see one, pal."

"Ah, come on, Wes. I don't kid myself. Don't you start."

"Listen, Curly. Now, look at me. It's not all of us going to be right up on that line. No army works that way. We've got to have front line men, second line men and reserves."

Bert brought his face up to search Wesley's eyes for confidence "Dammit, Wes, I can't wait at home. My brother's already said goodbye to his wife and kids and went off to the hall with his carbine."

"No, that's true. But you can maybe find yourself a spot in between if you want."

"In between?"

"Look." Wes stood to the window and pulled then released the cord so the shade shot around the roller. "See? Good lines of fire, right at the hall just in case they go for us. And once you fire--why, out the back you go. Head on home. We're not all front liners. Never will be."

"Well, thanks, Wes. I'll think about it," he said doubtfully.

Wes felt the bite of November wind, cutting south up Tower Avenue. They went straight for the hall.

Britt came up to him with the rattling of the door at his back. The bags under his eyes were dark as a funeral parlor.

"Elmer Smith just left, Wesley. He says he's got first hand, positive information they're gonna raid us. And we've got every right to defend ourselves. So that's it."

"Good enough," he said and touched the bulge of the .45 stuck in his belt. His friend had walked off to a small crowd at the other side of the room.

Men were still coming in the door. Most of them Wes knew were signed-aboard wobblies, but there were others they just had to trust as close hard friends who'd do anything for them, except carry a red card. Young Faulkner was there in his clean overalls. Wes waved to him. There was Hanson, he'd joined shortly after the picnic. Some had joined as late as the night before, and one or two were wobblies from other towns, just passing through. McInerney stood with another huge man, a distinguished looking worker with a mustache--he must have been nearing sixty. When Wes walked past them he heard the newcomer say in a thick, Celtic accent, "--DeValera's not an ass, James, he just looks like one."

Britt had his hand up, trying to be heard: "Our landlady," he shouted, "Mrs. McAllister. She went to Chief Hughes after Elmer left and Hughes told her he'd do what he could but he didn't think we'd stand 'fifteen minutes' against the businessmen."

There was general noise and clamor over the announcement.

"What the hell does he think this is," McInerney yelled, "a bloody football match?"

"To him it is," Britt said. "We know exactly where we stand now and what we have to do. We know exactly what our property rights are in this case and how far we can go defending them."

"I think we'd be wise for some of us to take positions up and down the streets. Two men in the Avalon, two more in the Arnold, maybe someone at the Queen. If they go to battering down our place, then you in the rooms fire over their head--"

"Why not shoot the bastards?" That was Loren, over on the other side of the hall.

"No, cool down. How about you, Roberts?"

"What--?" Loren was really agitated.

"You and whoever else wants to, checking out one of them rooms across the street?"

"What for? I know where best to be firin' from."

O.C. Bland stepped up to Britt--"I already got a room over at the Avalon. I'll be there, maybe Lamb with me. Right, John?"

"Okay by me, I guess," he heard Lamb answer from the group gathered around Loren.

Loren called back, "I just don't want nobody tellin' me where I got to be if there's a fight." Wes had lost track of Bert, now he saw him standing beside Loren, both of them armed with rifles. He must already have hidden it when he came to the room.

"Good, I appreciate that. All I'm talking about is protection, and being sure we're attacked before any guns go off. To me that means the first soldier boy makes for that door, not before. Wesley?"

"I'll be right where I'm standing now." He kept expecting to feel that sense of being nauseated and lost from himself that used to sweep over him before every dawn attack. Why was this different, he wondered. He was actually hungry.

"That's good, Wes. Who else? McInerney?"

"We'll be here."

"Now, Ray Becker and you, Faulkner--good. And where's that new man--I see you--Davis?"

The brown bear next to Wesley rumbled, "I'll be where you need me most, Mr. Smith, don't worry."

"Those two-bit patriots will be so damn' surprised we've taken a stand they'll probably run right over the county line before they look back."

They cheered him though some must have felt that they were whistling in the dark. When the noise died down, Britt picked up again--

"I want everyone that's next to me around this stove to stay on through the parade, and for you other men to stay close to the hall. Just keep an eye on them. Nobody's asking you to pack a gun or fire it if you don't want to--that's every man's decision for himself. What we're asking for is maximum support."

For a time it seemed that no one wanted just to sit and talk, everyone was milling around, pockets bulging with ammunition. One man clowned, walking stiff-legged with a rifle down his pants leg. Wes saw Bert and Loren disappear out the back door and the thought hit him like an axe head: he might never see them again, or hear their voices. Or Lucy's. That part he wanted to avoid, because it brought him back to his mother again, how in dreams women would appear to him. He would strain to hear the proper chords, but damned if it wasn't always the voice of any old body he'd heard the day before. Some teacher or shop girl.

He could not understand why, with the tension building around him in everyone else--why his blood had gotten so flat and cool. He remembered speaking to Oscar that sunny morning in his warm kitchen, how he'd wanted to use the word "fate," but had held back because it would have felt like a word newly made, coming awkwardly from the cavern of his mouth. "I will *will* her to you," Oscar had said. Ilsa, that was. He wanted to hold that little girl on his lap.

"Here."

Ray Becker had come up to him, a revolver in his belt, and was handing him a stained cup of coffee and a sandwich. "Thanks, friend." He would have expected such a gesture from Bert or Loren, not from Becker particularly. "Tastes good," he got out around the meat loaf and bread. Becker had left already.

He overheard Faulkner telling someone that they didn't have anything to worry about, and in the same breath saying he'd just run home to hide his red card. "Just in case," he'd added. Wes laughed to himself but wasn't about to doubt anyone's courage who stayed in this hall today. Faulkner was a little confused, maybe, but he wasn't alone in that. He'd been aware for some time of Tom Morgan, restless as a deer, first standing with his hands to the stove, then walking quickly back to the door. Opening it, walking out back, evidently. Returning and standing uncomfortably with his shoulder blades to the wall and his hands stuffed in his dirty pockets. He must be wondering, about now, why in the hell he had let Becker talk him into joining this miserable outfit.

McInerney was generally within Wesley's field of vision, skulking around the front of the hall, keeping the stove fired. Wes asked him, "This must feel like the Verona all over again, Jim." The big man stopped to consider.

"I suppose it's the same fight but I was more scared then."

"Younger, huh?"

"No, it was the water. I can't swim, Wes. Not a stroke."

Becker came back to him, holding out the gun. "I just got this thing. Why won't the button work that keeps it from going off?"

Wes held the weapon in the flat of his hand--it was a nice one, gangstery and smooth, the metal deep blue. He flipped the cylinder to the side, spun the cartridge wheel and snapped it shut again. The safety was a little stiff but he pushed it firmly off. "Now it's ready to use." He handed it back to him carefully. "Are you sure we're safe with you, brother?"

"You'll find out if they start kicking us around," he said. His hair and eyes were black as an Indian's.

"You know, Ray, it's too bad we never got to know each other better." He offered him a drag on his cigaret. Ray sucked awkwardly and outside a sudden squall of rain swept against the window panes.

"There's not that much to know," Ray said.

"You really studied for the ministry?"

"--what was that?" Ray called, releasing a tiny cloud of smoke.

"--drum roll."

They all stood frozen, straining to hear the sound again.

"God damn, that's eerie, ain't it?"

"They're just turning onto Tower, must be--"

The next roll of drums was like staccato fire. He could hear them now, the tramp, tramp, tramp; and some perverse little angel kissed his spine nostalgically and made his feet go Hup Hup Hup, rising first on one, then the other set of toes. He heard the steady lift and fall of uniformed legs and light packs slapping backs, then told himself to cut this shit: he reached for his .45, slipped the safe with his thumb and planted his feet firmly on the boards. The Legionnaires were in the lead and they marched severely past the hall without so much as a glance at them. He recognized a little man near the guidon as the druggist from over on Maple Street, and there on the other side of the column was Warren Grimm, his chest out, his mouth puffing little balls of steam.

"Who's the pretty one on the other side?" he asked. "The officer?"

"Van Gilder. Grimm's asshole buddy," Faulkner said from behind.

The hunger he'd felt before was swelling up again, but spreading out to the ends of his legs and arms. He made his buttocks flex and brought his gun up to the level of his waist. Becker glanced at him anxiously. He might as well admit that this hunger was the longing to kill. He'd not known this sensation at the front. It was defense there--this was the other side of the battle urge. Between the Centralia troop and the mix of soldiers and sailors from Chehalis rode a lean man on horseback. "Cormie;," someone said. "--owe this bastard thirty bucks." Beside the Chehalis guidon marched another officer, young but weathered. A part of his upper lip was shot away. In profile he looked like a grinning skull.

Then came the businessmen, the Elks, and then--he couldn't believe it! He shouted, "Jesus Christ, there goes a guy in a dog collar with a coil of rope!"

"--by jeeze, you're right. Who's the other one?"

"That's the goddam postmaster."

"Just doin' his job, deliverin' the mail," someone said.

The Elks weren't as disciplined as the soldiers. They craned necks and gave them evil looks.

The whole parade passed by, right down to the Red Cross girls who marched demurely in capes, and the Centralia High School cheerleaders, pumping pretty knees, shaking pom-poms of crimson, and blue, and leaping high in the air to scream for Victory, Victory, Vic-tory. They passed by, their shouts fading until there was nothing out in the street but drizzle.

Wes heard McInerney say, "Oh, hell, we might as well go home. They're up to nothin' more than takin' the air." Then the cheerleaders and the Red Cross girls were back, their heads and pom-poms bristling out the windows of a half dozen roaring autos. The whole line had about-turned and was heading with the wind up Tower Avenue. The midsection of the parade, the Chehalis division, came abreast of them and marched on past. Cormier shouted to them from his whirling horse, "Hey, you fellows, aren't you in on this?" His own troop halted before the union hall, marking time, their knees lifting up and down, up and down and Wes could see them breaking ranks, staring over. One of them yelled, "Eyes right!"

"Britt--Ray--Jim!" he yelled, jumping back from the window. "They're coming!"

It was like their front, double-doors had been rammed by a truck. Glass from the inner doors shattered in as far as where Wes stood with Ray Becker and Faulkner, the front line. Then the door splintered and three soldiers stood there wild-eyed, as if they'd blundered into the wrong place, a brothel or a hospital. In the next moment he'd blown in Warren Grimm's chest with one shot and knocked him backwards. He did not know if the other armed men fired or not because his .45 was lurching in his hand. He caught the sharp stink of powder. The soldiers were jammed up and pushing back, clawing for air and screaming curses. He heard bullets from outside slam into the building and men roaring in the streets like cattle.

Things went quiet and very bleak for a second. His hand was throbbing, he might have fired the whole clip. Britt called out, "Jesus, there's a hundred of them--we haven't got a chance--get in the back, get in the back!"

"Where?" Faulkner yelled, turning blind and bumping him off course. Becker was running ahead of them.

"The cooler!" McInerney hollered.

Wes and Faulkner ran on past the rest of them. No one was communicating. They burst open the back door and ran into a gang of soldiers coming up the steps. Wes leaped off the side railing still holding the gun and two men near him on the ground gave way in terror. He heard Faulkner cry from the steps and knew they were beating him.

He didn't know where the hell to go. Some instinct said, the river, and then he was going fast. He hit into a fence, pulled up and at the top fired a shot at a mob of about twenty, howling for him. One shouted, "Ain't that the secretary was into Axe Billy's?"

He was in the alley this side of Pearl Street, heading north. His throat scalded, tears had come up from the wind and bulged his eyes. A rifle bullet tore into the tree beside him making apples fly, so he whirled and fired again and again, not taking aim. They were crazy, screaming,

"Lynch that bastard!"

He halted and fired more deliberately and they stopped, too, so he ran ahead behind a house, kicking up a squawking chicken. He flipped out the spent clip and shoved in another, then looked up to see a little girl smiling at him from the other side of a white fence. "Hi," she said. He ran like hell.

Before he knew it he was running through a poor man's tumbled yard, past the steam plant. The Scoocumchuck was dead ahead; he could smell it. He vaulted the tongue of an old buggy and heard a door slam at the crushed-in house.

"There he is!"

It might be shallow here, and he figured maybe he could make it across and hold them at bay. But, Christ, they'd just hunt him down in the underbrush and one of them would take his scalp. He was in freezing water up to his crotch, the shock as hard as bullets skimming past. The next step might put him in over his head. He stopped and came back, aiming the pistol, first at one, then at another, till all but one man ducked.

"If there's bulls in the crowd, arrest me," he called back.

Three men started forward, two with coils of rope. He fired four times, but the third, stupid sonofabitch, kept on through the poor man's chicken yard down to the river's edge. Wes aimed and fired and knew he'd hit him because part of his uniform flew off. Still he lumbered forward. Wes could see his face, the bulging eyes.

He fired from ten yards, then point blank, hitting him both times before he plunged into the water at Wesley's knees, his uniform puffing up. Blood billowed out on the swollen water and the stink from his body was rank as an animal's.

"The devil's shot Dale--he's killed Dale!"

He threw aside the gun and the others were on him.

He hit the first man in the mouth and lost his footing, the next rode him down in the water. He panicked until he gripped a rock and lashed at the soldier's face as he pulled up to suck air. Two more caught him by the arms and dragged him to the edge. He could hear a rooster shriek; in the window of the shack was the outline of a startled woman.

They were a mob with red, sweating faces and beaming eyes. They all demanded, "Lynch him! Lynch the fucker!"

"I'm dyin' to kill him!"

"You haven't got the guts to lynch me in daylight," Wes told them. There wasn't a man among them he knew.

"Filthy wob--" A rifle butt slammed his mouth. He spit teeth, and blood rushed out on his tunic. He started to swoon when another blow exploded at the back of his head and he fell forward into darkness.

He came to in the street. They were untying him from the back of a car. His head was dulled by fumes, he was scraped and torn and bruised. The heels of both thumbs and the pads of his fingers were all worn off, blood packed hard with dust. They hoisted him, his left arm wasn't working right. There was a lamp post and more deranged townsfolk. The pretty-faced officer he'd seen from the hall was insane. He pushed aside the man who carried him so Wes fell on the curb.

"Warren Grimm is dead," he yelled. He was crying. Then he kicked his ribs and another soldier kicked his head so hard his ears rung like a cathedral bell. "And Dale Hubbard--the cream of this town!"

"What about this stinking wob?"

"An eye for an eye--"

He was up against the lamp post; there was a rope rough against his cheek. He saw bleary shapes. Then he heard through the ringing:

"Leave off! Leave off, there!" It was the constable and another, a woman, trying to assist him--"Let him go, you cowards!" Wes prayed that Lucy wasn't there.

"Who are you--wobbly bitch?" A man in the crowd went for her. Another was urging, "Leave that woman be--" Wes tried to pull away and hit the officer. He was butted in the pit of his stomach.

How many hours later? It seemed so. Hours, days. In the jail now. He couldn't see out of one eye; it was bleeding. He rose to see his fellow workers behind bars, staring out at him as though he was not something they liked to look at. He tried to reach for Britt's hand, but it was like trying to raise your head when you're heavy with a dream. From the same cell, Britt and Ray Becker were saying, "Sit up, Wes, sit up. We're all here."

Commodore lay on a bunk with a bloody towel wrapped around his arm. Wes could see through his cell window that it was getting dark.

He knew he was not in a cell. He was in the open with workers behind bars on two sides of him. Their faces blurred before him, wanting to look encouraging. He could see in their eyes that they were terrified for him. He tried to lean on an elbow, but there was no elbow there and he went down. He wanted to weep for himself, for the loss of his teeth. He remembered Frank Little, murdered in Butte. "Half Indian, half white man, all I.W.W. You'd have died before you cried out loud." He thought of Joe Hill. "If you've had enough of the blood of the lamb, then join in that grand industrial band." But who was the lamb? He would not be cynical. "This is my last and final will: good luck to all of you."

Shouting outside. The mob was outside yelling, "Wait until midnight, wobbly pricks. Here, now, stand off'a my new rope!"

He remembered, those weren't only soldiers and sailors in the street. The Reverend was there and the Postmaster. And the grocer and the druggist. And the man in the street. "--oh, the mob just went wild over me. . . "

Tom Morgan was squeezing bars and staring at him like he was a ghost. Wes wanted to speak to him, still too fuddled. Reason he wasn't in a cell--they didn't need one. Other reason--he was handier.

Big Irishman they called Sheehan in with McInerney. Bert Faulkner alive, looked like he'd taken a bad blow on the forehead. Two heads now, he sat on his bunk, his extra head in his hands. John Lamb lay on his bunk, knees drawn up, his hands around his head. It was through his window, mostly, they were hollering things. And, dear god, there under his bunk was his son, Dewey.

The door behind him crashed open. All faces shot up in fear and Wes saw Elmer Smith led to the first, nearest cell.

"Elmer," Britt called, "why you?"

"Don't ask me," Elmer told him. "They're making a pen out back, they're bringing in everyone--"

"Shut up!" the jailer prodded him.

"Where were you?"

"Out at the ranch, they surrounded us. There's men on horseback with lanterns, running people down and beating them. The jail in Chehalis is full--"

"Shut up, all of you bastards!"

"Where's Bert and Loren?" Wes got in, not sure that anyone heard. The cop whacked him hard on the flat of his boot with his night stick. He walked like a sack of shit. An instant later he came out of the door again.

"Tom Morgan!" he bellowed.

"What--what?" Tom was looking in the wrong direction.

"Got some men out here wanta ask you some questions, son, nothin' difficult." Wes could see behind the jailer, a man in a suit, just inside the doorway. He'd been in Axe Billy's that night, an attorney.

Britt spoke: "They want a confession. Say nothing, man." Morgan looked like a corpse.

Wes rolled on his back and tried to form some substance in his mind while they yelled at Morgan in the next room. "Be a man!" someone kept screaming at him. It was that lawyer, he guessed. Nothing to do with politics would come to him, only glimpses of his mother, and Uncle Jim in that tavern the last time he'd seen him, foam on his lip. The diving seagulls that clear day. Oh, god, his death would kill that old guy's spirit. Only a week ago--could that be? Then Lucy's face loomed, but she couldn't be there, really. He was stroking her; he remembered the details of her breasts, the nipples, the thin blue veins, wanted to push her legs apart and come inside her, and hear her whisper, Wes, I love you. Then he thought, Lucy, leave this place.

Morgan cried out in the next room then there was the thud of a stick on skull. The lights in Wesley's brain faded to ash.

He awoke to a drumming against the cell bars and an eerie cooing. The mob outside was larger and the cells stunk violently of piss. He thought he heard Morgan crying, then the door broke open and three men groped in, dropped a long pole, spilled light from a torch over him and hefted him up. He nearly passed out with the rush of pain but he remembered to say goodbye. "Tell them I died for my class," he said.

"Wait, Wes, don't go--" Britt pleaded.

They were in the street. One of them supporting him said, "We've got him." His voice was feverish with excitement. "Gangway," he ordered.

The thick crowd was quiet, backing away. In the stinking torchlight he saw a boy of about ten being hoisted high up on a crossbar by an older man. A big fancy Overland 85 taxi waited at the curb with drawn curtains, the motor rumbling. His captor snatched a hand away from him. "He's ours," he snapped. Service. Lights out all over town. Streetlights dimmed to coals, sucking air. Hundreds of frightened people waiting for the big event. He was that important.

Threw him in beside one man and two others jumped in. The last man in kept his face to the side, but the one on his left, who carried a bag and smelled of chemicals, he'd seen when the door cracked open. He was the skull who'd marched through town that day.

Sick quiet at first. Then the door burst open, spilling light, and another leaped in. "Where to?" the middle man in the front seat asked. He'd seen in profile the long-bladed nose. It was the rat-faced guy. "You wanta buy me another beer?" Wes asked him.

The other screamed--"You'll be drinkin' river water, soldier!"

"Take it easy, Dutchie," the big man beside him said. "Joe--take us out to the bridge. Go slow."

The man who'd just leaped in the door was nervous as hell--"Are you sure this is the man who killed your--"

"--good Christ, who is that donkey?" the big man muttered. He smelled of pomade. "Hold yourself together, man."

Someone else said, "We had him put right where we could find him."

"I am the one," Wes said. "--and I'd kill that hero again and any one of you--" The overcoated man on his right swung into him, screaming, "You'd *what,* young buck? You'd what? You'd *what,* young bucko--!" punching him again and again in his face and belly. He was tearing at Wesley's buckle, the stink of his perfume nauseating. Wes grabbed the slick hair with his one good hand and tried to pull the face close to bite the spongy nose but the skull on the other side had opened his bag. A man in front dived over the top of the seat and three of them had him down on the floor of the big car. They had his pants down. "No, stop!" he cried. But nothing could stop them, and they pulled his genitals until the air left his chest, and they cut and cut.

Nothing left of him but blood down his legs. Bridge over the river like the one in Independence. Cold air and rain. Cars at either end, blocked the bridge; lights criss-crossing in the dark picked out drops of rain. They were yelling, "Look, look. No balls at all--now he's just a cunt."

"Shoot me," Wes pleaded.

"He won't need no cock where he's goin'. Look at the killer faintin'."

"Here, don't be afraid of a little blood. . . "

"Boy, he is cut and cut good--"

He was dragged, the rope tight on his neck. One man was urging, "Are you sure this is right?" The skull and the fat man pushed him aside. There was a sailor with a cigaret in his mouth--no hat, dark thick brows, hair plastered down. Hangman, good with knots. Men crushed him up against the rail, eyes were beating out, breath up in steam. They stunk of filth. Rope's fast to the girder, short rope. His hands not tied. They hoisted him up and cheered. He was coming down through a rush of sea-borne air, grabbed at his neck and jerked. They were reeling him up again, calling for, "More rope, more rope!" Pressed against the rail, blackout. They were working in the dark. Launched again into the darkness.

They broke him.

Part 2: **Letters from Inside**

Back row, from left to right: Bert Bland, John Lamb, Britt Smith, James McInerney; front row, O.C. Bland, Ray Becker, Eugene Barnett. Montesano Jail, 1920.

Then the judge, he went wild over me,
And I plainly saw we could never agree;
So I let the man obey what his conscience had to say,
He went wild, simply wild over me.
Oh the jailer, he went wild over me,
And he locked me up and threw away the key;
It seems to be the rage, so they put me in a cage,
They go wild, simply wild over me.

from "The Popular Wobbly"

Montesano Jail
Montesano, Wash.
February, 1920

Reverend Ralph Burgdorf
Central Lutheran Church
Milwaukee, Wisc.

Dear Father,

I am writing to you, knowing how long it's been since we communicated, and not much hoping for a reply. I know your feelings about my beliefs and the life I've been living since leaving your house. I would welcome a letter from you or from Mother or from Bud; I would rejoice at a visit, but I fear that if you or anyone else from our home came to this hell hole of a town and heard the things said about me and my comrades or read the local papers, they would be hard pressed to know what they ought to feel. If they have written about us in the Sentinel, which I suspect they have, then I am Ray Becker. I am sorry to have to tell you this news in this manner, especially if you might have read about us already and started to hate us (and Ray Becker) as I'm sure the papers want you to do. I changed my name two years ago to evade the draft and have already served time for that choice. Father, I don't want to fall into a discussion of the rights and wrongs of the draft in a letter that has to stick to the facts of the case here at hand. I can see your face getting heated and I don't know if I can finish this letter.

I figure you as an informed man know what happened in Centralia on Armistice Day last November. I was inside the union hall when the Legion broke the ranks of their parade and attacked us. I was rounded up along with nine others for conspiring to murder the men who broke through our doors and were stopped by our gunfire. We were charged with murdering one man, Warren Grimm, a captain who we knew planned the raid and led the charge. They say he was hit by a .38 calibre rifle bullet fired from across the street. They want to avoid our plea of self defense.

All I'm asking you to do is just to read this letter and any others I may write to you. Father, if you cannot respond to me with any of the old filial feelings, can you find it in your Christian conscience to pass this message on, if not to your congregation then to the Wobbly Defense Committee in Chicago. It is so important, outside of what I feel about myself, that the truth about our plight be made known to the few people who haven't yet made up there minds about the Centralia defendants. Father, we do not choose to be here. We don't ask for the ill treatment we receive daily from our jailers. We only want to be heard and for justice to be done. We have little hope in this kangaroo court for anything but a conviction. We are convinced of our innocence but what we know makes little difference to our judge and the prosecution who keep the facts of the raid from the jury. We need to find any avenue possible to an impartial hearing outside this state.

Reverend, you are a Christian and you are my father. You know that poor men are treated badly by the courts. You know that Jesus was tried unjustly, then crucified. You know that this treatment was in part a political act. You have taught me about hell. About the stench and the ugliness and the terror of hell. I have been there. In the Centralia jail, jammed with innocent people overflowing into the open court between cells, we lay for two nights listening to screams and yelling, men riding by on horseback, rounding up and terrorizing everyone even suspected of being friendly to us. A game warden was shot dead on Seminary Hill for not answering to a posse's challenge. His family is not pressing charges. In the morning after my third night in jail a dear friend of mine named Wesley Everest was brought into our cell and dumped before us. He was a water-logged corpse, his neck a foot long from having been lynched. I can't think about it too much without risking nightmares. I have seen him in my dreams, the sockets of his eyes eaten by fish. Father, don't turn away, it wasn't a devil did this to him it was men. Men like you and me. They create hells. I know this. But listen, he was castrated by high officials of this town. It's true, damn you, listen! His body stank so that we couldn't sleep. I was in with a decent man named Britt Smith. Across the corridor from us was a decent man named Jim McInerney. Twice during the day of our capture they dragged Jim out and put a rope around his neck and threw it over a light standard. They asked him to confess to the fact that we had a plan to conspire to kill the Legionnaires. He told them to go to hell, we witnessed this. Isn't that horrible, father, for him to have said that? But he meant well. He only meant that they should visit us in jail. The stench, how can I say it? They made us sleep in our own filth. Don't put this down. I'm your son. Read this. Pass it on if you can't stand it. If you're so lily white and covered with Jesus precious

--My dear Reverend Burgdorf: forgive this intervention, and please find it in your heart to understand that the torture Ray has endured has made him at times rather short with those he too quickly assumes are his enemies.

I, as representative and counsel of these brave men, have asked that they try to write to anyone who could possibly be of service to us in this difficult defense. Prejudice against them is so great as to defy cataloguing.

We were allowed one change of venue--these men would all have been lynched if we had stayed in Lewis County. We were denied a second change of venue, though one doctor in this town advised that doctors boycott the wives and children of the men during their times of illness and need. We were denied the second request by the judge who presently presides, who between the two rulings addressed a body of local citizens, eulogizing the dead men and attacking my clients as "murderers." I hope that you can find room in your heart for a son who was once close to you. He is an intelligent, dedicated man, a model of devotion. Please write to him, and if you cannot, please find the time and the patience to listen to him, even if he sounds at times a little frayed and even wild. We need everyone's help. Families of the men have rallied here and are abused every day, but I'm sure that you are a courageous man and such action would not frighten you.

with all sincerity,
George Vanderveer,
attorney

Dear Father,

I will try once again to communicate a fraction of the pain and injustice that my friends and I have endured and expect will continue when this long trial is over. A copy of the Sentinel has been smuggled in to me. I read with dismay but without surprise that we are portrayed as "Copperheads" and "human reptiles" in the editorial section of my home paper. Father, if the prejudice is so strong against us 2,000 miles from where I sit, imagine what it's like here in Grays Harbor County. You don't have to imagine what it was like inside the Centralia jail because I'm bound to try once again to convey the atmosphere of that hell, which is something that you and I have often talked about. Now I have a version that runs counter to yours. All I know is that he was castrated and lynched, don't you understand? He did nothing but defend the hall where we are allowed by the country's constitution to freely assemble. I stood by his side. I too held a gun. Did I fire my weapon? I don't remember clearly but almost certainly I did. I was terrified by the sound of the soldiers' boots marking time in the street. I jumped when I heard Wesley shout warning, I reflexed when the doors caved in and those soldiers were standing there then their uniforms were exploding and I saw the blood. I ran to an icebox storage room with several others. The soldiers closed us in and yelled that they ought to burn us alive. We thought that they were going to do just that. I smelled burning, but it may have been my gun. I remember smelling it. It was an Ivor Johnson .38 special. I had just bought it the week before. I fired it twice. Ammunition is precious.

Our lawyer has asked me again to write something that you can understand and feel as I did, but in a fatherly way. You don't reply. That's your right, I guess. Really, I believe that though you may not answer, you do speak to your congregation, you do tell the old neighbors the truth about us. How could you do otherwise? How could anyone do otherwise who has a Christian heart as you do? Tell them, please. Or at least pass these messages on to the I.W.W. Defense Committee in Chicago. We haven't exactly got printing presses here in the Montesano Jail, you know.

I was telling you about the stench and the beatings. But I shouldn't forget the interrogations. They sit you down in the outer office with a stenographer over to the side and the city attorney, who is now our prosecutor, begins to ask you a routine of questions all designed to make you "confess" that there was a plan to kill the soldiers in the streets. Cunningham always maintains that the column was halted out there and we opened up. And we have to keep reminding him that they ran for us first. The interrogation was a relief from the stench of the cells and so I did not mind it, but after I had said that I might have fired on the soldiers, Cunningham looked over at the chief of police and the stenographer and they just stopped talking to me and led me back to my cell. But whenever fellow workers Loren Roberts or Eugene Barnett went in with them there was always a lot of yelling and they came back ashen. Roberts broke down completely the day that two of Wesley's friends came to retrieve the body. One of them was a girl named Lucy Neimi, the other I am sure was an in-law of hers, also a woman. Lucy is Wesley's sweetheart. We are all concerned for her. We haven't heard of her since that night. We heard her and her friend shouting, "All we want is his body." A guard cursed them and called them obscene names. We were yelling from our cells. I knew the girl, we were friends. I was frightened for her not for myself. My cell and Smith's was nearest the door. It broke open and the guard ran past our cell to tell all of us to shut up. I held the bars and pushed my face against them to get a look at Lucy. I called to her, I thought I saw a dress spread on the floor in the other room. There was weeping, then he was in front of me and I could smell his breath. He struck me with his night stick, first the fingers of one hand then the other and stood there rattling his stick back and forth on the bars and roaring like a mad man.

I don't remember pain as bad as that, not even when they dragged us out of the icebox and beat us. I passed out. But the body did not go away. I dreamed I saw Wesley and asked him, Please go away with them. Take yourself away, you're horrible to look at. Then I woke up sick with the pain and the stench. There was a small moon and his body glowed in the dark. I may have been crazed but I saw this. Please go away, I had asked him in the dream. I thought of Judas. I thought it was my fault that he stank, not his. No local mortician would perform the autopsy. They brought in a man from Portland to do the job. He came into the cell with another in white coats and trench masks and they dragged a hose. They hosed off the body. I heard the voice of the town coroner from the other room ask the man with the hose what was the probable cause of death. "It looks like suicide," this other said. "Then it's official," Livingstone said from the office. "He climbed up the girders, put a rope around his neck and jumped off." Then we heard laughter. Father, we have proof that the city leaders were in on the act of turning off the lights in town just before Everest was dragged out to be lynched. We know that our prosecutor here in Montesano took part in opening the jail to the mob. We know that the mayor must have condoned this action. We believe that the one who actually did the act of castrating Wesley was the town coroner. Now isn't that a more believable hell than the one you described to me and we used to argue about when I was in seminary? The hell you always warned that I would go to if I wasn't good? Well, I'm in one and I have been good. I was a good union man, a supporter of what workers want--an eight hour day, clean sheets, enough food to fill the bellies of them and their families. But they're going to jail me for thinking that that is a common good. Oh, to hell with you, you pale old fool. You don't answer. All you want is your lily white Jesus and your stupified audience.

Montesano Jail
March 1, 1920

Dear Father,

My lawyer has advised me to write letters, write until I drop. Get it all out of me, he says. He is a smart lawyer but I don't know why he won't put me on the stand. Sometimes I think the state is afraid of my testimony--everyone else has testified--but why should Vanderveer be afraid, too?

I don't want you to be concerned that the body is still lying in the Centralia jail, putrifying the air around my old jailers. On the fourth day of our stay in there we brought the body out. They picked me and Britt Smith, Jim McInerney and another Irishman named Mike Sheehan to do the job. Mike is 60 years old and never met most of us until the day of the raid.

We tore parts of our shirts off as bandannas though it was cold in the jail and getting colder every day. The bandannas were to keep us from closer contact with the stink. We rolled him onto a tarp they gave us. His arm was coming apart at the socket. I started to vomit and was hit on the back by one of the guardsmen who led the proceedings. Outside in the street there was a van parked with the words Transfer & Moving printed on the side. The truck was surrounded by National Guardsmen. By now we had him in a pine box and the lid nailed down. Britt nailed it. We bunched ahead in the van around the coffin and the guardsmen, armed with rifles, sat in back. There was an officer in front with the driver. The soldiers smoked cigarets.

We could see out the back of the truck over the tailgate. At one point we stopped. One guardsman leaned out as far as he could stretch. "Looks like a funeral," he said. "Must be a hundred cars with their lights on." We started moving again and saw the end of a long procession winding into the mist. Another soldier said, "Must be Warren Grimm's funeral." A third one said, "They finally finished with the autopsy." "One of these bastards," the first one said and they looked at us. We said nothing but I had the sense that Wesley had heard all of this.

I asked them for a cigaret and one of them told us to go to hell. Another of them moved and planted one cigaret on the coffin lid then asked if one of us "beggars" had a match. Britt said we had.

The four of us shared the cigaret, passing it silently. I'm sure we were all wondering where we were going. The town had long since fallen behind us and all we could see was the countryside dense and green through a falling mist. It looked so cold that I shivered to see it, yet I longed to be back in those woods again, cutting trees, burning slash, even a river pig's job would be better than what we had to do.

I had thought we were heading out in the direction of Grand Mound where Loren Roberts comes from. Along the way each of us was aware that out in the woods somewhere another friend of ours named Curly Bland might still be hiding. At the time he hadn't yet surrendered.

The truck came to a halt and the guardsmen jumped over the tailgate with their rifles held high. They helped us down, we were stiff and cold from the ride. The few puffs of cigaret smoke had made me dizzy.

One soldier said, "Okay, get the flap down and bring out the garbage." "On the double," another yelled.

There was a railroad behind us, somewhere I thought I could hear a river flowing. We carried the coffin about fifteen yards and then they ordered us to set it down. They handed us shovels and we began to dig at four corners, like directions of the wind. We dug without speaking for half an hour maybe. Occasionally one of us would drop down into the expanding hole and pull out a rock and toss it to the side. The soldiers stood at ease the whole time, smoking. The officer, who never said a word outloud that we heard, sat on the running board of the truck reading a mystery. We tired and took to digging just two at a time, two of us inside the deepening hole. Finally we lowered Wesley's body in, threw dirt on the box, filled up the hole and tamped it. I saw Britt drop in his union pin. I kept looking around, trying to fix the spot but out in those woods it's as though you are closed in by green like a jungle. Nothing sticks in my mind now except that railroad and the sound of the river like a memory of water. We tried to pile some rocks in one spot but the soldiers displaced them.

At last the officer pocketed his book and told us to drop our shovels and jump back in the truck. We did so, Jim McInerney stepping alongside the truck to cough and spit before he climbed back in. He came to us flushed and excited, "Britt," he said, "what was that fellow's name who came over to our side the night before the raid? The one with the brown and white mac and the mustache?" That is how we'd referred to him since the raid, but before he'd left the hall that day, I had asked him his name. "Davis," I said. He had carried a .38 rifle and said that he was taking a station in one of the hotels across the street to draw a bead on the first man in the parade that attacked us.

"Davis," Britt confirmed. "He went to the Arnold with Commodore and Lamb. But he left them--"

Jim said, "And no one's seen him." I had started to shake with the sweat and the cold. "Boys, I hate to tell you this," Jim said, looking at me, "But there's another coffin out there, big as life."

We sat staring at one another and outside came the sound of shovelling once again.

Dear Father,

The hardest thing about writing to you or to anyone about our trial, if it can be called that, is that everything I say sounds made up. We know of two men interrogated to death, one of them by the man who now leads the prosecution. Our prosecution is headed by the city attorney from Centralia; we know that he was also a party to the lynching of Everest, and we sit in this cold courtroom day after day and listen to him and Judge Cagey Wilson cut down our evidence or simply refuse to allow it to be heard. My mind just gets more and more sour hearing them. I write you notes and look at them at night. I have taken to sketching, I'll send you a drawing of our other prosecutor, William Abel, of Montesano--or "Monte" as the people around here call it. Abel is a round, slick-headed man with steel rimmed glasses and English accent. He is not as eager a prosecutor as Cunningham except when Jim McInerney and Mike Sheehan take the stand. Lawyer Vanderveer thinks that I sketch quite well. He says that I should "take it up." I'm doing the jurors now. Many of them are workers, perhaps there is hope, but there can be none if they never hear our witnesses.

This will give you some indication of just how this case has divided the town of Centralia. We all know and the whole town knows that on October 20, just before the parade on November 11th, there was a meeting at the Elks Club where they laid out a plan to raid our hall. This was done in the hearing of Cunningham, our special prosecutor, and was attended by Warren Grimm who was shot when he broke in the hall. I saw him myself. I didn't know him but he had been pointed out to me as "head" of the Legion in town. I know that at that meeting the Chief of Police presided, along with a man named Bill Scales, who was stepping down as commander of the Legion. We have a witness named Barnes and another named Jim Bengston who both attended that meeting and are both willing to testify that when asked about raiding the hall, Mr. Scales said, "I wouldn't advise it but if you do raid there isn't a jury in the land would convict you." Our witnesses to that meeting never get heard by the jury because every time Vanderveer gets them to the point of saying something, our black robed old hack of a judge dismisses the jury and they file out into the back chambers. They disappear through a door in a mural I stare at all day long that shows a pioneer woman, dragging a blond child across the prairie. If you look towards the cliff in the distance you can see smoke from Indian fires. In her other hand she carries a rifle, so don't worry about her.

Our prosecutor rests his case on the fact that we cannot prove that Warren Grimm himself intended to raid the hall. We are charged with murdering him alone, and my guess is that if they should fail to get us on

97

that charge then we would all be arrested again and brought in to face charges for murdering next Art McElfresh, then Ben Casagranda, and finally Dale Hubbard, even though Wesley was all alone with him and the mob when they chased him down to the Skoocumchuck. Of course we know that Warren Grimm was at the meeting where the raid was planned. We know that when Barnes was asked to serve on a secret committee to study the "wobbly question," he refused and Hubbard's uncle, the timber boss here, called him a "damned skunk" for refusing. We know that along with Hubbard, Grimm headed the secret committee that was to study the wobbly question out of existence.

The state's problem as Vanderveer brings out every day is that they know that the real conspirators were the Legion and the men inside the vigilante committee. They had the raid planned down to the command we heard just before they broke for the door. One of their leaders called "Eyes right!" when they were outside the hall. I heard the pounding immediately after that. Then they were inside, Grimm and Casagranda, anyway. McElfresh, a little druggist with a shop not far from our hall, was killed outside, the state claims by a .22 long rifle bullet. That could only be Loren Roberts' gun and he's so confused by now that he believes them,that he shot McElfresh. He has not spoken a word since the day after Lucy Neimi and her friend tried to get Wesley's body, when they worked him over to the point that he "confessed." Vanderveer says the prosecution is going to read the confession to the jury.

Father, you don't believe men capable of such evil, do you? Certainly not men who run towns and city governments. The Central Lutheran Church lies on a plot of ground that the city gives your congregation tax free. I'm not suggesting that your sermons are any way influenced by the fact that you sit without threat on a piece of Milwaukee soil, but if an action such as ours took place on the south side by the men at Cudahy and Swift and Chalmers, what would you think about it? What would you say from the pulpit?

I was telling you about the conflict that has been raised in the hearts of Centralia citizens because of our plight. This man Jim Bengston who attended the meeting where the raid was planned--he is a ready witness and Vanderveer has several times brought him to the point of allowing the jury to hear just what did go on at that meeting. The point is that here is a citizen, member of the Elks Club and friend of the Legion, who is driven to tell the truth in this case. We hear that he has been threatened in Centralia. He knows that he stands to lose his business there, small as it is. Now we look at his son, Ben. Ben was in the parade but he didn't raid the hall, he ran the other way and took a bullet in the calf (what calibre? that was never disclosed because his Legion friends, many of them sitting here daily in court with black armbands, were all supposed to be unarmed.) We know that Ben came home the night after the parade and told his father, Jim, that the boys had taken on more than they could handle and "got back what they deserved." These words of his son, Jim Bengston is willing to reveal on the witness stand. Finally, the day before yesterday, he was allowed to. We felt good for our cause when we heard him, but bad for him personally. Then Ben came to the stand.

Father, he came up there and told the jury that he'd never said they'd "raided" and got what they deserved. He was saying in effect that his father lied and that he'd been fired upon from the hall, that was how he got his bullet in the calf. Well, there have been some disappointments in this trial--maybe 30 a day--but that one hit me the hardest. The poor young fool was so intimidated, so much the cat's paw for those hoodlums that he would stand up there and lie about what he'd told his father just to save his own skin. I wondered what he felt about his poor father's skin. It was the subject of a long talk between me and Curly Bland that night, about family loyalty. Curly's brother, Commodore, is in here with us. He's 37, quite a bit older than Curly. Curly said one of the reasons he gave himself up after a week's run from all this mess was that he couldn't stand the thought of his brother going through such hell and him out in the woods only starving.

March 12, 1920

Reverend Father,

The fact that you do not answer my letters leaves me puzzled but no longer feeling any animosity towards you. I leave you to heaven, as the saying goes. I write to you now out of habit, like the sketching I practice every day in court. I am enclosing a cartoon drawing of our postmaster (former) and the Reverend Thompson, both of them recent witnesses.

Here is a little by-play from the courtroom that will give you an idea of what kind of a chance we have of being acquitted when the jury goes into session, maybe next week.

This is the Reverend Thompson on the witness stand: "I was mayor of this town once, I was elected in 1912. I have been going around the country telling people that this was an unprovoked assault on the marchers by the people in the union hall."

This next is from Maggie Stockdale, a pint of a woman, wears a black straw hat. "I was on Tower Avenue that day. The parade passed me twice. I saw the Reverend Thompson and T.H. McCleary carrying ropes. It was in the businessmen's section."

Mrs. Nettie Pierce appeared after Maggie, she is tall and stringy, reminds me of my old geometry teacher at South. "I was on the corner of Tower and Main. I saw about a dozen men carrying what they call 'wobbly neckties.' The men who carried ropes were in uniform. One of the men was Mr. McCleary and another was Mr. Thompson."

This is Reverend Thompson again, he has a tall black stetson hat that he carries in his lap when he's watching the proceedings. "Yes, I marched in the parade with T.H. McCleary and, yes, there was a rope. I picked it up in the street and made a lasso of it. I threw it over to T.H. and he grabbed hold of it and broke and end off. He carried one end and I formed another lasso. It was an old rope. I carried it until I came back pretty near to the Elks Hall. We were right at the last end of the Centralia Elks."

This is his friend. "My name is T.H. McCleary. I'm postmaster in Centralia. It was just an old piece of rope. We were playing tug-a-war. I and some of the other paraders."

I took these notes for your benefit yesterday. As always I am a dutiful son, trying to please and keeping you informed of our situation here. The attention to the testimony did my sleep some harm. I dreamed again of Wesley. I saw his face as he plunged down from the girders of the bridge. I saw his hands digging at the rope; his legs kicked in the glare of headlights. I woke up yelling and Curly had to slap me. He said the guards would come and work us over if I didn't shut up. You should take a vacation from your work (preaching) Father and come out and visit us. The men are in need of spiritual counsel. Imagine Curly thinking that my crying out might bring reprisals. That's how confused we've become here. There are trees in bloom, cherry trees. This state is rightly named after the father of our country.

March 21, 1920

Father,

The verdict has come in. We're appealing it. It isn't fair. They can't do this in an American court. The jury was manhandled and brought in first one verdict for 3rd degree murder and recommended that the court go easy. Cagey Wilson threw them back in session. He told them there wasn't any such thing as 3rd degree murder. Loren yelled at them, first time he's opened his mouth. They read his confession the last day but one of the trial.

I can't find it in this pen to say what they did. They gave us all second degree murder. Now, our lawyer says they can't do it that way. I don't know all this legal language. I'll have time to learn it. I'm going to college in Walla Walla. I know they can't do what they tried on us. They don't know or they don't care about human beings. To have conspiracy to murder charged against you it has to be proved it was first degree. Ours was second degree, so there couldn't be conspiracy with that. Father, the judge gave us twenty-five to forty years. Eight of us he sentenced to hard labor. Even at the worst I never thought it would go like that. John Lamb didn't fire a gun. Neither did Commodore Bland, neither did Britt Smith, neither did Jim McInerney. Thank god, Faulkner got off, and Mike Sheehan. Our lawyer, Elmer Smith,was released.

Why should I thank god? Why not thank you for having me in the first place so I could live this hell of a stupid life. If I'm living in hell I must be a devil. You shouldn't have had me. You should have restrained yourself. I've never known a woman. Why should you have? Why didn't you leave my mother alone, you god damned fool. I hope you die and go to the hell you told me about. I told Vanderveer to mail this or I'd kill him. He never brought me to the stand. Thinks I'm crazy or he knows something funny. They said Grimm was killed by a .38 rifle bullet fired from across the street. They said Eugene Barnett fired it. Eugene didn't shoot his gun, but they captured it at his house. It was a frame. They had to have someone across the street was the whole thing. They couldn't have Grimm shot in the hall by Wesley or by anyone else for that matter

II

Walla Walla
February 28, 1924

In replying refer to
9413

Dear Ralph T.,

It won't be much of a task to supply you with the facts and information that you request because by now I have most of the trial record off by heart. Until you began sending me books last year, which believe me are most appreciated, I had little to read and study except the trial record which Vanderveer secured for me. You have asked me questions about him and I've tried to make clear to myself and to others just what I found lacking in his defense. This is more difficult because I sense that you find him to be more than a competent lawyer, you remember that George stepped in on behalf of the I.W.W. in the Chicago Conspiracy trial after Darrow turned us down, and you know as most of the men here know that he won us an acquittal in the Everett massacre. My fellow prisoners here--all seven of them besides me--still think his work for us is worthy of praise. They say that my objections to his handling of the case are examples of nit-picking. That's me, to them. On the other hand they say my bead and leather work is the best in the place. Curly called it "exquisite" the other day. I asked him where he got such a word. He said he got it from me--"Who else?" Curly is in good spirits these days (for a change) having met a vibrant little woman who came all the way from Baraboo, Wisconsin, to talk to us here and cheer us up. She spoke to me as well. Seems she got our names from some list in a church bulletin: men in jail needing Christian pen pals. I asked her if she had ever visited Central Lutheran in Milwaukee. Yes, she'd heard my father preach, she said. "What a wonderful, inspired man, he is." I asked her if he mentioned us in his sermon. No, she said. But she was sure that I occupied a special place in his heart. I left her to Curly, and he seemed taken by her. The day after her visit I heard him whistling while he emptied his slop bucket.

This is Sunday, winter ending, we hope. It has been a bitter time for all of us. This climate is quite different from the western part of the state where most of the men hail from. It was below zero for three days in a row a month ago and still we worked outside on a pipe system for sewage disposal. They had us build bonfires near the trenches and tried that way to keep the ground workable. We all got scorched faces and bent backs from hacking away at the frozen earth with pick axes. When we are not out smashing granite for the roads, we are sent to the wheat fields to blister in the heat, which last summer rose at one point to 110 fahrenheit. We are all concerned with Jim McInerney's health but so far can't persuade the prison doctors to hospitalize him or to take him off the work detail. We are petitioning for a new look at our trial and there is some hope that soon we will be allowed to work inside in the apple sauce factory or on the license plate detail if things go right. There are rumors of a prisoner complaint board being organized and we stand a better chance than most of being elected to it because we are all literate and most of the men here are not. This place is not as advanced as San Quentin, say. I have two correspondents there, wobblies both of them, arrested at the same time that Tom Mooney was sent up.

Vanderveer is a class lawyer. (By that I mean classy.) Yes, he has worked extremely unpopular cases and done well by the men defended. Many like his flamboyant style, his ability to stand right up to a prejudiced court and blast the judge and the prosecuting attorney with invective and sarcasm. Curly and Lamb and Eugene Barnett thought him quite a hero at Montesano, when at a break in our trial he got in a scuffle with the Grays Harbor County sheriff, who had just indicted two of our witnesses for perjury. These were two young men who testified that they'd seen Grimm within the doors of the hall when the gunfire took place. I have heard him described as a man who loves the "underdog." A visitor here the other day told me there is a Seattle man already at work on his biography, the title to be 'Attorney for the Damned'. Do you get the feeling, as I do, that it would be better not to be defended by this guy if you're going to end up 'damned'? But my fellow workers only smile when I say things like this and tell me I'm too exacting. Well, so I am stuck with myself with thirty just around the corner and the promise of our getting a reconsideration of our case as remote today as it was two years ago. This is true despite the good job Elmer Smith has done, along with the Centralia Defense Committee, trying to work our release. Now, Elmer is the lawyer you ought to know, if you must be praising lawyers who risk their lives to defend unpopular causes. What a difference between those two men!

Vanderveer was disarmed in court, did you know that? Again, many of my comrades saw his carrying a gun as the act of a hero. I thought he was a fool to have a gun, though he claimed it was just to point up the fact that many of the Legionnaires sitting in on the trial carried .45's. His hotel room was ransacked, so he had reason to be frightened for his life. He got into the habit of signing into obscure little rooms in Montesano or Satsop or Aberdeen, using assumed names. Or of signing one register and going to another hotel, using his mistress' last name. Then in the morning he would go back to the first room to check for damage or to see if the lock had been tampered with. Of course he was given no protection. He took a cab every night after the day's trial right from the door of the Montesano courthouse, Kitty, his flame-haired mistress in tow, to whatever town he might be visiting that night. He used the same cab every night, and some said the driver was brought down from Seattle and trained as a racer should they ever be involved in a chase. I'm sure that Vanderveer enjoyed all this sensation. Some do, I don't. But it is probably true that his confidence and sarcasm worked in his favor to intimidate some who might be a threat to him.

He worked hard to bring out the Jim Bengston testimony and confounded Abel, the second prosecutor, on a number of occasions into retreating from their position that nothing should be heard of that October 20th meeting. The prosecution saw that eventually, with George's pounding, something of that proceeding must be revealed. All the time, of course, their assistants were working away at Jim's son, Ben. Here is an example of Vanderveer's style as it applies to this matter of the meeting. Abel objected that we must show that Grimm himself was making an assault on the hall before self-defense could be considered:

Vanderveer: "We will prove what was done by him by proving what was said by him and his associates at this meeting, because it was all done in words, and I now join issue with counsel and we will show that there was a plan to raid the hall on the 20th of October." Right at this point the judge allowed testimony, but refused Bengston the opportunity to reveal what various others said who were closest to Grimm, his co-conspirators.

Still Jim Bengston was heard.

And his testimony established for the jury the fact that there was indeed a plan on the town's part, but the thing I couldn't get over was the effect of Vanderveer saying, "because it was all done in words." That phrase kept coming back to me in my cell for nights afterwards. It seemed a monumental thing to have caught--but at the same time that it was true for everyone else in that courtroom, it was a lie for us defendants. When Judge Wilson said to us, "Twenty-five to forty years"-- I could have said, well, it's only words, they can't hurt you with words. But right there the words started becoming minutes, hours, days, years and those are the things that grind you down. The state buying my time-- twenty years of it maybe--for nothing. That's the difference I finally figured out between me and good old George V. and all manner of men like him. He doesn't labor by the hour, and for him time has a different meaning than what it has for me and for Britt and Curly and the rest of us.

The way to see Vanderveer best was when he worked in combination with Elmer Smith, Elmer on the witness stand and probably the brains behind the strategy V. took. Elmer was the best witness we had because he was more than just "our lawyer." He had taught high school in Centralia, coached football (coached Warren Grimm's brother, Polly) and was himself member of the United Mine Workers. He had worked wage claims for us and had been advising us for years. Elmer was an intellectual and like me a midwesterner, having graduated from Macalester College in St. Paul. But you know he was always one of us, and never gave us the impression that he was out to be a martyr or so caught up in a cause that he wasn't human.

Elmer Smith had never got over the business of Tom Lassiter being run out of town in the 1918 raid--and most surely killed by the same mobsters who burned his shack and burned us out of our first building. He had spent much time on this case, brought it to the highest court in the state and come back empty-handed. (Ex-governor Stevens had himself marched in the 1918 parade.) He and Vanderveer kept trying to establish that Elmer had good information that they were going to raid on November 11th. They named Elmer's informant--one Burrells--who'd been at the Elks Club meeting and told Elmer they would raid at the "psychological moment." That is, "when the soldiers were stirred up." Elmer testified that he passed this information on to us at the hall then went back to "defend his office against a raid."

When Vanderveer asked him if he had reason to fear his own property, Elmer said Yes and they went into the note he had received threatening him for attending our meetings, and referred to photographs of the old hall and the charred remains of Tom Lassiter's shack.

The judge didn't want any of Tom Lassiter in his court. He would allow no information about him except that Tom was "a wobbly." The two defense lawyers then shifted over to Elmer's "friendship" with Warren Grimm. They had known each other for years, both were lawyers, and Elmer had attended the Labor Day address where Grimm had called us "Bolsheviki."

What the judge tried to keep the jury from hearing was that Elmer and Grimm clashed after that address. When Elmer suggested that words in the speech made it easier for the town to justify destroying Tom's living and probably Tom himself, Grimm had told him, no. It was the "proper way" to treat such a man.

The judge stopped them after a roar of objections from both Abel and Cunningham. Vanderveer insisted that the information was relevant: "By going into the matter of Tom Lassiter, who was forcibly kidnapped, we will show that Warren Grimm approved of that action heart and soul."

Cunningham called out that Vanderveer's words constituted nothing less than "a threat."

Vanderveer's best words on the subject were these: "We are going to show that Grimm was part of the Lassiter business in 1918. We are going to show his mental attitude, we are going to show his prejudice against these people, and show that by being elected commander of this Legion post he had then the means to effect his prejudice. And we will show that he stood within four feet of the inside door with Frank Van Gilder when he was shot."

April 4, 1925

Dear R.T.,

Again, thanks so much for the generous supply of books. Yes, I had heard of Mr. John Dos Passos and I certainly admire his ability to keep his story alive and moving along. I admire what I assume are his political sympathies as well. The poetry I am trying out slowly. I like the sonnets of Wm. Shakespeare most; a few of these I had read when a high school student, but at the time I didn't understand them. Now they are a consolation to me and I have put one or two to memory (which I find is much more acute now that I have so much time at my disposal.) I'm not in favor of keeping to this room for the sake of my memory, however. Once out of this place I shall forget it. It is wonderful to think that one day I might meet you and converse with people who run in circles as lofty as yours where new books are got just for the asking. It must be extraordinary to review books, I envy you and admire your abilities.

You felt that I need say more about Elmer Smith; that won't be difficult. About Frank Van Gilder, I can supply only what the court record shows and something from memory will be easy because he made a lasting impression on me, and of course Vanderveer's treatment of him was classic.

Elmer's strategy was different from V.'s because he wished to show the long life of the prejudice, as it had existed from the time the I.W.W. first entered the scene. I didn't know Grimm or Van Gilder and I hadn't seen the first raid. I didn't know Tom Lassiter though I feel that by now I do because of Curly and Commodore's talk of him. They both assure me that Elmer's point regarding Grimm and Lassiter is well taken, that Grimm was seen out in the street when F.B. Hubbard was auctioning off our goods with the building burning behind him, shouting and leaping up and down, waving a couple of toy flags and "wailing like a banshee." Curly says that Hubbard yelled at the crowd, "How much am I bid for this I.W.W. Victrola?" Frank Van Gilder responded, "Who'd want a machine that won't work?" Hubbard said to him, "Why, posterity, young man!" So Van Gilder was shamed into buying the thing and coughed up ten bucks.

Elmer knew what he was doing trying to bring up Lassiter in connection with Grimm's love of violence. Their strategy was working, so the state got Frank Van Gilder up there to testify that he was with Grimm the whole time of the Armistice Day raid, and that Grimm was hit out in the street somewhere, a half block from the entrance to the hall.

When he was hit, according to Frank, Grimm shouted, "Oh, God, I am shot!" and Frank's response was: "Are you hit?" Grimm repeated, "Yes!" We knew better than to laugh at Frank's quickness.

Frank and Grimm had been named as the two men who first crashed through our doors by a schoolboy named Guy Bray, who was boycotted from the school basketball team and from running for school office since returning to town; and another man named Jay Cook, who has not worked since the trial. They both knew Grimm and Van Gilder and identified them, so Frank's testimony was vital.

Vanderveer asked Frank, "If we are to believe you, Warren Grimm was struck not only a long way from the hall, but actually a safe distance from it." Frank answered that this was true. Then he asked Frank what he did, knowing his comrade was shot. He answered, "I told him he ought to go to the hospital, and he started, bent over and holding his stomach." So Vanderveer asked, "Did he actually go to the hospital?" And Frank was stuck with saying, "I don't know."

"Why?" V. asked. Frank's reply--"I turned away and left him."

There was a moment of dumfounded silence in the courtroom, everyone sensing that either they had heard wrong or that things were pretty soon going to move in our favor, if the state had to resort to such blatant lies as these to keep their case together. But Vanderveer turned on the witness and began to harangue the court on the duties of a soldier in combat, the least responsible of them knowing that his first care was his buddy. Then he shifted back to Frank: "This man's failure to lift even a finger to aid his friend should impress even the most biased observer as abnormal behavior, and therefore I am moving at this point that his entire testimony be stricken from the record!" They yelled and objected and of course the record stood, but it was a rash and impressive move on V.'s part. One of the best chances I saw him take and Van Gilder himself was badly shaken by the action. He was already lying, and Guy Bray, who had spotted him and Warren Grimm in the doorway of our hall, had said as well that Van Gilder had come around when he was sick with the mumps the week before and tried to intimidate him into silence. Guy testified that Frank said, "I hope you never get well!" How did they know each other? Frank is Guy's brother-in-law.

The way the state got back at us was instructive. They hauled in one Vernon Ratcliffe, a Legionnaire and member of the parade, and had him testify that the man the witnesses Bray and Cook really saw was probably Dutchie Phitzer, big like Grimm, easily mistaken. Vern told the court that they were fired upon by us, while the soldiers stood in military formation. "I was looking back over the different platoons, as I started to look front again my eyes were resting on the wobbly hall, and I noticed the glass break in the hall windows. I turned around and about the time I got turned around the bullets was whizzing all around us. There wasn't a soldier had broken ranks that I could see, nor was there a soldier on the sidewalk at this time. Heinie Huss can vouch for that, he was there on the sidewalk. He knows Dutch. I just noticed like sudden holes come in there, three or four holes into the glass window. Then I finished making my turn to the right and a hail of bullets came and I hit for Second Street. As I started I noticed Dutch hitting for the wobbly door, to try to do something about it, I guess." Vanderveer said it sounded to him like Vern was doing a "ballet" out there and they objected; then he accused him of being one who hollered, "Come on, let's get them!". Vern denied this. Then he said, "Aren't you prejudiced against the I.W.W.s?" Vern said, "Yes, I am pretty much prejudiced against the I.W.W.s. Something should be done about them, but I don't claim to have enough knowledge to run this country and say what ought to be done with them."

Elmer had V. ask Vern about his involvement in the Lassiter kidnapping: "Did you know Tom Lassiter was an agent for the *Union Record*?"

"Yes, I knew he was an agent. And I know what kind of paper that is, that's a red paper."

"Weren't you one of them who burned that blind man out?"

"No, I was not!" Vern's voice was cracking, the prosecution was shouting objections and the judge was slamming his gavel.

"And isn't it true that you were also one of the men who lynched Wesley Everest?" Vern yelled "No," and that was the end of one day of testimony, a bit more stirring than the ordinary ones. The Defense Committee has a man on record as saying that two years after the trial he overheard Vernon telling a barmate of his: "That bastard never rattled me on the stand. I wasn't one of the lynchers, anyway. I was out there, I seen what they done, but I didn't hold any rope or kick him or anything."

Elmer Smith testified several times during the trial. He was brought back to the stand during this new barrage of lying on the state's part. They brought in several others who claimed they too had seen Dutchie bent over, clutching his guts near our doorway. The two defense lawyers kept reminding the state of the Lassiter business and the fact that the governor had not replied to Smith's request for a new investigation of his disappearance. Then Elmer was about his particular view of the hall on the day of the Armistice Day raid. Vanderveer asked him if he could "see the action on that day."

Elmer said, "I could not see the I.W.W. Hall. I could not see half way to it. I was watching the parade as it passed Tower and Main. But there were a great number of other people watching the parade."

Vanderveer: "About how many?"

"I think that there were about five hundred thousand in the United States, standing out in the middle of the street looking toward the I.W.W. Hall, looking north, at that very day and hour."

Elmer's words fix in my mind the principle difference between the two lawyers: he always saw the action as large and as significant as any civil rights fight going on in the country at the time. He saw political differences as one of the principal roots of all hatred and bigotry. And he was willing to say it and say it clear. Since the moment our trial ended Elmer has done more than any man to try and bring justice home to us. The Centralia Defense Committee, under him, is putting together a mountain of damning evidence against the state's handling of the case. He's got five jurors already who will sign affidavits that the trial was rigged, in effect, that they were blocked from bringing in their original verdict. He's got a line on several of the lynchers. He's helped us keep track of our families, consoling and bringing aid to wives and children left fatherless by this thing. From what I hear, though, he is in poor shape himself and neither is his home life all that secure, the way he runs himself ragged, now in Olympia, now in Seattle, arranging for rallies and collecting money.

May 1, 1926

Dear R.T.,

Yesterday the wind blew quite warm out of the Columbia River plain to the west of us, and reminded us that in less than a month we will once again be subjected to the extremities of this climate. Curly always tells me that the heat isn't so bad because it's "dry." So is a roaring stove dry. There are compensations, though most of the white cloud of blossoms in our orchard have blown onto the ground like a spring snowfall. The trees are strong and healthy and we can hope for a good harvest come this summer. It looks as though our pleas for a better work detail have been heard and soon we may be shifted from the road to the fruit trees and from there probably to the "applesauce factory." Eugene Barnett is busy organizing a boycott of all Ghirardelli chocolate bars sold here in the pen. This is to support fellow workers striking in San Francisco and L.A.

You have asked if our case was strong, and especially if it was strongly presented. Yes and no--Elmer's contention that 500,000 pairs of eyes were trained on our hall that November day is certainly true enough, though how many eyes were needed to see and understand some of the turns the prosecution tried on us is hard to know. Instance, Doc Bickford's testimony. During the pre-trial inquest Doc Bickford was so zealous or so sure of himself that he told investigators that just prior to the raid he had said to the marchers around him, "Well, if you want to raid the hall, I'll take the lead"; but before he could do so, "there were many there before me."

We were encouraged by that statement, which got printed the day after the raid in the Seattle *P.I.* It seemed to us like damning evidence that a raid was planned and that plenty were willing to take part in it, but before they could all get together, it had begun on its own accord. And at the trial Doc identified Grimm as the man in the lead, his foot up against the door just as the shots commenced, but added that no glass was broken as a result of his putting up his foot and shoving.

Bickford was a difficult problem for the state. Temperamentally he was on their side, but he had already made this incriminating statement that was quoted and would be used by the defense as evidence. I really wondered how they were going to get around what was already printed and circulated and part of everyone's thinking. They did a sloppy but effective job on his testimony. They got him to say that his words rose out of a conversation that took place before the final halting and the command, "Eyes right!" That the words "if anyone wants to raid the hall" were spoken casually before they got to a point opposite our door, that in fact he didn't know where we were located and was only aware of the hall because he saw our initials on the doorway. Now this in addition to the fact that he was "somewhat deaf", according to his own admission, could account for his not hearing the shooting until he was right behind the soldiers he identified as shoving in the door. Abel made a big thing of his bad hearing, but they couldn't shake him on the fact that it was Grimm up there with his foot against the door. So again, here came the lying witnesses to say that Doc Bickford was not up at the front of the parade when things went haywire.

This witness, Ansel Poundstone, is typical: "No, sir, no soldiers in my platoon had any ropes, clubs or guns. I know Dr. Bickford, and I could see him. He did not rush the hall before there was any shooting, and he was not standing up by the doorway when the shots came through there. I am connected with the Farmers and Merchants Bank and I'm a member of the Commercial Club. I am proud of my membership in the American Legion. Yes, and I am also proud of my prejudice against the I.W.W.'s." So you see, with testimony like that, what chance had we, even when trusted men of the town like Bickford would make the "mistake" of identifying Grimm at the head of the rush?

I have no idea why they couldn't just have gotten Bickford to lie about Grimm's position. He was an enigma to me. He got up there and told them that Wesley was a "desperate" man. He said that on a visit to the hospital with an injured logger named Olafsen, Wesley had remarked that if "he had the powder he'd blow up the hospital." Which is a silly lie. Bickford told the court that he worked on all four of the wounded soldiers, testified that the bullet that hit McElfresh was one of small calibre. That it "entered the posterior, or just back of the auditory canal through the petrous portion of the temporal bone on the right side, pierced the medulla and lodged a little lower down than where it had entered."

Now the authenticity of Bickford's testimony concerning the McElfresh wound is another example of how complex the state's case must have been: we know that Bickford was up at the front and saw Grimm, yet they can't get him to lie about it. Sounds like he's on our side: Not by the hair on anyone's chin--my idea is that he'll never deny being up there because he's so proud of the fact that he got that close to the lion's den. He doesn't want history to have him anywhere else, no matter how many liars they get up on the stand to say he wasn't there. To say something like "I would lead if anyone else would follow" means you're a frustrated non-combatant. He probably had dreams all during the war that he was in France, following the charge and damming up the wounds of heroes like Grimm and Dale Hubbard. Or he might have worked with the state to have himself discredited, having already been quoted by the *P.I.* Regarding the bullet, we're certain that a .22 long slug, fired over a distance of 300 yards, could not enter anyone's skull. It couldn't kill a man from that distance unless it hit him right in the eye. We're certain Art McElfresh is dead, we doubt that he was killed by a .22. But they had Loren in their hands and he was weak, they told the town that one of his bullets killed this other one, and so they held Loren in reserve over our heads. Loren in the meantime has never had the mental treatment they said they were scheduling for him, and still goes around at times bragging about his confession. He is one sorry lad and we have little to do with him, or at least I have little to do with him. The confession was beaten out of him, and by now he doesn't know what he thinks about us or anyone connected with the case. He told me the other day that Lucy Neimi had come to visit him. Knowing how wild he is, I doubted this, but I tried to verify this visit. The only person who saw him that day according to the record was the nurse from town who Elmer hired to look in on him from time to time.

Loren Roberts was officially, according to the court: Criminally Insane. But here's an instance of insanity on the other side (not that you haven't got proof of that already) that will either make you laugh or make your hair stand up. Late in the trial we were alarmed one day to wake up and find that the entire lawn in front of the Montesano Courthouse, about an acre, was covered with tents and about 500 troops of the U.S. Army.

Vanderveer was in a stew, as might be expected, the jurors were white with fear. Against the orders of the marshalls, they kept running up to the windows and looking out and then rushing back to their seats to whisper to their neighbors. I had heard a rumor all week that there were armed bands of wobblies out in the woods, making their way down from the Olympic Peninsula to attempt a jail delivery. Of course we'd laughed at the idea. But I can imagine the effect of that rumor on those unsophisticated men who were our jurors. What did they know about radical unions? If they believed the newspapers, we were an international band with Moscow and Tokyo on our side, not to mention arsenals and ships. We were a mysterious force of anarchy ready to boil over at any moment.

Vanderveer was demanding that Judge Wilson give him some information as to the reason those troops were stationed on the lawn. "There's no doubt whose side is meant to be hurt by their presence out there," he told the judge. "They're prejudicing the jury."

For a change the judge was dumbfounded. He didn't know how they'd got there and was a little frightened himself. He called to the prosecution to help him out. Abel and Cunningham threw up their hands.

Just then in walked the stiffest looking Captain you ever saw. He wore a peaked hat, leggings, a handlebar mustache, salt and pepper hair cut close to his scalp. He came stalking up towards the defense and prosecution tables. Someone whistled and the marshals cautioned us for it. He halted, saluted the judge and half-shouted, "Your Honor! Captain Carling, 35th Infantry, U.S.A.R., Camp Lewis!"

The judge acknowledged him and asked what was his authority for bringing on the troops.

"Orders from Governor Hart, Sir," was all that he would offer.

"But whose orders from Governor Hart?"

"Orders from Governor Hart, your Honor!"

The judge finally signalled him out of court and sat holding his head while Vanderveer got started again, this time shouting at Abel, "Surely Counsel hasn't brought in the troops as a precaution against the contingent of armed men already camped here?"

An explanation came at last from an unexpected source. The prosecution had a number of flunkies working for them, obtaining witnesses and so on. One of them was city attorney, Herman Allen. It was on his authority that Wesley's body was located and brought back into the cells. He finally spoke up and told the judge that he had contacted the governor personally and the governor had supplied the troops. "Why, for the love of god," Vanderveer wanted to know. "As additional protection for both sides," Allen calmly told him.

Vanderveer demanded that the judge must rule for a mistrial; this was denied. Finally Wilson concluded that the troops were not a distraction and they personally made him feel safer. He said that it would be "discourteous" to rule that members of our armed forces must leave a town on the vague possibility that they might influence a jury.

We lost on that ruling. Well, "loss" is not the point. We were in the hands of some rather strange men, that's what I mean. Elmer Smith has talked at length with Herman Allen since the trial. He is another of those enigmas from the Centralias of this country, who will admit to any outrage once the battle's over. He is no more morally dilapidated than your average Babbitt. He said to Elmer, "On my bare telephone conversation with the governor, the troops arrived. I'd met him only once, in 1918. Gifford Pinchot was in charge of the camp there. For me it was my most important contribution to the trial, except to be the one personally to indict those boys."

He'd heard there was agitation now to get us out of the pen, he knew that a number of jurors have been signing affidavits saying that the troops had a tendency to prejudice them against the I.W.W. But that wasn't his intention, "to prejudice anyone."

Elmer says he is absolutely sure of himself, even when he implies that maybe the trial wasn't 100% fair. Yes, he's willing to discuss the possibility now. He also told Elmer that it wasn't all bad that came out of having all that limelight focused on Centralia. There were some good things that came to people as a result of being in the public eye. Elmer asked him to name one. "Well, David Livingstone, our coroner, he went on to become head of the asylum up at Steilacoom." That was one. And, come to think of it, "he married Doc Bickford's daughter, too."

III

Walla Walla
July 16, 1927

In replying refer to
9413

Dear Julia Ruuttila,

I can't tell you how moved I was to receive your beautiful letter inquiring about my health after all these years! Did you get the note I sent to you, via your mother? Your enduring interest in my case has given me much pleasure, and I'm touched by your "confession" that you considered yourself naive seven years ago when you first approached me to try and help. Julia, you're not the first person who came to a political prisoner with high hopes regarding his release. I can point to many examples of eager young people flocking out of college classes with the intent of freeing all of us poor saps with one swoop of fevered humanitarianism. And when they fail after one burning effort, they usually find themselves on the other side, nodding their heads and saying, Yes, they are all depraved, and that's why they're locked up. Pass the salt, my steak's getting cold. I'm sure now, given the fact that you're still interested (and that your father was a wob--he had to lead you straight) that you can be an effective instrument. You have matured, you have fallen in love and seen that affair go sour with time. But you are a beautiful woman (as I remember you), and you can still expect happiness in that area of human endeavor.

The way you will be able to help me and the others will be to gather and arrange necessary affidavits from the jurymen. We know that most of these men are willing to admit that they were forced to be against us.

You must know of Colonel Edward Coll's investigation since you mention him. He might be one person to contact in order to give added support to his efforts. He is, or was, a member of the American Legion in good standing, yet his research has provided us with enough material possibly to effect the release of Gene Barnett, and maybe poor Loren Roberts. As you must know I'm no longer moved by the promise of a mere parole. I look to see justice finally done. A pardon, or nothing.

You should work closely with Elmer Smith and the Centralia Defense Committee obtaining affidavits from those one or two now ready to admit their part in the lynching. Elmer has had one man on the brink of a confession for three years. Perhaps you might be more effective than he's been, bringing the man around. Elmer is a very sick man and will need your help. You might be of help to him in locating J.M. Bengston. A document from him and his son, Ben, would show more clearly than anything else the state of civil war that existed at the time.

Any information that you might be able to find on the fate of John Doe Davis would be helpful. We may never know where Wesley's body lies; there are many rumors, no hard facts. Who knows what we could prove with the location of his body. With Livingstone out of town and no longer an influence, a new investigation might be mounted. I am hopeful too that you might trace Wesley's companion, Lucy Neimi. No one has heard a word since we saw her the night before we buried Everest.

Colonel Coll came out to Centralia from Illinois with the intention of clearing the name of Legion Post 126 by a thorough look into the case. Instead he ended up sympathetic to our position. He has appeared at a session of the parole board where Barnett's fate was on the docket. We feel very hopeful in the matter of Gene because of the Colonel's help. Edward Coll puts the blame for all four deaths on Everest.

Thank you for the latest issue of *New Masses*, it is good to read something that makes sense. The *Spokesman Review* and the *P.I.* and the *Times* are not the world's most liberal newspapers. I am hoping to find something in *New Masses* that will make me more hopeful about the fate of Sacco and Vanzetti. I see that there is a piece on the wobs still in Leavenworth. None on me, however.

My dog's name is Elmer. Best mutt I ever had. I have my own cottage now and am in charge of the prison garden. I think they put me out here partly to get me away from the rest of the men. Did your father know James McInerney? He remains very sick, is often in the infirmary.

I have another task for you and that is to keep a personal record, for some future unknown historian, of the difficulties these men faced trying to keep families and loved ones together while they remain inside. Here is a photo of a gathering of families who came all the way from Centralia and environs to see their men in jail. At times like these I almost wish that I might receive a visit from my own father or mother or brother. Almost, I say, because actually such a visit might bowl me over and leave me in a sick bed suffering from shock.

Elmer barks his good wishes across the state. One day, with the help of people like you (and there can't be too many) we will meet again outside the confines of this gray pile. Until then, thanks again for writing and for remembering.

Yours for a little decency and justice,
Ray Becker

Dear Julia,

Not a better witness appeared for the defense than young Guy Bray. You must see him this time through. Get from him an affidavit showing Frank Van Gilder's threat to kill him.

Thanks for the sweater, a perfect fit. I have become the envy of many of the guards with my library and my special gifts. One of them said to me the other day, "I thought you were an orphan." I don't know where he got such an idea. He thinks the trouble with us is that we have no parental guidance.

There were many who spoke up for us who played minor roles, but their insights into the case might still be valuable. Frank Nehring, who followed concrete construction and was in the parade, testified that it was F.B. Hubbard himself whom Warren Grimm ran back to find in order to converse about plans just prior to the raid. The command "eyes right" was Grimm's idea evidently. Nehring testified that Grimm brought Hubbard up to the front in order to use him as "right guide."

Of course we wanted to establish that Hubbard was a part of the parade and was in charge of the lynchers, but the state brought in a little rope of a man from Portland, J.L. Weaver, who testified that Hubbard was in Portland all this time, that his name appeared on the cash book of the Portland Hotel on the night of the 11th. "He called for his keys on the 11th, I know that," Weaver said.

"Who else called for his key on the 11th that you remember of?"

"Why all the rest that did not carry their keys, they must have called for them. Part of the time Mr. Hubbard *did* carry his key, though, I think."

Vanderveer called for the testimony to be stricken. "No," said the judge.

There was a dirt farmer named Cecil Arrowsmith who was most positive in his statement that he had seen Eugene Barnett coming away from town on the day of the shooting and that he had no rifle on him that he could see. Cecil still has a farm out east of the town, Elmer has directions. Anything we might verify as to Barnett's role in this is particularly useful just because the board seems to be leaning in his favor.

A meeting with Bert Faulkner would be instructive to you personally and will give you a better idea of what was happening at the time of the firing inside the hall. Faulkner stood between me and Everest and the door and claimed to have been hit by a bullet "from behind," shot through the overcoat; possibly by one of us, I've always thought, but Bert testified that he'd turned his back on the men rushing from outside, then got the bullet. He mentioned that he told his tale to Herman Allen at the time he took his statement, but that it never got passed on as information to the court. Bert was a good witness, made it clear that he could see the men outside and heard them say, "Let's go get them!" before anything occurred within.

"At the same time it sounded to me like they throwed a stick of wood, or spuds, against the door; just like a man hit the door with his knees or with his shoulder."

He will tell you what happened out on the back porch of the hotel, when Everest ran and he was pinned down and attacked by four or five soldiers and sailors, they thinking for a while that he was the one who had fired. Faulkner is a tough one for the Legion to hate. Have you seen their version of the fray? Here is Bert Faulkner, according to them:

"He of all the others was more the typical American youth, erect of stature, fearless of eye, clean in limb and features--good to look upon. He had served a home contingent of artillery during the war--" They had a tough time with any of us who had "served." Imagine how they must have worked to make Wesley a "bad man" as they kept insisting was the term we pinned on him when we referred to him around the hall. They have suffered over Wes, and this might be the subject for investigation on your part--try and find the extent to which people who were closely involved in the lynching and jailing us have since suffered anxieties, the most bizarre kinds of physical problems. You'll see what I mean. Look up Bill Scales, one who was first a planner of the raid, who later tried to stop the first attempt to hang Everest. Be prepared though.

Bert Bland has been a steady partner through all of these difficult years. He and his brother Commodore are down to earth, hard working companions. Like Jim McInerney, Bert has not been in the best of health these last few months or so. It is not exactly a warm weather spa out here in Walla Walla, except when the summer comes on like a furnace blast. I have no idea why they chose this place of all others for a state pen, except that it has to be in one of the loneliest corners of the world. And who would want to escape only to be run to death in a wheat field or to die of thirst stranded in a dry arroyo of the Columbia Basin?

Bert's activities on the day of the raid put him as far away as Loren. But closer in spirit. He figured that the soldiers would be armed if they broke for us. He and Roberts and Ole Hanson had been told by Everest that they could have his room in the Queen to use should they need their support. They went and looked at the room and found it too easy to surround if it ever came to that, so they all took off up to Seminary Hill, up behind the Eastern Mill, should you want to try and find the spot. Curly had his rifle in an overcoat that Davis gave to him, and they had a black bag with pistol, binoculars and some sandwiches.

They waited up there and tried to determine lines of fire, which was difficult with buildings being in the way. They saw the parade, and Bert saw the soldiers run, heard the glass fall. Right then he started firing and testified that he shot between four and eight shots. He did not try to pick out particular men and he did use field glasses.

They lit out east of there possibly a mile and a half and wandered around there possibly three hours. They were surrounded by soldiers at one point but sneaked out of the trap. They walked a long way back in a circle, heading now north and west. When they got to Galvin they found a railroad track, Hanson taking to it, so they left him. That was the last they ever saw of him. Possibly he boarded a freight bound for Seattle. The only word we have on him now is a rumor that he is safe in Anchorage.

Not so Curly Bland and Roberts. They continued out towards Grand Mound and there he and Loren said goodbye; Roberts was pooped and foolishly thought he could get a night's sleep at his mother's house. Curly pleaded with him to keep going. Roberts was arrested in his sleep at about three in the morning.

Curly continued slogging through the wet brush, following the Chehalis River, heading in the direction of Rochester and Independence. It was in this locale that the Neimis lived. Bland had the idea that he might run into Lucy and learn something of the fate of the other men. He survived mostly on vegetables gathered from farms. He told the jury that the only reason he gave himself up was that he "got tired of living off of fresh turnips." The Neimi store was his target. He describes himself walking into the place--he hadn't spoken to anyone in 5 or 6 days. He felt like Robinson Crusoe. He had on the tattered overcoat that Davis had given him to hide the rifle. He had no cap and it was raining. His hair was "full of twigs," as he put it and looked like a witch's. At Montesano, if ever the newspapers wanted a picture to show the public what a "radical" looked like, they dragged out Curly and told him to pose with his hands on his hips.

Curly was hungry and desperate, he also longed for news of us. He had no idea what had happened, except what he'd read in one hysterical article he'd found wrapped around some garbage. He prowled around the store under the glare of Mr. Neimi, pulling down a sausage and putting it on the counter. The store was dark as a cave, he said. He pointed to two loaves of bread behind Neimi and pulled a quart of milk out of the cooler. The old man stood with his arms crossed on his apron. Curly put down four cans of beans with the other things and said, "Can I put this stuff on the tab?"

I laughed when I heard this, remembering that stiff old Finn, and Curly claims it was half a desperate joke. The old man's sneer put him right on the brink of bringing out the pistol and ordering him to stuff the food in a bag. Instead they started talking, the storekeeper telling him that he looked "familiar", but he didn't have any damn credit with him that he knew about. Curly got tough, he wanted the man to remember him--"Bob Thompson will vouch for me," he said. "I been in here a hundred times. I worked that turtle-back ridge." He pointed towards Michigan Hill.

"Wait just a minute, young fellow," the older man warned him. Then Curly let it out, "You know my brother, you're Lucy Neimi's father, you must know Wesley Everest--" And at the mention of Wes's name the man leaped back and Curly was aware of a shotgun. Neimi grasped it by the stock, he was shouting, "They got a posse out for you!" Curly crouched below the counter and brought the pistol out. "That bugger Everest!" the man was screaming, then a shotgun blast tore out the window and the glass fell on Curly's head. Curly fired twice past the man into the cooler then grabbed the sausage. "It served him right what they done to him!" Neimi was still yelling. His second shot took care of a stack of cans that rolled on the floor hissing tomato soup. Curly stumbled out the door and made for the road. Neimi came to the porch to yell after him, "And where's my little one now?" Bland fired once more for good measure at a Coca-cola sign on the side of the store and saw the old man slide down the stairs with the smoking shotgun. He'd fainted with the shock and lucky for Curly didn't die of it. He died five months later, just after our trial.

Curly ran for a mile and threw up on the bushes. Then he hoofed it for the farm of an old man named Oscar somebody who knew both Everest and Lucy. He told Bert about Wesley. He described what he knew of the jail the night Lucy and the other woman came for the body. He said that the two women ran off to Portland, that was all he knew. The other woman is Eva Maki, and you might put out inquiries for her among your friends at the union. The effect of Oscar's story was to make Curly turn himself in. He describes himself at this point as"empty, just a sack of skin." A posse came riding up to the farm within a half hour of the business at the store and brought him into town tied to a horse.

I believe that I mentioned, regarding people who come a long way to try and involve themselves with men in jail, an Elizabeth Attridge, a school teacher from Baraboo, Wisconsin. Curly is still writing to her. She has been out here and in Centralia two summers since the first visit and seems sincere. There is much pressure now from Edward Coll and from Walter Bland, the boys' older brother, to get them both released. Let's hope the efforts prove successful.

Dear Julia,

You mentioned state's witness, Tom Morgan, whom Labor's poet, Ralph Chaplin, has immortalized for us as the "wobbly Judas" and he is someone you must try to contact if you can. It won't be easy. After he testified that we fired upon the soldiers from the Avalon and the Arnold while they were marking time in the streets, he was whisked out of court never to be seen again. I don't think they disposed of him exactly, I don't think they needed to. He was so frightened when they got done with him in the bull pen at the Centralia jail and during the sessions spent with Cunningham and Herman Allen and the chief of police that he likely never will draw breath again without it scaring him.

The state knew how to pick its "confessors." They knew a weak man when they found one, and Tom was one of those. The fact that he was often with me prior to the raid complicates my feelings for him. He wasn't quite a friend, but I did think I might influence him for the better. I know that was naive of me, but we were all a little naive at the time. Tom spoke right up and told the court that he was with me at Nevah River Logging Company when I bought my Ivor Johnson .38. He was very frank with the court, very open, and white with fear. How did he know for sure that they'd take care of him when he walked out of there--how did he know for sure that we hadn't someone outside ready to park his soul forever in the grass of Montesano?

He spoke right up and told the court the movements of every one of us inside the Roderick, told them what room I stayed in, told them about Elmer coming to us and advising us to be "ready," told the court that Britt ordered men to go to stations in the Arnold and the Avalon. Told the jury that Britt had asked Tom if he wanted a gun, and that Tom had said, "No." I can still see him up there, his jacket zipped up to his chin, the hair flopping down over his forehead as he always wore it when he used to appear "charming" to me in a boyish, movie-actor kind of way. I guess he's head-over-heels in love with death by now, having named every solitary one of us as being guilty of killing those men.

Tom: "I saw Bert Bland in there. I heard him tell Everest he was going to change his clothes. The man Davis was in there at the time. He had a rifle down his pants leg and he started walking stiff-legged, and they started laughing at him. Davis took the rifle and went across the street toward the Avalon, he went out just before Eugene Barnett went out. I think they both went to the Avalon. There was a remark made generally that if they should happen to get caught, why there not anything to be said about what went on in the hall." You can see how they'd worked on his testimony to cover the ground, and to pin Barnett down. Of course he never set foot in the hall that day, no matter. Not to them, not to Tom Morgan. He wanted his own hide. He got it, no holes in it, no flies on it, just the mark of the coward to carry with him forever. Yes, find him! His home was in Raymond, out on Route 6. Start there, use any method to locate him and if you do, wring the truth out of him. I don't see how the state can deny us, if you catch hold of his heart. If you can't find the heart, we'll settle for his signature.

Dear Julia,

Had Mike Sheehan been sent to jail with us it would have been an injustice worse than the state could have thought up, even in its ugliest mood. Have you met him? He's a big bull of a man with walrus mustache, very alert eyes. At the time of the raid he'd come to the hall only to drag Jim McInerney off to Tacoma to hear Eamon DeValera speak. He testified that on the night of the 10th of November all he had heard discussed in the hall concerned an article that appeared in the *P.I.*

condemning DeValera.

He came back on the 11th, he knew only McInerney, John Lamb and Ole Hanson among us. He just sat around, reading Big Bill Haywood's testimony before the Industrial Commission, waiting for the 4:30 train to take him to Tacoma. The only person who mentioned a gun, he says, was John Doe Davis who came up to him and said, "Have you got one of these?" pointing to his inside pocket. "No, what for?" he answered. Davis said, "In case there's any trouble in the hall," and Sheehan said, "There won't be any trouble around here."

In Sheehan's testimony you can locate Morgan, step by step, right into the Centralia jail, Sheehan with a close eye on him. Vanderveer had also in mind, through Sheehan's testimony, to positively identify Everest as the only man firing. He was sure that Mike would eventually be released.

I've often imagined sessions with the judge and the prosecution in which they bargained for our lives. Well, they didn't want to send Sheehan up. He was 60--he would have died here, how would that have looked? (I'm sorry, Julia, but I've had a tiring day, arguing with Britt and by letter with Elmer. They both want me to ask for a parole as the others are doing. "Solidarity," they argue, but I will not go that way. I want a reconsideration through a proper writ of habeus corpus. I'll write it myself if that lawyer, Cliff O'Brien, you and the others in the I.L.W.U. secured for me hasn't the stuff to get it done.)

Mike Sheehan was a good strong man. He survived brutal treatment while he was in jail as we all did. It wouldn't have been wise to torture him any further.

His back was to the action in the hall. He heard a "crash and a holler." When he looked around he saw "the door open and this man, Everest, firing out on the crowd. He had some kind of revolver and he was shooting fast. The crowd was in a semi-circle facing the door and he couldn't miss them. The crowd stood in one position, seemed to break quick. When he was firing all of them was getting away from the door. The farthest soldier from Everest was probably twenty-five feet, the closest around sixteen feet. My whole mind was concentrated on that man firing. I didn't see a gun on anyone else at the time nor was I aware that anyone else was firing. Right near me was McInerney and Britt Smith and Ray Becker was there. No one fired except Everest."

Remember those words, Julia. This is the version our defense committee wants to make clear to the authorities here and in the capitol.

Mike was in the icebox with us. He remembers someone shouting, 'Boys, here they are--let's set fire to them.'

He testified that he'd never been influenced in any way by Cunningham to "make a statement."

"It was all voluntary. But when I say 'voluntary,' I mean outside of jail. Inside I did see Wesley Everest after he was cut down and brought

119

back to jail. So did Tom Morgan see him."

Morgan curled himself up in the corner the whole time Everest lay there with his jacket drawn up over his head.

Mike had a friend at Montesano named Herb Edwards, a wobbly, a dockworker from Seattle. They were very close, and Mike's son, Will Sheehan, who was twenty-one at the time of the trial, was there too and did considerable leg work for us, talking to potential witnesses. He's a lawyer now, I believe. Mike has instructed his son that his body be cremated after he dies and that the ashes are to be sent to Herb Edwards in a shoe box. When Herb gets them, he will find inside the box some special instructions as to the way the ashes are to be disposed of. Mike leaves us in a dilemma: we don't want him to hurry up and die (though we know that the old fellow has worked his last shift) but we are all very curious as to the fate of those ashes.

August 9, 1930

Dear Julia,

My mood is not much better than when I last wrote. Forgive me, it is hard to live in this place.

It is not just the food, the climate, the loneliness, the day-to-day curse of things not working out the way you want them to. Our bodies grow more slack every day and they don't do anything productive. We don't cut trees, we don't mine coal. Every day I lose something and I forget to thank anyone that I'm alive at all. It is so hard to say what I'm leading to.

Today one of us got his release. James McInerney died of tuberculosis this morning in the prison hospital. The first of us to leave Walla Walla, and I suppose I should rejoice but I can't. It is all so unfair. He was the strongest of all of us. Even stronger physically than Wes.

Jim was born in Ireland and came to this country about thirteen years before he was arrested. He was never a U.S. citizen. He'd worked the woods and in construction and had joined the wobblies in 1916. He was one of those on the steamer Verona fired upon by the Everett sheriff and his deputies. He lay on the deck bleeding with a dozen other wounded men while the ship limped back to the Ballard docks.

Jim's testimony points to the fact that the thing he and others were doing principally in the hall before and just prior to the raid was union business. Passing out pamphlets. He reminded the court that he and Britt put together the appeal to the citizens of Centralia concerning the fact that we knew they were going to raid. He reminded them of the attack in 1918: "I had a picture in my mind of the first I.W.W. Hall that was wrecked during a parade. I have seen workers clubbed and tarred and feathered. I know what it's like to be fired upon."

He and Loren Roberts had a conversation about a gun about 12 o'clock on the day of the raid. He asked Jim if he wanted a gun and he said 'Yes.'

"Roberts gave me a gun; I took it. I put it on, it's right over there on the table. I wore it until I was captured in the icebox. I did not shoot it. The bullets are in the gun and in the belt as they were when I received it."

He described himself in the icebox with us: "I wasn't very comfortable. I was pretty well excited. When I got to the icebox was the only time I took out the gun. I just held it until the soldiers came. One turned the door and jumped back and said, 'Don't shoot, don't shoot!'"

"When I was first taken out of the icebox there was a soldier there who said that I was the man who shot somebody and he wanted to burn me at the stake. That was overruled and I was handcuffed and taken off to jail, but this same man later got me out of jail. He wanted me to make a statement. They had a rope and the mob held me. The rope was noosed around my neck and the end thrown over a telegraph wire support. They pulled the rope tight and finally I was on my toes, but since I didn't talk they came to a conclusion and took me back in again. This method of trying to get a statement out of me was tried twice more while I was in the jail in Centralia."

Jim's illness may have begun before the November incident, it may have started after. He was ill during the whole period of the trial, then he would improve, seemingly all his old strength would return, then he'd be flat on his back, flushed and spitting blood. He got quieter the years we knew him here. There will be a prison service for him which we will take charge of. There is no family here that we know of. He is the real American orphan, if my guard friend should want one. I have his father's address in Ireland, and I am hoping that we can get permission to cremate and send the ashes home to his native soil. He dictated the following letter to me last week. I made a copy of it. I want this preserved with the other items of a personal nature pertaining to all the prisoners:

Walla Walla, Wash.
U.S.A.
August 4, 1930

Liscanor
Kilshanney
County Clare, Ireland

Dear Father,

I am writing you from the infirmary in the jail here. Ray Becker, a friend, is taking this down for me. As you know I am sick with the t.b., much more so than when I wrote you last. No I have not heard from Donal and them. They have all spread like the wild geese you used to tell us about. I am happy to know that Sean is such a good son to you. I hardly knew him but he was a good little talker, I remember that. I am not surprised that he has turned into a poet. Maybe now there will be more time to read and write in our country. I think often of Clare and of Galway, of all the places where I grew up. The cliffs of Moher are a little less big in my conscious mind now but when I dream of them there is nothing bigger in the world. In my dreams I see the way the light shone through the rain between the cliffs and Aran. I think often of how I grew up loving my home and how that home was taken away from me by forces I still do not understand, though they are the same in this country as there.

I know Mr. Yeats that Sean mentioned only by reputation as as aristocrat and a senator. Yes, I remember Gort very well. I liked that part in your letter about going to the top of the tower and thinking about me and Donal and Gregory, and Michael and Seumas. Thank Sean for the book of poems, too. I liked them but I found them difficult. One that was not difficult went like this, "Parnell came down the road, he told a cheering man, Ireland shall have her freedom and you still break stone."

At this time I know only that I love my homeland, my father and my brothers and the memory of my mother. I have broken stone (here) and cut trees. Soon, praise life, I will be free of this tired flesh. I wanted to write you one more time to tell you that I remain,

Your loving son,
James

Dear Julia,

Frankly, I will be glad to see Loren Roberts go, but I fear for him once he is "outside." Julia, don't waste your time with him. He is a weak character and lacks initiative, and it's no pleasure to tell you this. Roberts was so proud of his confession that he frequently mentioned it among us while he was here. Yet the others are close to him and he was Everest's friend while he was alive. He and I are as unlike as rain and wind. What I'm more excited about today is the strong possibility that Eugene may be released in the same wave of understanding that's sweeping Loren out.

The matter of Roberts' confession and the question of his madness are the most puzzling aspects of the trial. He presented a problem for both sides: the state claimed him for his confession and the defense because he confessed. It was like Vanderveer was saying, all the time Loren was sitting up there struck dumb, "Here, can't you see? This youth sits before you beaten into senselessness." At one point Vanderveer openly accused Cunningham, "You more than any man are responsible for this boy's condition!" We had a psychiatrist come in and uphold our contention that Roberts was mad. The prosecution maintained all along that he was faking.

This will give you some indication how the state worked in the matter of the confession. Cunningham did read it over V.'s objection. After naming all those who were present the night before the raid, Loren says, "I don't believe there was a discussion with the boys again that night about defending the hall." At which point Cunningham read,

"Interlineation: 'I think there was.'"

"After the Foss meeting I believe I went home that night."

"Interlineation: 'I know that I did walk out home.'"

"Monday evening when I came to the hall again I remember seeing Everest and Britt Smith and McInerney. Davis is the guy that was in the Avalon, ain't he? He told his name and I forgot it. Davis is the guy in the brown pants, the brown suit and the mackinaw? I believe his hair is brown, wasn't it? I think he had a light mustache, very thin. There was something funny about him."

Something very funny, if you believe as we do that Cunningham turned John Doe to ashes. We should have put some of those ashes on Loren's forehead. Loren liked to identify people. "The man with the big black mustache? The Irishman? I don't know the name but I know the description, since you told me, and I don't remember whether his mustache is black, but I know he had a pretty heavy one, and he was there all right."

"The two Bland boys was there. I remember Britt Smith saying that this building across the street would be a good place for some of the boys to be, and I said no damn man need tell me where I was going to be, that I knew where I wanted to be. That is the way that conversation took place exactly. No, I don't know that Britt had an envelope with a diagram on it drawn out something like Tower Avenue, and that he had some mark here and another mark about where the Arnold Hotel was and a cross mark over here at the hill."

"What made us select the hill up there was, they tried to plan for us. These guys tried to plan for us to get in these buildings, and we wouldn't do that. I didn't want that at all and neither did Curly Bland or Ole Hanson. I knew this, that if any shooting started these fellows in the hall would be handled, so we went up on the hill. We thought we were watched--if we stuck our heads out of the window of any building we would get a bullet in it."

"We were instructed not to start any trouble of any kind until we heard shooting at the hall. My gun is a gun I always owned, I brought it down with me Monday night. It used to be my dad's. It's a .22 high-power Savage. Hanson's is one he owned for a long time, a .250 Savage. McInerney had a gun, Britt Smith had one, Everest had one, a .45. I don't remember Morgan. I remember that boy, Becker. I don't know what he had. He had some kind of little toy."

Well, you can see what he thought of me. It is not all friendship in a brotherhood. I must be fair to him, without damaging what I feel about the case. Make your own judgements about what he says. Does it sound like truth to you?

This is what he testified in that paper: "--and another thing, did you notice any bullet holes? I'll tell you where my bullets went. I think they either hit this brick building or went up through the glass up very high. I know that I was shooting high."

"I know what you and them others say, that Art McElfresh was killed with what looks like some kind of .22 high-power shell. I'm certain that I didn't hit anybody, because I was holding my shooting up. That's what I know."

It was what he *knew* while they were wringing this story from him. But at various times, at Montesano and more and more here at Walla Walla, he will claim that he did shoot McElfresh.

These are the words that hurt us most: "The first shots I heard came from the wobbly hall. I didn't see any soldiers making for the hall until after the shooting became quite brisk."

That was it. That's the confession. Vanderveer wanted the court to pity Loren for being forced to make it. Some pity he had coming to him, he was young at the time. But the silence he maintained--

I won't finish this. Julia, this is a dark area of the trial and the whole business. Maybe you should look him up. He might need help getting started again with the stigma of McElfresh's death hanging on him. He thinks he's going right back home and "get some work."

September 8, 1931

Dear Julia,

The story of Eugene Barnett is not an easy one to tell, it's not over though he was released today, and it may be more of a saga than a story. He rides into town one day, mails a package of geranium seeds to his wife's mother in Idaho, ties up his horse behind the Queen rooming house, and by the end of the day is arrested for murder.

Gene was very active among us, but a miner not a logger, and testified that on the day of November 11th he happened in by accident. He'd forgot it was Armistice Day. He'd been out coyote hunting since the time of the National Coal Strike that began November 1st.

"I was having some fun with my hounds out there in the woods, enjoying a vacation that workers seldom get."

His testimony that he spent the whole time prior to and during the raid in the company of the McAllisters, in the hotel adjoining the hall, was backed up by several witnesses who saw him there. Mrs. McAllister spent 67 days in jail, during which time they worked hard to get her to say that Barnett was not there but she stood her ground. She died of heart failure a year after the trial. Barnett testified to watching army men parking trucks across the street from the hall prior to the parade; he saw men with clubs and gas pipes in the parade. When he saw the attack coming, he threw off his coat and started for the door, but before he got there he heard the shooting and jumped back.

"They were breaking down a partition, they were coming in, one fellow had a hand axe. There was a fellow named Bill Scales I had credit with at his store. I told him to warn these fellows to be careful with the guns because Mrs. McAllister had gone back the way they were coming in. Their mouths were drawn like bows. You could see that they were scared and I figured that even if a chipmunk moved they'd be apt to shoot. I told Scales to please try and stop them. He looked at me but didn't make a reply. The next fellow who came in was a big strapping fellow in a sailor's uniform. His hat was off, his hair slicked down. I told him to be careful, there was a lady back there. 'Is that a wobbly c———?' he said and I started to struggle with him but he broke away when he heard that they had captured the men in the icebox.

Barnett told the court that Everest had been a wobbly even while he was in the army.

Cunningham: "Wasn't Everest known around the hall as the 'Bad Man?'"

Barnett: "No, he was not. He was about the quietest fellow I ever knew and the whitest, too, to my knowledge."

"And weren't you known as the 'Nervy Man?'"

"No, sir. My nerves may be good but I don't go by any name, except Barnett."

Cunningham asked him if he hadn't always been a radical himself. Hadn't he been arrested before on similar charges? Barnett replied:

"I was arrested two days before registration day, 1917. I've never spoken against the government, and the I.W.W. is not opposed to our government, either. They are opposed to the system under which we live, the capitalist system, the industrial system. I've been a socialist for a long time. That's not a crime."

"Why were you arrested?"

"I was arrested two days before the registration under the draft law, for remarks I made about the draft. Wages was the cause of my remarks. If you left the struggle for higher wages and joined the army for pennies more, why you were really hurting the American way of life--which is to improve the lot of the worst off."

"I was arrested for seditious utterances in Idaho, but I never served a sentence because what I said was the truth. I got into trouble only for objecting to working for $2.25 a day. That was the real charge. And that's the reason that the ten of us are standing trial in this court today--"

The prosecution objected; objection was sustained.

Like all of us, Eugene has served eleven and a half years in this prison, knowing that he is innocent. I am sure it goes even harder for him because they singled him out as the slayer of Warren Grimm. The time spent here has twisted him less I think than it has any of us. He leaves this place with the same stubborn head on his shoulders that he arrived with. His wife is dying of cancer--that's the state for you, showing more compassion for the nearly dead than for the living and vital.

You can see that this life twists me too. Eugene has decided to take his wife to a cancer treatment center in Missouri. He has some hope for her or pretends to.

Governor Hart made a special trip here for Gene's release. He called him and told him what a favor they were doing for him, and in return he expected that Gene would have nothing more to do with unions. He told him not to write for any more damned union papers, or it would be "too bad" for him.

Gene told him that he came in a union man and he'd go out a union man. He said that he'd see all of us on the outside before a year was out. He came over and took my hand. We were all grouped around my shack. He loves hounds and Elmer was licking his face and behaving like he knew Gene was going free. The day was cool and bright. He told me that he wouldn't take the route I've chosen but he understood my reasons for pursuing it. He asked if he could speak to anyone on the outside to help me. I reminded him about you. He said he might contact you, he couldn't say what was going to happen to him once he got his wife back to Missouri. Then he left and I felt a wave of emotion so complicated I can hardly describe it.

I was happy for him and part of me went with him, but I was frightened, too. I hoped that the state did not think it had salved its conscience with the release of one truly innocent man and one sick boy. Loren had left two nights before.

One reason for Gene's early release was that he made the other side particularly uneasy. Have you read the American Legion account of his testimony?

> A word for Barnett though he be guilty as Cain.
>
> Of those ten remaining defendants Eugene Barnett was the outstanding figure. His eyes were unabashed and unclouded, friendly eyes with the touch of fierceness in them-- far better gauges of a decent human soul than the sullen, shifty and morose brown optics of Elmer Smith, who was to be freed. One could believe that his convictions were deep and desperate and sincere--however greatly one shuddered at the deed he was charged with. Eugene Barnett, coal miner since his eighth year, molded and soul-scarred in a trade that undeniably has seen oppression beyond endurance might ask, as he would not, some word of understanding, if not of extenuation, for the hectic passions that drove him to blinded murder.

He might well ask.

> The defendant himself was calmly truculent, given to the logic of the propagandist in reply to question of counsel, and his story was a flat and impressive denial, in orderly sequence of commonplace conduct, to the charge that he passed a portion of the afternoon in Room 10 of the Avalon Hotel, firing a .38-55 rifle and slaying Warren O. Grimm. He testified that when he saw ex-sevicemen wrecking the front of the hall he would have gone out to engage them, had he not realized an instant later

that the affair was beyond fistic intervention.

Grim by-play was in that bit of testimony which concerned a verse from "Christians at War," one of the songs of the I.W.W. hymnal. Grimm, so the testimony had developed, was slain by a bullet which had been split at the nose. A number of cartridges had been similarly treated--to make the missile mushroom and inflict a more terrible wound. Prosecutor Abel had asked Barnett if he was familiar with the song, and had answered in the affirmative.

"Have you noticed in that song a suggestion about filing your bullet noses flat?" pursued the prosecutor.

"Many times," answered the defendant.

"Ever sing it?"

"Yes, sir."

"You do, then, believe in filing your bullets' noses flat?"

"No, sir."

Both the defendant and the counsel for the defense declared the song to be a satire on modern warfare, but in the minds of those who heard the verse, and who were familiar with the testimony regarding the "mystery rifle" and the death wound of Grimm, arose the hazard that through the song viciousness found its inspiration. These were the words of the verse:

> File your bullets' noses flat,
> Poison every well;
> God decrees your enemies
> Must all go plumb to hell!

Barnett said his anger was such, when he saw the hall sacked by the ex-servicemen in search of radicals, that he rode home at a gallop, intending to procure his rifle. His wife dissuaded him. His eyes flashed as he told the prosecution that had he returned Wesley Everest would not have died a victim to lynch law.

"You were not angered over the shooting of the soldiers, were you?" inquired the state.

"Not at all," was the calm reply. "I approve of anything that is necessary."

Julia, do you know the rest of that song? You dad ever sing it?

> Onward Christain soldiers!
> Drench the land with gore;
> Mercy is a weakness
> All the gods abhor.
> Bayonet the babies,
> Jab the mothers, too;
> Hoist the Cross of Calvary
> To hallow all you do!

When Gene and I were first here and happened to line up across from one another, on laundry duty or in the license shop, we used to sing parts of the song to pass the time. Since I've moved out here, more and more isolated from the others. I think of such moments as cherished memories from a relatively innocent childhood. I shall have to teach my dog the song for old times sake.

Walla Walla
January 22, 1932

In replying refer to
9413

Dear Julia,

Last week John Lamb, Britt Smith and Commodore Bland went home; there's only me and Curly left. Lonely times.

I think sometimes John Lamb of all of us had most to lose. Five children at home, a wife he sorely missed, very little money except what came in from the Defense Committee and what Dewey earned, and he the oldest among us. I am glad to hear that you have met them all and stayed with the family. John will be a most welcome addition to have back among them. He is a stable man, he plans to go right back to his old friends, the same old streets. I understand the town hasn't grown much. But why should it?

On the day of the raid John went with Commodore to the avalon. As he puts it, "When I went to that room I was just the same as Commodore. I had been threatened at home and on the streets. I was there in order to be out of the way. I had no intention of using the rifle or any revolver. I was in that room to keep clear from mobs."

They both registered their right names. John watched the parade go by, then left the room briefly. He heard Commodore yell they were going to raid the hall, then he heard a breaking of glass.

"I know he broke out a glass of the front window and when he turned he said, 'I've hurt my hand.' I saw his hand. It was badly cut. No shots were fired in the room."

John suffered bouts of depression from loneliness that the rest of us could not cure with talk and joking. It did little good to remind him that we all were brothers. He told me he was getting too old for that. He just wanted out. Some time ago he came to me with a letter. He was going to send it to his wife but he was torn. He didn't know if it would do more harm than good, if it would do any good at all. I read it and put it to the side. He talked to me till curfew about the way you get when you have a woman who loves you on the outside and you can't do a thing about it with your arms and legs. You have only a silly pen. I've often wondered about the same thing. What would it be like, these letters of mine, if we were what you call closer? But I can't know that and I will not pursue this line further--I might find myself in a state similar to John's. This is what he wrote, Julia, because he walked away forgetting the letter, and I happen to think it touching. It also gives you, as our recorder, a first hand

128

look at what one man suffered during his time here. Multiply that feeling by 100,000 and you might approach the loneliness that all of us in prisons feel. No sad songs, just a little truth. Tell me what you think of it next time you write.

Walla Walla
December 6, 1931

In replying refer to
9416

Dear Mrs. Lamb:
My dear Bunny! It is me, fooled you.
How are you? How is everybody? I am fine considering. How is Dewey's poor lungs and his right hand healing? Hope he continues to be ablebodied and a big help to you.
My dear, a pernicious rumor has reached me that you do not even have to bother to dispute. I only bring it up for the sake of keeping lines clear between us. Someone of the local Defense Comm. (probably a secret scissorbill or a communist) has written to the Def. Comm. Hq in Sacramento that our boarder, Fellow worker Hacquist, is contributing more than he ought to in keeping our family together. Not only in just money the story goes. I'm sorry even to have to say this considering how swell it was between us when last you were here. How I look forward to your xmas visit! Well maybe we can get it all cleared through the gov't mails and by the time you and the kids get here it'll be all over and done with. A dumb tale to tell, don't you agree? and I am enbarassed to have to say anything. But here in this (blank) place where Dear John letters go begging they are so cheap, a man gets looney sometimes in that department.
Enough of this. The guy who started it probably had a secret crush on you himself. Why anyone ought to, you're pretty enough. That's probably why I had so many youngsters by you in the first place. As you always say I'm not such bad shakes myself. In other words, Bunny, I'm jittery! Ha.
Ray Becker says to say hello to you and Dewey. He says if Dewey had taken the stand we could have won. He is still going on in that same vein.
P.S. I'm learning a new "trade" still with my hands. It'll require that I hang out a "shingle" when I get out of this place.

Please write soon
and kill this sickening talk
all my love to you,

your *Dear* John

You can also see by his letter that John sees my cause as a little less than practical. It's true, from one way of looking, that John did not waste his time here. He looked ahead to the future, and he will be engaged in "curing" people, he is convinced, while my way of carrying on must seem to him obsessive.

You will meet O.C. Bland when he gets out, another family man, and a good one. I don't think he plans to stay in town, that's only a guess. His wife Martha is an emotional woman. I hadn't met her before her visits to O.C. and Bert. I found her strong at times, but she often verged on collapse. I don't know how they kept their home together except with help from the larger family. Sometimes when I'm lying in my bunk hearing nothing fall on my roof, since little does fall out here besides the driest of snow flakes, I try to imagine how much others close to a person must suffer with a man's or a woman's convictions, should the man or woman bother to have them. I guess I'm too self-centered to take that very far.

O.C. was armed the day of the raid, he had his rifle. You can look back to Robert's statement for the exact calibre. He and Lamb went straight to the hotel.

"I went up there and emptied the rifle cartridges out on the bureau, set the gun down in the corner and sat down on the bed. The gun was loaded. We were conversing about casual matters until the parade came along."

When the raid started he saw "the lead man hit the door with a rush with his foot, glass flew out. He hadn't any more hit the hall door until I had my rifle in my hand, shoved the muzzle of it through the window light. I was down on one knee. I had my hand up near the muzzle of the rifle and run my hand, rifle barrel and all through the window, broke the light with my hand instead of the rifle. I did not shoot."

"When I left the hotel I went straight home. I changed the towel on my hand and tried to get Lamb to pull this flesh back on my hand and he started to faint. My haste in getting away was, I could do nothing. Why should I stay and be beat up? I couldn't do anything because my hand was numb to my side. There was nothing I could see but to be with my family, to afford them a little protection. We'd all been threatened before, to our faces. I wanted to be with them."

And now he is back with them. Britt is home, too. John Lamb and Loren are home; Eugene is in Missouri by now. I have no word from him. For all of these men, life surely has changed, their children grown up, no longer children. Their wives, it must be true, tired and bone weary, past their primes. This is an aspect of prison life connected to the loneliness that one day--praise the gods outside--I may take up with you. I really do long to see you, without a partition between us!

In replying refer to
9413

Walla Walla
April 4, 1932

Dear Fellow Worker Mooney,

Well, they have all gone home. Bert Bland was the last of us, save me, to receive parole. I wrote to you when Jim McInerney died in the prison hospital, didn't I? I suppose some will say it is stubborn of me to hold out for complete vindication of the crimes against us, but I was never a man for half measures. I will have my day in court through a lawful writ of habeas corpus. For the last ten years and more I have gone over the facts of our case in such detail that my head sometimes won't let go of the words when I try to sleep at night.

No need to tell you about that feeling!

I am still working on my own writ. It is hell but I am getting used to the terms. I have help, if you can call it that, from a new lawyer in Portland, Cliff O'Brien. Did I write to tell you that I fired Irvin Goodman? Elmer grows worse, we all fear for him. He has worked himself nearly to death, and here I am still in jail. I am a problem for him, but I ask myself, and I ask you (though I'm sure you'll agree), are we right or are we wrong? If we're innocent, then shouldn't the record say so? Yes I do care what history says about us. You don't turn up innocent with a mere parole.

I am not a hero nor especially a martyr. I am just a man who wants to see justice done.

Hope that I see you one day outside these walls. You've said that you will visit me, but I wonder who will visit who first? No, I won't bet on it. I have a trusteeship and a small garden I'm in charge of. Things could be worse. Oh, yes, and the care of a nice dog who somehow has managed to get "with pup" though there are no signs of potential mates around. On such facts are miracles based, I suppose. Wish I could work one as easily myself.

Yours for a little decency and justice,
Ray Becker

*

Dear Julia,

I am passing this note from Bert Bland on to you. I don't trust myself to keep it safe. Too many newspapers and legal papers strewn about my cabin.

Madison, Wisconsin

Dear Ray,

Name of the lake here is Mendota. I heard this song on the day me and Elizabeth got married. "High above Mendota's waters, there's an awful smell, it's because those sons-of-badgers really stink like hell." I thought you might like that seeing as it's about your home state. After the ceremony we went sailing on the lake, my first time, hers too. She is a little older than she first told me when she came to see us all the way out to Walla Walla. A little more of a Christer too. I think we're going to leave here pretty quick. Too many young hot shot radicals.

She and her brother and sister have a farm up in Baraboo. That's the home of Ringling Brothers, Barnum and Bailey. She says I could possibly get work at the Badger Ordinance Works. I says I don't think I would. I'm going to spend my time instead reading Merchants of Death. Get that fellow R. Trowbridge to send it. It's about the Nye committee investigation. The way the munitions makers and bankers moved us into the Great War.

Heard from Eugene Barnett. His wife died out in Missouri. Poor bugger. He's going to come through here and have lunch with us. I miss you and our bull sessions very much, though there is plenty out here in the way of cows. Have not been feeling too good lately, must be something I ate (back there).

best to my old buddy,
Bert

Walla Walla
September 24, 1934

Dear Julia,

Mrs. Warren Grimm and Mrs. Elmer Smith sit on the front porches of their adjoining homes, they have not spoken to each other since Warren's death, now they are both widows and there is still nothing going between them. No ill will, just nothing to talk about. Don't bother trying to obtain an affidavit from Mrs. Grimm. She knows her husband ran for the hall but can't admit it now out of simple pride. Can't say as I blame her, but some word from her would be a rare find. I have told Ralph Trowbridge about you. He says you must be a wonderful individual indeed. I knew that first. He has sent me in the neighborhood of 1000 books.

I believe I told you that he is going through the process of adopting one of the I.W.W. prisoners who was in Leavenworth. He has invited me to come to New York and stay with him for as long as I like when I get out of this place.

I agree with you that Elmer Smith was one of the most courageous men among us. When he made that remark about everyone in America looking at the I.W.W. Hall that day, it was all I could do to keep from standing up and applauding. His disbarrment proceedings as you can guess were a farce and grew directly out of their fears that he might actually win his campaign for prosecuting attorney of Lewis County. Could they risk his investigating the lynching, now when so much of public sentiment has swung in our favor? It would be some work but well worth the effort if you could determine the actual vote in the disbarrment proceedings and record what were the reasons given for their decision. Elmer was always a hot item for this state, his investigation was tireless and impeccable and he worked seemingly around the clock. The work he did for the Centralia Defense Committee (now the Free Ray Becker Committee) was what finally did him in. Your account of his death sent me into a deep depression, one of the reasons I did not reply to you immediately.

Yes, Elmer and I quarreled, when I first heard that he wanted to run for office I was angry with him. It seemed a threat to his energies and maybe I replied selfishly. I know that I cannot allow myself to forget the lynchers and of course they were much more apparent to Elmer, living and walking among them, than they are to me having lived so much alone. Please overturn every obstacle to get into Elmer's office, take help with you if you need. But get the records that Elmer has compiled before they are all destroyed by some well meaning citizen from the Elks Club or the city office.

As Elmer said, there were at least 500,000 Americans looking down that street, but what did they see? And this was my central argument with Vanderveer's conduct of the case. I say they could have seen more and they could have seen differently. Julia, there is a Pathe photographer, who may still live in Seattle. The name is Judson, I think. He came into town the night after the raid and put up at the Elks Club. He heard things, and the next day he took pictures of the way the bullets entered the I.W.W. Hall. He was willing to testify as to the angle of the bullet holes entering the building and to offer his photos as proof. I know that George V. knew of this potential witness, knew he had been threatened, run out of Centralia and his equipment broken. But he did not bring him in.

I have met and discussed my case with Cliff O'Brien, the lawyer the Committee sent. You know him, I am sure. I paid him $2.50 to draft a petition for habeas corpus and represent me in court. He promised to have it done in a month but a month went by and I suspected the worst. I was right, he hadn't started it when next he got into contact. But what I fired him for was not the worthlessness of his promises but because he refused to say in the petition that George V. had betrayed the Centralia prisoners.

I argued with Britt Smith in Montesano about Vanderveer's handling of the case. Britt's view was shared by many. Mine was the minority view, and here am I and where are they? Perhaps they settled for less than I, maybe in the long run they got more. I keep thinking of the Wild Geese, those Irish rebels spread all over the globe that Jim used to tell me about, his last days. I feel much in common with Jim these days and with Elmer now that he is gone. Dear Julia, it's not morbidity that brings these associations on. I know that death is a kind of purity and also a final truth. I sit here day after day, or I move about my trusteeship like some steward of the middle ages, keeping my grove of trees and my rows of wheat, but living so quietly that maybe I'm not living at all. I ask you, is there still a life out there? Does Portland bustle and thrive? I imagine the lights of the city at night seen from that high hill behind it. It must be exciting, your life must be exciting. Or does the work you do for me make your life as narrow as mine? How I wish we could share more deeply what I feel at this moment.

Dear Julia,

I did not know you and Mr. O'Brien were so close. I'm not sure what good I might gain by apologizing. I am sorry that alcohol is such a problem for him but then I didn't invent drink. I had nothing to do with inventing prisons either, but here they stand, nevertheless. I am moved, though, I can't say how deeply, that you and your friends went to such lengths to copy and put the brief together. It looks as though the debt I owe to the city of Portland continues to grow.

I'm sure that Mr. O'Brien thinks me a little mad. Well, put him in here for a few years, I wonder how he would fare? What else, he wonders, was wrong with Vanderveer's defense? The whole range of testimony regarding the .38 bullet that entered Grimm was never faced or gone into by Vanderveer except obliquely. He kept inferring that it was probably fired by John Doe Davis, the mysterious man in the brown mac, and that it probably was shot from across the street, from the Arnold.

Since we all know that Davis was made to disappear by some mayhem or other, Vanderveer was hedging, trying to please both sides. You see, 'I'll give you the concession of having the bullet come from across the street and not from within the hall, if we all keep in mind that it was shot by someone no longer with us. And no longer with us because of some death sentence dealt out before the trial.'

We never had to concede putting the killing bullet across the street. Colonel Coll, whose investigation was so helpful in getting the other men released, states flatly that everyone in town now believes they pulled .45 slugs from all of the soldier victims.

Thanks very much for the latest copy of *The New Republic* and the new magazine, *Partisan Review,* which I eagerly read--most impressive in its quality and its politics. There is still some faint hope for the Scottsboro boys, the way I read things. And with people like you working for me, even more hope for Ray Becker. When I get out, what would you say to a cross-country trip to New York? Ralph T. wants very much to meet you. Please say yes.

I hope that I do not sound too demanding in the midst of all the chores I have been sending your way, to ask you to try once again, the next time you are in Centralia, to find any information you can concerning the girl, Lucy Neimi or her friend, Eva Maki. It is a mystery that seems not to want to break, yet I believe that she must still exist, somewhere, and maybe with a child of Wesley's if the rumor proves true.

Elmer barks his good wishes over the Columbia River, across the state and over the five bridges to the city of Portland. I dreamed of them again last night. Hopeful sign?

Dear Julia,

This came yesterday. I have no comment to make, I grieve quietly and alone.. It's raining for a change. I wish that I could weep with the day.

I feel as dry as the dust bowl north and west of here.

Baraboo, Wisconsin
September 12, 1935

Dear Mr. Becker,

It grieves me to have to write to you the news that your friend and old comrade, Bert Bland, was the recent victim of a heart attack. He died last Sunday, the day before Labor Day. We had only a short year of married bliss together before he was called away. He will be sorely missed.

It also grieves me that I must at this time try and straighten some misunderstanding that must have grown as a result of Bert's and my jail courtship and our hasty departure from the northwest he loved so well. A letter from you came addressed to Bert alone, which I took the liberty of opening and reading.

On the matter of how we met in the first place you may remember that the National Churches' Relief Council prints in its Washington memo the names of all prisoners desiring correspondents. This it did in 1924, this it still does. I wrote to Bert and I wrote to you at random, so to speak. You must remember that you replied that I ought to go hear your father, the Reverend Ralph Burghdorf, preach. I made the trip to Milwaukee and I did just that. No, he did not mention the Centralia prisoners that day, but it was his inspired preaching that convinced me to make the trek westward. As you know, since you introduced us, Bert and I met only once in Walla Walla. It was, as he often said, love at first sight.

I do not like the term Do-gooder and I'm sure you did not mean it to apply in any way to me but only generally. There are such people drawn to the downtrodden in life's race, but in the eyes of Jesus they are as hypocrites.

I only mentioned Badger Ordnance to Bert because it was the only place hiring a year ago. Bert did not work the year he was with us and I'm afraid my brother and sister saw him rather as a burden upon us. We are not wealthy here in any way but in land, which as you are well aware, you cannot eat.

Give my best to the young guard with blond hair who allowed Bert and I a longer stay that the rules allowed. He was a fine young gentleman. Gene Barnett came here about six months ago and Bert and I went down to Madison and had lunch with him. A fine handsome man he is, and so are you all, good strong men.

I did not understand the reference made between "some kinds of marriages" and "living off turnips for a week." Perhaps you could explain it to me.

I remain yours sincerely grieving
in Jesus Christ,
Elizabeth Bland Attridge

Dear Julia,

Sorry to have taken so long to congratulate you on your new interests of the heart. In the interim I endured one brief hearing with His

Honor Hiram Daniels, district court judge from Spokane. I'm afraid I did not behave as they would have me and the whole thing was short lived. Please ask that sod Cliff O'Brien to keep from my presence all human dross like the "psychologist" he sent snooping around me a week ago. He looked exactly like Major Hoople in the funny papers but was a sight less funny to me. I smoked him out in about ten minutes and sent him packing. Does O'Brien not know the meaning of the word "fired?"

If Doc Equi calls your new fellow "handsome," than handsome he must be. I haven't met her but heard of her by reputation as an untiring picket marcher and champion of women's rights. Wesley knew her, I think.

I hope you will be happy with this new man, Julia, I sincerely do. What more can I say? My head aches tonight like a grindstone without lubricant, still working on the bloody writ. Thinking of Jim, thinking of Bert, thinking of all of you safe and sane outside.

Walla Walla
November 12, 1937

Dear Julia Bertram,

A cold, the first in more than three years, kept me from feeling like doing much of anything and is the reason I am so long in thanking you for the socks and book. I like them very much.

How is the little one doing? Walking by now, I'll bet, stepping out gamely if she is anything like her mother.

Last night's dream was as unpleasant as it was vivid. I returned to my cabin after a day's work, my back bent with pain, and find pinned to my door a curt note, informing me that I am to have a chance of a new hearing, not in Spokane but in Montesano! That's it, a very grudging note and the next thing, I am in a huge touring car with the blinds down, so dark that I suspect that I am being driven to my own funeral. When finally I talk I ask the driver and a faceless passenger to lift the blinds. We look out upon a swirling snow storm and soon we are stopped at the pass.

There are no garages, no chains for the tires, only the towering evergreens, a road proceeding over a crest of hill and the snow obliterating all distinctions. The men with me--sometimes they are two, the driver and the faceless man, and sometimes they are several--stand with hands in their pockets beside the car. Then the mountains are gone and, magically, we are in court. It is the same court. I look to the mural on the wall. The pioneer woman I remembered now is dressed in black, and her blond child has an enormous head on a long neck and a mouthful of white teeth.

They sit me down in the front row of the court. We are waiting for His Honor. The jury is out, permanently, the witness chair is empty, there are no lawyers present for either side. I can't turn my head to see if there are any others behind. Yet I feel their presence with such intensity that it's as though I have a wound in my back or my thighs that unknown to everyone but me is bleeding me dry. The feeling is that behind me, around me, next to me are massed all the people I have ever known. I look up, someone has entered, he is familiar and I do not like the feeling that he is.

From two wing doors two lawyers enter. And it is clear to me what's happening. One is Vanderveer right down to his sandy hair and his lantern jaw. The other is oval-headed Mr. Abel, with pince nez and suit of conservative cut. The judge is Cagey Wilson. I leap up to scream at them and to run from the court to roll across the lawn outside, to throw myself into the Chehalis, but stop short, straining so that the cords of my neck must burst. From my arms and legs hang massive chains.

This letter, Julia, is meant to be a lullaby. Not for you, for me. I did not think I could sleep tonight unless I told it all to you.

Dear Julia,

I can think of nothing recently that gave me more pleasure than the sight of you escorting those five jurors from the old days into the visiting room. What a gesture, what work it must have taken you and Sig Olson and Shorter and Stevens and the rest of them to round up those men and to bring them all the way out here. Could the Board and Warden Hardin be less than impressed by them and their mission: to get me out.

I was especially taken by Mr. Hulten, what a gracious man. They were all so humble meeting me. I suppose it must be quite a confirmation of their guilt to see me here. It's one thing to be a part of sending a man up when he is 400 miles away from you but quite another when you see him in prison clothes. I wonder what they thought, I really wonder.

It was interesting seeing Goodman again after all this time. It's amazing what a hold I must have on these legal types who keep on "helping" me despite the fact that as far as I'm concerned I have dispensed with their services. He reminded me again, that my case was a "class action." I asked him, then, why wasn't my name as known among political circles as Tom Mooney? For the fourth time he and I stopped speaking.

One other thing, who was the driver of that second car? I got the strangest reaction from one of my fellow prisoners here who was a wob and worked the docks in Portland. He said, That's some friend you got driving that big car. I asked him what he meant. He laughed and said, You never heard of Major Milner?

No. Have you? A mystery to me. Anyhow it was wonderful to see you again, my dear, and I'm sure the jurymen made a deep impression on the heads of this household.

My Dear Julietta,

What a coup that Tom Morgan affidavit was! It was very clever of you to have represented yourself to his family as an estate investigator, to have guessed that greed might be the most likely way to find his path. I am sorry you had to travel so far to discover him. Does it occur to you, as it does to me, how strangely the names of the places reveal the people in this case? Did you say to yourself, I must go to Raymond to free Ray? Did you shout Eureka! once you'd found the spot where Tom Morgan was hid? As you know, I grow more and more peculiar over words. But I love these:

> that while affiant was in jail, he was threatened with hanging if he did not say what the legionnaires wanted him to say. That the said legionnaires came after him in this manner ten or twelve times. That finally affiant promised to sign what they wanted him to say. That he was told he would be "rewarded"; he understood this to mean that he would be released from jail and that he would not be tried with the I.W.W.s for murder. That a stenographer was called into the room. . .

It's all music to me, Juliet, and you are the composer. My god, that description of him shaking still, though you were alone with him! The guilt that man has lived with would keep my father's entire congregation in line for the length of his tenure. And to think that I was the one principally responsible for bringing him into the union. My friend, life is strange and gets stranger every day.

September 4, 1938

Dear Julia,

That must have been some discussion between you and the F.R.B. Committee and the Lieutenant Governor! Vic Meyers has never struck me as any more sympathetic to my case than the late governor, Mr. Hart. What did you use on him? Threats? Charm? The promise of my lasting conversion to the commercial class? "Ray Becker, if freed, will establish the most prosperous horse hair belt business this side of the Rockies and bring untold revenues into the state." I am so moved by this turn that I am not yet able to allow my thoughts the least celebration. Some dark spot must still lurk in all of this "good news." Take it any way I want, though, I like the news! And you.

To think that I will see you outside this place, in the river-scented breezes of Portland! I must admit that I am bewildered, too, by the prospect of altering what has become a rote existence. Maybe I will manage to change with the times. I will seem a fossil to some, I know, when I emerge from this pile, winking the sun out of my eyes.

I have to close this. That last sentence brought up the emotion I feared I had lost. The spots on this page are the first parts of me to be released. Save the letter.

Yours in Solidarity,
Ray

Part 3: **I Was Born Here**

Will the roses grow wild over me
When I'm gone into that land that is to be?
When my soul and body part in the stillness of my heart,
Will the roses grow wild over me?

from "The Popular Wobbly"

Some think they're strong, some think they're smart
Like butterflies they're pulled apart,
America can break your heart,
You don't know all, sir, you don't know all.

from Songs "VII"
by W.H. Auden

The next month. . . is a window
and with a crash I'll split the glass.
Behind it stands one I must kiss,
person of love or death
a person or a wraith,
I fear what I shall find.

from *Selected Poems*
by *Keith Douglas*

One wiper blade had gone spastic, dancing madly on the windshield. I jumped into the rain and jammed it tight again. Said to myself, Freelance photographer, to get my mind back on making a living. Shifting gears, thought about the $700 I paid for this truck--savings going down, down. I was raised in this town that already was beginning to send me little telegrams of bad feeling.

Brought up in that boxy green house whose front porch I was just kicked off. I asked the old woman who lives there--

"Would you mind very much if I came in?"

She wore a black dress and patent leather shoes that were perforated. Her tiny eyes squeezed together. "What's that?"

"I used to live here. I was wondering if I could, you know, come in and look around--"

"You what?"

"--used to live in this house, when I was a kid. I was wondering if you'd mind very much. My name's Rivers, I'm just getting started in town." The rained flushed down my hair and fell coldly on my neck. I had the collar of my denim jacket up. The little eyes opened wider, maybe my camera unsteadied her.

"So have alot of people lived in this house, but thank the Lord they don't all come asking to get back in. No, I don't think I can trust the likes of you."

Like a fool I said, "Oh, you can trust me, all right."

"Don't contradict me, young man, on my own property. You'll just have to go and find some other house to bother." The door closed firmly.

Okay. I'm sorry.

I only wanted to see if the kitchen was really as big as I remembered it, room enough in the winter for my brother and me to ride our trikes round and round the oak table. I wanted to see if the cherry trees in back still blossomed like clouds above the grass. I remembered the bedroom with brass knobs on the bed and my mother and father deep in the folds of a crazy quilt one May morning when I crashed in on them, my fingers in the dripping red gills of my first bass. "Mom, Dad! Look, I caught a fish!"

He rolled away from her and shot up wild as though wounded in the head. His eyes were bloodshot. "Get that god-dam thing out of here!"

I had a dream once that I was the reason for his chronic bad feeling. Remember the fights he had with his old man? Grandad Rivers was a fancy dresser, a carpenter with carefully manicured hands. He could flim-flam three cards so fast that the old boys gawking and betting round the battered tables at the Olympic Club never did find the red Jack. Except when he let them. I waited for him every day after school, my paper bag stowed, my fingers itching to get hold of those cards when he stopped to show me how.

Gold Street turns to Tower, I am two miles out of town, moving past the "Yardbirds." Giant plaster bird, eighty feet high, straddles the entrance to the biggest shopping center in southwest Washington. The bird has on levis, big spurs at the back of its clumsy feet. Yellow beak comes way down on its chest like a takeoff on a Jew merchant's nose. The Yardbirds sprawls and grows. Whenever I drive under the bird I look up and wonder if there's a cock and balls under those sailcloth pants, or nothing at all. If there was something it would have to be as big as the cannon on the lawn in front of the library where the monument to the soldier sits. Ed Asuja reminded me of that monument the other day when I found the photo of that wobbly guy.

Keep driving south along Tower, now a highway. I know that sign's coming up:

BEFORE THEY TAKE IT ALL AWAY
TAKE AMERICA BACK FROM THEM!

My little town. But it isn't every day your mother comes into a farm and asks you to live there and take care of it. Could the timing have been better? Me without a job. Darkroom's about complete, lucky to have my neighbor's help. Good neighbors out in Finn Valley. Ed says the photo looks just like the guy they lynched. Long time ago.

I pull into the lot in front of Ken's Studio. His secretary is friendly. "Mr. Rivers, you have such bad luck, I'm afraid Ken's out again. But I think he did like your pictures. Can I have him call you? Oh, that's right.."

"..still don't have a phone. It's okay, I don't mind the drive. Be back in a day or two."

Coming home I'm hit by the words on the other side of the sign:

ONLY FREE MEN OWN GUNS

I find that if I view the sign with irony, I can actually feel better about my town for being Heartland America, rather than stuck out here as it is fifty miles from the cliffs of the Pacific. "Centralia" becomes central, "mid." The feeling doesn't last, the sign pisses me off. It also frightens me.

But here I was home after twenty-five years. I'd just arrived, I had to start somewhere. I wasn't going to teach again. I had a divorce from my first wife (well earned): it all came together on the night she cold-cocked me with the ketchup bottle. Drove me to the emergency room, crying all the way--"Are you hurt? Talk, godammit!" I mumbled, "Nice shot, Jean. . . " "You bastard!" she cried. The R.N. on duty tasted the ketchup and thought for a second it was all a bad joke.

So far Carol and I are living happily on our new farm. I must get into a frame of mind where I'm not thrown off by every breeze from the garbage pail. It's going to take time. My neighbor, Ed Asuja, says the town never grew after the "war" they had on Tower Avenue.

"What war?" I asked.

I was going through some sepia prints I found out in the shed and slid this photo onto my slate. Ed was home for lunch. An old brown and white of a soldier with a good-looking woman on his arm. What appears to be our sauna shed shows up in the background of the print.

When Ed came back from lunch I asked him about the photo and he stared at it a long time, slumped down on a pile of potato sacks, his back against the concrete wall.

"I vas only six years old at the time, in first grade. . . your mother vas in t'ird. Dat school building down the road. She loved her teacher, dat vas his girl, I t'ink. After the fighting, you know--" He rolled his balding, freckled head back and forth against the concrete as if to force himself on. "--dey cut him up bad. Den dey hung him from the bridge."

Outside my darkroom a hen squawked in the mist and pecked at dirt. I remembered that when I was a kid they called the bridge in town that spans the Chehalis, "Hangman's Bridge." I never asked my dad or mom about it, I just knew that I could never cross it for fear that ghosts out there would grab me and string a rope around my neck.

I turned left onto Main and headed for the library. There was the cannon and the monument in the middle of the broad lawn. Standing in the rain I raised my head to the helmeted statue of a 1918 soldier stopped at parade rest on a granite pedestal. He was greening around the helmet, holding his weapon in front of his face and his tarnished brass eyes. He was wrapped up in a flowing overcoat, strapped with cartridges, a gas mask at his hip and an entrenching tool in the pack on his back. There are two set of brass likenesses at the north and south sides of the pedestal, four names under the soldier's feet: McElfresh, Grimm, Casagranda and Hubbard. "Slain on the streets of Centralia, Washington, November 11, 1919, while on peaceful parade wearing the uniform of the country they loyally and faithfully served."

But how "slain"? Ed says in a war with the wobblies.

Finding the photo was the first of a series of small connections between our farm and the town's past that began to force my attention away from the new routine and back upon history. I remember quite well the circumstances that led me to slide that photo out onto the slate. I had been busy going through a box of stuff that probably belonged to my mother's Uncle Oscar. I found two boxes of letters and photos under a tarp on the flat bed of this old White truck that Ed said was made in 1917. The truck is wedged in one corner of our garage that is not only huge, it could be a museum of out-of-date tools and gears and wheels. The grease in there smells pre-war, like my dad's old brake shop in West Seattle. The letters were in Finnish and signed, Jussi. The photos were of people I didn't know, and I couldn't tell if they were taken in this country or over there. All the time I'm going through this stuff I'm wondering if maybe Mother's got some property she doesn't know about in Finland, too. I figured the way her luck was running when she came into this place, maybe we ought to try some remoter possibilities.

Meanwhile I was making a fair collection of brown and whites, thinking as much as anything else about technique. I couldn't get the print off my mind and several times during the day I studied it--the curious, desperate way they held hands, his rather erect carriage, yet he was powerful. She was vital, too, especially her eyes.

That night I showed the print to Carol. She hadn't quite the same response as mine, but she sat with it a long time and I hadn't prejudiced her to be shaken by it. I just said, "Here, I found this, what d'you think?"

"They look strong," she said. "I think she's trying to keep him from going to war."

"Do you feel strange about them? They really walloped me." Then I told her what Ed had said about the lynching.

She put down the photo and rubbed the joints of her hands that were already beginning to rough up from the work she'd been doing. Her face glowed when she was tired.

We took our coffee into the dining room and sat at the table in front of the oil heater with Judith. She's in her mid-fifties; she stayed on at the place after my Uncle Pete, the former owner, died and she's been here ever since, helping Carol and me. We always say, "She was Pete's housekeeper," and people stare at us. But we're sure she was no more than that. Long years of celibacy have a way of appearing in a face. I guess you have to be a photographer to know that. Maybe not--anyway, that's how Carol and I felt about her. She sat at the table reading the *Farm News*, which she subscribes to.

I handed her the photo and she held it away from her at first, looking through the upper part of her lenses, then she brought it up close.

"Never saw them before in my life," she said and went back to her paper.

We got the farm down here first because my Uncle Pete, my mother's brother, died of a bad liver. When Pete and Ilsa were orphaned over fifty years ago, they were brought out here and raised by two different sets of relatives on two adjoining farms. Ilsa got Uncle Oscar, a great old guy--a liberal for his times from what my mother says. Pete was brought up strict by the Kilpis, who were hard-liners, and so thrifty that once they got Pete, they said to heck with having any more. When the Kilpis and Uncle Oscar died in the same season, Pete found himself suddenly the biggest landlord in the valley; and last year when Mother learned that she was the only one named in her brother's will, the shock spread finally, in waves, out to Carol and me. My mother was happy with the inheritance but couldn't uproot herself and come down here to live. She could only think one step at a time: she was just leaving Anchorage in order to come to Seattle to be closer to us and to dry out. We saw her through that ordeal, daily visits to Swedish Hospital, then got her into a motel room but no further. She wouldn't come with us to Centralia--sure, we could live there, but after fifty-eight years, she convinced us, she was still shy of what the neighbors might think of her. Soon she'd come down, she said. "Give me some time alone, I've got to be able to do things on my own." Then, a week after I'd found the photo, she called to say that she was "ready now."

You want things right for your mother. Ilsa was sixty-four, a gentle, loving woman. She was cured now though I worried about her. After the rush I got from looking at the photo of the soldier and viewing the monument in town, I'd gotten out all of Pete's albums. I rummaged through trunks in the upstairs hall. There were a couple of pictures of a little girl I assumed was Ilsa. One of her leaning into the leg of an old man. Oscar, probably.

We have a string that runs through loops from the one hanging light. There's an old Victrola with a disc on it. I turned the crank and set the spiky needle.

> When   John-ny Comes Marchin' Home a-gain
>   Hur-rah!   Hur-rah!
> We'll give him   a   Heart-y   Wel-come then
>   Hur-rah!   Hur-rah!

It was very squawky, and I sang under my breath the rest of the words--

"The men will sing and the boys will shout and the ladies they-ay will all turn out. . . da da da da dah, when Johnny comes marchin' home!"

The walls of the upstairs were gray-white, rough plaster. The tall baseboards were a cold steamship blue. Wind sucked the leaves of our tallest apple tree and the branches scraped the window. I knew that I was not held by any job. The concrete storage shed next to the house was a darkroom now. I could work there by the hour.

We were working on a garden, filling rows with lettuce seeds and corn. We'd have some beets and cabbages. I thought I might raise a cow for slaughter.

Rummaging through trunks, I do not know what day it is. Her old report card: Ilsa Roukoja--Spelling 90. Arithmetic 90. Citizenship 80. "Ilsa is an intelligent girl and well meaning. She needs to contribute more to the class. She is shy but very energetic and well-liked by all." 1922, Grade Seven. Independence School.

I see myself in the kitchen, our tiny house in West Seattle. Must have been about sixth or seventh grade. "Mom, what was your name before you changed. . . ?"

"Roukoja," she said with a smile. She liked her name.

"Oh--" I was puzzled and she knew I wanted to take it further.

"Finnish names are like Indian names, they're pictures," she said. "It means--" She watched me get the impact. "--food of the rivers." I felt my blood run suddenly cold like water. "You're my little Indian," she said.

"See our faces, yours and mine." Our faces coupled in the glass. "The Laplander Finn is Mongolian," she said.

I made my mouth sag grotesquely. "No, no," she laughed, "look in the mirror at your eyelids and cheekbones, look at your arm now it's just as dark as an Indian's."

I looked down at my arm and saw it all copper and sinew. "But why Rivers? That's his name, isn't it?"

"It was as close as I could come," she said, drawing away from the glass.

I had a pile of stuff stacked on the floor. The string broke on a bunch of papers and they sloped into the corner of Pete's wallpapered trunk. A little red booklet fell out. "I.W.W. Songs." I grabbed it up.

"To Fan the Flames of Discontent." I felt funny, turned the pages.

Everett, November Fifth
Strange when a book mentions a place you've always known.

Song on his lips, he came
Song on his lips, he went--
This be the token we bear of him--
Soldier of Discontent

I liked the way it chilled me. Ilsa, how old? I wondered whose it was. I thumbed and read. It was strong stuff. The worker on the cover was stepping out at me from a smoking factory with raised hand. I took it to heart, maybe what I needed on that last teaching job was a stronger union. They were radical songs. "Bayonet the babies"? Jesus. I read it, sometimes I laughed. It was really pretty good. Joe Hill's name everywhere, he was familiar.

Then I came on the picture of him:

"Wesley Everest--Murdered by the Lumber Trust
Centralia, Washington
November 11, 1919."

I stood on washed-out legs and went to the light of the window. It was the same man as in the picture I'd found a week ago. As murky as the man in the songbook appeared, there were the same eyes, the same broad facial bones. I leaned my face against the cool, humid glass. It *was* Everest. Murdered. Someone at this house had taken his picture. I read on:

There's a little western city in the shadow of the hills
Where sleeps a brave young rebel 'neath the dew.

"'--'neath the dew'"? Not so good. Says it's written by a guy named Barnett. "Another Centralia victim." How many more?

Where the old Chehalis River flows its way.

That was better. The line moved me the way Mukilteo does. Or Duckabush, Satsop or Cle Elum. Docewallips, Hamma Hamma, Upper and Lower Lake Lena. Quinault, Quilliute, Queets and Makah. The Chehalis runs right out there. I can see it. My mother's name. My kids will fish it when they come down this summer. I sat down heavily in a corner of the hallway in a battered chair, the book slack between my knees. It was suddenly claustrophobic, messing around in stuffy trunks.

I left the house, squeezing the photo between the pages of the songbook.

The library was cold and smelling of old gradeschools. The librarian, a young guy in a tweed coat and a striped tie, was helpful, interested in me and my work the little I talked about it. He knew all about the monument.

"Offered to the city by the American Legion," he said. "It wasn't quite a war but not much different when you consider that to belong to the International Workers of the World was practically treason in those days." He told me about the march down the street and the attack on the hall, about the lynching and the trial.

"But the lynchers, they never got the lynchers?"

"Oh, no," he said, almost like, What did you *think*? "The picture you've got is certainly like Wesley Everest in the songbook and the ones in Chaplin's book. He *was* castrated, one of the pamphlets I've got has it that one old boy went out to the bridge when he was hanging and looked. That's rare, that picture."

"What about the uniform?"

"A number of wobblies were returned servicemen, he was one of them. I've got some stuff you can read, both sides. Until I got here people had only the Legion pamphlet to read. You're only about the third person who's asked about the incident, though, since I've been here." He had some old newspapers which he offered to xerox.

He paused to think. "There was another raid, you know, on another parade day a year before that, Red Cross and Liberty Loan rally, and that time the union men didn't retaliate and were beaten and run out of town. One man, a blind man who sold labor newspapers, had his stand burned down--then he was taken out of town and never seen again."

"C'mon, they burned him--a blind guy?"

"Yep. Still want to make a living here?"

"'The times they are a'changin',' right?"

"That's what they say." He stopped before a picture of an old colored gentleman, cottony-haired. "D'you know about this guy?" My mind jumped back to stories my grandfather used to tell me about a black man who was supposed to be the "founder of the town." He used to sing this song to me--

> Stacy Coon, that lazy ol' loon,
>> lives under the bridge and sleeps till noon;
>> rows his boat by the light of the moon.

> Stacy Coon, telling his woes,
>> just under Main Street, he rows, he rows.

I never understood that line until he told me that there were canals running under the streets. In the 'nineties the Skoocumchuck and China Creek "joined hands," he said and flushed the whole town out, so they rebuilt over the creek and now you could travel the entire downtown in a rowboat if you wanted to, though who'd want to run into the ghost of Stacy Coon, I couldn't imagine. Sometimes you could hear him if you listened at that manhole across from the Timber Inn, laughing or crying out for what they did to him--

I started to say the name my grandfather had brought me up on, but was surprised when the young librarian interrupted. "George Washington was his name." I looked appropriately surprised. "Really. He was supposed to have owned the whole downtown at one time. Washington School, right? Pretty safe name when you think about it."

I told him my version of the legend and asked, "I wonder what it was they did to him?"

"It's something to do with the flood," he said. "Who knows? One fellow told me that they figured after they rebuilt, the old property laws didn't hold anymore for the fill, so he got taken."

"Think they left him anything?"

"George? I don't know. . . maybe a cherry tree."

I read the xeroxed sheets of the newspapers and a book by a labor man named Chaplin. I came out heading for Main and Tower, listened briefly at the manhole across from the Timber Inn (when I was a kid I'd once put my head right down on top of it), heard nothing but water lapping. I wheeled into Tower where soldiers, Elks, sailors, cheerleaders and a whole contingent from the Washington State Employers Association left-turned on those two parade days that crushed the I.W.W. in my town. I was wired especially to two men--Wesley Everest and the blind man. I had his name now, it was Tom Lassiter. In the Centralia *Hub* that came out the day after the parade in 1918 it is reported that he would no longer be seen at his familiar stand on Tower Avenue.

I passed the Lutheran Church, it was the same building as stood here in 1918, where the Reverend J.J. Woody preached to his congregation the day after the first raid:

"By his action in ridding this town of scoundrels, vagabounds and mockers of Christ--"

As I stop by the brick front of the church, I swear I can hear a murmur, a fragment of dead voice droning out to the street.

"--Mr. Hubbard and the members of his Association together with our brave Legion have proved once more that God has cast them in a mold a little lower than the angels and crowned them with honor and glory. . . "

A detour across the tracks and back again at this point takes me into the neighborhood of Washington School, through the territory of my earliest recollections. The streets are Gold, Buckner, Kulien, Everson, Rucker, Washington. In 1918 you could rent a house in this working-man's district for $12.00 a month, running water and central heating nonexistent. An outhouse and a woodshed in back, and I can remember ours--the two-holer stunk of lye and piss, but the woodshed held wet alder, dank and peeling. I pulled a hundred slivers out of my forearms every night after school.

Here in the paper is a mention of a man named O.C. Bland, lived on Kulien. On the day after the 1918 raid, it's reported that a child of O.C. and Martha Bland died in Scace Hospital of Spanish flu, aggravated by malnutrition. It mentions that O.C. was spending a "rare day in town" on the day of his baby's death, usually he "stayed nights at the camp on Michigan Hill." I stop, arrested by the beat of old blood; Michigan Hill is the huge mountain-like ridge a mile south of our farm. And there behind a curtained window in a falling house before me I glimpse a woman with a baby in her arms. She appears to be suckling it.

Back to Tower Avenue, heading north, I pass under the ticking windows of the Centralia *Hub*. I hear the whip and sting of the editor's eye-witness account of the 1918 raid:

> Mr. Hubbard brought out for all to see an antique Victrola from the smoking darkness of the Hall. 'How much am I bid for this I.W.W. Victrola?' he demanded of the crowd.
> 'All proceeds go to the American Red Cross.'
> Though their methods were swift as an avenging god, the men who vented their fury on the wobbly hall have delivered this town of all that is ugly, discordant and demoralizing; from now on the industrial problem of our community will be built upon the ideas of mutual recognition between capital and labor.

This should be about the spot where blind Tom Lassiter sold his papers. The *Hub* says it was across the street from the Olympic Club, and east of the railroad station. About where this little grassy plot is next to the sporting goods store should be the place where he sold *Solidarity, The Seattle Union Record, Red Dawn,* besides the *Hub* and the *P.I.*

In my mind I see the shack where Tom lives. It's out of town a ways. It rests beside the Chehalis, he likes the sound of the river. It's reassuring, you can tune it in any time you need it. In the middle of the night, say, when you wake in a cold sweat, dreaming of the defective cap that left the stump intact but blew the eyes right out of your head, and you stumbling into camp to demand of the cook, "Is there anything left of them--look at me, you bastard, don't pull away!"

One night they come to get him. They wade the river in high boots, carrying torches, trampling down the bank to his house. The stink of creosote billows ahead of them on the wind and Tom sees in his mind's eye their red stupid faces as they crash around his falling down shack and yell at him to get his newsstand the hell out of town. He slides under his bed with a revolver trained on the door and bellows at them--"The first one through, I'll blow your guts across the river!"

They leave his shack with the threat, but the next day he comes to town to find his papers a heap of wet ashes and the two-by-fours of his stand gutted to sticks. His friends in the I.W.W., woodsmen he'd worked with, rebuild the place. But a month later on the day of the parade it is a foregone conclusion: they'll raid and burn the wobbly hall and get old Tom, this time for good.

He hears them marching past, proudly, the war is still going strong, this rally's for blood: "Hut two tha-ree four! Who th'hell're we fight-ing for?" There is a command to halt, then a roar like the ocean and a chorus of screams from the women watching on the corner. He can hear the turbulence as the Legion hits in there, throwing books, clubbing workers, dragging them out and pulling them up by the ears into the waiting trucks.

He is so scared he starts to sweat and to yell; has no defense sitting under his tarpaper roof. His friends run past him screaming for him to, "Get out, for Christ-sake, Tom. They're stripping men's clothes off, they've got ropes and tar!"

He doesn't hear them coming to get him. One minute he's hypnotized by the noise and the next they've torn his tarpaper roof back like they were scalping him. The rain hits his face as he lifts it numbly to the unexpected breeze, then he smells gasoline.

They're yelling at him and tearing and throwing his papers. Smoke catches his lungs, then he's going crazy, swinging and scratching at the moldy hogs. He hits one crack in the face, grabs his hair and yanks him close. He bites through skin and cartilage till the man's scream is a rush of pain as they club him senseless.

He wakes up bouncing in a car. The upholstery's dusty, he licks the blood out of his mustache. His head is split.

Then what? I can't quite get it. I know this thing about old cars, they have that back to them that feels like the nap of old armchairs, hairy and itchy to the touch.

But I'm out in the sidewalk with my eyes pinched shut, my camera sense lost to me and I can't take it further. All I can feel is the car, and I'm straining to hear voices as Tom must have done, to know at least before you die who's doing it to you.

This is serious business. These guys want him underground, these guys have burned his living down. Twice. Who are these men who would do such a thing?

The sign outside of the town: Before They Take It All Away, Take America Back From Them. But what could Tom "take?" Their daughters? Their land? Their hearts? Why *these* poor fuckers? Why were they such a threat?

I feel a nameless panic. The car? Whose driving?

In the dark of Tom Lassiter's brain, he struggles to know them. Maybe he works it out, maybe he works it out by some clue, maybe the guy whose nose he bit, he names and they swing into him. But he leaps to seize the driver's head, to take them all with him if he can, and punch his fingers into the man's eyes, tear his throat apart. The pitch and swerve of the big car throws him to the side and again they punch and curse him. They aim to please, to kill. All good old American boys, they want to kill just once before they hang up their spikes. To make a killing.

And they slow down and just dump his ass so he goes tumbling, banging over gravel, tearing through grass like a torpedo, till he comes to a sprawl and half dies while they u-turn and come whining the gears of the touring car back towards him. He scrambles towards the river bank, he can smell the green water, and they holler, "Stinking commie cocksucker--stay out of town!" and fire a pistol shot that wallops the air past his head.

He can't cry anymore because the tear ducts caved in with the accident but a memory of tears builds up in a familiar region of his face. He stands there broken and grimy with the river tumbling before him. And he smells himself and knows he stinks--stinks with fear and panic, just as the little kids always say when they pass his stand--"Old Blind Tom stinks like a goat, stinks like a pig, stinks like a dirty, blind old man."

But he takes heart and knows where he must be. County line crosses just 300 yards down from his shack. The river speaks to him and says, "come across". He thrashes down to the edge of the water through nettles and broken down alder, comes to the lip of the bank, hesitates, figures to wade it. Instead the ledge gives way and he is into sharp cold water over his head. He comes up spitting and grapples with the bank but more dirt and mud and debris falls on his head, so he kicks off from the edge. Colder now, it's colder, he must be mid-river. A dragonfly skims his ear. Puts down feet to touch, no bottom. Loses momentum, river booms in his head and he does not want to think of her. She left him; what else could she do? So little time left, he must embrace her. Her arms were bare and tan, shadows of leaves played on her back. Her hair was washed and reddish in the sun. She stripped him down. He's seen enough, he's seen all there is to see. . .

Now you pop your eyes open and what do you feel, photographer, standing here at the spot where his newsstand stood? I sway with the shock of light; a cop eyes me from across the street and faintly I hear a newsman cry, "Pee-Yii. . . Pee-Yii." Do you want to touch Tom's hand as you slip him a nickel for a paper? Do you believe that the spot where blood or seed has been spilled is more special than any old place where nothing happened? Yes, probably: my Centralia, the literalness of it. Since your father's dead, is he your father? No, can't reach that. I'll make Tom's father a miner in Idaho. "He died in a cave-in about a mile below Kellogg."

Next day I left the house and walked out between the chicken sheds and the big cedar barn with the green and orangey rust running all along the top, walked on through the scabby-trunked orchard, on to thistles. Bending through the fence I heard a bird call. *"Burned him--" "One old boy went out to the bridge when he was hanging and looked. . . "*

I crossed fields of yellow tansy to the railroad bed. Got to kill that tansy, it bloats the cows. Moved down the tracks, river sang beside me. Sings me down, on down, river bucks and curls in swollen March. Heavy-muscled river's a dirty green, far away are glaciers, is the foot of Mount Rainier where my mother was born in a mining camp, where her mother bled to death with an unborn child, waiting for the doctor to arrive. Where'd she come from? One remove from Finland? Two? Walking across the trestle, it's like balancing on a tightrope. River turns in a big elbow bend, high sides, almost cliffs--dark down that passage.

Up above me on this side is an old torn and broken homestead. A rotting scar where someone tried to live. This is where Judith, our friend, Pete's housekeeper, my mom's ally, was dragged through adolescence into womanhood. Like my mom she was another stray. Like Tom Lassiter, like thousands who beat their way westward to the coast. To find what? A wet abyss. "At the bottom of the cliff America is over and done with."

Ilsa told me Judith's story. She was brought out to the coast by an aunt on a train from Montana after her mother died, told she could stay with an uncle on this dark green spot. Just for the summer. Then the aunt left her. Aunt went home to Montana, left her like you'd leave a cat in a cattle barn. Bruises she has for a childhood. Doesn't say much. Judith was alone when Carol and I came. The animals were starving, she was digging the last of the spuds to share with them. She's such a servant she can't sit down to eat with us. She gets mad when I insist. See her cradling yellow chicks under her chin at night, to warm them, those endangered. Her glasses on her nose, reading the *Farm News*. She has a chicken jail where she puts "bad" chickens, a box up above the pen, all closed in. She warns them and scolds them and threatens them with jail when they don't lay. Heard her yesterday, "Bad chicken. Bad!" Then a squawk as she grabbed its neck.

My mother's friend. They played here, the homestead's all on a hillside up from the tracks, a scooped out socket above the river. In the middle of a dying orchard a split giant of an apple tree still blooms. All the buildings are shacks now. The house sinks into the mud of the hillside. At some point Judith ran away--900 yards--to Pete's house, after Ilsa had left. This February she advertised at the store to sell her one suitcase. The guy stood in the kitchen, he looked like a migrant picker. Offered her five bucks for it. She let out a sly smile; she thought it was a steal, then she figured she'd better look inside it. There were all her old clothes! Exactly as she had packed them when she'd run away forty years ago. She scooped them up in her arms and I saw beneath the clothes, swordferns pressed into the bottom of the case like fossils, a thin glass vase and a long, yellowing envelope. Right then she knelt and laid the dresses back inside. She told the guy, "I'm sorry, I guess I can't sell it," and that was that.

II

"You knew the guy?"

"Well, I didn't exactly. I was just a little girl. Where'd you get this picture?" she asked, holding it and studying me. She put it down carefully beside her cup. Mother's hair was white and thinning, outside I could see sun hitting the trees through a halo of frost.

"What about the girl?" Carol asked.

"The girl?" Ilsa repeated. "She was my fifth grade teacher. That was such an awful time, just to think about it upsets me all over again."

"You never told me about it," I kept on.

"Well, it wasn't something you wanted to bring up. But we must have--"

"You and dad--?"

"Your father wouldn't have been one to have much to say for wobblies, you know. He was always independent. But out here there was Oscar and the man at the mill, Bob Thompson, who hired the men. There's still some things down at the old station the same now as they were then, if you're really interested."

Carol and Ilsa had finished breakfast and couldn't quite leave the table. Judith went gunning for the dishes. Sun glanced off the linoleum and the room was rosy and yellow with morning warmth.

"You were just a little girl. . . "

"Joe's age," she said, saying the name of my third boy.

"She never sat still," Judith offered cagily from the pantry where she flushed water over the dishes.

"Oh, I was such a tomboy," Ilsa said, laughing as though she saw herself in funny old togs.

"What about Everest?" I persisted.

"What do you mean?" She began to redden. "He died--"

"No, no--you said before, he 'saw' you. I mean, just that?"

Judith came past us sticking her arm into the sleeve of her mackinaw.

"Goin' out and shake up the chickens?" I asked her.

"If that Erica doesn't have two eggs today she's in trouble," Judith said. "Yesterday there was nothing under her but straw."

"'Erica?'" Carol asked.

"The big Rhode Island red--she ought to have her head examined," she added, closing the door.

"What were you saying, Mom?"

"It was just. . . that man Everest--he slept one night out in the barn and the next morning I was out there and his little red book was on the floor."

"The thing I found?"

"No. This was their by-laws. They said, 'The workers should own the machinery, not the owners because they worked it with their own sweat.' That bothered me. I read it without understanding but I could feel somehow what it meant, then he was up there looking down and I just tore out of the barn. That's so clear," she said.

"What was he like?" Carol asked.

"He looked like a giant. Big and handsome," she added, laughing and blushing. "He was so powerful that I ran off and hid in the chicken coop. Then later I heard them talking very serious--him and Oscar--they were talking about me and it made me so excited I could hardly stand still. I remember as a kid always wondering who my father was. I'd never seen him and I thought since they were talking about me that maybe this could be him. Then I'm sure Oscar said that he ought to *have* me, only that was a joke, or that I was his 'girl.' In my mind right then he was my father--and I never talk about this but it's quite real to me even now, remembering."

"What did you do?"

"I didn't know what to do--I had some crazy idea that I wanted to sit on his lap, but that was just too much to imagine. I ran outdoors, down to the river."

Carol said, "Then it must have killed you when that happened."

"I never quite understood the details of it. I just knew there was a 'war,' and by this time he was in love with my teacher and . . . she did all the suffering, really. Besides, Oscar was so good to me that I kept right close to him, and he was more my father just because I saw him all the time."

"So that was it," I said, feeling strange that my mother's childhood, which I did not think I knew at all, was suddenly vivid to me. "But who do you think took this picture?"

Again she hesitated almost as though she wanted to conceal something. "It might have been a woman named Eva who lived here off and on with Oscar. She was a free spirit. She'd been married to one of Oscar's sons."

"Was I ever out here when Oscar was alive?"

"We used to bring you out. . . no, he died before that. Remember how we used to come out here from town and you and Bob would swing from the barn loft on that long rope down into the hay?"

"Yeah, I do remember. I'll have to put one back up there." My four boys were to visit us for part of the summer. I could see them swinging in the dusty light of the hay-filled barn and walking through alfalfa fields, fishing all day, jabbing deep into the cool water of the long pool at the bend of the river.

"Oscar was funny," she went on. "He wouldn't let me spend one dime on government savings stamps--you know, like the ones you put in the little books in the second world war, and he'd always argue with people about the draft and go out on Sundays deliberately and work his fields. But that woman who was married to his son stood by him. . . and my teacher, too." She drew in, looking out the window abstractedly.

"What about her?"

Again she seemed puzzled.

"What was her name?"

"Lucy," she said. "She was very young."

She said that on the day after the shooting in town her teacher wasn't in school, and the day after she missed again. Then she came in for the morning period of the third day, and Ilsa watched her move around the classroom as though it was a foreign place. A boy asked her a question and she cracked the chalk in her hand with a sound like a rifle going off, then ran out of doors. One boy looked out the window--they were all petrified--and he yelled, "She's down by the river!" Ilsa ran after her, stumbling and calling, and the girl scooped her up and crushed her hard against her chest. She told Ilsa to go on back home, to be "good," to forget her.

"Her last name was Neimi," my mother said. "Her folks had a store-- it's still down there, I showed you when we came down before."

Carol and I had rummaged through the place. The floor was falling in but the counter was there, resting on beams, the glass still intact.

"We got a big metal Nesbit's orange pop sign," Carol said. "And a Coke sign, 'five cents.'"

"Yes," Ilsa said, "and one of them was caught down there, I think. The Neimis left not long after they hung him. It affected so many people. It was terrible--" Carol went to hold her but I couldn't stop.

"Your schoolteacher, Lucy--" I checked her out in the frame of the photo. "Whatever happened to her?"

Ilsa took one of Carol's hands, tilting towards her. "She's gone, we never heard from her again."

Later that afternoon, showing her the garden, I learned that she thought that Lucy had left Centralia with Oscar's friend, Eva, but she wouldn't take it further and I realized it was too painful an area for her to remain in, but my need to know was like an appetite. It was much easier for her to talk with Oscar, though she said he was never the same afterwards. He loved a great many people and to have so many leave him in the same cloud of hatred just about ruined his gentle nature. "He got closer to me, though," she said.

"He told people when he knew he was dying that I ought to go on and get an education. Girls weren't supposed to do anything then. I went, too." She became animated. "--to junior college. D'you know, that's the oldest one in the state down there? I took care of a house and went to school for two years--I had the best English teacher. I still like poetry because of her, and she taught me how to speak correctly. I had such an accent people could hardly understand. . . then I got married," she added

"--and there went Roukoja," I said.

"Almost."

I asked her about the bridge--"Dad always referred to it as Hangman's Bridge. You remember him telling me that?"

"You know, it's an odd thing," she said, speaking easier, "the actual one in town's been fixed and changed, but that bridge down there in Independence is exactly the same. . . the one with the wood road over it? Now the mill where Bob Thompson worked and where Fors worked and a bunch from this valley is right up the road from it on Michigan Hill."

I remembered the sense of coming into a new dimension when we had first driven down from the Peninsula and crossed that bridge. In my eye, too, I saw the dark green turtleback ridge that dominated the valley. We were walking back towards the house when the dog we call Kanga started barking like hell. I yelled to calm him. His back two legs are paralyzed. When we came up the steps he was pulling his trim collie body around the porch with his forelegs, whimpering. It seemed colder now than it had been at nine in the morning.

The things my mother knew pleased me yet made me feel strange about her, as though she, and I wondered how many others in that town, were all in it deeper than I'd first imagined. It wasn't just the doubt that sometimes clouded her voice, and which often struck side by side with a surprising clarity of recall. It was a way she had of looking at me but obviously seeing the past. She carried her thermos of coffee with her everywhere she went--out to the darkroom that night where Carol and I kept our private stash of homegrown weed: that and the sauna were our principle pleasures on the old homestead. Ilsa wouldn't smoke with us. "What's the difference?" she asked. "I'd probably end up hooked on that stuff just like the other."

In bed that night I stared at the wall and the face of Wesley Everest faded and came clear on the darkness of my retina. How real he looked, stubborn and broad cheeked. He was goading me to know more. I wanted to pull back the bruised flaps of skin, to peer into the gills of the place where I was born. To open wounds? Yes, take the chance. I wasn't a fool about knowing things. Outside the dog barked, wind blew, rushing air through stunted trees. I strained to hear the river sing.

On the day Mother left I was alone with her out in the driveway. There was a silence and a reluctance to leave on her part that began to be awkward.

"I want to tell you something," she said, "and I've been debating whether or not to say something ever since the day you were so sure you wanted to know about the troubles. There's a piece of paper. . . "

She said that one time a woman who seemed to know everything about the case stopped by the farm. She introduced herself, she was friends with one of the men still in jail. Oscar helped her locate one of the men in the jury who lived out near Oakport. She had a briefcase full of material, some of it she showed to Ilsa. She was in college, and had only happened to come out that way to see Oscar, who was failing. One of those pieces of information this woman forgot and left behind, but they didn't discover it until days later.

"Do you think you could still find it. I've gone over so much stuff in the garage and the attic--"

"No, no, I know where it is."

"Where?"

"It's in Judith's bureau," she said simply and cracked open the door of her Falcon. "Don't let her know, and you'd better not keep it. Just read it, I don't think she'd bring it to you if you asked. It's by a photographer."

"But how come you waited until now?"

"Because you were right about wanting to know more. There is more, and I don't want to see you stalled on something that might be important to you." She started the car, revved the engine mildly and leaned out to kiss me goodbye.

"Take care," she said and backed into the shade of an apple tree.

Judith's room was down the long dark hallway and to the right just as you turned to climb upstairs. I don't think I had ever been inside it until that day. I knew her schedule to the minute, she'd be out with the animals until about one, then she came in for a cup of bouillon and a cookie. The breeze blew curtains in that were like old bridal clothes, lacy and gray. There was just the bed, sagging with the weight of years and a single bureau. Beside the bureau was her suitcase. She had one picture on the wall, a triptych of Cupid in varying moods; with his dangling locks he stared at me from all three frames. In the top drawer next to her long johns was the yellow envelope I'd seen when she emptied her suitcase in front of the migrant worker. There were two sheets of paper typed rather roughly:

Will E. Hudson, being first duly sworn, does depose and say: that in 1919 and 1920 he was an employee of the Pathe News Service in Seattle, Washington. That on the evening of November 11, 1919, the affiant and three other photographers were sent by their firms to Centralia, Washington, to take pictures of persons and places connected with the shooting which had occurred that afternoon. That affiant drove down to Centralia in a black Oldsmobile, together with another photographer, T.G. Randolph. That they arrived in the evening of November 11, and they had difficulty in finding lodging, all the hotels being full-up. That affiant was a member of the B.P.O.E., Seattle Elks and he suggested to his companion that they try to obtain rooms at the Elks Club in Centralia. . . all the beds being taken there, affiant and his companion stretched out on the floor in front of the fireplace in the lobby on some blankets. That during the night other persons wandered about the room, talking. . . that he and his companion pretended to be asleep and heard many remarks passed to the effect that: "We got more than we bargained for. We got in a row and we got the worst of it. We started something and we got whipped."

That on the following morning of November 12, affiant took pictures of the I.W.W. Hall on North Tower Avenue. That he was struck by the way the bullet holes had apparently been made by shots fired from the street and at close range; that they slanted upward from the street level and could not possibly have been made by shots fired from an upper story window across the street or from a hill top, as the legionnaires tried to assert.

. . . affiant took pictures of some of the men who were in the city jail in Centralia. That a large crowd of persons was gathered around the jail and that their attitude toward affiant and his colleagues was hostile and threatening. That about ten-thirty that morning affiant was told by someone in the crowd that "you better get out right away; a bunch is fixing to destroy your equipment." That affiant stored his camera in the safe at St. John's Titus Garage. . . affiant then went to the Centralia Post Office and mailed a dummy package wrapped and sent as films addressed to the Pathe Office in New York. That he then boarded a southbound train for Portland, Oregon, and mailed the real package of undeveloped films on the train. That when he returned to Centralia he was told by T.G. Randolph that the Legionnaires had stopped every Oldsmobile leaving the city and searched them for films. . . later he learned that the dummy package's arrival in New York had been greatly delayed. That some time after the events described above had transpired, he received a threatening letter at his home in Seattle from some anonymous person. That the letter contained threats upon his life.

That later affiant was sent to Montesano, Washington, to take pictures in and around the courthouse while the trial of the case of Britt Smith, Ray Becker, et al., was in progress. That on this occasion he was approached by a man whom he identified as a legionnaire because this man wore the insignia of a soldier, and told not to make any pictures of the defense attorney, George Vanderveer; that affiant had just finished taking such pictures; that the said legionnaire threatened and abused him.

. . . while affiant was taking pictures of the I.W.W. trial, he stayed at hotels at Aberdeen, Washington. . . on one occasion he had registered at the Saray Hotel. . . sometime later, when he went to his room, he found his door smashed in. That after this, for his own protection, he often registered at one hotel and stayed at another under an assumed name. That sundry other efforts were made to influence and to intimidate him into leaving town, both while he was in Centralia and later while he was in Montesano. That at all times it was his desire only to photograph persons and places as they actually were to get at the truth; but that he found the atmosphere of Grays Harbor Lewis Counties hostile and unfriendly to this purpose.

16 May 1936

I thought I'd start with the bridge. I strode down there, past the Neimi store, out onto the timbered roadway. It did not arouse my natural fear of bridges. I kicked it and it hurt my foot. The Chehalis was a dense forest green, moving determinedly. I felt too easy with the sweet weather and the cows in the field beyond the bridge. I tried again to think what a lynch mob smells like, tried to imagine the faces of men wanting to see another die. I had done it that day with Lassiter, why not this man? Was I too innocent, already becoming part of the town? I had been hurt and had hurt others, but to cut a man up and string him from the beams--it just seemed too much for me to get. Ilsa's connection with him intrigued me but it bothered me, too. Everest was the man she would have chosen for her father. That brought him very close to me, but every time I worked with the image, the memory of every lynch mob I had ever conjured up began to insinuate itself into my brain and I wanted my head clear of ugliness just now.

Nothing hung from this bridge. But I took shots from every angle I could manage, even one from the top rigging, looking down like some heroic Richard Nickel, photographing the Chicago Stock Exchange Building one last time before it was crushed to ruin. And took Nickel with it, I reminded myself.

I wandered up the tracks on the downriver side from the old train station. We had the signboard for the town--INDEPENDENCE pop. 234; elev. 114--nailed onto the tool shed at the farm.

I humped it uphill a ways through heavy wet underbrush, glad to be wearing my trusty climbing boots. My levis were soaked, my head a tangle of twigs when I came onto an overgrown roadbed that led higher up the slope. I found a clearing and there was the remains of a mill. There was a long, heavy timbered shed with a corrugated tin roof. I climbed a rickety ladder and surveyed. I shot a long view of the inside from what must have been a manned station in the mill's operation. Here was a huge rusted saw that could cut through timbers as big as my waist. The sawdust at my feet was soaked with oil and three or four inches deep-- drifts of it curled up the sides of the building like cove moulding. A conveyor belt was like a giant bike chain with hooks. It ran the length of the interior, and along one wall was a black scar from some forgotten fire. The place couldn't have been abandoned too many years ago because it was crudely wired for power. I came upon a complicated piece of dead machinery with gears and wheels, a flat bed, rusted beyond hope. There was a plate beneath the metal bed with instructions:

> Never babbitt on a cutter-journal, it will be sure
> to spring it and once sprung cannot be
> permanently repaired

I read that and realized that I didn't know what in the hell it meant, but someone who ran this machine at one time had to know. The camera sat idle on my chest. I conjured and conjured, I worked to make the man who'd once run this machine come into being. But it was like squatting in a graveyard, nothing comes up but grass.

III

The next morning I milked Geoduck with a sense of purpose and by 9:00 I'd driven off down the dirt road through a cloud of barnswallows, blue and gold, diving for fat bugs. I bought a couple of rolls of .35 mm film, dropped by Ken's to deliver more prints, then doubled back to the town library. I returned a pamphlet that the Federal Council of Churches had done on the Centralia affair, then went out to get a few shots of the monument. A closeup caught those words that years after must have stuck in the throats of a growing number of my fellow citizens: "Slain on the streets of Centralia, Washington, while on peaceful parade. . . "

I got another of an old man with glasses and a thick white beard, his head tilted wonderingly up, his hands clasped behind him.

I'd taken down a bunch of names from the library books, then got hold of a phone book and wrote as many numbers as I could that even resembled those involved in the case. There was one Bland and several Lambs still listed, but when I called Marion Bland as a first try, I got the information that she had a private listing.

I looked at the list of Lambs. There was one Dewey; I thought I remembered, that was his son. I was intrigued but couldn't get on it right away. I checked my list of those who'd testified for the defense--there were a number of Brays, but no Guy Bray. But there in the book was Cecil Arrowsmith. It must be the same name as the one who'd supported Gene Barnett's alibi.

Then I came on Bert Faulkner, a Buckner Street address. That I wasn't expecting. He was twenty-one in 1920--okay, say seventy-three today. It was our old neighborhood. Maybe my father once fixed his car. No, he probably never had a car and my father left Centralia practically broke. Once more the thought rushed at me--was he like these men? No, very unlike. Never mind, I couldn't know that for sure.

In a sense I watched myself driving away from the library across Tower Avenue, across the tracks, past the little house where I was born, down Buckner--there!--I saw an old man in a cap at what might have been the address. He was outside with a pole, leaning against the garage as though propped, with what appeared to be a pint in his hand.

Drunk? I couldn't keep away. I parked the truck, checked the address. It was the right one. With my Nikon around my neck I approached. Self conscious or not, I wanted this image. He straightened up briefly when I came up the yard. The pole was done up on the end with a bright cloth--the pint was full of dark liquid. His old man's smile under the cap shone with gold fillings.

"Want some bees?" he said.

I'd heard him right, I thought he was selling hives.

"Well--" I was considering it, remembering I was a husbandman now. "Are you Mr. Faulkner?"

"That's right--you the man about the bees?" He looked at the camera.

"I--I'm not sure--"

"Sorry, can't stand up straight. Got arthritis in m'hip." He leaned back into the shade of the garage. "Called the exterminators down there, got me some bees up in m'roof." He pointed up at the gutter, where it terminated at a corner of his tiny house. They were yellow jackets, tight in a mean cloud, buzzing in the heat. "Thought you were the man."

"No, no. I'm working on a sort of project--just getting started." That stopped us both. He was suspicious.

"I got some gasoline and lysol on this rag and ever now and again I shove it up there and watch them scoot around--doesn't seem t'do no damn' good at all."

"Your name's Bert Faulkner?"

He eyed me closely. There were large freckles on his cheeks and I realized that he'd spoken haltingly, as though out of breath.

"That's right--"

I was very eager. "The same man that was in the labor troubles here in 1919?"

"That's right."

"I'll be damned--"

"Yep."

"So. . . well, I guess I've come to the right place--" I felt like I was having one of those dreams where you're standing in the aisle of a bus in just your t-shirt that doesn't quite cover your ass and balls.

"But I don't talk about that no more."

"No?"

"Nope. Too much trouble over that."

"Just--?"

"A lot of water's passed under the bridge since then. Don't ever talk about it now."

"You were part of it?"

"Yep--"

"You were acquitted?"

"Dropped charges," he corrected. He kept looking up at the bees.

"You been in Centralia ever since?"

"Oh, no. Just came back here this last year. My wife died. Well, my second one died. My first one died thirty years ago. We was out in Richland, then down to Tenino. Then I come back here."

To die, I wondered. Why here? "Mind if I take a picture?"

"What for?" He looked at the bees again. He was about ready to poke.

"That's what I'm doing just now, taking pictures."

"For a newspaper?"

"No. Just myself."

He eyed me. "Just yourself--"

"Yep, just me." I was calmer now; we listened to the hum of yellow jackets. "Did you know Wesley Everest?"

"Oh, yeah. I worked with him. Then we was around the wobbly hall a lot together."

"He was quite a man."

"Oh, yes. Different. Different from the others."

"From--?"

"From Becker. Not wild like him, or that man Roberts."

"Becker's dead now--?"

"Oh, I think they all are, all except me. That was a long time ago."

"You were in jail, up in Montesano."

"Oh, yes--they had us in two tiers up there in Monte."

"You remember much about it?"

"Sometimes I do. . . had us a hunger strike up there."

"Really? You started that?"

"Wasn't nothing, just some flies in the food--some of us threw it out in the hallway."

"It must have been a great relief to be let go."

"Oh--" he started then breathed deeply to catch up to what he wanted to say. "Yes, it was."

"But you didn't miss the other men?"

"Miss them?"

"Well, I was just thinking, if all of them but you and Smith and

164

Sheehan went on to jail, it must have been hard, too. . . to come back alone--"

"I got no complaints about that." He moved stiffly with the pole, propped it up into the nest, then hustled back and we moved with hunched shoulders away from the swirling-out of angry yellow jackets.

"That ought'a piss 'em off," he said. He eyed me again in that way between curiosity and fear.

"No, I don't talk about it no more--that was a lot of trouble."

He was being final with me and now I wanted to leave him be.

"Maybe I can see you again--"

"Don't really want to talk about it."

"Just to talk--"

"You'll get me loosened up and I'll say too much. Maybe somethin' I don't want to."

"But what could anyone do to you?"

"What?" he demanded and the breath left him once more.

"I mean, there's no one now. . . " I trailed off, knowing somehow that he knew better. At the edge of the lawn I brought my hand up. "Well," I said, "it was good meeting you. I hope I'll see you again."

He followed me with eyes that were shaded by the cap. "Say," he said.

"Yeah?"

"Do you work?"

"What?"

"Are you a worker?"

"No," I said. Then I thought to add, "I used to teach."

"Oh," he said, "I thought so."

I hustled for the truck. I looked back; he was at his pole again, peering up. When I developed the negative of the one shot I got of Bert Faulkner, the swirl of bees clearly shows at the corner of the house.

I had the Tower Avenue adress of both the wobbly halls. It was hard telling exactly where 803 might have been, except that it must be this rather squat, faded place on the corner of Tower and 2nd, double windows boarded up, two dwarfed stories high. Like any kind of returning, things appear smaller because of what time does to your natural belief in objects. There were some old men up street from the site, smoking in the doorway of a very downtown garage.

"That old wobbly hall?" they said looking at one another. The one with the pipe had on a greasy, quilted, brimless cap like my dad used to wear in his shop. "Why, that was right down there on the corner, wasn't it, Ed?"

"Believe it was. But, god damn, that was. . . how old y'think we are, boy?"

"I thought the whole town knew about it."

"Some did, some didn't." The hatless man had a large blue kind of mark on one cheek and was half-bearded in that territory. He appeared to be a joker.

"Just gettin' some pictures."

"Writin' a book?" the one with the greasy hat said. They were both amused.

"Diggin' up old evidence," I said, playing the ironic man.

"Oh, now--wait a minute!" the man with the hat shouted to a helper, who had just dropped a muffler on the concrete floor. He retreated to a car that was up on a rack in the interior of the place.

I started back to the tired facade of the Roderick Hotel. The other man followed me--"Hey. . . hey." He rubbed the half-bearded mark on his cheek. "You wanta know all about that wobbly deal you get yourself in touch with Vern Dunning. D-u-n-n-i-n-g. He was the postmaster here for so long I don't wanta count. He's about ninety years old, knows every damn' body in this town. Don't bother talking to that fella back in the garage, he don't know anything. Then there's another one might know something, you get in touch with a guy they call Dutchie--you see him around here. He wears a patch on one eye sometimes. . . done time in the pen, I hear."

"You're kiddin' me."

"No, no." He stopped short. "Yeah, this is the place--this here's the old hall, all right, and right off through there's where they were firin' from the hill."

There was another dead building across the street, and through a corridor of space we could see the barest of green rises, distant a good half mile.

"Looks like a long shot."

"Oh, it was. They had binoculars." He watched me readying my camera. "See this arm," he said. He thrust the left arm, fist high, elbow out. "You doin' a book on this stuff, you wanta get the goddam cops around here, too. Goddam copper bent this arm half way around my back th'other night."

"No kidding--for what?"

"For nothin'. For 'resistin'' arrest.' And they beat the shit outa a young girl here the other week. Two-bit bastards. You wanta stir up some trouble writin' a book, you wanta get after the cops of this town, yes sir. And the sheriff's department, too, while you're at it."

"Thanks."

"It's nothin'. You wanta talk, come and see me down the street: Bengston's Garage. That's my employer now. Come to think of it, they might know something. . . big sign outside says, 'Brakes a Speciality,'" he added and hustled off.

I got Cecil Arrowsmith the first try on the phone and he was the same man from the trial in 1920. I felt lucky, like my grandad doing card tricks. He said that he'd gone up to "Monte" towards the end of March. He couldn't talk with me just then, he was planting. But he knew someone I would want to meet.

"Who's that?"

"Loren Roberts."

It was like the phone went dead.

"Loren Roberts? He's still--"

"--still alive and kickin'. Went bowlin' with him last Friday out at Riverdale. He lives out to Bucoda--just ask the man out there in the post office. It's only a piss-hole in the snowbank."

"Jesus, I had no idea. I thought they all were dead."

"Well, that one's pretty lively, and I think he made contact with Barnett, too. He may be alive someplace over east of the mountains."

"Barnett--no kidding? This is a gold mine."

"Why, you another one of them doin' a book?"

"Well. . . kind of. My own man, you know? Just getting started. This is a help, maybe we can talk sometime."

"Glad to be of help, maybe next week. Those were mean times--Loren's never really got over all that."

"I sat down to my toast and coffee and said to Carol, "You want to meet Loren Roberts? I can't get over this--fifty years ago and he's still bowling. Let's go," I said, scraping up the car keys. "First stop's Vern Dunning."

"I'm with you," she said.

It was as if the old men of the town were all in their cupboards, waiting for us to find them. Vern Dunning didn't mind my taking pictures. I got two of his blue-veined hands in repose, one of his face that stresses the sharp white blade of his nose. There was a freckled rose on his left hand. He had no hair at all, just tufts of fuzz over his huge ears.

"Everything grows, bears fruit and dies," the old man said. "If you do something the wrong way, you can't expect any good to come of it."

His housekeeper was off somewhere in the kitchen. We were on Buckner Street again; you could see Bert Faulkner's house from the front porch. Vern Dunning sat bent in a faded chair with his gold watch chain the only color in the room. "The owners start by wanting men in their pockets--that's it, they want to own them, too. Then the men have to get outa that grip. . . *have* to.

"I knew John Lamb and Britt Smith and Elmer Smith--hell, John lived right over there in that little house on the corner--" He pulled himself rigidly higher by an inch or so. "--right there." Carol slipped a look over her shoulder. "Him and his wife and kids."

"Dewey?"

"That's the oldest boy, still around here. Might talk to ya, it's hard to say. John, he learned this thing from a man he was in jail with where you work with your hands into a person's back. Oh, John had big strong hands."

"Chiropractic?" Carol said.

"Yes! That's the one, and he set up practice when he got out right in his house there, worked on people for years. He's dead now, oh--died 'bout fourteen-sixteen years back--he was a pretty old man. Still chipper. I knew this man--retired supervisor at the P.O.--had this trouble with his back, so I sent him over to John, though I knew the man had testified against John and them. Don't know why I did it, kind of curious, you know, to see what could happen. John could've slipped and paralyzed him. But he came back cured and happy, never even knew that John was one of them he sent up, or didn't recognize him, and John didn't hold no grudges. It was just a business. Doctors around town got to sending people to him for help, those they couldn't cure, you know--and John in turn would send people to the doctors. So, what I mean, he was respected."

"He did what he could."

"Oh, yes--he did more." The old man's eyes leaked, he wiped the mucus. Breeze blew the dotted curtains onto the arm of the worn chair. He had a standup radio under a panoramic photo of a pioneer scene labeled, "Centralia 1889." Looking at it was like peering through a wall.

"Grimms, now, I knew all of them. And McElfresh--he lived in this neighborhood too. They was good boys that just got mixed up in something rotten. I ain't saying they deserved what they got, they just run in there into something a whole lot bigger than they thought could ever be."

He grinned at my wife.

"Hell, I oughta know everyone, I came out here on the immigrant train when Washington became a state in '89. People pourin' in from every state in the union. Come out to claim a lot of mud and a mess of trees. Come out from Michigan, had to bring your own blankets for the train, do your own cookin' on kerosene stoves, bunks everywhere you looked was packed. The state ran the trains.

"Yep, come out here--worked at Onalaska, where I met Britt Smith the first time, worked with him before he left to go out to Oakdale. He was a quiet sort of a duck."

"That's near where we are."

"Oh, yeah, he lived out at Rochester."

"That's right where we are."

"Yes, there's a mill out at Independence, too."

"Yeah. I came on that old mill in the woods. My mother says there were several wobblies working out there."

"Knew all those old boys. Knew all the Grimms, too. Sometimes I think I knew everyone in this town. Mary Grimm used to sit out on her porch--this was years after all the trouble passed by--and ask me, 'What's the latest scandal, Vern?'

"Yes sir, that was a terrible thing they got into. My feeling is that that man they chased down Pearl Street to the Skoocumchuck did all the shooting."

"Makes it even worse, doesn't it?"

"Couldn't be worse."

Besides the early photo of Centralia he had on his wall a fairly standard picture of the black man I'd nearly called Stacy Coon in the library. "I see you've got a picture of George Washington," I said. "I beg'pardon?" "Isn't that George Washington in the picture?" "--how's that?" He got up painfully and moved to the wall, passing George by.

"I gave this picture to the mayor of Centralia about two years ago. I says, 'This here's a baby picture of your city.' Oh, he was impressed, he thanked me. Since then he's had copies made, gave me back the original."

We stood peering into the picture, down towards Tower Avenue when there were still trees standing. There were horse carts that looked to be stuck in the mud. It was raining even then. It was wide as a street from a Russian novel, probably done with one of those fantastic hand ground lenses that come right out of Rochester, New York.

"Well, the town came a long way from this picture to 1919. We thought we was really on our way--you know--but that trouble here was like a stroke or heart stoppage. The night of that raid a man run up to my house awful scaird of what the posse was up to. I told him, 'What the hell you doin' here?' Then I said, 'You oughta be home with your wife.' He tore off. You could see from any porch in Centralia the torch lights and lanterns of about twenty separate posses. They shot one man out of town here a ways, just a game warden, walkin' through the woods. They gave him some challenge or other and then they just blasted away. Said they figured he was a wobbly. Even men without red cards was in peril of their lives that night."

Vern turned to the picture of the black man.

"You know about this hombre?" he asked.

"A little."

"Yeah, well, this here's a picture of George Washington. That was his name, kinda funny. Supposed to be the father of this town, owned all the land 'round here at one time."

He added,

"You can tell he's Jewish by the look of him."

We were speeding towards Bucoda. Sun blasted through tall firs.

"Do you believe that?" she asked.

"What?"

"That Vern says he's Jewish?"

"Yep. Believe anything now. Believe more and more each passing day. Believe in god pretty soon."

"Are you going to ask Loren Roberts about--?"

"--what? The insanity plea? I don't know, play it by ear, you know?"

The postmaster in Bucoda got us right to the house. We parked, looked. It was a place like all the others, but especially with Roberts I couldn't help wondering--How could he still exist in this context? He was firmly fixed in my eye as a victim of third degree tactics that were like a prelude to Buchenwald. I knew that picture of him by heart, the stooped and confused looking kid in overalls. But sly, and very very strange.

I got a shot of his purple Plymouth hardtop parked between two budding apple trees. We couldn't put it off much longer.

He answered the door. Loren Roberts was smaller than I am and I'm not big. He just looked at us; he wore a Sears flannel shirt and house slippers under his green work pants.

"You wanta ask me some questions?" he said quickly. "Sure. Come on in. I'll talk to you."

He was hustling us into a tidy room. I spotted a sunburst clock in the kitchen and behind me two bronze-winged ducks slanted up one wall, straining for airspace. The mantel and a shiny corner table beside me held pictures of kids. "These your children?" I indicated, thinking that might be an easy line to start things rolling.

"Nope, haven't got no kids." He stared right at me--his hair was still brown and tight to his scalp, the eyes flat in his head. He sat unnaturally close on the couch, perhaps the better to hear.

"Oh."

"What'd you wanta ask?"

"Well, about the labor troubles. I been talking to people."

"Oh, yes." His hands were strong but stiff, brown tinted, no age freckles. He sat slightly bent, but as a spring is bent. Only then was I aware that there was a rifle leaning against the wall near the couch.

"You wanta ask me questions, go ahead--shoot." There were two more rifles poking up just behind the stuffed rocker where Carol sat. I realized that I was just plain nervous.

"You--ah--"

"Just fire away."

"You--"

"I may not talk so good. I had a stroke here a while back, makes me talk funny. How do I sound?"

"Oh, no--fine."

"Sound okay?"

"Fine--"

"Okay, ask me anything you want."

"Well, this is going back a ways--fifty years."

"Do the others talk as good as me?"

"Huh--?"

"Do the others talk better'n me?"

"Well, I just talked to Faulkner."

"What--Faulkner's alive?"

"Oh, yeah, he just moved back here--"

He jumped up and went for a pad. "You don't happen to have his phone number? I been thinkin' all of us was dead."

"Cecil Arrowsmith said he thought you might know about Barnett, too?"

"Who?"

"Gene Barnett."

"Oh, yeah, I know him. What about him? He was out in. . . what's that little town in the middle of the state?"

"Ellensburg?"

"No--"

"Yakima?"

"Nope--"

We went through ten names that way. When I lucked onto Clarkston his eyes lit up--"Yeah. That's where I seen him last."

"He's still alive?" Carol asked.

"No, I doubt it. Had three or four strokes I heard."

"Oh."

"How does Faulkner talk? Does he talk as good as me?"

"Well, not as good, no."

"Had this stroke, affects my talkin', you know what I mean?"

Sounds fine."

"Ask me anything you want."

"Okay--"

"Go ahead."

I felt that I was at the center of delicate ganglia, crucial to synapse-- like one wrong question and he'd simply go haywire.

"Well." I rushed way too far ahead: "About Vanderveer--?"

"Oh, yes."

"Well, was he okay?" What I probably meant was something like, was Insanity a planned strategy, as the Legion would have it, or can one really fall apart from pressure of the kind they must have used? I wanted to believe in him.

"Oh, yes."

"No problems with Vanderveer?"

"Nope."

"Because Chaplin, you know, maintains that there were some who weren't all that convinced--"

"Who?"

"--I. I was wondering if you all stuck closely together in prison, as a unit?"

"Yes. Oh, yes."

"Because I got the impression from something I was reading that there was one or two among you who had an entirely different strategy

171

from Elmer Smith and the Defense Committee and were a long way from Vanderveer at the end--"

"Oh, no."

"Nothing of that kind?"

"No. . . . How do I sound?"

"Oh, fine."

"Ask me anything you like."

"Was there a hunger strike at Montesano."

"No."

"Did you--?" I was drowning.

"I went straight to prison from Montesano after the trial. Went to Walla Walla three months before the others. I didn't go to no hospital like they say in the books--went straight to Walla Walla. Spent my whole time there, come out eleven years later, come back to my mother's place in Grand Mound. That's what they call me, 'Grand Mound.' That was the depression then, that was supposed to explain everything. I come out and just hung around the house there for twelve years. I used to go into town and try and get work. Nobody would hire me--they'd use that I was in jail or crazy as an excuse. Twelve years--then, hell, I don't know. Guess I come out here."

There was another terrific silence. I couldn't resist looking at the gallery of 3X5 faces of kids on the table next to me.

"Got me a wife now." He looked at Carol, then a huge smile knocked his face into daylight.

"Know where she is? She's off somewhere playin' Bingo!"

"Does she ever bring home a pot?" Carol asked.

The huge smile was still there; it was a total change in personality. "She does every once in a while, mostly she loses."

We hit another impasse, the smiles subsided, then as quickly he was sunny again and jumped up.

"Wanta see my gun?" he said.

I was standing with him in the middle of the room. He had handed me a rifle, which I held as though it were a mystery or a reptile. Stunned, I was aware of rubber shoulder pad, grooved stock, dark clean meatal barrel, and--as though it had to be--a scope.

"It's nice."

"Beauty, ain't it?"

He reached and pulled out his wallet. I looked, there were no greenbacks. He slid out five or six pieces of paper. Each was perforated with a smudge-ringed, round hole a half an inch across.

"Shot them today. 300 yards--believe that? You stick them papers up on a green dummy."

"What kind of gun is this?"

"Rifle."

"--right. No, what I mean--oh, hell--was this the gun you had up on

Seminary Hill?"

The big smile returned. "No, no. That there was a twenty-two long we had up on the hill. Belonged to my daddy."

"Oh--" A voice was urging me, Get to it, get to it.

"Could you see right to the doorway of the hall with the scope?"

"Oh, yeah."

I plunged into the next question as into a bath: "Are you satisfied that you killed Art McElfresh?"

The way the grin came back was like he'd shot adrenalin:

"That's what they say!"

"Yeah, well--"

"I might have. That's what they say, anyway, that a twenty-two bullet got him. You never know."

"No, for sure."

"Now that there's a thirty-aught-six by her chair, and that other one's a carbine, use it for deer."

We sat back down. I felt somehow clean having gotten to the point.

"Oh," he began, "I see this cousin of Art McElfresh all the time. Went fishing with him here a while back. Nothing between us now, we don't even think about it. . . 'course it was different at the time."

"I would imagine."

"Oh, yes--you read all about that." He paused. "Where you from?"

"Out a ways from town--Independence."

"Yeah, well, you know about Bert Bland. He told me he had quite a shootout with that storekeeper out in Independence."

"Really? I think my ma mentioned that. I suppose it's the same place." I had one more question then I wanted to get him outside.

"What did you think of Wesley Everest?"

He looked at me as though this time I had finally touched bone and said, "He was the best kind of man there ever was." The conviction had given strength to his voice, but his face darkened in the terrible act of remembering.

Carol asked, "We have a picture, we're pretty sure it's of him. He's standing by our sauna it looks like. He's with a very attractive girl."

He was turning to stone again. "Where d'you say you live?"

"Out past the store. It's a farm. An old man named Oscar used to own it."

He gestured, "I know, I know--she was--"

"What?"

"The girl, I knew that girl. Lucy, we never saw her around again. No. See, I had this stroke. . . . Can you understand me? I don't talk so good anymore."

Carol touched his arm. We stood by the door.

"You talk fine," she said.

IV

Loren Roberts had no offspring--by choice, I wondered, or by someone else's design?--but John Lamb had fathered five children. Something regarding Lamb had been working on me since our visit to Vern Dunning. It was the fact of having come right back to Go after eleven years in the pen and, instead of chopping trees for a living, finishing his days cracking and rearranging the bones of Centralia citizens, some of whom were party to his sentencing.

I did not call Dewey Lamb, but drove to his address on South Tower Avenue. The house was tiny and white and perched on a loaf of green lawn above the street. There was something written on a board above the door. When I parked and came closer I could make it out: it was the single word: MASSAGE. Pink flowers formed a border down the walkway to the front door.

"What do you want to remember all that horrible stuff for?" he wanted to know once I got inside. He was broad shouldered and strong, but his voice was mild as tea, his hair soft and white. When his wife realized what I wanted to talk about, she walked painfully away from us into the kitchen. She appeared to be sick as well as lame. Dewey brought me into a room dominated by an old-fashioned surgical table, a white flat bed on tall wooden wheels. He sat on this, kneading his forearms. I took the only chair. I expected to find little glass jars of cotton swabs or that he would put a thermometer into my mouth and look at his watch; instead he stared inquisitively at me through thick glasses. "--that was the most miserable period of everyone's life around here, the gangsters when they remembered what they did afterwards, and for us for what we suffered at their hands. There ain't much like that nowadays, unless you're living in Portuguese Africa or in Chile or someplace where they just go out and gun you down for what you think."

"You suffered, too. I read that they got you with your dad. . . in a car or something--"

"I'd say I was mistreated by my fellow townsfolk, I think that would be a fair statement to make." He lit a cigaret, Lucky Strike. The pack was empty and he tapped ashes into it and slowly crushed it as he spoke.

"My dad came home about 2:30 from the parade, we lived over by the gradeschool. He said the Legion had gone for their hall. They'd fired into them. Hit some. Very soon there was a mob of about 150 soldiers, sailors, high school boys and Centralia businessmen all around our house, yelling for us to come out. They knew my dad better'n the rest 'cause he'd been around awhile. By this time we'd slipped over to a neighbor's house, Claude Borne's house--but a friend of his named Bud Hansen told them where we were and soon they came over there demanding that me and my father surrender to them. We refused but they ordered us out with guns. These guns were cocked--let me tell you--

and pointed at us by shaky hands. I was grabbed by three big fellows, all wearing the uniform of the U.S. Navy, and pushed into a car. In the car they swore at me and knocked me around. They asked me questions I had no knowledge of and when I couldn't answer they prodded me with guns and said, 'You sonofabitch, you *do* know--you'd better tell everything.'

"When we came to the jail, I was taken out of the car and held at the jail by two sailors. A third man took a run of ten yards and gave me a kick. When I came to I was lying on the floor of the jail still retching from that kick.

"When my father got there I was locked up with him in the ladies' cell or women's quarters where the mob could see us through the barred window that opened out to the street. They pushed rope through that window and told us that as soon as it was dark they would take us out and stretch our necks.

"A necktie party, they called that," he went on, still speaking quietly. "You've heard of Wesley Everest, I imagine?"

"Yes, I have."

"Wes fired the first shots. Then he killed that kid, Hubbard, after they'd chased him down to the river. Well, shortly before he was kidnapped from the jail, I was taken out of my cell for questioning. About this time the lights went out. As the mob came through that jail door, someone turned on a flashlight. I saw F.B. Hubbard, that was a big timber boss around here, he was the first man to set foot across the threshold. He screamed, 'Turn out that light, some I.W.W. sonofabitch might see our faces!' Wesley Everest was lying on the floor of the corridor bleeding bad. When they came on him, he got up and tried to fight but it was no go--a stream of blood run from his mouth to the door of the jail office ten or twelve feet away. I was pushed under a desk and hidden away from the mobsters. I heard a police officer say it might be a mistake to lynch a kid as young as me.

"After the mob took Everest out, they dragged me off to the jail at Chehalis. They put me in a cell by myself for the rest of the night, but the next day they turned me into the downstairs bull pen. The air was poor down there and the only food we got was just leftovers scraped from plates in restaurants. I guess I lost about forty-five pounds while I was in that jail.

"Every day I was taken out of the bull pen and put through a third degree. They hit me, they poked guns in my stomach, they kept all of us from our sleep. Sometimes seven or eight of them would question me at once, then curse me for not saying what they wanted. This went on for nearly two weeks. Then just like that I was taken to the Wilson Hotel in Centralia; they told me, 'Order anything you want to eat, it's on us.' It's my opinion they figured I would have died if I'd stayed longer in jail. By this time I was a sorry sight--I had t.b., I was half starved.

"Four weeks I was in that hotel, living like a king, then they took me to Martin's Mill. One of the Legionnaires took me. He got me this job and said from now on I had to earn my mother's and sister's bread because my father would 'never be home' to do it anymore. So I was taken away from school and put to work.

"When the trial started, I was subpoenaed by the State and held by the Legionnaires as a witness just to make it look like I was ready to testify against my own father. But I wasn't ever called to the stand because the Legion knew I'd tell the truth and damage their case."

"How old were you--?"

"I just turned sixteen."

I could hear his wife coughing in the kitchen. I looked down at my hands to see if they were shaking, then he asked me if I thought I had an extra cigaret kicking around in my pockets. "I--" Never had I felt so guilty for giving up a bad habit. "I might. . . why don't I run out and buy some?" I said absurdly.

"Oh--*no.*" It was the first time he'd smiled. "Lousy, filthy habit anyway."

"Do you know something?" I asked, focusing back on his weak blue eyes. "I've never had a massage, never in my life."

"Oh, well--"

"I mean, how much does it cost? Do you have different rates for different times, or what?"

"Here, get up here," he said with more vigor than he'd shown since I'd come in. "Lie down here, stretch out face down--that sheet's clean. Just lie down there and I'll give you a free one. Take your shirt off. Don't worry," he added a little ambiguously, "the wife ain't looking."

His hands were articulate paws, jabbing in, shoving my shoulder blades up over my ears, it felt like, then rearranging my spine in such a way that all the tension that had started to accumulate in my back from listening to his tale was dissipated to a fine neutral itch, brushed aside the way you'd shoo a fly from a picnic table.

"Now you tell me," he said, boring in, "why you want to live in this pipsqueak of a town?"

"I don't know," I said. "It ain't for the money."

"No, it ain't for the money or for the lovin' care. It's just that you happened to be here, and maybe some of your family blood was scattered around these streets."

Something deep inside my structure popped so rapturously that even my calves went limp. I felt my back yield itself hopelessly to his incredible hands.

"And maybe one day when they get through with you and me and my poor wife--they told me last week she was 'terminal.' Maybe one dark day when they get through with the likes of me and you and that sweet woman in there. . . they'll let us die in peace. And no more bloodshed--right?" The knuckles ground in. "--and no more hatred. Ever. Amen."

By the reaction I got in Bengston's Garage--Brakes a Speciality--I must have appeared just slightly off key. The guy with the grease spot mole who was paranoid about cops and who led me to the Bengstons two days before would hardly give me the time of day. On his overalls was stitched in cursive the name Chick. He said, "There's the man you wanta see--" pointing to two men behind the glassed-in office at the back of the shop. One was middle-aged, wearing a Pendleton flannel shirt, the other was very old and sat bent forward in a swivel chair. "That's Len Bengston and his father, don't let them see me talkin' to you, bud, they'll get the wrong idea. Give me a break, huh, I ain't exactly their favorite flunky."

The younger of the two men in the office was black-browed, fierce looking. He stared at us with his hands on his hips--"Anything wrong, Chick?" he called. I came right over and walked in. The white haired man wore clean overalls and never moved a muscle when I introduced myself: "Ivar Rivers," I said. "I'm Len Bengston, this is my father, but he don't hear for shit and he can barely see. Little senile, you know. What's up with Chick, you a parole officer?"

"Oh, no, nothing like that. Free-lancer," I said, making it sound like I might be a roving surgeon or a British soldier gone A.W.O.L.

"Well, that's nice for you--do you work a job, too?" He put down an empty coffee cup on a wooden table strewn with papers.

"Got a farm. . . no, I'm new in town and I'm trying to put together a feature story, maybe. I'm interested in that old labor fight that took place on Tower."

"Oh, yes. We know all about that." He looked at his father and yelled, "Don't we, Dad!" but the old man never lifted his head. On his overalls was a yellow tag that said Oshkosh-B'gosh. His hightop shoes looked professionally shined, the black leather thin as skin. "He could tell you a tale if he had his tongue."

"He testified?" I asked.

"He did. And so did his old man, my Grandfather Jim. He's dead now, died in Oregon fourteen years ago. We have the distinction of being the only family in this town to have two different members testified against each other. Old Ben here, my dad, he wrote out an affidavit in 1937 to help some little lady who was going around trying to save the only one of them prisoners still left in jail. Can't remember his name, or hers. I think she was the one found Grandpa Jim, too, and got a statement from him. Ain't no secret what my dad did, everyone around here knows he lied on the stand as many another did in this town, for what he said was 'business and social reasons.' But you can't print that, mister."

"I'm not a reporter."

"I thought you said. . . "

"I'm just a photographer--photo-essay, you know--"

"No. But it don't matter. It's one thing that everyone knows and it's another that it gets said in a paper. My dad was in that parade, he broke ranks when the shooting started and got a wound in the leg that still gives him trouble to walk. He went up to the hospital to get it dressed and later that afternoon he had a talk with his father, in the shop here."

We were located on Main, right across from the library and the monument to the soldiers killed in the raid, not half a block from the Legion Hall. "He told my grandad that the boys in the parade had attacked the union hall before the shooting and that some of them were killed or shot and he was sorry about it but it was really their own fault.

"Well, that was the bit in the horse's mouth--old Jim told the truth about what his son said but when it came to Ben's turn here, why, he said things like, 'I don't remember having said that to my father,' though he damn well did--right, Dad! Christ, you'd think he was deaf as a post-- because when he made a statement for that little lady whose name I can't recall, why he said that he *did* remember and probably remembers to this day. . . not that we can get much out of him.

"The other day he said something, what the hell--? It was like *toi-toi* or *toe-toe* or something, I don't know. Anyway, he opened his mouth.

"You see, the pressure he was under to tell a lie was just tremendous, and Grandad Jim understood that and never really held it against his son. The Legion was around Ben every day before the trial and town lawyers like Lloyd Dyhart all tellin' him he had to clear the Legion and the businessmen in the parade or it would be the end of his livelihood in Centralia. What did he have? He couldn't live on his integrity, like his old man said, so he let himself be manhandled. . . though, f'r Chrissakes, our family was pro-Legion to a man before this whole thing blew up, and it wasn't only the Legion did things by a long shot. Hell, I'm still welcome up there, they know now, most of them with a memory, where the guilt lies. But it was Ben and others like him who went through hell in the time following the trial. He was a pretty mixed up man for all those years though he claimed that making that statement about his guilt took a lot of the pain away. I'm not so sure, he was one tough titty of a father to have on your neck, I'll tell you that--*right, Ben!*" The old man actually looked up at him. His face was white as concrete. He blinked at me as my cow did whenever I had to switch her into the stall to be milked.

"By god, he brung me up honest, you can be sure of that. At least my butt is sure of it. Which is one reason why it don't bother me none to tell you what you wanted to know about our part in the thing. And there's more. . . my old Grandad Jim, I admire him more than any other man I know in the country, president or not. . . and I'll show you why in a minute here. I had a copy made of this here affidavit he made for that pretty woman I mentioned. Usually keep it in the desk drawer--here, *move, Ben--"* He reached for the wood beneath him and literally picked the old man up chair and all and moved him away from the roll top desk that stood under a shiny-skinned Vargas girl with tits like summer squash. The calendar date was 1946; Christmas was circled and as red as the nipples of the girl in the picture. He had to force back the top of the desk, then fumbled and yanked out a drawer that clattered to the surface. The paper was in a long, company envelope marked with black thumb prints. "Here, young fella, you read this and see if it don't tell you something about courage and decency in the face of bitter odds. Tell you something about this town, too. In a funny way I find I can be proud of Centralia because of men like Grandad Jim. He was raised here just as sure as the lynchers were--"

> . . . on the afternoon of Nov. 11, 1919, I was standing on Maple Street, not far from Pearl Street, with my son, Roy. I saw a bunch of men coming down Pearl Street, dragging a prisoner with them. My son and I walked towards them; we saw that the prisoner had a belt fastened around his neck. The men were pulling on his belt and kicking and spitting at him. I saw a man run up and hit him with a gun. His face was bleeding. He had been terribly beaten and he looked bad. I could hardly stand it.
>
> . . . the mob stood under or near a telephone pole. One man had a rope in his hands; I thought the prisoner would be hung then and there. A woman unknown to me rushed into the crowd and called the men curs and cowards. I heard the prisoner defying the crowd; he said something about: "You haven't got the guts to go through with this." William Scales pressed up close to the prisoner, I saw that he was crying. He said, "Don't hang him, men, don't hang him." I remember thinking to myself, "You instigated the whole thing and now your conscience is bothering you." Finally the prisoner was taken to jail.
>
> Early in the evening of November 11, 1919, I was walking along the east side of Tower Avenue, in company with my father-in-law. We were walking north; when about midway of the block between Magnolia and Maple Streets, our attention was attracted by a group of men hurrying from the direction of the Elks Club. Among those I recognized were David Livingstone, Hank Andrews, John Stephens, Fred Cormier, Ted Patton and Henry Huss.
>
> We followed them and just as we reached the alley between Tower Avenue and Pearl Street, the lights went out. In the darkness I lost track of my companion.
>
> I was standing on the curb at the alley corner of the south side of Maple Street when a car drew up and turned its

headlights on the jail door. I heard a man yell, "Douse those lights!" He ran up an kicked the headlights out. Before the lights went out, I saw Sheriff Berry and Attorney C.D. Cunningham among others near the door of the jail.

. . . I saw a group of men break into the jail and drag a prisoner out with them. They shouted "Gangway, gangway!" I saw the mob thrust the prisoner into a taxi in front of the jail.

During the trial of the case of the State of Washington versus Britt Smith et al, I was called to Montesano to testify for the defense. Judge John Wilson sustained the state's objection to testimony I tried to give concerning the meeting of the 20th of October at the Elks Lodge, which proved they planned to raid.

When it became known that I was to be a witness for the defense, I was threatened, both in Centralia and in Montesano. I was approached in the courthouse by a legionnaire who made threatening remarks to me.

On the day the defendant Elmer Smith returned from Montesano to his home in Centralia, I was working in my leather goods shop at 117 S. Tower Avenue. A legionnaire employed at that time was salesman for Carstens Meat Company came into my shop and asked me to make a holster to "fit a forty-five." He said he had to have this holster by evening. I said, "Man, it's quitting time; I'm not going to make a holster today." Not long after this, one of the boys working in the garage across the street from my shop came into the shop and told me that the boys in the garage were laying plans to lynch Elmer Smith. He said that they were planning to lynch him that very evening. In order to prevent any further trouble and bloodshed, I asked my two friends, Jesse Downs and Charley Beavers, to go with me to Elmer Smith's house. We walked around said house and otherwise showed ourselves to be present. . . during that entire evening and part of the night which followed. I refer to this incident to show the sort of feeling which existed in Washington at that time.

After my appearance on the witness stand at Montesano, my trade fell off alarmingly. At the time my two sons, Roy and Ben, had a body and fender business in the same building. Townspeople came to them and said, "We will boycott you if you don't get your father to leave town." For these reasons, I moved to Denver in 1921. In 1929 I returned to Centralia for a visit. At this time my sons had a body and fender works on Main Street. As I had no employment, they offered me bench room in their shop and I started up in the leather goods line. Soon afterwards, Claude Carter, a member of the Elks Lodge and connected with the Legion crowd, came to my son Ben and said, "Get your father out of your shop or I'll throw my business to someone else." At this time Claude Carter was in the business of selling Chrysler cars, he was my son's best customer. Rather than see my son lose trade, I again moved away from Centralia and have lived away from there ever since.

I make this affidavit in the interest of justice; I am not and never have been a member of the Industrial Workers of the World.

A day or two later I was in town checking out a new health food store. I was getting in the habit of asking questions. The woman at the counter, it turned out, had been in town the day of the parade in 1919. She was staying with her mother's sister, who lived over on Pearl and it was down that alley between Pearl and Locust that they think Everest was chased.

"I was standing in the yard and this man came up all red and sweating and he had a gun but I thought it was only a toy like my brothers had. I just looked and said, Hello, and he jumped when he saw me. Then there was all this noise and about twenty soldiers came running down the alley carrying ropes, hollering so wild that I thought it was a game--like Hide and Go Seek. But you really want to talk to my father. He ran a mill out where you're living, I think. He's often mentioned that he knew some of those men--the Rand boys, were they?"

"Blands?"

"Yes. And a couple of others. For all I know, Everest."

"What's your father's name?"

"Bob Thompson."

It took some doing to locate her place, out towards Raymond on Route 6.

Bob Thompson sat in a wheelchair, big as a horse, with a friendly, round face and one leg off at the thigh. He was nearly deaf but articulate when he caught your drift. The alertness was all in his eyes; the rest of him was firmly committed to the wheelchair.

"Yes, we had us quite an operation out there where you're located. I do remember your Uncle Pete and Oscar, why he was very well known in those parts--what you might call today a sort of protester."

He laughed at the idea.

"Yeah, they was well known out there, and Britt Smith worked for me running a cut-off saw. Everything was simple then. You got a top saw and a bottom saw, edgers, cut-off saw and a plane in those old operations. We used donkey engines in the woods and the railroad runs right along the river there for shipping. Both the Bland boys worked for me in the woods chopping trees."

"Do you remember much about the posse that got Bert Bland?"

"How's that?" He thrust his bulky neck forward.

"I was kind of wondering--" I repeated what I had said.

"Oh, well, you know there's posses and there's posses. Oscar helped put that one together of men he knew would protect Bert going into town. Bert wasn't fighting none and he wasn't going to leave his buddies altogether. Once the jail people got him it was a different story."

"I can see that. Do you happen to know what 'babbitt on a cutter journal' means?"

"How's that?"

"I just. . . *what did you think of the I.W.W.?*"

"Oh, them boys was just doin' what they had to do. We had government regulated wages, in effect, during the war. Most unfair system I know of--it was all the boys could do to make a livin', and most of them didn't have families, partly because they couldn't afford them. They said a lot of funny things about the wobblies but one thing they done was to bring sheets and pillowcases into the bunkhouse.

"That may sound funny but that was an important thing, to stress conditions and do something about them."

"*Were they practical?*"

"Where they--? Oh yes, I know what you mean. Yes, I think so. First of all they knew what they wanted in the way of conditions and they reminded you of it ever' chance they got."

"*What about their songs?*"

"Oh--hah--the songs. Yeah, well, they were all right. Gotta do something with your time. And they were persecuted, no doubt about it."

"Read a *song* about *Everest!*"

"Did you? I hired him, you know."

"*Really?*"

"Oh, yes. Come up to me one day in March--I remember--that was two-three weeks before a Swede we had out in the woods with Blands got cold-cocked by a falling limb and was disabled. Everest was a big man, stone cold eyes, big feet and hands on him. A real he-man, you know?"

"Got a picture of him--" I reached for it in my manila folder.

"Yes, that's him--and that there's the girl whose dad ran the store. . . by god, where'd you get this?"

"*Boxes* of stuff out at the *farm.*"

"Ain't that somethin'? He was an all right man. In a way kinda ahead of his time--"

"How so?"

"I don't know. Lynchin's a funny thing. It's like people trying to get rid of all the bad in the world in one rash move. Then they all find out they done wrong. I seen this movie on tv about five times, *The Ox-Bow Incident.* You can see the same thing in it as what most of us saw in Everest's killing, hatred of their own worst side. My god, you want to talk to this little weasel of a prick that hangs around town--little Dutchie Huss, or Hess."

"*Dutchie?*"

"--or Heinie. Or some calls him Pus. Now there's one of the lynchers, brought this town so much disgrace, you know, that for ten-twenty years afterwards people would come to Centralia and they weren't sure but they'd remember that there was something real bad about this place and then they'd just drive on through. We never grew because of that."

"Hangman's Bridge--"

"Yep."

"*How* th'hell does *Heinie survive* without someone *killing* him?"

"Oh--him--hell, you look at him you wouldn't want to with a ten foot pole. He's got an eye out and emphysema and this damndest little hole right here above his nostril that when he talks without puttin' a finger over it, he gets a little toot-toot or whistle between every word."

"Jesus."

"He's somethin'. He says things like he was Wesley Everest's friend, stuff like that. Told me once he helped Wesley Everest get his first job. I ain't seen him since, not likely to, either."

"He served *time*?"

"Done a jolt in the pen for some kind of fraud, I think. He was a pet of the business people for a year or so after the trial, then they dropped him on his striped ass. Maybe you don't want to mess with him, he's like a touch of permanent bad luck." He winked, eyeing the camera. "Photogenic, though."

He was a lovable old fat man with the thickest stump of a cut-off leg I'd ever seen. Then I thought 'stump,' and laughed to myself.

"I had a mess of friends out your way. Ol' man Fors, you know him?"

"No."

"Well, he was down at that mill, too--funny man--wild like a lot of Finns. He thought Oscar was a magic man. Said so, anyway. Anyway, him and me was both supposed to go in the army in World War I, then we got into defense contract work and I was safe from it; we was making staunchions for aircraft, supposed to be. Well, Fors he was always real worried, anyway, he'd be called up. He hung around his farm--he didn't want to leave that farm no-how. Finally it just blew over and he'd stayed out and he couldn't quite believe it. He said that if he ever went into the army, why his wife would go 'all funny' was the way he said it. Of course, no one wanted to go, and the I.W.W. were the most open about that: Be a Man not a Soldier! They had signs. Don't Kill Fellow Workers. People just weren't ready for them."

"Weren't they idealistic?"

"Oh, I suppose. . . sure. . . you never been that way?"

"Not yet. No, well, maybe once--"

"They were tough people. In Aberdeen their women joined picket lines. Stood right up to the police when they knocked them down with hoses."

"You've been *around.*"

"Eighty long years, my lad. Now that is a long time to live, whole or half whole. I wish I knew more and not just about our little 'war.' About lots of things. I could'a been a little more careful with my life, as you can see. There was someone, though. . . yes, let me think. There was a woman I talked to as long ago as 1936. Oh, she knew so much."

"A woman?"

"A little woman, not yet thirty years old. Why she was up to her neck in that Centralia mess. What was her. . . I got a paper, still, somewhere. I was in Arcata, California at the time. She was tryin' to locate an old wob named Tom Morgan--yes, all the other prisoners were free but one of them stubborn sons-of-guns refused to take parole. Wanted to be freed completely. She was a friend of his. She needed affidavits from this Morgan to try and get this last prisoner out. Morgan was a wob who turned state's evidence under pressure. I knew where he was working, then she got an affidavit from me about the general effect the lynching and trial had on the town. How any of us with any sense knew where the guilt lay, some of my reasons for leaving this place when I did, you know. I got that woman's name on the copy of that affidavit I signed somewhere in this house, and with my good daughter's help I will locate it and call you. See, she was someone who knew the real inside poop about the lynchers. She lived in Portland at the time, maybe still does. Worth a try, anyway."

Two days later the phone rang. Bob Thompson had found his copy of the affidavit.

V

We headed out route 6 along the Chehalis, following the passage Tom Lassiter's body took bumping down the Staircase Rapids, on through Raymond, the traitor Tom Morgan's town, angling through the left end corner of my state towards Astoria and the wide mouth of the Columbia River. Our object was Julia Bertram, who was alive in Portland and waiting to see us.

We drove beside tidal rivers that soaked in salt when the sea came up then flowed languidly out to mix with the ocean surf. We passed tangled logs peeling in the pale sun; the sound of gulls on the far rocks came to us filtered as children crying down the block. We counted ten blue herons on the great mud flats of Willipa Bay, mincing through brackish water and tufts of spiky grass. The air was salt, our lips were dry, we ate one meal--rank and messy oysters and washed them down with beer.

The bridge to Astoria starts out flat and unspectacular, the lanes are tight and mean, little separates you from the oncoming traffic, then about two-thirds of the way over the spreading Columbia, the road widens then takes off, a rollercoaster ride. It climbs higher and higher, the superstructure grows more and more complex and taller, like something out of Feininger. She was driving by this time and I looked down the skyward pointing stack of the Nikki Maru, its flapping sun on the rear deck a tiny flag my father gave me to stick on the best toy I ever got, a tanker that exploded if hit amidships by a torpedo spring-launched by a tricky PT boat.

This getting to Julia Bertram by the less direct way was a routing based on the confused urgency of a definite need to know. We moved on an arc but resloutely towards a point.

Julia was short, rather young looking. The house was the kind I'd always known, the living room small and book filled, like Ilsa's when we were living in Seattle. The kitchen was bigger than the living room. A typewriter sat on the vinyl kitchen table with a sheet of paper in it, as though she'd just come from working. She was slightly impatient.

Her voice was strong and clear and she tended to watch us with her clear green eyes, taking me down in her mind. She was a labor reporter for the *Timber Worker*, her father had been an I.W.W. and she'd been a part of the labor struggle since she was a kid, or that's how it seemed to her. In her freshman year at Oregon she'd gotten involved in the Centralia case, transcribing letters by hand for the men who were then in Walla Walla. They were limited as to the number of letters they could send, and she helped them contact many more people than they could alone. It was her father's wish that she do this; a trip to Walla Walla was part of her work. There she met Ray Becker.

"I've got lots of stuff here just waiting for the right person, or for the Historical Society as soon as they change the guard over there," she told us. "It's too bad you're not doing a history of the Centralia case--you're not, you say?"

"No, not really a history of it."

"Oh. Could I ask you why you're not?"

"Because I'm not a historian, I'm a photographer."

"You can do justice to this story with photos?"

"I don't know anymore. . . speaking of which, I guess I should have brought the photographer's affidavit with me. I told you on the phone the reasons I can't yet."

"Well, if she's terribly possessive and strange, as you say. . . I suppose you might get a copy for me eventually by the same means you read it." She sat across from us, next to a blackened fireplace and rather dwarfed by her overstuffed chair, but most degfinitely in charge of the situation.

"Yes, I could do that. It must have been upsetting to you to have misplaced it."

"It was, though how much difference it would have made is hard to say. We had other documents stronger than that one that made little dent on any official feeling. Ray was very keen on Hudson's statement, though, and I never admitted to him my. . . misplacing it."

"My mother says Oscar was thought of as a magic man, maybe you were under a spell."

She looked at me as though, frankly, that were a dumb thing to say.

"I know all about Finns and their magic," she said, "but your Oscar seemed pretty real to me. Since he had our best interests at heart, he'd hardly want to slow us down." She spoke this last to Carol, as though hers might be the more sympathetic ear.

"It's kind of special to me that you stayed there. You met my mother?"

"Yes, I remember, a college girl, very charming--"

"And Judith?"

"Who? Oh, the one whose room you entered. . . that's a cloudy area for me, I'm afraid, though I know you mentioned she was living there for some time. I'd met another woman from that household, Eva Maki, who was occasionally in and out of Portland. She was the one I thought I might meet. . . and the girl, Lucy, of course."

I brought the photo out. It was wonderful to see how it affected her, to know that as much as she had seen and known of the case, here was something new. "He was special, wasn't he? And she--"

"Yes?"

"How much easier it would have been to have had this face to go by," she concluded.

"It's strange, you know, the feeling I'm getting is that I have to track down these people. . . and for you, it must be--"

"'Water under the bridge?' Is that what they still say up there? It's not--it's quite immediate," she said. "I'm glad you're here, I don't mind sharing what I know about the case, it's just in a way I keep waiting for the person who'll do the story as I would have done it, or *should* have done it, though I haven't. Well, that's neither here nor there.

"This thing that took place so long ago, and I'm not really young, you may have noticed. The one man I knew in all of this experience was Ray Becker, and he was a most unusual man, one of the most exceptional people I've ever met. You can see by his correspondence how tangled and complicated his mind was. But he was so persevering, to carry on his fight for as long as he did, then to come out of Walla Walla and visit us here in Portland on the train, that was quite a moment for us and for him."

"You must be exceptional, too--" She stopped me, as if it were a wrong line.

"I met him when I must say I was still too much of a girl to understand his situation. It is so difficult to really understand the psychology of a man confined as he was. I must have seemed to him someone capable of helping a great deal, and I suppose it would be fair to say that he was taken with me personally, then I lost contact, years went by and I married. I was always attracted to loggers. Then came this letter to my mother's house, wondering where I was and chiding me for being one of those who preys on men in prison, but still it was gentle and he could be vitriolic. I felt so odd, then I took this money I was making selling true confession stories to Bernard McFadden and sent it to Irvin Goodman in Portland. He was Ray's first lawyer--the International Labor Defense had hired him."

"How many lawyers did he have?"

"He had Irvin, then Cliff O'Brien and before either of them, Elmer Smith, who worked hard for all of the prisoners until he died of a burst ulcer. They were all good men, really, but Ray tangled with them--he did not really believe in the men who run the courts but he maintained his faith in the law. After all the work and study he put into his own case, Ray was like a lawyer himself.

"But Goodman worked hard, even if Ray did eventually fire him. . . and even poor Cliff O'Brien--we foolishly paid him in advance for the brief he finally did file. A few days before the date of filing, we found he had not written it yet. Other lawyers interested in Ray's case forced him to buckle down and finish it. I remember staying up half the night in his office helping to staple pages together. The Free Ray Becker Committee had to pony up some more money to Cliff so he could eat while he finished the brief. Ray was through with him from that time on. Cliff was a brilliant man but even then an alcoholic."

"Who was on Ray's committee?"

"They were a lot of old wobblies. As they got less active they got more involved in legal matters, and of course many of their old leaders were in jail. When the I.W.W. was dying out a lot of them drifted into the Federation of Woodworkers which eventually became the International Woodworkers of America. The I.W.A. when I knew them was full of wobs like S.P. Stevens, who was chairman of the Free Ray Becker Committee and Sig Olson was another leader. They went from meeting to meeting and sold Ray Becker buttons and horse hair belts that Ray made in Walla Walla."

"Why did Ray fire Goodman?"

"One story that may or may not have had something to do with their disagreement involved a trip I made with Irvin to Walla Walla with two car-loads of former jurors who were ready to sign affidavits in favor of the prisoners. In the second car, and driving it, was a Major someone, who turned out to be a stool pigeon for the Portland police red squad. Irvin, of course, knew nothing of this, but it was a part of their coming to a crossroads. Irvin complained that Ray had lost his faith in the working class; the thing is, they were at odds. I think they kind of fired each other.

"But when Ray came out of jail he took the train to Portland, and went from the station to the hiring hall where a big contingent of loggers joined us and from there we were going to the union hall. It was such an ordeal for him. He got off the train, we marched right up 6th Avenue, and the traffic got to him. He hadn't heard it in years, and the noise and confusion must have seemed horrendous. One minute he was there, beside me, the next he was running down an alley. I ran after him--he was terrified, his face against a wall and his hands over his ears. I brought him back, though, and you know he still went on and made a speech. They had a picture of him up on a wall, as big as Lenin's, and when he came in everyone turned and cheered--1500 people. He wasn't a speaker but when he was asked to, he'd do it. Sometimes up there he looked as though he was going to fly apart.

"Jail had an extraordinary effect on him. It does on most men. He could never get out of the habit of collecting bits of string, he had a big roll with him all the time. And he had an awful time with money. The police claimed that when they found his body there was over $700 in cash in the house, which they described as unbelievably filthy, the money strewn about. He died only eleven years after he got out of jail, he had a little cabin over on the Washington side of the Columbia. They found him there, he'd fallen from a ladder from one of the trees in his orchard. The autopsy showed some damage to his head but nothing that couldn't have been caused by a fall.

"The Centralia's prisoners' sentence was hard labor, but eventually Ray was a trusty and a gardener. He had his own little world and something else, he didn't seem to age. You'd look at him, it was like his skin was tight, like an apple kept in the refrigerator for a long time, it looks fresh but really it isn't. He was preserved, and when he came out he went rather quickly into decline. He was subject to real bouts of depression. I feared for him many times.

"His real name was Ralph Burgdorf and just prior to the incident in Centralia he'd done time in Bellingham for resisting the draft. I think, in fact, he'd escaped. What was so special about him was that, looking at him or talking to him, you'd never believe he'd done these things.

"His brother came out here for the body. That was the first time we even knew he had a brother. We used red roses for funerals of Socialists and I.W.W. members then. When I placed the red rose in Ray's buttonhole, as he lay in the coffin, the Secretary of the I.W.A. took the dress button from his coat lapel and pinned it on Ray's lapel. His body lay in state for two days, and union people visited the mortuary. The brother wouldn't allow us to have a union funeral, that was the only concession he would make, that we could visit the undertaking parlor."

As I had listened to her story, the room not only darkened, it was as though the space at the sides of my eyes pressed to a center--occlude was the term I thought of. My view of her was as my listening, confined to that overstuffed chair and her quiet, firm voice. Hearing her tell of her friend Ray was at first almost a vacation from the sense of flood waters, rising in the barn, up the porch steps. I was brought up on original sin, assumed for years I'd shaken it: but if I thought clearly I knew that you don't escape what's in the superstructure. She was so practiced and smooth in her telling that whenever she paused--despite the fact that I was deeply moved by Ray Becker--I had the sense of someone knitting, rather than talking.

Carol had asked her something concerning Bengston I had missed, but Julia was answering her in that animated way women have when they feel that they are speaking essentially to women (she might have sensed my doze).

Carol had said, "Ivar saw it, in his grandson's garage."

"Yes, they might well frame that document for the city library. Cliff O'Brien, who'd reformed a little and went on working for the committee though Ray had fired him, found old man Bengston down in Salem, where he was then living. Anyway, at about this time I had become very interested in Elmer's office. It wasn't much, he built it himself, but after he died, knowing what was in there, I and an old wobbly named L.L. Dietz tried to get access to a closet in that office where we were sure was some really sizzling material. But Elmer's partner was stubborn. I don't think he cared for what Elmer stood for or did. . . We were there in his office one day about noon and the partner was being uncooperative, so when he left for lunch we stuck around--and this was not my usual way of doing things--and we just opened that closet door and lifted this great cardboard box, covered with cobwebs, and took the whole thing out to Dietz's car and took off for Portland."

"Oh, that's great," my wife said.

"It was now or never, we figured. Unfortunately we stored some of that material--and this was stories or personal and family conflicts those prisoners suffered--in the I.W.A. secretary's houseboat. It was swept downstream in the Vanport flood in 1948, it was a total loss. Everything, just completely washed away."

"Did you know Barnett?" I asked.

"I had a long talk with Gene Barnett. He came to see me once out here to talk about obtaining money to buy a ranch for raising mink. I gave him the money I had in my purse. His wife was with him, his second wife, and two lovely children. . . my it is late," she said, sitting now almost in darkness. "You know I wouldn't rush you but the union's got me running off to Aberdeen day after tomorrow, and I've got to finish another article before I leave. Could you come back later, say in a couple of hours? I know a number of inexpensive restaurants around town, in the meantime I'll dig up the Clifford affidavit. He was 'of the party,' you might say. The lynchers." She had moved back into the kitchen, now she returned to the dimness, younger. "Here, this is an extra copy of a short piece I did on gathering material for this case. I hitch-hiked, you know, all over the state, My transportation costs weren't high; Ray's funds were limited. But people were so surprised! You know, to see a girl out hitching rides. In those days they often stopped out of curiosity. You come back, now.

You're both very nice," she concluded.

We sat at a table waiting for Julia to come back from the restroom. Her statement was titled: "Some Remarks on Research." It described the way she coordinated notes found in Elmer Smith's files with instructions from Ray Becker, how she put these together with material she had stumbled upon in the basement of the courthouse in Chehalis, helping the clerk look for the inquest into the death of Wesley Everest. (There was none.) Besides these efforts, she took leads from interviews and from discrepancies in the trial record, which she'd studied in the courthouse in Montesano.

Whenever she returned to "that territory" (my Centralia), she would re-contact friends and good contacts made on the previous trip, letting it be known that she was back at her cheap hotel, that she would be there with her rented or borrowed typewriter between certain hours each day, writing up her notes. It was surprising how many people came to see her voluntarily, or left unsigned notes under her hotel room door. The rest of the day she would be out, trying to verify reports, interviewing people, checking, re-checking, and cross-checking stories told to her.

The Lamb family, the Blands and many others became friends with whom she kept in touch for years.

She was back at our table. I was aware of her folding her napkin carefully in her lap. She had told us that our visit had brought back vivid memories. Carol sipped a drink. Julia had written:

> I shall always remember my surprise at the impact time has upon the personalities of people; how the part individuals had played when they were younger--cruel, brave, criminal, or merely weak--had colored their lives, their family relationships and the pity I felt (unwittingly, it is true) for several who had played very discreditable roles.
>
> It was interesting to learn what had become of the members of the lynch party and others who helped break in the jail and who had participated in overall conspiracy plans to raid the hall, and to cover up responsibility for the tragedy.
>
> One man I interviewed was suffering from a then-undiagnosed disease, which had eaten away his ear, one eye and a part of his face. I shall always remember my horror when he drew off the cloth or bandage he wore over that side of his face, and showed me what was underneath. Another deeply involved man had committed suicide, several had moved away, one was dying of some disease (I forget the name) which was slowly turning his body to stone, two had died in unexplainable accidents, one had gone insane.
>
> One man asked me again and again to try to understand why he could not sign an affidavit admitting what he himself had done what he "knew" because of the suffering and shame this would bring to a family he had not had at the time and who knew nothing of his connection with the events on Armistice Day, 1919.

The statement left me with little to say, except the obvious--that often I had wished to leave this outback of a country.

"I'm not sure myself to what extent I live in *this* country," she said, "since I work for a union that admittedly is on the edge of things and in a state that everyone calls 'maverick.' Well, that's not it. Let's just say that more moving than the horror I discovered was the courage and dignity that revealed itself everywhere. . . in men who had been beaten, lost their jobs, been jailed just for sticking to their guns, or for telling the truth.

"I should tell you about a man named Hulten," she continued. "Of all the jurors, he impressed me the most, yet he never voted to acquit, he voted for second degree. You see--this was our push, to get these men out in the open after ten years and to admit that they had wronged the others.

"As I recall he came down from some remote place near Lake Quinault to meet me in Aberdeen. He insisted on taking me into the dining room of the best hotel for lunch, then on paying for it. He was a solid man, heavy, dark and very simply dressed. I have no idea what he did for a living, he may have been a farmer or a fisherman, and I thought maybe he was part Indian. I know that he had immense dignity and it was a pleasure for him to be buying me such a fine expensive lunch. I have a very exact visual memory and if I look right there--" (She was pointing at the napkin in front of me.) "--I can still see those gnarled, weather-beaten hands moving with grace over that white cloth. His manners were almost courtly, and then this careful way he spoke, almost as if he had thought out every word in advance. It was the most moving thing anyone had ever said to me: 'Saying he is afraid is not what a man can say. It would take a long time to say that to yourself; if you are a man you know this.' Then he looked at me, and I sat at that table with its dazzling white cloth and fine silver. I was hardly breathing, and at last he said, 'I have said it to myself, and now it can go on your paper.'

"Hulten was not a man with that quality we sometimes call 'political understanding.' I know that's a glib term. But P.V. Johnson did have it. He was the man who almost hung the jury, he was the last one to insist on innocence, and he knew exactly the politics of the case. That must have come to Mr. Hulten slowly over the years, just as the fear deepened gradually and he finally came to know what had happened at Montesano.

"P.V. Johnson was the juror I came to know best, and I was responsible for getting him to leave his exile and return to Portland. I never knew anyone to suffer more from guilt. It had caused him to leave Grays Harbor County and go to Portland, but even there he sometimes thought that people might know 'he was the one' who sent them all to prison. He'd finally given in on the jury, of course. So he had retreated into an almost inaccessible spot in the forest, far from any road, between Scappoose and Vernonia. That a'way--" She smiled and pointed generally south. "He carved out a sort of homestead in the woods, packing on his back things he couldn't make himself. Even his shoes were handmade of wood, like ones you'd see in Finland or Sweden. Anyway, I found him, after a long walk through the woods, along a sort of track.

"I sometimes thought Johnson would gladly have traded places with Ray Becker, and that way got his proper penance. He was brought up a Lutheran and there was a lot of that faith still with him. He had been a union man and I suspected he was also a wobbly sympathizer. He tried for years to think that 'what he had done' in hanging the jury was a noble action. And he still had moments when he insisted that, 'This is what saved them from first degree.'"

I sipped coffee and studied the lines of her face--

"I feel as if I know him."

"He was a real Hamlet," she said.

Carol asked her if the jurymen's affidavits most swayed the parole board.

"They were important, of course. And then two carloads of them agreeing to travel in the flesh all the way to Walla Walla. . . " She was pulling something from her purse. "--but they were also aware that we were capable of being even more explicit. When you get a town to the point of admitting to a lynching, you're on the way to the jugular vein."

I was shaking out the folds of the document in the table lamp's soft light. Carol shifted closer.

"Capitalist governments are most sensitive to that," Julia said.

"Affidavit" the paper said boldly.

> State of Oregon
> County of Multnomah
> I, Claude Clifford, being first duly sworn, on oath depose and say:
> That on the evening of the 10th day of November, 1919, I attended a meeting of the American Legion at the Armory in Centralia. The meeting was dominated by David Livingstone.

Among those present, the paper went on, were C.D. Cunningham, Joe Borgard, a taxi driver, Ted Patton and Hank Andrews, who was some sort of peace officer. These last names were vaguely familiar to me.

According to Clifford, Livingstone gave instructions that all those present were to march within the ranks of the 91st Division, despite the rank one might belong to. The purpose of the grouping was to demolish the I.W.W. Hall, and if they encountered any opposition the instructions were to "take them as they come."

On the day of the parade, with the 91st opposite the hall and a military command for breaking ranks having been given, a "great number of men led by Warren Grimm" made their attack. Clifford claims that he, along with about twenty-five others, moved in the other direction across the street and watched the fracas at the hall, heard the shooting and saw Grimm fall in the street. Thereafter he was witness to the mob's attempt to lynch Everest. He suggests that, but for the intervention of Mrs. Bray and Constable Patton, Everest would have been hung there in the street.

At about 5:00 P.M. that same day, he attends a meeting at the Elks Club presided over by William Scales. Four men are sent to the armory for guns and ammunition. Scales then challenges Clifford's right to be there. Is he an "overseas man", Scales wants to know. Does he belong to the Legion? Clifford is neither an overseas man nor a legionnaire, so Scales concludes publicly that he must be holding a "Red Card". But Claude defies them to throw him out and is allowed to remain.

Claude goes to the armory with "the committee" and takes a Colt .45 and a .30 Craig, then legs it back to the Elks' Temple. At 6:00 P.M. there is a meeting called by several men, including Dr. David Livingstone and C.D. Cunningham. A man stands on the desk and shouts that anyone not belonging to the Elks or the Legion should get out for, "We're going to hang this bunch of rats."

Before the jailhouse now, someone from the Elks crowd loses his nerve and begs them not to break in but the mob persists. A utility pole is used to crush the door to the jail. Everest is dragged out. He is dumped in a taxi.

> Not knowing in which car Everest had been thrown, I jumped into the front seat of said taxi. Everest was most of the time on the floor of the rear part of the taxi. Besides Borgard the driver, Everest and myself, the following persons were in the taxi: Dr. David Livingstone, Dick Wyatt and two others unknown to me. During the raid on the jail, C.D. Cunningham took charge of the raid and shouted directions to the raiders.
>
> The taxi was in a line of cars headed for the Chehalis River Bridge. Just after the cab crossed the railroad tracks, Everest hollered and screamed, and at the bridge he was taken to the front of the car where its lights shone upon him. The front of his clothes had been torn off and his privates had been cut off; Dr. Livingstone had said privates in his hand and laughingly said he would pickle them in a jar; Livingstone's hands were bloody and I saw that he had his doctor's instrument case with him.
>
> At the bridge Wyatt, Cunningham and Livingstone, and a small man who runs a clothing store in Chehalis were the moving parties among a large throng. They threw a rope over Everest's neck and suspended him from the bridge, but it was not long enough to snap his neck. However, the drop tore flesh loose from his shoulder.
>
> I estimate that more than 100 persons were in the crowd. Everest was then hung on about 30 feet of rope, but still his neck did not seem to be snapped. Flashlights shone on him, and a lot of shooting started. I left the scene.

I make this affidavit solely in an effort to accomplish justice; I related some of these facts to counsel for defendants in the case of State vs. Britt Smith et al, and was called as a witness, but the court refused permission to relate these facts. C.D. Cunningham, who acted as special prosecutor, was active in all the events I have related as having transpired at the Chehalis River Bridge and at the city jail.

My wife lighted a cigaret. I finished reading, folded the paper and gave it back. There was no one in the room but us.

"I think. . . " I started.

"Yes?"

"I think we'll try to sleep on that, and hope to see you for a while tomorrow."

"Come by about eleven," she said and stood behind her chair.

That night there were two dreams. In the first I thought I was watching on the tv screen a man going hand over hand up a steeply sloping tower-like precipice, struggling with a rope that was as heavy as a steel cable. At first he was Everest, then he was Ray Becker. Then there was no tv and it was me. I'd gotten to some terrifying height, the tower of a broken bridge; I could hear the water rushing through the gap beneath me. Carol climbed into the bed beside me and I felt secure again as the toilet gushed to a pause. But I'd no sooner fallen asleep when someone was ordering me down concrete steps that led into the depths of the earth. I went down them it seemed for three months, then I understood that I was to come back up. I took the stairs at about 100 per hour and rested, then on again and again, satisfied that I was saving myself that way from fatigue and possible heart failure, but somewhere near what I figured should be the top, the steps ran straight up into a ceiling of dirt and roots.

Julia wore a white dress, just slightly formal, with a patent leather belt, but she was warmer with us than she'd been on the day before. We walked north from her tiny house. She had a bundle of letters and photos.

"You ought to stay another day here, there's a very cheap motel in the neighborhood by the park up here with all the roses."

"We may do that. I want to try and locate Barnett from here."

"You are an ambitious person."

"I suppose."

"Well. . . here, I'd forgotten. This is Ray as he looked at Walla Walla, this was when he was a groundsman--must be summer, you can see how tight and tanned his skin was. I know nothing about the other men with him. The dog was one a guard gave him. Wheat country--right? At least from this angle. Are you old enough to remember argyle sweaters?"

"Um hmm."

"He is," Carol affirmed.

"I may have sent him that one. Here he is in '39 when he got out. That's the two of us here at this house. He wasn't a terribly big man, he doesn't exactly tower over me."

She looked kind of windblown in the '40's cover-girl sense, a dress to her knees, hair curled and unruly, her profile to the camera. She is "well-endowed." He does not look really happy to be out of doors.

"This was just before he left us for New York. He wanted to meet Ralph Trowbridge, who'd sent him so many books, and gave him his first education--outside of the seminary.

"I think much of what 'wobbly' once meant you can see in Ray Becker, and this is despite the fact that he left the I.W.W. He renounced all organizations because he continually felt that he was being either forgotten or used. The way he devoured books. . . that wasn't exactly typical, but during one of the California trials, either Mooney's or the Ramsey, King, O'Connor case, the union men complained they'd read the whole town 'dry.' The working class really goes for education as long as it has a hand in it--the wobblies had their own college up in Duluth in the 'thirties.

"But it was Rays's obsession with justice, with seeing the right thing done by people that is most typical of the I.W.W. and it's a rare thing today, you know, especially if the only thing you see resembling it is youthful enthusiasm for this or that party (my god, the Young Republicans!), or for no party. These 'apolitical' youth, aren't they sweet? Oh, god, I just thought, there's an old wobbly up in Seattle named Herb Edwards who knew Mike Sheehan, who told me one time that so and so was a 'Pig Hoosier,' and I said, What? And he said, in this heavy accent I won't try, 'You know, Julia, someone who thinks Nixon is their best friend!' You must see him, he was sent Mike's ashes after the old man died, had them in a shoe box for years, finally his wife objected so he took them--as he'd promised--down to the Chehalis Bridge. My, he said, the way this young man ran off when he asked him where Hangman's Bridge was, carrying that suspicious looking box! Then he dumped Mike's ashes into the river.

"Anyway, no one thinks anymore as they did, that's why they're so rare, and Ray, believe me, had this quality in the extreme. He was puritanical in his obsession with justice.

"Here are some of the very first letters written to me, and these are the later ones. Now one thing, notice how the handwriting changes the longer he's in jail--it's amazing. Here, these first letters are written in almost perfect--I should say, tortured--Palmer penmanship--"

I read out loud:

Dear Julia:
    The superscription may seem somewhat queer and is partly a consequence of my hatred of bourgeois titles. It came as a result of what I thought I saw in your letters, a fellow meeting on less formal grounds than Mr. or Mrs.

"Just a bit stiff," I ventured.

"Yes, you have to understand he'd devoured a ton of books that Trow had sent, who was like a father to him. Ray's own father had abandoned him. Here he asks, *'Prometheus Bound,* was it so radical?' 'It is a thousand pities that Shelley came to such an untimely end.' Ray could be so pious! He read almost all of Victor Hugo in translation, all of Dos Passos--the list goes on and on, but the point is that when he got to writing to people, but especially to me because I'd told him I'd majored in English, he'd occasionally get in the habit of being arch with me, I suppose partly to impress.

"There is the same kind of thing in his references to women, and there are a number of them in the early correspondence. Here, he's telling me about a girl he was in touch with from the University of Missouri: he talks about 'replying to a letter reflecting disappointment of which she was the author.' And, 'she mocked me with deceitful promises concerning publicity.' There was a distrust of women, but it may have been just a way--the only way he had at first--of keeping me on the track, or hoping that I wouldn't be one of those who'd simply abandon him. You know, you couldn't be the same about women again after years of confinement, and I'm not talking the usual stuff about homosexuality. It's more like a kind of celibacy and it lasts, it eats at you.

"Now we go on to the later letters, this is such a jump in time, but the handwriting changes, all the swirl is gone, maybe not all the flamboyance and now there is more of grace and controlled feeling. Everything is meticulously printed, caps and lower case, almost every sentence is brief and to the point and entirely concerned with 'getting his case to the proper authorities.'"

The next letter began:

We should have a joint affidavit, if possible, from the Pathe motion picture photographers' helper whose camera was wrecked. Get this with a pictorial record of the way the bullets entered the hall. It would prove that the witnesses who testified that the hall was not attacked before the gun shots, that Warren Grimm was elsewhere than in the hall the instant he was shot, were giving perjured evidence. Other eye-witnesses may be able to identify the mobsters who destroyed the camera. With this kind of evidence it can be shown that the charge that peaceful paraders were massacred was fabrication coming from a corrupted and putrid source.

"And that's the one I have," I said.

"Yes. . . " She sat on a stone bench, her legs not quite touching the ground.

"I feel like I ought to run off and get it to some proper authority."

"Of all the material we collected, and the miles and miles we travelled in search of signatures--it turned out finally that it was a kind of blackmail more than anything else that got Ray out."

"How so?"

"I'll get to that, not even Ray knew the true story. . . you remember former Lieutenant Governor Vic Meyers? Yes, everyone does, he was rather colorful. He was also more persuadable than the average politician."

"You knew all these people? You knew the cameraman?"

"Yes, Hudson. I remember *of* him, didn't meet him. You might try and locate him but it's very likely he's dead and gone. He was a good man. . . a little fellow, I gather. There is a rumor that actually he was a woman. That he or she used the disguise in order to gain easier access to the kinds of stories normally denied to women. Who knows? Right?"

She'd said this last in her earlier manner of keeping me to one side. She had another photo--"This may be a picture Hudson took of Vanderveer."

"Hmm. Mr. Jaw. Tough looking." I was trying to get her to keep it out there so I could study the style, if there was any. She put it away.

"Ray never trusted him."

"But he must have been a powerful lawyer."

"I'm sure he was, Ray knew this, too. But that's it, you see, there is a glaring little difference between them and then this grows. Maybe this doesn't have to be. It's just that in this matter, you must know that I'm on Ray's side, if side is even the right word. Well, in the instance of the .22 bullet that is supposed to have been removed from Art McElfresh's head. I have an affidavit from one of Art's relatives that says that when she went to the mortician about the body she was told that his skull was crushed by a blunt instrument. That in fact he'd been hit from behind, probably accidentally by on of his own comrades."

"If only Loren Roberts knew that!"

"What?"

"Loren Roberts," Carol said. "We saw him, it's very sad the way he goes on about guns. He thinks he killed him."

"There's something you know that I don't. Yes, that poor man, I can imagine what he thinks. . . and here is an area where I was influenced by Ray against my own best sense of things. I wanted to look up Roberts as you've done, I wanted to talk to him. Ray told me, though, that it would be a waste of time, that Roberts was weak, but really it was a matter of their being different. Was he cogent?"

"Yes--well, off and on. Like the sun on a cloudy day."

"He didn't go to any hospital after the trial."

"We know that. . . something that's bothering me," I said, pursuing what seemed like a new line, "is the thing about the .38 bullet. Did Ray have an idea about who shot Grimm. It was a .45, right?"

She carefully considered and looked at me peculiarly.

"Do you think that matters now?"

"I think so--everything matters."

"You know, it's funny, your bringing that up. I did ask him once, and he answered me. I asked, despite the fact that I was tending even then towards pacifism, and I never thought that guns mattered to me much."

"Well, they don't to me either, but the point is--"

Carol said, "He answered you--?"

"Yes. I'm not trying to be vague," she said, checking us out again in that way she had of weighing the evidence. "I'm honestly trying to remember. Why not have lunch on it?"

The restaurant was modest; hamburgers seemed the safest thing to order. As the harried waitress approached our table, Julia spoke to her, rather challengingly, "I'll bet that's scab lettuce--" "What?" the waitress called back, totally serious, "no, I don't think so. This here is iceberg." I could feel forgotten laughter bubbling up as though from behind me, just to keep its disguise in all of this heaviness, then it was in my throat, and I knew that I loved that answer, so curiously innocent, and I hoped to Jesus Christ that Julia had a sense of humor, but my laughter came first, then Carol's, and as the waitress--now pissed at being part of a joke she didn't get--placed the hamburgs down, Julia turned to me with the faintest wry smile and said: "You can have all of mine, it's good for your digestion."

"We ate and talked, about her grandchildren, about teaching them to read from the Blue and Red Fairy books. She was an asthmatic. During certain seasons, she said, Portland was like a death trap to her. She had to get to the sea. I finally asked her in the midst of our new lightness, "You think you remember now--?"

"What? Yes, the bullet. . . this man's nearly as obsessed as I once was," she said to Carol. "About the bullet fired at Grimm."

"Just to keep everything in line," I said.

"Of course. Yes, I do remember. The answer seems more pertinent now with your interests than I think it did at the time I learned it." She looked into the palms of her hands. "Ray answered that either he himself or Everest killed Grimm."

The new motel was across from the park, one end of which was given over to roses. Their scent and color gave head to my excitement.

"I see what Becker must have done now," I said, stretching out with a gin and tonic on one of the twin beds in the new motel room. It was a little more expensive than last night's, a little dirtier, but handier to Julia.

"Don't be too sure," Carol warned.

"No, it's not hard. He was near the doorway with Everest--she said that--he's got a .38, according to her. He fires at the same time as Everest, but, man, a .45 going off, maybe three or four times, who hears the .38? The coroner really does find a .38 slug in Grimm's body, they can't fake that. But if you pin it on Becker you take the chance of it being self-defense, you know, and him a preacher's son, if that comes out. Whereas you're sure that if it's across the street, it's cool. So you look around for .38's--here's one, belongs to John Doe--whoops, he's dead. No good, like Everest, looks very bad. Well, here's Barnett--a good man, a rotten thing to do, but what else can we do? Right? We've got to win for the sake of the country! And we can keep mentioning the .22 slug in McElfresh just to show that it we *had* to we could go a hell of a lot further away from 'self-defense.' So forget about Becker, but make sure we hang him or send him up. And of course we *can* . . . "

"I don't like it."

"Well, they're cool. The wobblies knew that they were all in it together, but think of the guilt Ray must have felt."

"Like she says, does it matter? Guns and numbers?"

"Yes!"

"I agree with Carol, I can't see it your way. . . 'guilt' is an old-fashioned idea, and I don't like using psychology on him."

We sat on the same stone bench as on the day before. There were red and yellow roses behind her, and another that was a pretty shade of salmon. I hadn't slept much but I felt better than I had for days.   .

"But I wonder how Barnett felt all that time, if he knew Ray shot the bullet."

"I don't think he could have thought much about that part, except that he was innocent, as they all were of the charge of murder, including Ray. They had only their solidarity to keep them going, and at times they must have seemed like something less than the sun and the moon. One gets a little strange in jail, he says extreme things. Ray's attitude coming out of Walla Walla upset the Defense Committee so much at one point that Cliff O'Brien sent, without my knowledge, a lawyer who was also a 'psychologist' to see him. Ray bounced him out pretty quickly.

"once in Seattle I heard Ray described as a 'megalo-maniac' by someone supposedly sympathetic with the case. I jumped on the man--I told him Ray was more consistent and courageous than he was, and that by using a trick name on him he was only trying to shirk his own responsibility. I was furious. I knew better than any of them Ray's peculiarities, I also knew better than any of them what jail does to a person's concentration. Put your average psychologist in jail and he'd end up catatonic in half an hour. With Ray being locked up made for a sharpening of his intellect, and the work he did with his hands reminded me of--what is that?--sailor's craft, *scrim*shaw. He was very deft, but that didn't mean that jail was good for him. Jail is never good, for anyone. But whenever I heard this kind of analyzing--'megalo-maniac,' can you imagine?--I knew it was just someone going through a reactionary phase, categorizing him out of existence, because to get a man out of jail *is* a hard thing, and how much easier to call him strange and leave him be."

"You think I'm categorizing?"

"Not at all, if I thought that I wouldn't have anything to do with you. Here, how silly. I'm afraid we're talking as though he were still alive and fighting to get out. You coming here has put me pretty high the last couple of days, and brought up some painful memories, too.

"There was so much suffering over that incident. Not just the men, families were put under tremendous strain. There was a rumor going around about the Lambs, absolutely ridiculous. I knew them, they were great together. Barnett's wife died, but they were on the brink of divorce before that, or so I understand. The Bland brothers died within two years of each other--one in Port Townsend, the other out in Wisconsin someplace.

"It's funny, now, carrying around Ray's letters. It's like Ray Becker's 'works,' and to me it is a story. I really was a part of it, he was fond of me. And I was of him but not romantically. My only love affair was with a union--" She said that with a kind of irony, but not the sort that I was familiar with. Since I had been warned against 'psychologizing' I looked at her and took what she said without a grain of salt.

"This is an earlier letter from him, long before our relationship got to be one where I was almost exclusively a person on the outside, researching.

> Your registered letter was read only twice before I sat down to write my reply which has been mulled over many times in my mind. Of course I remember your visit to me. It was an enormous while ago. All the intervening years I kept only the good thoughts of you. True, I was sorry that you stopped writing to set up a home but I couldn't think of holding it against you that I did not make you like me. In reading my letter you made the mistake, I guess, of thinking that you and I were the only people in the world.

"You can see that he was hurt or confused, if only a little. Maybe I oughtn't to comment more on that side of it. After this letter, anyway, he 'gets it all together,' as they say."

We came upon a couple of other personal references that I couldn't keep from asking her about. One concerned a Dr. Marie Equi; Becker mentions her casually to Julia and says casually in the same line that he 'trusts that Everest's offspring is doing all right'! In another place Ray says, 'That you are becoming an author is, dear girl, wonderful news.' I asked her about these references and she became quieter.

"There's no big thing about my becoming an 'author.' I'd written poetry and short stories for years--some of which I'd sold--I was also at work on a labor novel. Ray was impressed by my writing and in fact when he left us in Portland to visit R.T. in New York, he took that book with him."

"To show around?"

"Yes, because Trowbridge was a man with connections. Well, the less said. . . The other, the reference to Everest's offspring I want you to understand is an extremely touchy and difficult subject. I have some information, but again it's of a special kind involving people who could be hurt. It's simply a fact that Dr. Equi was a friend of mine, she was also a feminist and she did perform abortions here in Portland. The town fathers would like to have arrested her all the time she was practicing, but she had too much on them, knowing certain things. As soon as she died, in the early '50's, the police moved in on her clinic. She was an important person for the radical labor movement in the early years. She finally did serve time after the Centralia trial, in San Quentin, but that was supposedly in violation of the sedition laws--for speaking against the draft.

"The tricky part of this whole thing is the persistent fact that she adopted a baby girl whose birth certificate says the parents are Wesley and Lucy Everest."

In the sunlight we heard the traffic pop and crawl along the freeway not so distant, and nearby a bird sang fresh in the intervening silence.

"You said Lucy?"

"Yes. That's what the certificate says. And Doc Equi, who I must say had her eccentricities, periodically told this girl, the daughter, that she was her mother and at other times that she was not! She actually told the girl at one point that she'd had her, by Everest, as a cure for a back ailment."

"What did you ever learn about Lucy?"

She was watching me again, as she had on the first day. "I know this much--a few months after the Centralia trial, Doc Equi spent about a month away from here at the seashore near the mouth of the Columbia. I believe there was a young woman with her and another who was a few years younger still. One of them may have been Eva Maki but she's not been seen again, either. The younger one might have been Everest's Lucy, I just can't say."

I was on the point of saying, 'You know you really can trust us.'

Instead I asked her what her novel was about.

"My novel? About a Finnish woman who edited a labor magazine. She lived in Astoria. She was a suicide."

The bridge rose up; I heard the seagulls crying down the block. "A Finn? First or--"

"Second generation. But, you see, whenever I brought up the matter of the child's parents with Doc she became so evasive that I felt I might irritate her if I went too far, so I didn't push it. The child appeared, you might say, in the late 'twenties. There she was, walking along at Doc's side."

"Where is she now?"

"Where?" She tilted her head slightly towards me as I sat, almost breathless. It was the first gesture that suggested anything other than complete self command. "Maybe it's as well that you don't know. Not that you'd penetrate her privacy, not that you aren't perfectly decent people. But you see there are some areas of life that just won't take too much probing. Finally they have to be left alone. She exists. Isn't it enough to know just that and rest easy? I think so, anyway."

We walked her back to her house. I wanted her to stand right in front of the steps.

"Don't glorify me," she said as I squinted at her diminished figure. "I couldn't stand that. Just take me as I am."

VI

All that bright day we drove the Columbia River, then crossed over on the ferry to Merryhill, Washington. Throughout this long dazzling trip, I thought of Julia and about the eight men who made the trip in June of 1920. I imagined them driving out over the mountains in a car like Joe Borgard's taxi, through the desert of eastern Washington, and finally into the wheat country of the state's lonely lower border.

Loren Roberts had said that he thought Barnett had landed in Clarkston, so we headed there to take the chance that somehow he existed. We stopped at a restaurant; it was about 6:00 at night. Clarkston is located in the lower east side, dead end corner of the state, east of Walla Walla and, not surprisingly, right across the Snake River from Lewiston, which is in Idaho. The ground went out flat from the restaurant window, then soared up slanting, brown and massive, 2,000 feet or so to what we knew were the Palouse Hills. We could make out a roadway on that distant rise that cut its way with crazy hairpin turns to the top.

Carol asked, "Do you believe water ever fell over that edge?"

"What makes you think so?"

"Here, on the back of the menu, 'a thousand Niagaras'. Get ya wet, huh?"

"Oh, yeah? It would take that much."

"What? To clean things up?"

"Naw, I'm running out of blame. . . to put us back a billion years. Start again as lichen or plankton. . . no?"

She put aside our menu. "What's our next move?"

"See those old folks over there eating their lettuce? I'm just going right up to them and ask them about Gene Barnett and see what they say."

I caught them between cash register and swinging door. "Barnett? Married to what's-her-name," the man said. "Yeah, wasn't there some old feller out Asotin way, had him a mink farm. Silver something."

The old woman said, "Yes it was, you're right again, Claude Taylor." She winked at me. "He's always making brags about his memory, thinks he's keen."

"Yes, but that old boy, he left that business long ago, I heard he had a stroke or something." The old man's head was bent as though he was listening to his own heartbeat.

The wife said, "You want him, you want to get hold of his in-laws. You contact a woman named Grossmickle, Mrs. Elmer Grossmickle. She'll know. C'mon, Claude, I'm driving us home. You're in no condition."

I used the restaurant's phone. Amid the sounds of clanging pots I listened to Gene Barnett's in-law denounce him.

"Yes, I know Gene Barnett and, yes, he is still alive but, no, I won't help you out in any way, shape or form for the reason of what he done to my sister, Neva."

"He married your sister? What's her name?"

"My sister's name's no concern of no one but us here."

"But you do know where Gene's located?"

"I do but you won't get that kinda help out of me for the reason that Gene Barnett ran out on my sister and never supported her or those boys in any way, shape or form. And if she doesn't want to get back what he owes her that is her business but nobody's going to bully me into helping him out."

"This is the same man. isn't it? The one who did time in Walla Walla? Did you know about the charges against him?"

"That's right. Yes, I knew all about that."

"I guess I see him differently. I can't help but see him as a really good man."

"What. . . you mean for that business he was in on over on the coast?"

"Yes, sure, for all of that. . . and for being framed."

"Oh, well, I know all about that. Family has a way of knowing them things."

"I heard that he's sick. He had a stroke, didn't he?"

"That's true. Fact is, he's had him about three or four strokes.

They're just waitin' for the one that'll carry him off for good."

"Well, that's it, I'd like to talk with him before he's gone."

"Might be dead this minute, might a'died today for that matter."

"That's right, like you or me could go, too--just like that. Walk out of your house one day, get run over by a truck."

"Well, I, for one, would make some provisions for my family before I did any dyin'."

"No, sure. I agree with you. Is he in a home?"

"He is. . . who is this, anyway? Why d'you want to know where he is?"

"I'm F.B.I."

"Uh-oh."

"Do you have the name of the home?"

"There's three rest homes in this town. I can tell you the names of the ones he's not in."

"Great."

"Oh, you can find him, all right, that's no big problem. But he won't talk to you."

"What? He won't want to?"

"Oh, no. . . what I mean, he can't."

The starched but helpful nurse sent for Gene Barnett. There was a list of names behind her tacked to a bulletin board under the instructions Please Oil Scalps. The nurse looked at us with interest. We weren't family, she knew all of them. She may have known that Gene was once "important." She warned us frankly:

"The last stroke rendered him almost speechless. He can understand you all right, and he really wants to talk. It's not going to be easy on you. . . . Here he comes, why not take him down to the tv lounge?"

He was capsized in a wheelchair, rolling himself along with one fairly good left hand. He wore a flannel shirt, stained work pants and pathetic slippers. The right hand was useless in his lap. His hair had not yet thinned, the face was long, the nose weatherbeaten. His sunken eyes swept our faces, trying to see if he knew us.

"Gene." She spoke rather loudly. "Here's a nice young couple to see you. They wanta talk to you, I guess."

"Gimme gimme," he said.

I will never get over him. The way the left hand went again and again into his mouth as if he were gobbling everything we said, and he punctuated every bit of information we passed along, concerning his friends and his cause with "Gimme gimme." It was as though he could never get enough of Union News.

When he couldn't understand, the words were the same but exasperated as, "Gim-me gim-me," drawn out and there was definitely a change in his tone. As if to say, "I'll never get it!"

The most painful part of our meeting was that he wanted us to know something special about himself, I guessed about his life since getting out of jail. The feeding motion of the left hand changed to plucking, as if he was trying to pull something out that was deep in there and wouldn't budge, like a stuck bone. His brow broke into waves at his efforts, the fingers went into the mouth. He gave up on "Gimme gimme." His throat said, "Ahhh-ah-ah-ahh--" and concluded with, "god demn'it."

The nurse brought a letter. It was addressed to Gene and it came from a newsman near Centralia who claimed to have studied the case for decades. He mentioned Barnett's "writings"; he said that he'd written to Barnett's publisher and to one of his daughters in Texas concerning a book or pamphlet but that there were no copies left.

We asked him, "Is this what you want to talk about?" I pointed to the passage concerning the pamphlet, "The Art of Hitching Horsehair."

He nodded, "Gimme gimme."

"Do you have copies of your book?"

His face twisted. "Ahhhh-ah-ah-ahhhh. . . god demn'it!"

Carol asked, "Do you want to know about this man who wrote to you?"

"No-oooh-oh-ah-ah-ad--" He shook his head.

Again my wife had a better sense of the situation than I, "Do you think my husband's this man?"

"Gimme gimme."

"No," I told him. "No, we're just interested people."

Carol added, "Like we said, we met Loren Roberts and Bert Faulkner and a woman who knew Ray Becker. We started moving and here we are."

"We started out by taking pictures," I offered.

Barnett brought his left hand down on the fancy stationary before him. The hand scurried around, he couldn't coordinate his desire with specific lines of the text. I figured it must be something to do with his book. The nurse had stood to one side under the color tv. She said, not really callously, "I think he still wonders about the sales of that little book." He seemed half to hear her and nodded eagerly, but he missed her suggestion of the hopelessness of the situation. He was dying, that was the message hanging over him that everyone saw every day. What he still seemed to want, to demand--because despite the destructive power of the strokes you could see that he was as fiercely willful as an eagle-- was recognition. I am Eugene Barnett. I still live. I was treated by this state like a lump of dirt. I am so much more than that. So much more.

When we left I shook his hand, then put my arm around his broad shoulders. It wasn't enough. I pushed him down the hallway first to his room, then he made another demanding noise and I understood and pushed him in the direction of the men's room. I hesitated, hoping he wouldn't need help. He did but the nurse was there, professionally useful. I waved, he waved, then I noticed for the first time that stenciled on the wide lower strap of his wheelchair was the name Walla Walla.

VII

We went home to the farm to catch up on the chores, wash up and get some rest. I told Carol at breakfast that it was coming on me again--I had to get to the ocean. She said, Okay, we'd go to La Push and stay over with friends. You need fresh images, the ones in Centralia were beginning to cling. She drove us into town for supplies; we'd leave the next day. I bought a roll of TX 135 at The Shutter and was coming back down the street to the truck when I heard a funny fluting voice saying, "Paymer, Misthur? Pee-yih, Pee-yih. . . Paymer, Misthur? Pee-yih?"

I turned, reaching into my jeans for a dime. The guy was up close enough to stink, with a bundle of papers under his arm. There was a kind of shit colored stain of snot down his gray shirt. His pants hung from his hips so low his underwear showed at the beltline and the cuffs that flowed over his shoe tops were all torn up. On his speckled head were hairs rather than hair. The left ear was like trimmed down. One eye was right out of his head, the patch off to one side and dropping.

"Paymer, Misthur, paymer?" He took his hand from his nose and showed a hole in the nostril big enough to push a pencil through. "Hope-phoot-you-phoot phoot-god th'righ-phoot-change-phoot."

He held the paper and looked me over to see if I'd come through. Now he tucked the paper under his other arm and put two fingers to the hole. He seemed to pinch.

"Wha-th'fuck ya starin' ad?"

"I'm starin' at you. You gotta be Heinie Huss or Hess."

"Oh-yead? O-yead? Well, I don'know how you kno'dat, bu' dat's close, all righ'. Dutchie. You one of dem hippies? Here, take dis paymer."

"Buy you a cuppa coffee."

"Buy me any'ding you wand, pretty'boyd."

He led me through an alley into the Bungalow Lunch. And ancient painted-on sign said, Meals 25¢ and Up. Hamburgers 10¢ and 15¢. He dumped his papers sideways in a wooden booth. I slipped the Nikon from my neck, aware of his one-eyed stare. A cook came out of the clanging kitchen, wiping his hands on an apron, smeared with grease and blood. He dug under his apron as though to loosen the tightness around his balls.

"What'll it be, Dutch, bean soup?"

"Make dat coffee wid real cream, Lou," he said. "Hippie here's payin'."

"That's good. What for you, bud, same--"

"Same-o, plus one donut."

"--oh, good." Heinie gave off an odor that seemed to come right from his open eye socket.

"Make it two donuts."

"Jelly, mak'id."

The guy left, picking gingerly at his backside. When he came back with two pancake-like donuts, red oozing out on the plate, I found I had stomach only for the bone-black coffee. Heinie scoffed both donuts, dripping runny sweet down his stubbly chin.

"So you know my name, hippie. . . how'd'you kno'id?"

"Heard about you and read about you--"

"Dat'zo?"

"That is. . . been reading all about that old wobbly fight, fifty years ago."

"Oh, dat." He took away his hand to gesture. "Dem-phoot-sonso'bitches-phoot." Gripping the nose, he added, "Now dem wad dengerou'd times. We was lucky to be rid of dem slimy, snaky-sons a'moldy dogs. . . hey. Wha'da hell's y'r work, hippie?"

"My name's Rivers, I'm a photographer."

"Well, ain'dad a kick in d'head? I knew a'Rivers 'round the Olympic when I was still a man an'nod a'nold piece of cow dung like I amb now. You believe I was once a man dad stood tall?"

"I believe you were something."

"Meaning? Whad'th'hell's dad s'posed to meade, long hair?"

"I just mean, like you say, you must have been something--a man."

"Still a man, nod like some oders I could name 'round here, wid der clothes. Fairies, you know?" The good eye winked, the heavy lid rising slowly. He put his head out into the aisle, as though searching an illustration.

"No, I guess I don't."

The eye fixed me again. "--den whad do you?" The hand came away to send a fly dipping crazily off. "--phoot-fuck-all, pro'bly. . . kids-phoot, what do they-phoot know-phoot?" He grabbed the beak and twisted it, thrusting his head at me. "See dis node?"

"Yeah, I see it."

"Know how I god diz fuck'id node? I'll tell ya how I god diz node. I wad in Walla Walla, see--?"

"Yeah, I guess I knew that."

"Well, how d'ya kno'd thad? Ya followin' me arou'd? Wha'th'fuck are ya--?"

"No, I'm in a town, you know things."

"Nodey Parker, are ya, like me? Tha'd how I god dis, hear? Wad in the pen wid a bunch a'rads and fuck'id ra'cals. . . pud id to me, know whad I mean? Dey fuck wid me. . . fuck wid m'node."

He had conjured up an image even more disgusting than himself--now he waved, "--phoot-call me, 'Nosey-phoot,' see? Den day do diz to me, down the laun'ry room. Pud dere cigarets oud, all a'dem, one after anoder, pud'em oud. An' I wad fightin' like ten wil'cads. But whad am I, see? Jud one man. An'whad are dey? Niggers, some o'dem. . . doctor geds me, cud it ri'doud. Cud a hole, dere, an' whad dad leaves me, goin' rou'd th'rest a'my life sayin', 'Hey-phoot-paymer-phoot-read-all-'bout'it-phoot!'"

He pinched his nose and struggled to bring coffee to his lips. The blades of a giant fan beat the air lazily above us--I spoke more or less to his empty eye:

"Better'n bein' blind, though."

The cup crashed into the saucer. "Wh' th'fuck thad mean?" He brought an index finger to his cheek under the empty socket--"You talkin' boud dis?"

"No, but even one eye's a whole lot better'n bein' blind," I repeated, "or hounded through a rotten court. . . or being castrated."

He pushed himself flat back against the booth, his broken teeth grinding viciously. "--yer one a'dem, I could tell id, should a'know'd bedder. You clean a town oud, an' what d'dey do, come back in, crawlin' like rads. . . hippies and pimps like you."

"You got your monument," I told him--our faces nearly whacked over the center of the table.

"Do it-phoot again-phoot-best-phoot thing we ever did-phoot!"

I crashed my fist down, meaning to hit emphatic wood, but instead struck both saucers, catapulting cups and coffee over him and the wall.

"Lou!" he shrieked. "--guy'd threaten'in my life! Tryin' t'kill me!"

Lou was there, a great ham of a hand pushing me down. I was trying to get my camera on, urging myself against the hand.

"You broke anything, you'll pay, buster," he was saying, but backing off. "--outta here, botherin' old men," and he was gut-bumping me down the aisle. Grizzled faces checked me out, breaking into lopsided grins.

"Blue-eyed twirp-phoot!" I heard and burst into the sunlit street, squinted and saw her making towards me behind a line of parked cars. She grabbed my arm and spun me towards her. "What's wrong. What is it--you seen a ghost?"

"Yeah, and he stunk," I said and spat. "And he's ninety years old." I looked into her eyes. "Where's the truck? Get us out of here, okay?"

Four days at the ocean and I wearied of the convalescent power of tide pools. Cruising up the Hoh in an Indian's long boat, we reached a landscape so dripping in green that it was as though I'd discovered the color of memory (it is a monochrome of smooth, water-swept, mossy stones and grottos filled with grass). Within that dense interior I began to miss the sense of daily discovery and surprise I'd gotten used to working with the thought of Everest and the Bland boys and Ray Becker. I came home with a letter to Gene Barnett already composed, asking him, in effect, to keep his pecker up. I called Loren Roberts to tell him a little about Gene. He was pleased and told me that one day he'd like to see me. A week later he drove over in his Plymouth hardtop.

"Going to take you fishing," he said. He stuck his creel on the hood of his car and propped his pole against the bumper.

"I'm game," I said, "coffee first, though." I got him into the kitchen, seated at the table with a Danish roll and some black coffee. He couldn't keep his eyes on me but kept gawking around the room, looking for familiar signs. Everything must have looked new to him, except maybe the pantry.

"You were in this house, weren't you, Loren? You must have been."

"Oh, I guess--maybe a hundred years ago."

"You say you got a fishing spot?"

"Oh, yes."

"Far from here? Should I take a lunch bag or a thermos?" I don't know why I wanted to toy with him like that.

"Nope. Near. Just down the tracks a ways." He got up and stooped to pull the curtain aside and peer across the back fields. "Nice pool back there, unless the river's twisted all around. Fished back there and hunted back there but, lord, it's been how long--?"

Judith came into the kitchen, as usual silent over guests. I saw him look at her with sudden interest. "Loren, Judith. Judith, this is--"

"--hello," they said in unison. I felt as though she was counting the crumbs we had spread on the oil cloth. It had been sponged just fifteen minutes ago.

"He knew that couple. . . the one in the picture. Right, Loren?"

He had his narrow ass propped against the cooling woodstove, sipping the dregs of his coffee and trying to look at her. She grabbed up the last of the rolls in their crackling cellophane, took my cup and saucer from me and said, "Oh, is that so."

"Oh, yes," he said, abstracted but watching her at the sink now.

"Just leave that on the table when you go," she instructed.

"What?"

"Your cup," she said over her shoulder. "Just leave it."

The blue heron coiled its neck into a tight S as it came up laboriously, even with the tops of the scrub maple across the lake, the long legs tucked up to the belly. I wanted to give him a tour of the farm, which he kept trying without success to work into his memory. "Nope, that don't click," he would say. We walked beside a tiny lake choked with lily pads, where as a kid I used to swim and fish. I had worked hard that morning before he came, prints were dripping all over the dark room. It was good to be off with him, and I squeezed my bamboo pole as I had when my dad used to whisk me off to the Sound.

It was good to work, it was good to have the break, and all in all, I had begun to think, was this so bad a place to be?

Loren had said that he couldn't get over the fact of Barnett's disability.

"And I thought I talked bad. . . what's he say again?"

"Gimme gimme," I repeated.

"Ain't that a sonofabitch."

But what if the lead should fly again?

Then make sure you're on the right side. Stand tall with Wesley, or like Ray, persevere.

Or, like Loren?

"I wanted to ask you something else?"

"Oh, yes. . . ?" he said.

"How did you happen to pick a spot that far away?"

"When you mean?"

"That day in November, with the rest of them in the hall?"

The flat brown eyes studied me calmly. He shifted back his creel.

"When you decide you're gonna shoot for someone, you know what I mean--? Then no man ought to tell you where you got to do it."

"You weren't just a little--?"

"We knew the terrain. And, no, we didn't want no copper hands laid on us."

Take him at his word, I said to myself. Still I pushed: "You weren't just a little scared? You were only--what? Nineteen?"

"Aren't we all?" he asked.

"What?"

"A little scared?"

I'd asked for it, I guess, and why I couldn't simply have said to myself, This man survived. That is a value in itself, maybe the greatest value.

We had come a fair ways down the tracks; they were much easier walking than the deep cut riverbank or the rise of land above us.

"What was your work?" I asked him. "Before Walla Walla."

"Oh, I worked punk and whistle, you know, when I was really green, then I set choke. Logs so big in those days they looked like the Chinese Wall. They was bigger then--this is all second, third growth," he said waving his pole at the green tangle around us.

"Then when you came out, not much work, huh?"

"Well, no, not really."

"Did you boys stay together much after?"

"I saw O.C. Bland for a time before he died. Went hunting with him out to the Black Hills west of Rochester there and killed a deer, about 1940 that was. But I didn't. . . I got away from the organization along about then."

"I can imagine."

"Well, you see, the trouble was more in Chicago. They started to split up there because of the communists."

"Because of--?" I wanted him to stop. I did not want to hear of any God-that-failed conversions.

"They got the only idea," he said casually. "The communists. I haven't been a member for a long time, but there were alot of us, many were good friends, who came over to the CP. Oh, that was--"

"You joined the CP *after* you got out of Walla Walla?"

"Let's see, it must have been. . . I was a member 25 years ago. Yeah. That's right. Well, they were 20 million strong, and what were we? Four or five hundred, it felt like. I gave it all up, though."

"From pressure?"

"No, hell no. Reason was I figured the communists wouldn't get control for another hundred years, and what am I? Seventy-plus, anyway," he said thoughtfully.

The spot he had in mind lay just beyond the big elbow bend in the Chehalis, above which was the scooped out wreck of land that Judith's uncle had tried to homestead. I wanted to show him that place as well.

We pushed gingerly through nettles, stepping high in waders rolled up to our knees. The scent of breaking nettles rose sharp and green in our nostrils. I had rolled down my sleeves and was careful when I did touch one of the stinging plants to avoid the stems and the underside of the leaves. Still I felt a sudden pain twice on my right hand and once on my cheek when a bush that he was sliding through swished up to graze my face. I saw the twin tops of the split apple tree, all tufted green with leaves. Caterpillars at it, probably. Then just as we broke the brush, I caught sight of an image at the base of the tree so white that for a moment I thought all the available light had fallen onto one shape and focused her so sharply that my first thought was for a camera. "Lord, what's she up to?" Loren said.

We stopped at the edge of the clearing, held by the sight of a woman in a torn white dress, bending over a cairn of rocks. Near her was the stone well; I had seen the pile of rocks before and never paid it any mind. Her face was bent towards her hands, her hands down on the pile so that it appeared she might be praying. My heart revved furiously when she lifted her face, sightless, looking into the sun. It was Judith, but no Judith I'd ever known. She looked younger, with her hair hanging down her back, her face glowing. She was mouthing words, then turning to add rocks to the pile. Loren and I bumped against each other and I feared that if he lost balance, it would be hell trying to keep quiet.

"Damn," he whispered, "what's she up to? Thought she was peculiar when I seen her."

Then he was moving away, discreetly at first until, reaching the thicker bush, he started to walk fast. When I sensed that I was alone, fear came at my throat and I was following him with large strides like an animal not wanting to be struck from behind. Two emotions were at work in me: I wanted badly to know what she was doing, or what she thought she was doing; but the sign that warns you, once you've run a course, not to push along it any further kept me moving less and less cautiously as I slashed at nettles that turned my skin to lumps. Just as I realized I had lost Loren entirely, forgetting how high I was above the tracks, the ground gave way and I was sliding down the bank. My shirt rode up to my armpits and the skin on my back went clammy with dew as I slid down grass and blackberry, coming at last to bump hard on my spine, then hit heels first and pitch forward to lie across the tracks, my chest heaving and sore. I brought up my hands to see that they were crusted with mud and scraped raw at the base of the thumbs. I wiped mucus from under my nose, gripped my pole and followed him up the tracks.

Epilogue

We were in the older of the two farmhouses, the one where Pete had been raised. The kitchen planks were worn and there was nothing in the room besides a woodstove, a center table and cupboards. The sink you reached through a glassed-in pantry that was larger than the kitchen. Sitting with Ilsa at a table with coffee was such a forgotten but familiar act that I whacked my shirt pocket for my Camels though I'd quit smoking two years ago.

She had the Thermos raised. "You want more of this?" She held her own steaming plastic cup in hands that hardly shook anymore.

"Okay." I sipped, the craving for a smoke cut deep, then was gone. I realized that what I really wanted for her to do, to live here, was not something I had to be anxious about.

"You've been awfully busy lately," she said. "Seems like I never see you anymore, always in the darkroom or running around the farm."

"You weren't worried that I'd discover his daughter?" I asked to put her on my track.

"No, because she's not been out there that I know about in years. I thought she'd stopped."

"It might have been what I told her that morning, that Loren was someone who knew the couple in the picture."

"Yes. How did he take it?"

"He left without his pole."

"Wish I could remember him," she said. "There were so many that came around."

"When did she get like this?"

"It must have been when the one she used to call 'auntie' brought her here to live."

"And she lived out there alone?"

"Sometimes. She used to tell me that her mother was buried out there, and sometimes it was her father. But really it's been ten years since she's gone there. I honestly didn't think that you'd find her out, just the paper, and the way the picture keeps showing up in one place and another."

"What does she say about him?"

"Her father? She doesn't know the story, or she's blocked it. She told me one Armistice Day, without build up, 'My father was a great patriot.' Just like that."

"He was," I said.

11 February 1980

213